KU-684-169

MR. LUCTON'S FREEDOM

THE NOVELS OF FRANCIS BRETT YOUNG

UNDERGROWTH
(with E. Brett Young)

DEEP SEA

THE DARK TOWER

IRON AGE

THE CRESCENT MOON

THE YOUNG PHYSICIAN

THE TRAGIC BRIDE

THE BLACK DIAMOND

THE RED KNIGHT

PILGRIM'S REST

WOODSMOKE

COLD HARBOUR

SEA HORSES

PORTRAIT OF CLARE

MY BROTHER JONATHAN

BLACK ROSES

JIM REDLAKE

MR. AND MRS. PENNINGTON

THE HOUSE UNDER THE WATER

THIS LITTLE WORLD

WHITE LADIES

FAR FOREST

THEY SEEK A COUNTRY

DR. BRADLEY REMEMBERS

THE CITY OF GOLD

FRANCIS BRETT YOUNG

MR. LUCTON'S FREEDOM

THE BOOK CLUB
111 CHARING CROSS ROAD
LONDON W.C.2

THIS EDITION 1941

PRINTED IN GREAT BRITAIN AT THE WINDMILL PRESS
KINGSWOOD, SURREY

For
Leonora and St. John Ervine,
affectionately

CONTENTS

Part One

NORTH BROMWICH

CHAPTER | PAGE

I THE GRINDSTONE 1

II POST-PRANDIAL 15

III REAL ESTATE 34

IV EASY DESCENT 51

Part Two

THE COUNTRY OF STRANGE ADVENTURES

I SCHIZOPHRENIA 63

II WARMEST WELCOME 74

III TIBBERTON'S FARM 87

IV TRANSFORMATION SCENE 112

V SIR OWEN WENT WEST . . . 128

VI FOREST OF 'ARRY 148

CHAPTER PAGE

VII THE ABBEY 169

VIII THE DRIVE 185

IX THE YOUNG DAMOSEL 202

X DOUBTFUL AUTHENTICITY 227

XI THE DAMOSEL OF THREE SCORE 256

Part Three

QUIETEST UNDER THE SUN

I THE "BUFFALO" 281

II POPLAR COTTAGE 289

III STILL LIFE 305

IV DEA EX MACHINA 322

Part One

NORTH BROMWICH

(I)

THE GRINDSTONE

THAT buff envelope with the words *Income Tax*, *Private*, printed on its left-hand bottom corner had assumed complete possession of Owen Lucton's desk. Ever since he sighted it on entering the office that morning its presence had tinged the atmosphere of the well-appointed room with a vague discomfort, casting a shadow on the habitually rosy surface of Mr. Lucton's mind and undermining the conscious thoughts which he successfully applied to the ordering of other people's balance-sheets with a cavern of disquietude and foreboding in the pit of the stomach, resembling that which, of late years, he had been accustomed to associate with the word "dyspepsia". Impelled by a childish obstinacy, Mr. Lucton had determined to put off the evil moment of opening it; he had craftily concealed it under a pile of business papers; but though he pretended to dismiss it from his thoughts, he had continued to be conscious of its imminence, like that of a masked battery which sooner or later was bound to open fire.

During a lull, towards the end of a busy morning, his secretary, Miss Jenkins, had presumed, officiously, to remind him of the damnable document's existence.

"There's that notice of assessment which came this morning," she said. "I put it on the desk, sir. You must have covered it. Hadn't I better check up with the return and make sure they haven't made any mistake? They generally do make one, don't they?" she added; and as she spoke, the focus of disquietude under Mr. Lucton's waistcoat—a dove-grey waistcoat with a row of pearly buttons and a slender but elegantly expensive watch-chain of platinum—had suddenly, without a moment's warning, diffused itself into a rising wave of irritability that was manifest in a reddening of his high, shiny forehead, and could be felt as a sensation of engorgement inside the glossy collar that constricted his neck. His eyes glared at Miss Jenkins; in his flushed sensorium the words "Kindly mind your own business!" flared up like a spurt of flame; but before they had reached the speech centre, whose duty it was to give them articulation, Mr. Lucton became aware of their victim's person. He saw a clumsy, middle-aged woman, inclined to stoutness; a little gold cross suspended over a cream silk blouse; a black velvet ribbon encircling a throat inclined to goitre; a pair of watery blue eyes, magnified by pince-nez, which already blenched before his unspoken asperity; and in that instant of clarified vision Mr. Lucton's harshness faded into a mood which was almost sentimental.

"Poor Miss Jenkins," he thought, "she's growing old like the rest of us; twenty years with the firm—she'll never marry now—not a ghost of a chance; I suppose that's why she hangs that cross on her chest: consolations of religion—I hope she finds them, poor soul! She's as good as they make 'em, and a first-rate secretary. Thank God she's not better-looking! The world's quite full enough of distractions of that kind."

Mr. Lucton smiled, and immediately the apprehensiveness faded from Miss Jenkins's watery blue eyes.

"Never mind about that, Miss Jenkins," he said. "I'll deal with it after lunch. By the way, have you made arrangements yet for taking your holidays?"

Miss Jenkins blushed faintly; but even that tinge of colour could not make her attractive. "It rather depends on you, sir," she said. "I don't like being absent from the office when you're away. Things are bound to crop up. They always do, don't they?"

Mr. Lucton waved her aside. "Oh, don't worry about me. I doubt if I shall manage to get away at all this year. There's so much to be done, getting into the new house and all that."

"I quite appreciate that, sir. You've an appointment at four, at Wilburns' office, to complete the sale of the old one. There's a note on your pad to remind you."

"I saw it. Thank you. I don't need reminding of that, Miss

Jenkins," he answered ruefully. "It's a bit of a wrench, you know, leaving a place where you've dug yourself in for twenty-five years. Men are creatures of habit, anyway, by the time they've reached fifty."

"The new house is a delightful place," Miss Jenkins consoled him—for she knew that consolation was part of her duty. "I'm not at all surprised that Mrs. Lucton insisted on buying it. It's extremely dignified, isn't it?"

"More in keeping with my station than the old one, you mean?" Mr. Lucton teased her.

"Well, we *are* an important firm, sir, aren't we?" Miss Jenkins replied.

Mr. Lucton laughed. "As witness the taxes we pay." (How that damned thing stuck in his mind!) "Well, never mind. Get your holiday fixed up without thinking of mine. Where are you going, by the way?"

"I think I shall spend most of it with my mother, near Lesswardine in Shropshire. Quite a tiny place; it's called Mainstone—not far from the Radnorshire border. I don't suppose you've heard of it. You see, my father *was* Welsh, sir, wasn't he?" she added, with a timid eagerness, bending forward slightly and then, with a nervous, an almost confiding gesture, touching the edge of the desk between them with a finger reddened on one side with ink and purpled at the tip with typewriter ribbon. Indeed, as she spoke, Miss Jenkins's face became tender and transfigured; her blue eyes misty and soft, like a rain-washed landscape; but Mr. Lucton was unaware of this shy, instinctive gesture of approach. That quiet word, Shropshire, endowed with an alchemical quality, had released in his mind soft echoes of a remembered music which, dwelling there, generally subdued amid the activities of his business life, had a way of emerging, like those waves which, wandering through ether, may be transformed into sound by the sudden turn of a switch. So, now, staring straight before him, yet unaware of the orderly litter of documents on his desk or of Miss Jenkins's inky fingers, a rhythmical figure of words took shape in his mind:

In valleys of springs of rivers
By Ony and Teme and Clun,
The country of easy livers
The quietest under the sun . . .

They ran through his brain like an ambling music of muted strings, half-gay and half-sad, and suddenly his unseeing eyes saw—not that sumptuous accountant's office, the fine fruit of excess profits, with its mahogany chimney-piece, its book-shelves of gilt-backed Transactions, its mottled deed-boxes, lettered with the names of the gilt-edged firms whose figures he sifted—but a green bank that shimmered in the blowing weather of June. The hornbeam and sycamore along the wood's verge were whitened by every gust of it; the great elms, newly come to leaf, dipped their swaying tapestries like the flounces of stately ladies who bowed and curtsied; and there, downhill, with the blowing wind behind him, downhill, through an air made sweet by wreathing honeysuckle, his feet tucked up on coasting-brackets above the spinning pedals, sped a boy on a safety-bicycle: a slim boy with a freckled face, wearing a red-and-black striped blazer and white flannel trousers girt at the waist by a red-and-black belt with a brass clasp shaped like a snake! Mr. Lucton's right hand strayed mechanically to the back of his waistcoat, where a buckled strap had reached the end of its tether. He thought: "This damned tailor makes my waistcoats too tight." He said: "Ah, Shropshire. . . . When I was a lad, Miss Jenkins, I rode all through that part of the country on a bicycling tour. Yes, my old dad rode with me. Stopped at a pub every night and slept together on feather beds. Eggs and bacon, morning and evening. Nothing to beat it! Now nobody would dream of riding a bicycle in these days."

"Oh yes, sir, *I* do, when I'm at home," Miss Jenkins declared, with enthusiasm, bringing an instant vision to Mr. Lucton's inward eye of a long flat road and Miss Jenkins, viewed from behind, pedalling along it for all she was worth. It was a vision that failed to give him æsthetic pleasure; so he banished it, saying kindly: "H'm . . . Now fancy that! Well, well . . ." which was his way of implying that the conversation was closed. But Miss Jenkins was not to be cheated of her opportunity; having advanced so far along this easy road to intimacy she refused to turn back.

"You know, Mr. Lucton," she began, "I can't bear to hear you say you won't take a holiday; because I'm perfectly sure, if I may say so, you need one much more than I do. It would freshen you up . . ."

"Do I need freshening up, Miss Jenkins?"

"Well, you know what I mean, sir. You never will spare yourself. You're at it all day and every day, and then, what's the good of it?"

"Ah, now you're talking profoundly, Miss Jenkins! You mean that if I went away for six months the business would go on just as well as if I were here? Well, you're probably right."

"Oh no, sir. You know quite well I meant nothing of the sort." Miss Jenkins was horrified yet persistent. "But if you would only delegate a *little* of your work to Mr. Leith. When we're through with Hingston's audit . . ."

On the last words she lowered her voice and stopped suddenly; she had heard the door-handle turning. Mr. Lucton, his right eye screwed up, continued to regard her with a quizzical smile, while the door itself opened and his elder son, Leith, swung into the office. He was a tall young man, with an extremely polished exterior, but with a hardness beneath the polish that gave it an air of jet. He had hard, dark, shining eyes, and fine, white, shining teeth; every word that issued from his firm lips was clipped and shining like a newly minted coin—for Mr. Lucton, whose own accent was that of an educated Midlander, had sent him to a public school which, if it taught nothing else, produced a standardized variety of the Cockney dialect and a pattern of manners—both of which Mr. Lucton was prepared to admire without attempting to emulate—which made their possessor free of polite society. There were actually qualities in Leith which Mr. Lucton admired even more: a dark torrent of energy—(Mr. Lucton, though conscientious, was naturally indolent) a fierce fixity of purpose—(Mr. Lucton indulged in dreams) an entirely ruthless realism—(Mr. Lucton was incurably romantic), and a mind which had the edge and precision of a surgeon's scalpel.

The admiration which Mr. Lucton conceded to Leith's attainments—and, in private, he was not above boasting about them to his business friends—was tempered, in secret, by a jealousy of which he was ashamed. Leith was his mother's boy, not his; his mental and physical opposite. He knew, again, but was reluctant to admit, that the brain of this lad of twenty-four worked more keenly and swiftly than his own; he was disquietingly conscious of Leith's growing preponderance in the office over which he himself had presided since his father's death. Old employees of the firm were beginning—not exactly to question his decisions, for, wrong or right, Mr. Lucton's word was still law—but to say, with a guarded obsequiousness, "By the way, sir, Mr. Leith suggested . . ." or, "Oh, I forgot to mention, sir—Mr. Leith asked me to remind you . . ." and the perception of this rising influence so sharply antagonized Owen Lucton that, more than once, he had turned down Leith's suggestions, though he knew they bettered his own.

At this moment Leith's name, newly trumpeted by the loyal lips of Miss Jenkins, whose soul Mr. Lucton had regarded for the last twenty years as his private property and herself as the unquestioning slave of his least prudent caprice, filled his mind—already disquieted by the unopened income-tax assessment—with a new sense of insecurity which her falling to silence increased. His quizzical glance grew hard. He said: "Please go on, Miss Jenkins. Mr. Leith will be flattered no doubt and interested to hear what you were saying."

Miss Jenkins's neck reddened under the black velvet ribbon. She hedged.

"Oh, I think that's all, sir, thank you, isn't it?" she said. She turned with a nervous smile in Leith's direction, and minced out of the office.

"Of course! the old goose is in love with him," Mr. Lucton thought. "Preposterous at her age! Bicycling! Upon my soul!" Then his eyes fell on Leith standing there in the attitude of studied deference towards paternal decrepitude which Winchester had taught him; he was aware of his son's jetty elegance, and of the fact that Leith's waistcoat positively went in at the waist, and said, with a kind of uneasy importance: "Well, Leith, what is it?"

Leith smiled a most charming and deferential smile. "It's past one o'clock, sir." (The "sir" had an old-fashioned flavour and pleased Mr. Lucton in spite of himself.) "If you're lunching at the club, I'ld like to go with you. There are one or two things . . ."

Mr. Lucton rose heavily. "Very well, come along," he said.

They descended the stairs, Leith a little in the rear of his father, and stepped out into Sackville Row, the most elegant street in North Bromwich. At that hour and on that day the "Row" had a gay, irresponsible air which emanated from the spirits of a multitude of young women employed in business offices whom the hammer-stroke of the Art Gallery clock striking "one" had unshackled at a blow from their desks. Emerging from their morning's captivity on a harlequin flight, these creatures filled the pavements with a brisk linnet-like chattering which seemed, somehow, in keeping with the bright June sky, the gay window-boxes on the sills of the Grand Midland Hotel, the sheaves of blue Spanish irises in a flower-seller's basket, the leaves of plane-trees shivering in the light breeze against the sandstone curves of the cathedral's dome.

Leith Lucton, striding along at his father's side, seemed singularly unaware of these fluttering bevies. Though not actually insusceptible to their attractions, he looked upon women, as he looked upon the rest of life, with a canny and entirely unsentimental eye. At this moment Leith's crystalline brain was still grimly fixed on business, and therefore hermetically sealed against any such intrusions. Mr. Lucton's, though theoretically divided into the same kind of watertight compartments, showed a tendency to leak. He was just old enough, but not too old, to notice young women. He noticed them now, with approval. During his thirty years in business he was prepared to say that the standard of female beauty in North Bromwich had definitely improved. He was happy to observe that skirts were lengthening, for he had, as he proudly admitted, an old-fashioned, romantic prejudice in favour of mystery. It seemed to him odd that Leith kept his eyes to himself while his own glance wandered.

"When *I* was Leith's age . . ." he thought. . . . But when *he* was Leith's age, he remembered, he was already married and Leith on the way to be born at the snug little house in King's Road, Alvaston, which Leith's mother—and Leith in collusion—had just forced him to sell.

"Twenty-five years ago," he thought. "That's more than a third of a lifetime. *And take from seventy springs three score*—two and a half score to be precise—*it only leaves me twenty more.* Only twenty years more, after thirty of drudgery!" Mr. Lucton reflected. "And what have I got out of them? A biggish income, of which the tax-collector bags half; a wife and a family of four who are completely self-sufficient and don't really care twopence for me; a prominent position in the business world of North Bromwich. That policeman is going to salute me . . ."

And indeed, as they crossed the road in front of a block of traffic, Mr. Lucton's wilting self-esteem was revived by a smile and a spectacular salute from the white-sleeved officer on point-duty which made him stiffen his back and even gave an air of importance to his gait till, having passed through the glass swing-doors of the Constitutional Club, a newly presented portrait in oils of the late Joseph Hingston, first Baron Wolverbury, brought him back to the sombre mood from which the policeman's salute had diverted him.

"Success . . ." Mr. Lucton thought. "Success . . . Yes, that's what it means: a handle to your name or your wife's (wouldn't Muriel give her eyes for it?); a big place in the country to keep up, with thirty damned gardeners; then, after you're dead, a portrait in your club which members subscribe for and promptly forget. But what else did Hingston get out of it? Not too much, to judge by his face, though he did have a longish innings. Eighty-three . . . eighty-four. Joe always looked after himself. Never smoked, never drank; always ate a milk-pudding for lunch. . . . Of course, that's what *I* ought to do."

At this point Mr. Lucton's conscience became a prey to conflict. Their silent progress had brought them to the enormous buffet of the club dining-room on which, displayed with all the temptations of art, he perceived a luscious assortment of cold viands, cunningly glazed and frilled and garnished, that instantly made his mouth water with desire and swept every ascetic resolution (in company with the late Lord Wolverbury's milk-pudding) out of his mind.

The carver leant over towards him. "I've a beautiful bit of prime beef here to-day, Mr. Lucton. Just suit you. I know I can't tempt Mr. Leith—but you couldn't resist it, sir. Only look at it!"

Mr. Lucton looked; he wavered; he fell. "Not too much, Charles," he weakly pleaded, just a second too late.

"Oh, *that* won't hurt anyone, sir. Can't tempt *you*, Mr. Leith?"

Leith laughed. "Bread and cheese for me, Charles."

The wine-waiter hurried up to them. "The usual for you, Mr. Lucton, sir? Half a pint or a pint?"

Mr. Lucton pursed his lips in reflection. One might as well be hanged for an ox as a plate of red beef. "A pint, John," he said. Leith poured himself out a glass of water, so pointedly that Mr. Lucton felt under the necessity of defending himself.

"When I was a lad, Leith," he said, "many years before you were born, Marie Lloyd used to sing a song on the halls, and the last line was this: 'A little of what you fancy does you good.' Well, d'you know? I'm inclined to agree with her."

"So am I, Dad," Leith answered coldly. "*A little*. . . . By the way, do you mind if I talk while we're eating? I have to meet a fellow at the office at half-past one."

Mr. Lucton disliked talking business at meals, but felt himself cornered.

He sighed. "Carry on," he said.

"Well, it's Muriel . . ."

Mr. Lucton went red. His pint-tankard was already half-empty. "I do wish you young people wouldn't call your mother by her Christian name. I know I'm old-fashioned, but it always gives me a jar."

"Mother likes us to call her Muriel."

"Very well, go ahead."

"It's about the new house. We've been discussing the question of bathrooms. You see, there are only two, which is ridiculous for a house of that size, and we're all agreed that we can't possibly do with less than five, and another for the servants."

"Six bathrooms? Who's going to use them?"

"Well, there's you, and Muriel and Rupert and myself and Dorothy; and if Patricia and Hugh come to stay and bring the twins, or if we have any visitors, or if people come in to play squash when we get the new court. . . . Honestly, Dad, I can't see us doing with less than six as a minimum—and Muriel ought to have one to herself by rights."

"By *rights?* What d'you mean? What rights?"

"Well, in these days, particularly in a house of that size, a married woman expects a little privacy."

"Privacy? Privacy?" Mr. Lucton gulped down the rest of his bitter. "Let me tell you this, Leith: the first year your mother and I were married, we lived in two rooms and we lived in them happily, and on Saturday nights I lit a fire under the copper and carried up buckets of water and tipped them into a tin bath. Once a week, mind! And when you were born, my lad, it was a question of a kettle and a basin, and me sneezing my head off, like hay-fever, with your beastly baby-powder. Six bathrooms! The whole British nation's gone cracked on baths; and so far as I can see, we're not any cleaner than we used to be. You'll be wanting a swimming-pool next!"

"Oh well, we can easily do without that till next summer," Leith answered mildly. "But this bathroom question. . . . Honestly, Dad, we must have them. You don't want to have people lining up in a queue."

"Why should they line up in a queue? Let them stay in bed till somebody shouts for them. If your mother particularly wants a bathroom as well as a bedroom to herself, I suppose she must have one. What'll all this cost?"

"Oh, not much. About two hundred pounds." Mr. Lucton gasped. "You see," Leith went on, "Muriel's seen one at Lady

Astill's. Black marble surround for the bath and rose mirror all round the walls. She's set her heart on it."

"What's the rose mirror for?"

"To see oneself in, I suppose. Rose mirrors make you look younger and fitter first thing in the morning. Women love mirrors, anyway."

"Why should a woman want to see her own body in her bath? The idea's revolting. It's indecent. It's decadent . . . that's the right word. I tell you what, Leith: when people begin to take that amount of interest in their bodies there's something radically wrong with our civilization. You read your Gibbon. Decline and Fall. We've gone soft. What people need to-day is a good old cold douche to brace 'em up again. Two hundred pounds! Do you realize what this fancy move of your mother's has cost me already?"

"To within a few pounds. It's cost roughly eight thousand four hundred. Say nine thousand in all, when the squash-court and one or two minor things have been paid for."

"Nine thousand pounds! Have you any idea what that means to me?"

"I know what your income is, Dad."

"H'm . . . so do the damned Commissioners of Inland Revenue."

"It's hardly likely to go down. The business is always expanding. It's the biggest in the Midlands——" ("Yes, and who made it *that*, young man?" Mr. Lucton thought.) "After all," Leith went on, "what's the good of earning a pot of money if you never spend it?"

"What's the good of earning it if you spend every penny you do earn on rose-coloured mirrors? Why not blue all our capital in one jolly week? Am I never to be allowed to retire and enjoy a bit of leisure?"

"Well, you're only fifty," Leith answered reproachfully. "That's young in these days. Old Wolverbury didn't retire till he was close on eighty."

"*And since to look on things in bloom*," Mr. Lucton thought, "*Twenty springs*". . . . He said: "Now, look here, my boy:

suppose I refuse to give in on this bathroom question and allow the architect two hundred and fifty to play with, what'll your mother say?"

"She'll remind you you're just taking delivery of a new two thousand-pound car for your own private use. By the way, you know Rupert's burnt out one of the Bentley's big-ends?"

"Rupert would. I suppose he ran her without any oil in the sump. He's no feeling for machinery. He hasn't enough engine-sense to manage a Model 'T' Ford; and yet he's the cheek to keep badgering me to buy him a second-hand aeroplane! One of these days Rupert'll burn out his big-ends two thousand feet up and come down flat as a pancake in Sackville Row. It's time Rupert settled down to a job of work, Leith. He's not fit to fly."

Leith smiled. "Oh, old Rupert's all right. He's got his pilot's licence. I forgot to tell you. He's flying down from Heston at this moment." Leith looked at his watch. "Twenty-five minutes past. I must scoot. Look here, Dad, you know, you'd much better give Muriel her head over this bathroom business. It's *her* house, when all's said and done."

Mr. Lucton laughed ruefully. "There's no doubt about that," he said.

Leith rose. "Don't forget you're handing over the deeds of the old one at Wilburns'. Four o'clock sharp."

Mr. Lucton nodded. "All right, my boy. I shan't forget. See you later."

(II)

POST-PRANDIAL

STARING moodily at his empty plate, Mr. Lucton lit a cigar. A sense of suffusion in his neck and forehead reminded him that beef, pickles, blue gorgonzola and a pint of beer at luncheon were a mistake. He regarded with envy, regret and admiration the remains of Leith's frugal repast.

"A good boy," he thought, "altogether an exceptional boy. I ought to be proud to own such a son—if one did own one's own sons, but one doesn't. That's the devil of it," he thought, "from the moment they're born we regard our sons as possessions and then cut up rough when they regard *us* as a kind of ambulating cheque-book. Why shouldn't they? The whole trouble is," his mind ran on—for the heavy luncheon had somewhat disorganized his powers of consecutive thought—"the whole trouble is that everything and everybody in these days move too fast. I can't keep up with them. In this damned age nothing stays put for two minutes at a time; life's just like a cinema news-reel, bobbing here, there and everywhere. People behave as if they'd been bitten by one of those what-d'you-call-'ems—tarantulas: they can't stop jigging. They're so busy living, as they call it, that they forget they're alive. Speed . . . speed . . ." (Mr. Lucton had a vision of his younger son Rupert droning northward at that moment from Heston; and a shiver ran down his back, for, in spite of the boy's wild ways, he loved Rupert, who was blond and wide-eyed and freckled like himself, not dark and intense like Leith and Muriel, and he distrusted aeroplanes.) "Yes, speed. . . . And where does it get you?" he asked himself, paying three and ninepence at the desk and moving heavily from the dining-room to the smoke-room of the club, where he counted on neutralizing the effects of the beer with black coffee.

This long room, blue with the reek of expensive cigars firmly clenched in the teeth of a number of solid gentlemen more or less recumbent in saddle-bag chairs of maroon-coloured leather, showed small evidence of the precipitate speed against which Mr. Lucton rebelled. The majority of them, like himself, had lunched well and unwisely, as was betrayed by the fact that their voices were raised and their faces flushed. For the first time in twenty years, Mr. Lucton surveyed his fellow-members with distaste. Those surroundings into which he had previously fitted as smoothly and snugly as a well-oiled piston in its cylinder, no longer pleased him. Depositing himself in a solitary corner-chair, he rang for coffee and sat like a rock bespattered with flying phrases that were flung towards him out of the murmurous sea of talk:

". . . so I said: 'My Lord Bishop, I'm only a Protestant Englishman, but as *I* read the Thirty-Nine Articles . . ."

". . . Sleepy-sickness, not sleeping-sickness, my dear chap. That's Africa . . . Quite . . . Yes, nobody knows the cause of it . . ."

". . . three hundred and forty for six, on a drying wicket, mind! I bet you, if Hobbs . . ."

". . . five hundred Consolidated Main Reef at one and twenty-nine thirty-seconds. . . . Oh, copper, my dear fellow . . ."

". . . the third cook in two months. . . . Well, I just made her shut up the house and go to the seaside. . . . Yes, yes. . . . I'm a temporary bachelor. . . ."

". . . six months in the second division, and, by gad, he deserved it . . ."

". . . Czecho-Slovakia's only the beginning, he's after the Ukraine. Unless he happens to take a fancy to Rumania . . ."

". . . So last week, Joe came down to breakfast on Thursday morning and said, just as casual as be damned: 'Look here, Hazel, I'm going to leave you.' Walked out of the house there and then . . ."

Mr. Lucton woke up. "What's that, Parkes?" he asked.

Mr. Parkes, a lanky solicitor with a head like a skinned rabbit's, turned round and grimaced.

"Hello, Lucton! You there? I'm talking about Joe Astill. He's left his wife. Bolted."

"What for?"

"The usual reason. Joe's fifty years old. A young woman."

"What kind of young woman?"

"Oh, the usual kind. Irish. Name of O'Brien. That's all I know about it. But it's catching. That's the third case of the kind come my way in the last two months. You be careful, Lucton."

Mr. Lucton grunted. "Well, I always knew Joe was a lout, but I thought they got on all right. Lady Astill's an attractive woman. Pretty rotten, I call it. They've been married twenty-five years. Where's Joe gone to?"

"London. The honeymoon will be spent in Italy," said Mr. Parkes, with a jocular air. "Well, I must be moving. So long!"

The club lounge was emptying. "The slaves returning to their galleys," Mr. Lucton thought. "I suppose I ought to go too; but, after all, why should I? Leith's perfectly capable of running the office without me—even Miss Jenkins hinted at that. In an hour and a half I shall have to turn up at Wilburns'. Why shouldn't I stay here and be comfortable?"

He crushed the glow out of his stub of cigar and lay back luxuriously. A club servant in livery threw open two windows facing on Sackville Row. A soft purring of rubber-tyred traffic permeated the room; the wreaths of hanging cigar-smoke twirled and eddied; discarded newspapers fluttered where they had fallen; the soft, irresponsible breath of June filled the club—that temple of Midland middle-class orthodoxy—and Mr. Lucton's head, with a frivolous invitation to relax, to expand, to escape.

In the back of his mind he was still shocked by the particular kind of escape which his contemporary, Sir Joseph Astill the brewer, had suddenly achieved. Mr. Lucton was a family man, a domestic traditionalist; he believed in the sanctity of family life as he believed in the stability of the Crown or the Bank of England or the M.C.C. He had never approved of Joe Astill's "ways", and their latest development disgusted him. Yet, while he condemned it, there arose in his mind, unbidden and indeed discouraged, a sneaking sensation of—how could he describe it?—of awe?—of envy, rather. Yes, envy was the word. Joe Astill, rotter though he was, had actually displayed a decision, a ruthlessness, of which he, Owen Lucton, knew himself to be incapable. Joe Astill, at fifty, had succeeded in renewing his youth; with no more to-do than a casual good-bye, he had calmly shelved every single domestic responsibility. Joe Astill, the lucky blackguard, had made a clean cut; was making a fresh start in life. How many men of his age would give their eyes to do that?

"Though, by Jove, if I ever put up a show like that," Mr. Lucton thought, "I wouldn't start in by getting messed up with a woman. I should want to clear off by myself and go my own way; I should want not to have to listen to anyone talking when I wanted to be quiet; I should want, most of all, to be free from answering questions; I should want to read all the things that I've never read and ought to have read, and to see the places I've longed to see all my life, and drink beer in village pubs—not in clubs—with real people. Why, I've been hurried through the best of my days," Mr. Lucton thought, "like a tripper hanging out of a char-à-banc: never time to take anything in or think things over. Lord, what a life! And supposing I *did* lose my head and bolt, like Joe Astill, would anyone miss me?"

Debating this question, he found himself peering backwards towards events which, at twenty-five years' distance, grew hazy with sentiment. It was a sinister sign of advancing age, he supposed, that the future no longer interested him; that his thoughts of late had tended to flutter back, like tired birds, on the past. He remembered now, with a poignant renewal of youthful ardours to which his heart had long been a stranger, the dance at Mawne Hall, where he had first set eyes on Muriel. In those days of swinging waltzes and kitchen-lancers, dancing had been dancing: not a languid shuffle accompanied by the wail of saxophones, but a stirring and strenuous exercise, an affair of thudding pulses and crumpled shirt-fronts. In his days dancing had been the joy of hot youth—not the pastime of elderly matrons, bald-headed satyrs and effeminate gigolos. In his days dancing had been gay, full of zest and laughter, and a ball a festal occasion, not a mere alternative to bridge as a digestive routine.

He remembered the moment when Muriel and he had met. She was descending the staircase at Mawne on the arm of Edward Willis (killed in the War, poor fellow!), her face flushed beneath her splendid coils of dark hair; he supposed she had been "sitting out" in one of the labyrinthine corridors upstairs, which was a daring thing to do, but not nearly so daring as the red satin slippers that showed beneath the lifted hem of her white satin dress. Owen Lucton had gasped, yes, literally gasped at the sight of her; she was the most "stunning" girl he had seen in all his born days. Blushing violently—he had always been subject to that disability—he had placed himself in their path.

"Won't you introduce me, Edward?"

"Why, surely you know Muriel Davies?"

Muriel Davies? He had remembered, distantly, a sallow, lanky little girl with long black stockings who could have no possible connection with this red-slippered glory. Then Muriel had laughed that low, provocative laugh whose deep tones her voice still kept, though the laugh had now lost its provocativeness. "I've a better memory than you," she had said. "You've not changed a bit. You're Owen Lucton." Edward Willis had hurried away—he was an odd, shy fellow—and left them to a coquettish struggle over her programme, which Mr. Lucton insisted on seeing and she denied him. It was awfully full, she said—(as it would be, he thought); she had nothing left but a polka and a quadrille, which he eagerly booked.

"And the extras?" he asked.

"No, I haven't booked those. Would you like the first?"

"May I have them all?" he said boldly. "Well, really, Owen . . . !" But she smiled; and in the surpassing, soft sweetness of that smile Owen Lucton was lost eternally.

Well, hardly eternally, but for a period of five or six years which had the quality of eternity. They were years, Mr. Lucton remembered, of astonishing hopefulness; years of eager scheming and infinitesimal triumphs which seemed, at the time, world-shaking in their importance. The world which they caused to shake was small: its axis stretching between the two poles of Mr. Lucton's father's office, where he worked for a junior clerk's salary, and the particular seaside resort which was gravely chosen each year as the scene of their holiday in August; and its equator the warm fireside of the little house (which had seemed so enormous when they first dared to take it) in King's Road, Alvaston.

It was a tiny world, yet so centripetal, so introspective, so self-contained, that its inhabitants—Owen Lucton, Muriel, the young cook-general and the regular accretion of babies, four in six years—hardly knew any other. Its quietude had suited Mr. Lucton's easy temperament. In spite of their narrow resources—his father, that shrewd old man with his handsome Victorian beard, believed in self-help for the young—Mr. Lucton now looked back on that period of his life with regret and yearning. He still kept in the dressing-room to which, twenty years later, his wife had banished him on account of his snoring, a silver-framed photograph of the miraculous Muriel of those ecstatic days in which the fading of the print had given a bloom to her smiling lips, her young, unwrinkled features, her voluminous shadowy hair, recalling the long-lost vision of lazy voluptuousness which he had watched, possessively contented, through half-closed eyelids when, lovers still, they lay late in bed on a Sunday morning. In that far-off age they had always been busy, excited, happy, but never tired; too engrossed in the business of living to notice the weather, which, later, had become the chief subject of their mutual condolences. Looking backward, Mr. Lucton could only remember halcyon days: days of tufted lilac-plumes and golden cataracts of laburnum, the green smell and soft touch of mown grass that flew from the blades of the clattering machine he pushed to and fro in his shirt-sleeves, proudly aware of the pattern of stripes on the little lawn; days of summer stillness, when odours of honey drooped from one shady lime; himself in a deck-chair smoking his pipe and listening to the drone of bees, and Muriel—the Muriel of the silver-framed photograph—sitting smiling, sewing, beside him—so silent, so richly contented to be silent—and there, on the rug at her feet,

Leith, a baby, gurgling and crawling; golden days of autumnal fulfilment when the dahlias sunned their velvet and drowned wasps hung in bottles of sugary beer, and the Michaelmas daisies he had planted made a mist of amethyst through which they walked arm in arm, slowly (another baby was coming), with no need of a spoken word between them nor any sign but a sudden slowing of their steps, a sudden pressure of clasped arms against the side.

And when the dahlias shrivelled in one night of frost and the evenings closed in—as they did with surprising swiftness in the age before "daylight-saving"—then, indeed, came in the richest season of all. He could remember the discreet explosion with which, when he came home from work, the gas took light round its incandescent mantle; the sensation of pure relief with which he sank into the chair by the left-hand side of the fire which was flanked by his bookcase. From the first they had decided that this smallest of the three rooms on the ground-floor should be his own, and for twenty-five years it had remained the inmost sanctuary of his inner life, acquiring, from his habitation, not only an untidiness (which was Muriel's despair) and a characteristic aroma of leather and tobacco, but also an aura, a kind of spiritual patina, which was an extension of his own personality and made the place as much a part of him as his own skin.

During the first years of their married life (when it was called the "den") Muriel had spent almost as many hours in this room as Owen himself. It was cosy in winter because of its smallness; and there, when the children had been safely tucked-up in bed, she would sit with her needle-work (how busy those neat fingers were!), only occasionally interrupting the flow of Mr. Lucton's thoughts as he sat there reading, with a pathetic "Oh, I'm sorry, I've disturbed you, darling!" which was a statement of fact, but which Mr. Lucton gallantly denied: she was so naïve, so meek, so richly contented with simple pleasures, so angelically patient.

In those days the thread of his reading—for nothing could stop that—was broken by many kisses and just a few tears; but this combination of culture and domesticity was not unpleasing to him, for he was still in love and not more selfish than most men; but after the second baby, Patricia, had been born, he began to insist that Muriel, for her health's sake, shouldn't sit up with him, and remained downstairs, reading and smoking, into the small hours, when, reluctantly, he turned down the light and stole on tiptoe to bed.

By the time that the third child, Rupert, came, in the fourth year of their marriage, Mr. Lucton's bearded Victorian father had died; the "den" in keeping with its owner's new importance had become the "library", and Muriel rarely visited it. She was increasingly busy, for one thing, with the care of three children; and, for another, her husband's sudden emergence as the head of the oldest accountant's business in North Bromwich had given her a sense of her own social importance in the life of Alvaston. The house, which had seemed much too big for them when first they married, was now just a trifle too small for their dignity. It became incumbent on Mrs. Owen Lucton to compete with the wives of other professional men in entertaining. So the drawing-room and dining-room were re-furnished. A frilled and starched parlour-maid, who had actually served the Hingstons at Stourford Castle, was added to the faithful cook-general and the "lady" nurse. Muriel's tea-parties and her monthly "days"—second Thursdays—became celebrated for their rich confectionery, and within six months the household expenses were doubled.

Owen Lucton stumped up willingly. He was sufficiently sly to conceal the fact that, when once the death-duties were paid his income was at least six times what it had been before. By this time—and even more when their last child, Dorothy, was born—he had begun to regard his wife's always increasing exactions as a kind of Danegeld. She made it quite clear that the four children came first in her interest and himself a bad fifth; that he was, admittedly, in comparison with herself, a dull fellow, a social failure, only tolerated as a sharer of her bed and board because he was privileged to provide the money that supported her extravagant elegance. That her dress and manner of life did him credit, that she was an excellent mother, he could not deny. He was moderately rich—far richer, thank heaven, than Muriel ever guessed!—and since the bloom, and rather more than the bloom, had faded from their romantic marriage, he had settled down, like the bachelor he really was, to the secret enjoyment of the things which still made life sweet for him: the books which automatically accumulated in his shabby, deserted library (the only room in the house that hadn't been renovated); the nursery, where Muriel regarded his visits with undeserved suspicion (for the nursemaid was pretty), and the newly-built garage, his only personal extravagance, which Muriel grudgingly approved of, because the possession of a motor-car, in those days, conferred social distinction.

And then came the War . . .

At the moment of its outbreak Mr. Lucton had not considered the Great War to be any of his business. To him it was no more than a gigantic spectacle of a new and thrilling variety, provided, like the exploits of Suffragettes, for the entertainment of those who read the penny newspapers. Even the first grim casualty-lists in those newspapers failed to move him, for he belonged to a middle stratum of society, from which very few officers and no rank and file of the regular army were drawn. The motto of "Business as Usual" suited him splendidly—for business, in North Bromwich, became better than usual, and business in his own office began to boom. However thunderous the skies of Europe might be, at home it was his obvious duty and opportunity to make hay while the sun shone—the more so since men whose judgment he respected assured him "it would soon be over." But when the New Year came in and the first spring followed—he had been forced to lay up his precious motor-car for lack of petrol—he found that most of his friends were enlisting or building new factories to make munitions.

The "Derby Scheme" came. With Muriel's approval he found himself going to the office with a crown and the King's initials in red on a dark blue armlet, and, a few months later, he discovered what that armlet meant, waking up from the placid dream of which, till then, his life had consisted, to find himself the cynosure of all eyes in a khaki tunic with one gilt star on the shoulder, canary breeches innocent of saddle grease, and new leather leggings that chafed him below the knee when he walked.

For a man of peace of a meditative temperament, this breaking out into fancy dress was an exciting experience. One of the more surprising effects of his transformation was a sudden and flattering rise of his prestige in the eyes of Muriel, who proceeded to atone for her neglect of him during the last eighteen months by a display of affection to which he was so unused that, at first, he found it embarrassing. There was, he perceived, an element of irony in this renewal of love, his wife's ardent attentions resembling those which the Aztecs, in Prescott's History, lavished on the prospective victims of their bloody sacrifice; yet the raptures of their last days together in England, and the proud tears, sternly repressed, with which she bade him good-bye, made him feel that, after all, perhaps he had misunderstood her, and convinced him that there was something heroic in the sacrifice which he had unconsciously slipped into making.

The memory of those tears and the vision of that brave but agonized face kept him company, for the best part of four years, in Mesopotamia, where he found himself transported with as much understanding or volition as a tick on an elephant's tail. He saw them, romantically (for such was the spirit of those times) through mirages of heat, through pestering clouds of flies, through the pungent smoke of fires of camel-dung. He wrote and received some hundreds of passionate letters, more high-pitched in their tone than those they had exchanged in the days of their courting. He dreamed of her—talked of her with a lowered voice in some of those odd moments when men who were strangers and inarticulate shared touching confidences, and again, to a pretty nurse in a hospital at Alexandria, just to convince her that he wasn't (as he undoubtedly was) a little in love with her. In those strange and, oddly enough, not unhappy years, Owen Lucton created—out of the debris of the past, out of the poetry with which much solitary reading had crammed his head, out of the poetry which that exalted and perilous time discovered in himself—a new Muriel of the imagination, surpassing in beauty, in sweetness, above all in tenderness, the wife he had left behind. When finally, thinned to a scarecrow by dysentery, Mr. Lucton returned to the arms of this wifely paragon, he found . . . a stranger. Desirable—oh, eminently desirable—but still, a stranger.

"And we've been strangers, practically speaking, ever since," Mr. Lucton thought. . . .

Sitting there, in the empty lounge of his club—the waiter, having flushed the smoke out of it, had pulled down the window-sashes, so that the newspapers fluttered no more and the steady rumour of traffic in Sackville Row was hushed—he endeavoured to recapture the mood of that surprising home-coming. He saw, by some wilful vagary of fancy, the banks of the Suez Canal, the pale, opaque, olivine water spreading from the green-banded stem of a hospital-ship on to thirsty sands, and the face of a man, whose name he had forgotten for the moment, who had died as they left the mouth of the canal at Port Said.

"Suppose I had been that poor beggar," he thought. (A red beard, he had, and a curt, saturnine humour: a Scotsman, no doubt.) "Suppose I'd changed places with him and died, would it have made much difference to her?"

He felt doubtful. It was only when they found themselves alone renewing their most intimate relationships, that he had been shocked (for he was easy-going and inclined to take things for granted) to realize the magnitude of the gap that separated them. Muriel tolerated his embraces with the resignation of a martyr nailed on the cross of patriotic duty: but it soon became clear that there was no prospect of their recovering the earlier rapture. He was surprised to discover that her life during his absence had not been one long, aching void. She had found hard work and absorbing interest in Lady Hingston's officers' hospital at Stourford Castle. Mr. Lucton was not at all sure that she hadn't found something more. On the drawing-room desk at which Muriel dealt with her housekeeping, he saw a "snapshot" of a man with a crutch, rather older than himself, in a major's uniform. Sniffing round the familiar, unfamiliar room on the morning after his return, Mr. Lucton had idly asked who the subject of the photograph might be.

"Oh, nobody you know," she had said. "A man I nursed. He was a gunner." Her eyes met his with a steadiness in which there was a challenge. "Be careful," they seemed to say; "you may easily hurt me." Then they hardened, as though a portcullis had fallen behind them. "He was killed on the Somme," she added. Her voice had a painful tensity beneath its willed composure; and Mr. Lucton knew, as surely as if she had whispered the words in his ears, that this man had been her lover, or could have been.

He left her, with a casual commiseration on his lips: "Poor devil, was he?" and wandered away from the drawing-room to his own little library, not angry, but curiously shaken by the mute revelation. In his four years of absence, bereft of his dreams, that room had given up the ghost; it was a dead room, deserted, reduced to a mortal rigidity by Muriel's material attentions and her emotional neglect. It smelt faintly musty—for in the war winters fuel had been scarce—and the books on the shelves, once warmed by Mr. Lucton's loving fingers, felt dank and uncared-for.

Even so, the sight of that familiar fire-side, of the arm-chair so moulded by use that it had not yet forgotten the shape of his body, of the friendly volumes from whose companionship he had been divorced for so long—his Boswell, his Gibbon, his *Don Quixote*, his Borrows, his Fieldings, his *Morte d'Arthur* —atoned, by the solace that inanimate things afford, for the shock of having lost the romantic human relationship on which he had counted. "We expect too much of marriage," he told himself; "I have had as much out of it as most men and more than many. If we can't start all over again on the old lines, we shall have compensations. The children. . . ."

Mr. Lucton had been prepared at that time to be sentimental about them; they were no longer mere babies, amusing little animals whose fumbling antics one watched like those of piglets in a pen, but small human beings with sharply-defined characteristics and temperaments—the dark pair, Leith and Patricia, were like their mother; the fair ones, Rupert and Dorothy, resembled himself. But if he supposed that they were his in anything but their surnames, the new Muriel soon showed him that he was gravely mistaken. She had rigid ideas—the latest—on the education of her children; the haphazard processes which had produced Mr. Lucton and herself were not good enough for them. She made it quite plain that their lives were not going to be botched by the affections of a clumsy amateur, who had played so small and so selfish a part in their creation. In addition to a pseudo-scientific professionalism derived from text-books on the newly-fashionable "cult of the child", she developed a fiercely exclusive jealousy, a tigerish possessiveness. Whatever the colour of their eyes and hair, their children were hers, not his, all four of them. Their father's functions in the matter were clearly defined by the word's etymology. Mr. Lucton was nothing more nor less than a father, a feeder. It was his privilege, by keeping his nose to the grindstone, to see that they were fed.

He had achieved this function to some purpose. During the early post-war boom, when the relief of Europe showed itself in a feverish attempt to rebuild, against time, the material it had wrecked, Mr. Lucton's business took toll of reviving industry; he became wealthy—far wealthier than he had ever imagined was possible. As for Muriel, she was too deeply absorbed in her children to be aware of his growing fortunes. During that period—and it lasted for twelve years—all she had asked of her husband was that he should not interfere, in return for which she was thankful to leave him alone—to his irritating bachelor ways, his books, his club, his motor-cars (in which his thwarted passion for everything mechanical displayed itself), and to his boring business friends whom she tolerated because they were useful and kept him quiet.

Mr. Lucton, cannily, lay low and asked less and less in return. They were passing, as he gathered from comparing notes with his fellows, through the period of adjustment which complicated even the happiest of marriages: the final balancing of give-and-take between human beings of different temperaments. When this trying phase was over, experienced friends told him, he might look for a happy renewal of married life, a period in which their children having chosen their own lives, man and wife "came together" once more, all differences forgotten in a kind of autumnal serenity.

Mr. Lucton secretly yearned for this happy issue—he was placid by nature and well adapted for domesticity—but the event belied what his friends had led him to expect. The children grew up, more or less according to Muriel's plans; he was bound to confess, on the whole, that they did her credit. Leith, the eldest, brought into the business his keen, hard intelligence; Patricia, the second, married a young man to whom he could find no objections and produced unexceptionable twins; Rupert, the third, harum-scarum by nature, not too richly endowed with brains, was more simple than either of his elders, and nearer, therefore, to Mr. Lucton's heart; while Dorothy, the baby of the family, was a darling, and the principal object of her father's generosity and love. They appeared, to the casual observer, a happy and united family—most united of all in their patronizing attitude towards poor Mr. Lucton, whom they had been taught to regard through their mother's benevolent but faintly contemptuous eyes. It was an attitude that Mr. Lucton, not unnaturally, resented. After all, though his tastes might differ from theirs and were, frankly, old-fashioned, he *did* pay the piper to an increasing degree, and might surely expect to have some word in the choice of the tune.

It was his misfortune that the tune they chose should be as unintelligible and as distasteful to him as most of the dance-music with which, through the medium of strident gramophone-records and wireless-sets, his peace was shattered. He yearned, figuratively and in fact, for a little Gilbert and Sullivan, unexciting, tuneful—something better-mannered (as he would have put it) than their barbaric tom-tom rhythms and chromatic blues. His mind was too rigidly fixed in the mould of the pre-war world to take on new forms, and the war itself had crystallized rather than dissolved his prejudices. He found himself, in short, a back number, and ended by glorying in it, feeling himself old and wise and almost uncomfortably sober in a dizzy world, like a solitary teetotaller at a bottle-party.

But when he expected Muriel to share his point of view and to settle down at his side to a dignified old age, she did nothing of the sort. With the flight of her nestlings and the birth of her grandchildren she began to flap her own wings. Mr. Lucton didn't mind that—in moderation. He admired the way in which modern middle-aged women contrived to retain their complexions, though he did call the beauty-parlour business—(dishing out cocoa-butter and extract of witch-hazel in imitation Lalique pots at a guinea a time!)—a barefaced ramp. He was flattered when his business friends told him how young Muriel looked; he could even tolerate—though not without shocked surprise—her sudden hatching-out (at a time of life when her mother and his had finally resigned themselves to lace caps and elastic-sided boots) into a platinum blonde: after all, he reflected, though she fooled the rest of the world, she couldn't fool *him*. What disturbed him more deeply than this change in the colour of her hair, which, when you came to think of it, had a pathetic aspect, was the corresponding change in the colour of her soul.

He had taken it for granted that he knew Muriel through and through. Now he couldn't be sure of it. There was in her a new hardness, a new ruthlessness, a new greedy frivolity which he couldn't recognize. It might be natural and even becoming for a mother to identify herself with the interests of her own grown-up family, but it was neither one nor the other to compete with them: to flirt with boys who were young enough to be her own children, to whip herself up with cocktails, to talk with a license which made him shrivel with shyness, to plaster her lips with paint and (more shocking still) to redden her toe-nails.

Up till this, Mr. Lucton had always, with some satisfaction, regarded his wife as a prude. Those reddened toe-nails shook his faith in his judgment, and her latest scheme for a rose-mirrored bathroom destroyed it. He began to wonder if, all the time, she hadn't, perhaps, been the worst kind of prude: a prude with suppressed inclinations towards debauchery; and the thought of those secret fires, which possibly smouldered beneath the frigidity he knew, was frightening—for when once women started "that sort of thing", particularly at her age, there was no knowing where it might end. "Rejuvenation"—everyone talked and wrote of it. And there passed through his mind, to his acute disgust, a hateful example of Hollywood slang of the kind which at that time infested the English language. Was his cold, proper Muriel, in fact, a "*Red-hot Momma*"? Impossible, he assured himself; there was really no harm in her. Her only trouble was that, for some cracked reason or other, she resented growing old gracefully. Well, nobody liked growing old. He himself disliked his bald patch and his protuberant waist-line. But the disquieting symptoms in Muriel's rejuvenation were not merely connected with her sex. The thing, from his point of view, had an ethical, social side.

The Luctons—his father with the stern Victorian beard and his grandfather before him—had always prided themselves on the modesty of their private lives. Though the family had now been wealthy for three generations and in a position to compete in social splendour, if they so wished, with the new industrial aristocracy of North Bromwich—big brewers and ironmasters such as the Astills and Hingstons and Willises—its members had always avoided the least suspicion of display. At this moment, with social unrest in the air and unemployed on the streets, Mr. Lucton felt this attitude more than ever justified; but Muriel, once released in her second blooming, had quickly grown impatient of any restraint. She had begun to spend money to an extent that made Mr. Lucton shiver—not because he grudged or couldn't afford it, but because of the infinitesimal value of what she got in return. He hated to feel that anybody connected with him should find pleasure in the society of people like the Astills and their flashy friends; yet Muriel (and, what shocked him more, the children as well) appeared to take pride in cutting a dash in this vulgar company. That was why—and here the old gnawing grievance against being uprooted came out—the whole family had insisted on his selling the snug little house in which they had been born, and had dragged him with them to the elaborate Victorian Tudor of Alvaston Grange; hence the demand for six bathrooms, the squash-court, the bathing-pool.

Even Dorothy, the darling of his heart, had deserted to her mother's side in this last and most bitter of all his losing battles; and, thinking of Dorothy and her simplicities which, because they appeared to resemble his own, he adored, Mr. Lucton experienced once more the disquietude and foreboding he had felt that morning at the sight of the income-tax envelope. Even Dorothy's innocence, on which he would have staked his life, appeared to be in danger of pollution by the ways of this abominable age. Mr. Lucton remembered how, only last evening (and now that he came to think of it he believed that this was the real cause of his depression that morning) he had gone to her bedroom in search of a missing volume of poetry, and found there, flagrantly displayed, for every housemaid to see (there were three of them), a highly technical and richly-illustrated treatise on Contraception. Mr. Lucton had gone hot and cold at the sight. With a feeling of mingled horror and shame he had pocketed the book and slunk downstairs to show it to Muriel. But Muriel, seeing it, had laughed . . . she had actually laughed!

"My dear Owen," she had said, "will you ever realize that this is the twentieth century?"

"But you can't leave things like that about for the maids to see!" Mr. Lucton protested.

"I suppose you'ld prefer the poor creatures to get into trouble and have babies?" Muriel replied. "As for Dorothy, I hope she knows more about 'those things', as you call them, than I did when I married you."

"Well, what shall I do with the damned thing?" Mr. Lucton asked helplessly.

"Put it back where you found it," she told him. "It's none of your business."

Mr. Lucton did nothing of the sort. After a careful perusal, during which he was astounded at his own ignorance, he had taken the book into the garden and thrust it, guiltily, into an incinerator, where it had refused to be consumed as obstinately as a murdered corpse. He only hoped to goodness the head gardener (of five), who was a licensed lay-reader, would not rake out any decipherable remains. When Dorothy came down to dinner that evening (for a wonder, she was dining at home), Mr. Lucton scarcely dared look at her for fear of finding new traces of depravity on that innocent face. He himself had passed through a shattering emotional crisis of alarm and anxiety. . . . His daughter, on the other hand, appeared not in the least embarrassed. Instead of ignoring the ghastly subject, she promptly broached it.

"Muriel tells me you've borrowed a book of mine, Dad," she said mischievously. "I hope you've enjoyed it."

Mr. Lucton went red in the neck. He was used, more or less, to Dorothy's teasing and patronizing him. He submitted to both, pitiful coward that he was, because, having lost so much, he was frightened of losing more; because any intimacy—even one in which scorn was involved—seemed better than none. But now, while his mind grew incandescent with indignation, he kept silence; for there was contempt in Dorothy's voice: the unassailable contempt of the young, to which there was no answer but something beginning with "When *I* was your age . . ." or else "In *my* day . . ."—words which carried with them their own condemnation by admitting that he was old-fashioned and thus making argument futile.

Yet if Mr. Lucton was silent, his silence made him still angrier, not only with the modern world which went spinning away from him in this giddy fashion, but with Dorothy herself. At that moment, perhaps for the first time, he became aware of his daughter as what she was: a luxurious little cat whose pink tongue delicately lapped the cream from the surface of life; a sleek, lovely little thing who, liking to be stroked and petted and, occasionally, sensuously stimulated by such attentions, condescended to rub herself up against him, but, beyond that, gave nothing in return. Shrinking back into himself, Mr. Lucton left it at that. He felt lonely—lonelier than ever before in his life; and that sensation of loneliness returned and weighed on him now (reinforced by the heaviness of his imprudent luncheon) as he sat in his club and thought:

"A mad world. One must either adjust oneself to it or retire from the struggle as gracefully as one can. To do that would be cowardly in a man at my time of life—one can't throw up the sponge at fifty!—yet adjustment takes time and thinking, and I've no time to think. Too busy making money for these people to spend. No time . . . ever since the War. If my soul were my own . . ."

(III)

REAL ESTATE

It was not. The clock on the wall above the mantelpiece gave a discreet little cough, reminding him that it was about to strike.

"Three minutes to four," Mr. Lucton thought. "How time flies! If I'm to keep my appointment at Wilburns' I shall have to buck up."

Fastening the top button of his trousers, which he had found it convenient to undo, Mr. Lucton rose and made his way to the office of Wilburn and Wilburn. He went there automatically. For the last thirty years he had been going to Wilburns' office. When first he visited it, as a boy, there had been two active Wilburns, Ernest and Dudley. Ernest Wilburn had shot himself; Dudley, in middle age, had married a young widow, Lord Wolverbury's daughter-in-law, and died. Middle-aged men should not marry young women, Mr. Lucton reflected. The less they had to do with young women the better. Now there were no Wilburns left—only a Mr. Flower, who had been shoved into the firm during the War, and three junior partners, whose names he didn't know. But though the present partners were new or newish, they preserved, Mr. Lucton was consoled to recognize, a sense of the past. They still occupied the original Wilburn and Wilburn office in Sackville Row, still kept the brass plate from which the lettering had been almost polished away, concealing rather than proclaiming the firm's existence; one still approached the office by a steep stone stairway with iron banisters and a mahogany rail; the outer chamber in which one was received still looked and smelt like a lawyer's office in Dickens, and seemed—for after the War the practice had recovered and was now immense—to affect an air of shabbiness, a disdain of show, in deliberate contrast with the spick-and-span legal "chambers" which had sprung up on every side of it. Mr.

Flower, the senior partner, himself accented this formal note by enduring the kind of dress which was worn by family solicitors at the beginning of the century, displaying at noon and in the heat of summer a quantity of starched linen such as is rarely seen before sunset, and a starched manner to match.

It was all, Mr. Lucton told himself, a little theatrical, and, in real life, ridiculous; but in spite of that it happened to reflect his own mood of rebellion against all things rapid and modern. It seemed restful and dignified and was not, necessarily, inefficient. He was even pleased—for he had time to spare—by Mr. Flower's insisting on the old-fashioned rite of handing over title-deeds formally and in person and of receiving payment for the sale of the house not by the fallible expedient of a cheque, that might be dishonoured, but by the inconvenient passing from hand to hand of legal tender of the realm in the form of bank-notes. That was the only way, he knew, in which Wilburns did business. It took and gave a lot of time and trouble; but at least it was safe.

Mr. Flower received him with the compliments due from one leader of the professional classes to another. "The purchaser is late, Mr. Lucton," he observed. "But you, I notice, are precisely on time." That showed the difference, he implied, between the manners of the ancient aristocracy of business and the upstarts of to-day. "And then these fellows complain," he went on, "that business is bad! Now in our day, as you know, Mr. Lucton, punctuality——"

At this point the purchaser, who had probably been held up by the red-tape entanglements in Wilburns' outer office, was ushered into the room. Mr. Lucton had never seen him before, and disliked the looks of him now: no doubt he would have disliked them in any case, not for themselves, but because this man had been allowed to buy him out of the house he loved. The purchaser was a bustling, truculent type of small manufacturer, and appeared to be more irritated than impressed by the formalities to which he had been subjected.

"Please take a seat, Mr. Hogget," the lawyer said. (Mr. Hogget had already taken a seat and mopped a fiery forehead.)

"This is the vendor, Mr. Owen Lucton." Mr. Hogget nodded; he pulled out a bank-envelope full of notes and threw them on the table. "Here's the brass," he said, "though it beats me, if I may say so, why you can't take a cheque through the post like any other business 'ouse I've ever had dealings with. You gentlemen may have time to spare, but in my line, I don't mind telling you, time means money. Now, is there anything else?"

Mr. Flower waved his hand up and down in a soothing gesture. He picked up the bundle of notes and began to count them methodically. Mr. Lucton, who had been studying his supplanter's flushed face with an ever-increasing hatred, felt he ought to be polite.

"I can't tell you, Mr. Hogget," he said, "how much I regret giving up this house."

Mr. Hogget regarded him incredulously. "That's an odd thing to hear, if I may say so, from a man who's just bought Alvaston Grange. Alvaston Grange, Mr. Lucton, is my bow-ideel of a business-man's residence."

"Well, I've lived at Number Fourteen for more than twenty-five years, and naturally it's dear to me."

"H'm . . . You've not made it cheap for me, either, have you?" Mr. Hogget said. He looked impatiently at the lawyer who, having counted the notes with a professionally-moistened finger, proceeded to count them again. "I'm not saying," he went on, "that the 'ouse isn't a nice little 'ouse; but if you'll do me the honour to look round there in six months' time, you'll find, if I may say so, a great change in it."

Mr. Lucton was chilled at the idea. "You mean, Mr. Hogget . . . ?"

"I mean, first of all, that I'm going to 'ave all those trees down in front—the lilacs and such-like. My missus, she can't abide trees blocking up the windows. She likes to sit in the front room after dinner and see what the neighbours are doing and watch the traffic. You-see-what-I-mean?"

Mr. Lucton saw. He had planted and pruned those lilacs himself; he had watched them grow from straggling bushes into a perfumed barrier of tossing plumes, white and purple, between himself and the dusty world outside.

"Then that lawn at the back," Mr. Hogget went on. "Grass, as such, is all very well; but grass, if I may say so, means labour. If you capitalize that lawn, Mr. Lucton, in terms of wages . . . Well, we needn't go into detail, but I got out the figures, and we decided it would pay us to clear the whole lot away—you don't happen to want to buy any turf, do you?—and put down an 'ard court. It'll add to the value of the house when we want to sell. Of course, that means cutting down that old tree, that lime, or whatever you call it."

"That sounds very drastic," Mr. Lucton sighed.

"Drastic. That's the right word, sir. Drastic! And that—if I may say so without giving offence—is what's been wanted all through in that 'ouse of yours. You wait till I've finished with it. I don't grudge the expense. Now take, for example, that little room on the ground-floor, the one looking out on the lawn at the back with all those fixed bookcases. You-know-what-I-mean?"

"Of course. We called it the library."

"Exactly. Well, books, Mr. Lucton, are not much in my line nor my missus's either. I don't know how long it is since I bought a book. Waste of money *and* time, I call 'em. So got a friend of mine in the building and contracting business to 'ave a look round. He's a practical man, and he saw what was wanted at once. It's as simple as A B C. All you have to do is to pull down one wall, and you've got a beautiful lounge-'all, or 'all-lounge, whichever you call it, that 'ld do credit to an 'ouse twice the size of this. Now you can't deny that's a brain-wave, an inspiration!"

Mr. Lucton shivered. An inspiration of the devil. For a moment he felt inclined towards a foolish gesture; he would call the whole deal off; refuse the money, and let the house at a loss or leave it empty. But by this time Mr. Flower had finished his second count and was ready to hand over the deeds.

After all, Mr. Lucton thought, life was full of climatic moments like this, in which death or disaster or good fortune ruled a double red line at the foot of an account, after which a clean page must be turned and a new account opened with its inheritance of debit or credit.

Mr. Flower handed him a pen. "If you please," he said . . .

Mr. Lucton signed his name, swiftly, boldly, with its accustomed flourish, and knew that he was signing away something he could never recover. Mr. Flower formally presented him with the packet of bank-notes.

"Two thousand four hundred and twenty-six pounds," he said, "that is twenty-three hundreds, nine tens, one five, and thirty-one one-pound Treasury notes. Why the bank chose to give you all those small notes," he added "I can't imagine."

Mr. Lucton negligently thrust the envelope into his trouser-pocket. "The price of my happiness," he thought, "of all my old happiness. Well, well . . ."

Mr. Hogget had risen and was shaking hands with him. "Pleased to have met you, Mr. Lucton," he said. "Give me six months to get things straight; and then, any time—well, you know-what-I-mean—you'll always be welcome to take a glance at the improvements. I bet you you won't know your little old 'ome when you next set eyes on it! Good day, sir. Good day, Mr. Flower."

He went, and Mr. Lucton dreamily followed him. He returned to his own office and the clattering of typewriters, with the sensation of a man emerging from a quiet backwater on a turbulent river. He entered his room by his own private door, unnoticed, and sat down at his desk. In his absence the careful Miss Jenkins had disinterred the income-tax envelope from the pile in which it had been buried. It lay on the blotting-pad under his eyes, demanding attention, and—almost as if the accursed thing had the gift of spontaneous generation—another, a demand-note, of the same shape and colour, lay close beside it, reminding him that the second instalment of tax would shortly be due.

The sight of an unpaid bill always made Mr. Lucton unhappy. His horror of indebtedness, drilled into him in youth by his bearded Victorian father, had been heightened of late to a morbid degree by Muriel's careless ways. Her housekeeping desk (where the photograph of her Major continued to fade) lay buried beneath a litter of "accounts rendered" which she had neglected to pay. When he reproached her she merely begged him not to be silly.

"My dear Owen," she would say, "these people know that you're perfectly solvent; they know they'll be paid; *they* don't worry, so why should *you?* As a matter of fact, they like longish bills."

"Well, I don't," Mr. Lucton replied. "I prefer to know where I am."

It was his anxiety to know where he was that impelled him, at this moment, to open the demand-note before he looked at the assessment. He read:

INCOME TAX

Second instalment due on 1 *July.*

Application is hereby made for payment of the undermentioned instalment of Income Tax for the year 1938–39, *due on July* 1, 1939 *and payable on or before that date.*

and, below, an astonishing figure—twelve hundred odd pounds.

His mind's reactions to the sight of this impressive figure were complicated. Its first emotion was horror, stark horror at the magnitude of the sum—in his early married life he had lived comfortably, and actually saved, on an annual income of less than half of it; and even in these later years, when large sums rolled in automatically to the firm's banking account, he was always impressed when he saw their figures on paper. So now, though he knew that the payment of twelve hundred pounds would not embarrass him, he had a sudden and (as he knew) unreasonable sense of insecurity, like that of a man who has a hole in his pocket.

His next emotion was one of pride, of self-satisfaction. It was rather magnificent, after all, that he, Owen Lucton, who, only twenty-five years ago, had started his business life on so small a scale, was now in the proud position of paying, in tax alone, four times the total income on which he had begun. There were not many men in North Bromwich, he reflected, and none in his own profession, who had earned the privilege of being bled so drastically and were equipped with a financial constitution that could stand it without blanching. It was with a feeling of swelling importance and the vague sense of a patriotic duty performed that, although it still wanted some days till the date on which payment was demanded, he took out a cheque and filled in the name of the payee: *Commissioners of Inland Revenue*. Yet when his well-mannered pen (Mr. Lucton's script had a clerkly, old-fashioned, formal quality) proceeded to inscribe the figure, twelve hundred and sixteen pounds fourteen shillings and ninepence, a third emotion, more complicated and more powerful than either of the others, overwhelmed his mind—an emotion in which, as it seemed, all the doubts and questionings of the last seven hours became crystallized.

Indignation, resentment, hot anger: all these Mr. Lucton felt—not merely against the anonymous Commissioners of Inland Revenue, but against his business, his family, the British Empire, the world—against every condition of life in the disordered age in which he was condemned to live.

As he gazed at the half-written cheque the ideals of material success, of professional reputation, of the good citizenship which it symbolized, filled him with disgust. He saw these, suddenly, clearly, as questionable values; he saw himself as the slave, the victim of these ideals, and asked himself, perhaps for the first time in his life, what his body or soul had gained by respecting them. And the answer was: nothing, nothing compared with what he had lost!

He thought: "Supposing I had the courage to be a coward; supposing I struck work; supposing I simply declined to go on sweating my life out year after year to earn an income one-third of which goes in taxes to finance the dole, and most of the rest on Muriel's extravagances and social ambitions; supposing, after I've signed this cheque, I just quietly stepped aside, taking with me enough to live on (that wouldn't be much) and left Leith, who enjoys it, to carry on with this wretched business; supposing, without any fuss, I just did a bolt like Joe Astill—would anyone care a damn? Miss Jenkins, perhaps, with one or two old hands in the office. Would Muriel? Not personally: she might resent the humiliation. Leith? Not he! Patricia? I never set eyes on her unless she wants something. Rupert and Dorothy? Perhaps. Rupert likes messing round with engines, and Dorothy, in spite of the shocks she gives me, is fond of me, I think. No, when once it was begun, the whole thing would be perfectly simple. It's the *premier pas* that *coûtes*, and of course, I'm a coward."

Leith entered without knocking. "Oh, there you are, Dad," he exclaimed. "I didn't hear you come back. Did you finish up that business at Wilburns'?"

Mr. Lucton nodded. "Got the cash in my pocket. Flower made the chap pay it in notes."

"Better shove 'em in the safe. The bank's closed. What about this income-tax?"

"I've written the cheque. I was signing it when you came in."

"It's not due till July the first," Leith said disapprovingly. "After all, Dad, the interest on twelve hundred pounds for the best part of a month . . ."

Mr. Lucton smiled. "It's worth a lot more than that to have the thing out of my mind. Do you want me for anything?"

"No: Miss Jenkins gave me all your letters to sign. By the way, I had a 'phone message from Rupert. He landed at half-past four."

"Well, thank God for that," Mr. Lucton sighed. "If the letters are signed, I'll go and collect that car."

The thought of his new car was, at that moment, the one thing in the world that could be relied on to raise Owen Lucton's spirits. All his life he had been obsessed by a passion for machinery. As a boy he had delighted in prying into the great engineering works on the outskirts of North Bromwich: indeed, if the opportunity and duty of succeeding to the family business had not diverted him from his bent, he would gladly have become an engineer himself.

The invention of the internal-combustion engine, during his early manhood, had given him the excuse of indulging this passion in his private life. "Motoring", in those early days, had been regarded (not without reason) as a mysterious and hazardous pursuit: the rudimentary automobile, with its hot-tube ignition, its chain-drive and its inadequate brakes, was a creature of temperament which had to be coaxed rather than driven. Owen Lucton was a skilful coaxer: he had not merely a mechanical sense, but a born mechanic's hands. In that era, when the chauffeur, usually a Frenchman, was the priest of an esoteric cult, when words such as "camshaft" and "differential" and "carburettor" sounded strange on the lips of an ordinary Englishman, Mr. Lucton's passion had emerged, of a sudden, as a social asset; he had become known as one of those mystagogues who, cheerfully grovelling in the oil and dust beneath a spidery chassis or sunk in an "inspection-pit", had the gift (it was more than knowledge) of discovering what had "gone wrong" with a motor-car in an age when something always "went wrong" as a matter of course.

If at that time he had chosen to hitch his fortunes to the rising motor-car industry, he might easily have become a millionaire, like his acquaintance, Sir Robert Tregaron. As it was, he had followed the new machine's evolution with an interest as romantic as that which he applied to his library—an interest which Muriel regarded with much more sympathy than the other, since the distinction of parading the town in a series of motor-cars off-set the indignity of living in the King's Road.

Owen Lucton knew this and was thankful. The possession of a motor-car was the only one among his intimate pleasures which, at some time or another, had not met with Muriel's disapproval. So, carefully concealing the cost of his darling hobby, he had slyly proceeded from one cylinder to two, from two to four, from four to six—and now from six to eight. So long as she was allowed to choose the colour of the body-work (and later that of the chauffeur's uniform) she let him have his way.

Though she had learnt to drive a car herself, with an equally superb disregard for the rule of the road and the pinions of her gear-box, she was far more interested in the shape of the bonnet than in what lay inside it, displaying, in moments of emergency, a childlike naïveté that could melt the heart of the sternest policeman, and save her delicate hands from contact with oil and dust by persuading chivalrous strangers to change punctured wheels for her.

This summer, for the first time in his life, Owen Lucton had decided to have a car of his own. With a cunning that was the product of years of experience, he had chosen an open two-seater body of a draughty design in which no woman who flattered herself on her personal neatness would be seen dead. The new car was a miracle of deliberate selfishness. The seat was immovably fixed to suit the measure of his own legs, so that neither the women (who were shorter) nor the boys (who were taller) than himself could drive it in comfort. The colour of the bodywork was in the strictest sense protective. Although he did not admire it himself, it was one which, as he happened to know, his wife detested. Externally, this car was the negation of everything his family admired: the finish of the paint was dull; in all its fittings—even in the radiator—there was not a square inch of chromium. But the paragon of mechanical ingenuity and efficiency that this modest exterior concealed—the latest eight-cylinder Pearce-Tregaron "fifty" with the new fluid fly-wheel transmission and synchromesh gears—represented the height of his present desires.

As he hurried down Sackville Row towards the garage in the lower part of the town where this wonder was housed, Owen Lucton's whole life was sweetened, like that of a man in love, by the mere fact of possessing it. From the medley of cars of all ages and hues and conditions with which the garage was crammed, the shape of the new Pearce-Tregaron detached itself instantly, and flattered his eyes with its unique aristocracy. He walked up to it eagerly, and caressed the radiator as one who pats the muzzle of a horse. (Not one horse, but a potential two hundred, lay hidden behind it!) A faint thrill—it was that rather than a vibration—communicated itself to his fingers. The engine was actually running—and ready, at the pressure of a finger-tip and in the winking of an eye, to exert this tremendous power! Its quietness, its perfect balance, ravished him. Even the induction's whisper was silenced. While he stood rapt in contemplation of this sublime work of art, the proprietor of the garage approached him.

"Well, here she is, Mr. Lucton," he said. "What d'you think of this for a job?"

"Not so bad," Owen Lucton said modestly. "I've come to fetch her. I suppose she's all ready? Have you tried her yourself?"

"You bet I have! Took her out for a spin this morning. All O.K., so far as I can see, apart from the front-wheel brakes. It's a tremendously fine adjustment, you know, and if you jam them on suddenly she's inclined to pull to the left. Of course, that's a trifle: I didn't expect you round quite so early or I'ld have had it seen to. If you can spare ten minutes I'll put a man on it now."

Owen Lucton hesitated. At that moment his most urgent desire was to step into the driving-seat, to be alone with this beauty. More than this: nothing gave him intenser pleasure than tinkering with minute adjustments; he knew that no soulless mechanic would tackle those brakes with the delicacy he would give them himself. He said:

"Oh no, don't worry about that. I can put the brakes right in a jiffy when I get home. She's warmed up nicely; so I think I'll jump in and get off. By the way, you might send up the breakdown van to tow in the Bentley. Big-end's gone, I'm afraid."

"H'm . . . I guess I know who's done that. That young man of yours passed me the other day like a streak of lightning—and I was doing eighty myself! I hope you won't let him play any tricks with this bus."

"You bet your life on it! This car's private property. Nobody's going to drive it but me; I can promise you that."

He climbed into the seat. It fitted him immediately, like an old glove. With no more sound than the whisper of grooved rubber on cement, the obedient monster moved forward and stole out of the garage; with unhesitating delicacy, with superbly balanced power, it slid through the checks and openings of traffic in the Halesby road. Like a great bird gliding on fixed pinions close to the ground, those two tons of tempered metal seemed to skim the earth rather than rest on it. So secretly they moved, at Owen Lucton's bidding, that drivers of other and meaner cars looked round in surprise when the grey shadow stole past them. After five minutes, with the daintiness of a plover alighting, the new Pearce-Tregaron came to rest beneath the red-brick Gothic porch of Alvaston Grange.

Owen Lucton switched off the ignition and entered the house on tiptoe—quite unnecessarily, for Muriel's new Turkey carpets deadened the sound of his tread—and once more an acute distaste for the place overwhelmed him. It was as impersonal as a railway-station hotel, and even less sympathetic; for in a station hotel one was welcomed at least by reception-clerks, or hall-porters scenting a tip, while in this new house of his (or Muriel's) the relays of haughty domestics who condescended to appear, and decided to disappear as soon as it suited them, regarded his presence as a bore if not as an intrusion: an attitude in which they took their colour from Fowler, the butler, that portent of stateliness and stupidity to whose judgment on all matters of social usage Muriel deferred on the strength of his five years' service with the late Lord Wolverbury, and who spent his life (so far as one could guess) between polishing "his" silver in the pantry and enjoying his meals in the servants' hall: a corpulent pasha surrounded by a twittering seraglio renewed month by month, or a heavy-browed bull, replete and slowly browsing, in a field full of heifers.

Owen Lucton hated his butler. It was the conviction that Fowler—who, with Muriel, adopted a fawning, an almost sentimental air—not only disliked but also despised him, that got on his nerves—especially at meal-times, when a sense of this superior being's unspoken criticism boring through his back reduced him first to discomfort and then to silence. A later and more definite reason for this detestation arose from the fact that Muriel, distressed by his failure to live up to her new standards of smartness, had recently entered into a conspiracy with Fowler to supervise his outward appearance. It was time, Muriel said, he had someone to valet him; and Fowler—as though this were a concession!—would be pleased to do so.

From that day, the shadow of Fowler, which, till then, had merely acted as a reminder of propriety in public, had fallen on his intimate life. Mr. Fowler knew how real gentlemen, who were used to butlers, behaved in private. Owen Lucton was not even allowed to pick out the clothes he wanted to wear or turn on his own bath; Mr. Fowler's taste in clothes (particularly in neckwear) was not his master's—with the result that his selections, laid out on the bed and the chest-of-drawers to await Owen Lucton's return from the bath to which he had been summoned, were usually rejected. An intelligent man, Mr. Lucton thought, would surely have seen what a failure he was as a sartorial adviser and would have tactfully retired; but Fowler was either too stupid or too conceited (or both) to realize with what contempt his suggestions were turned down, and continued to make them, remaining, in face of all Owen's rejections, a martyr to his principles, so consciously superior in his martyrdom that Owen Lucton hated the sight of him and evaded him whenever he could.

That was why he now found himself treading on tip-toe through his own hall. He was hoping to steal upstairs and get rid of his hot city clothes before anyone became aware of his arrival. Unfortunately, the window of the butler's pantry, where Fowler habitually slept off the effect of his midday gorge, commanded the drive. Mr. Fowler slept so lightly that the whisper of the new Pearce-Tregaron's tyres on the gravel awakened him, with the result that as Owen set foot on the stairs he heard behind him that impressive clearing of the throat with which the butler prefaced his least important announcements, and Fowler's voice booming after him: "I beg your pardon, sir."

Mr. Lucton turned and said "Yes?" impatiently; but Fowler was not to be hurried.

"Madam asked me to inform you, sir," he went on, "that she and Miss Dorothy are dining out this evening. Mr. Leith will also be habsent, as he's going to a dance; but dinner will be served, sir, if that is convenient, at eight."

Mr. Lucton hesitated. The prospect of a lonely meal eaten under Fowler's supervision was not inviting. He made up his mind rapidly.

"I shall be dining in the country as well," he said. "So you'd better let the cook know. If you want to go out yourself, you may. I shan't want you any more this evening."

Mr. Fowler bowed, with an air that said: "Thank you for nothing."

"If you're dining in the country," he said, "I'll put out a black tie, sir."

"No, no. Don't do that. I shall pick up a meal at a pub."

Mr. Fowler's face expressed intense disapproval at the possibility of such behaviour on the part of anyone socially sponsored by himself. The late Lord Wolverbury, it seemed to suggest, had never lowered himself so far as to pick up a meal at a pub. Nor did the prospect of being released for the evening cheer him; for he was a creature of slow habit, and needed long notice of any change in routine. Furthermore, the expression of any emotions, gratitude included, was not becoming to his station: so, with a doleful bow, he resigned his employer to his disreputable fate.

Owen Lucton mounted the stairs with a springy step. The absence of his family on this evening which, above all others, he would have preferred to spend alone with the memories and regrets they refused to share, was a blessing of providence. He had planned to escape from being dragged into some "celebration" of the kind with which Muriel's excited sociability filled every evening by getting into dungaree overalls and retiring to the oily desolation of the garage to deal, at the greatest possible length, with the front-wheel brake which pulled slightly to the left. The sudden realization that he had nothing to evade made him change his mind in an instant. The adjustment of that brake would provide an excuse for escape on some future occasion. He was free, for once, to behave according to his nature: to get into old clothes—the older and shabbier the better; to slide into the driving-seat; to steal away, without any precise objective but the breathing of country air and the exploration of dim green distance with the aid of that exquisite piece of machinery, his new Pearce-Tregaron.

"The sooner the better," he thought; for at any moment the conscientious Leith might return to ask questions. The fact that nobody—not even himself—knew where he was going, spiced the adventure. His mood, indeed, had changed like that of a sombre landscape enlivened by a sudden burst of sunshine: even the varnished staircase of Alvaston Grange, with light pouring through the anonymous "transfer" coats-of-arms in its mullioned mock-oriel, was enchanted at that moment, into a charming effect of bright spaciousness which almost persuaded him that the change which the family had thrust on him was not so bad after all, and that the new house, at the worst, had really been something of a bargain.

He was, he supposed, beginning to get used to it—if not to Fowler—and the small bedroom at the end of the landing which Muriel had allotted to him (she had chosen the dressing-room next her own for the black marble bath) seemed already to have acquired a little of the patina which comes insensibly from an intimate and personal habitation. The alien and hostile frame which had at first offended him was gradually becoming subordinate to its familiar contents: the bedside-table with its reading-lamp, its bottle of aspirin tablets, its litter of books; the chest-of-drawers on which mirror and nail-scissors and shaving-tackle were so methodically disposed that he could have put his hand on each in the dark; the cheap mahogany wardrobe in which, at a moment's notice, he could find the suit he wanted.

But could he? Even now, as he stood in his shirt and pants, Owen Lucton was puzzled. His most ancient suit of Harris tweed, made up from material he had bought in Oban before the war—that well-beloved suit, with patched knees and elbows and cuffs, whose shape (or shapelessness) had adapted itself so patiently to his body's changing proportions, whose indestructible aroma of peat and heather was the very perfume of youth—no longer hung there on its accustomed peg! When he missed it, a spurt of hot anger filled Owen Lucton's brain. That precious garment, he guessed, had been spirited away: the victim of a snobbish conspiracy between Fowler and Muriel. He had tolerated many interferences with his private life; but this was the limit. He rang the bell, fiercely determined to give Fowler a piece of his mind, and waited impatiently for the irritatingly measured impacts of the butler's feet.

Not a sound . . . save the flapping of a blind which stirred in the breeze and, far away, the clatter of a motor lawn-mower. He rang again; and this time, to his embarrassment, a timid under-housemaid appeared. She looked terrified, as though she expected to be ravished on the spot; and Mr. Lucton, hurriedly retreating, spoke to her through a crack of doorway. Mr. Fowler, she said, had gone to his cottage to change, and she was packing her box, as her month's notice was up and she was going home to Dorset to-morrow morning. She knew nothing of the missing suit: Mr. Lucton's room, she said, wasn't her work; but, now that she came to think of it, she *had* seen a parcel which might contain clothes put ready for the post in the butler's pantry.

Mr. Lucton roughly commanded her to bring this to him at once, and she ran like a frightened rabbit, returning with an oblong brown-paper parcel tied up with professional accuracy and addressed, in Muriel's decided hand, to St. Martin's Vicarage, Alvaston. On the corner of the label he read the words: *Jumble Sale*. As he snipped through the string with his nail-scissors, the odour of peat reached his nostrils, and he knew the worst. It would be futile to indulge his indignation. Through the half-open door he thrust the bundle of cut string and brown-paper into the housemaid's hands and told her to take them away and burn them immediately. Then, still hot with rage, he proceeded to put on the stolen suit.

"The sooner I get away out of this the better," he told himself. But now, once having been rattled by this annoying incident which, trivial as it was, appeared to symbolize all his frustrations and irritations, he found nothing that would go right. His socks had holes in the toes: in the old days Muriel had darned them. A worn shoe-lace snapped as he tightened it. In the end he was half-way downstairs before he remembered that he had left the two thousand four hundred odd pounds which he had received from the lamentable Hogget in the breast-pocket of his city clothes.

It was his duty, he knew, to lock this money away in the safe in his library, for all Muriel's servants were strange birds of passage, and he trusted none of them; but by this time the mere thought of any further delay was irksome, so he compromised with his conscience by ramming the envelope into his trouser-pocket, only just in time to escape an encounter with Leith, whose respectable Austin, as smug and reliable as himself, crunched cautiously into one end of the gravelled drive at the moment when the grey bonnet of the Pearce-Tregaron stole out of the other.

(IV)

EASY DESCENT

It spoke well for the resilience of Mr. Lucton's nature that he had no sooner left the suburb behind him than he had almost forgotten his bitter preoccupations. The smell of the recovered tweeds embalmed him in an incense of holiday and youth, and the general atmosphere of that golden afternoon, together with the exquisite behaviour of the new car's engine, convinced him that, even at fifty, life had not lost its savour. This was no solitary joy. He himself was no more than a unit in an adventurous multitude; for, by this time, the North Bromwich business-day being over, the smooth width of the Halesby Road was scoured by a multitude of other motor-cars, each of which, like his own, appeared to be set on escape.

It is one of the peculiar (and redeeming) features of North Bromwich that such an escape is easy. The suburb of Alvaston itself wears a woodland air, and the slope over which it straggles climbs upward towards an escarpment, eight hundred feet above sea-level, which is, in fact, the brim of the high Midland plateau: the watershed between the cold, sodden lands that are drained by Trent's tributaries and the warm brooklands of Severn. The plateau reaches its highest point and its end in the recently-debauched village of Tilton, where, of a sudden, the contrast between these two worlds is magnificently revealed.

Here, within half a dozen miles of the city's centre, Mr. Lucton slowed down, slipped the gear-lever into neutral, and, allowing the stream of west-bound traffic to flow past him, lit a pipe and let his eyes idly rest on the prospect displayed. To the north, the Black Country smouldered beneath its perpetual smoke-pall: there lay Wednesford and Dulston and Wolverbury, clasped in the grimy tentacles of North Bromwich itself, beyond which the line of the Clees and the dome of the Wrekin marked the ultimate skyline. Full in front, at his feet, the spire of Halesby Church pierced the film of smoke that settled in the valley of the Stour, the debatable land between the black and the green. Beyond Halesby rose the undulant line of the Clents, last outpost of the mountainous west which, in the motorless age of his boyhood, had marked the limit of his romantic wanderings on foot.

Mr. Lucton knew well what wonders were visible from those twin summits: not merely the Clees and the Wrekin, but all the hills beyond Severn—Woodbury, Abberley, Ankerdine, the Malverns, and, westward again, the mountains of Wales. It was odd, he reflected, how, all through his life, that prospect had drawn his imagination westward—as though, like the wistful St. Brendan's, it had expected to find there some lost paradise, some Isle of the Blest. Yet to-day his mind shrank from the stimulation of vague magnificence. It demanded quiet and solitude, in a setting free from any emotional distractions—a landscape warm and green and soothing to the nerves; and so, as he canvassed the possibilities, there came into his mind—led thither, unconsciously perhaps, by the lines of Housman he had quoted to his secretary that morning—a vision of Bredon Hill (Bredon Cloud, as the old maps called it) rising gently out of the orchard-lands of the Severn Plain, with the slow Avon meandering about its feet, and larks overhead.

"Yes, that's what I want," he told himself, relighting his pipe and automatically groping to turn on the ignition of the engine, which was still running silently. "No main roads for me: not even a map! I shall keep to the lanes and trust my sense of direction for a hunk of bread and cheese and a pint of cider. On a long summer evening like this it doesn't matter a damn how late I come home—not that it'ld matter all that much," he smiled rather grimly,—"if I never came home at all."

He reversed the car and turned right-handed into an "un-adopted" road which had been cut, only a few months before, through a virgin field, and was already fringed with newly-erected bungalows, hideous to behold. Each of these shoddy, brand-new little homes had been built to house the typical unit of the new suburban dormitory: a young married couple, a radio-set on the hire-system, a dog and a Baby Austin or Morris Minor. How mean they were, Mr. Lucton felt, how alien to that wind-swept plateau with its stupendous views, on which they turned their backs, preferring to contemplate their neighbours; how insensitive—and yet how snug!

He could not help feeling vaguely and sentimentally envious of these hopeful innocents in their jerry-built bungalows: the kind of folk to whom men like himself paid a salary of two or three pounds a week. However blind they might be to the beauties which, indeed, their bungalows had already defaced, they were blessed with another blindness which he, alas, could never recapture: the blindness of young married love with its tender ardours, its pathetic, unconquerable hopes.

There was, he remarked, in these homes, a significant absence of the perambulator: the kennel and the garage came first. It shocked Mr. Lucton faintly to notice this deficiency; and yet, when he came to think of it, the perambulator, so far as he himself was concerned, had long since ceased to be a symbol of happiness—if not of domestic virtue. He remembered a broken sentence he had heard in the club that morning: "Czecho-Slovakia: only the beginning, he's after the Ukraine—unless he happens to take a fancy to Rumania . . ." Were these young people, after all, perhaps wise in their generation—or in their lack of it? Hadn't they the right to "have a good time" while they could, to make the best of a war-shadowed, precarious youth—particularly when the contents of the perambulator seemed destined for the void of unemployment or the vortex of war? What right had he, rich and secure, to lay down the law to them?

He could not answer this question, and refused, in any case, to allow it to trouble him. What he did observe, with increasing satisfaction, was the perfection of the springs of the new Pearce-Tregaron, which swayed over the brickbats and crevasses of the unsurfaced roadway like a well-ballasted yacht unperturbed by a choppy sea; and, a few moments later, these insults to the car's suspension ceased: it had emerged, in fact, from that scarred no-man's land upon a naked trunk-road which had lately replaced one of the favourite lanes of his childhood.

He crawled into this, crossed it cautiously, and left it again as soon as a grass-grown by-road offered him the chance. Even within so short a distance of the city's centre, a number of these winding lanes had escaped such embarrassments, there was always the arterial roads, which acted as main-sewers draining the town's excreted traffic, they had become more secret and solitary than ever before. A man in a big car, and a new one at that, should enter such by-ways warily.

They were sunken by centuries of use and deepened by storm-water; low-hanging boughs often scraped the roof of a motor-car; trailing spurs of bramble and briar might scratch its wings; if one happened to meet, by bad luck, another car, there was the devil to pay—a retreat to the nearest field-gate and, in winter, the chance of becoming mired axle-deep; and even if one escaped such embarrassments there was always the chance that the track would peter out in the yard of an unknown farm or of an isolated barn.

That, Mr. Lucton reflected, was the spice of such adventures, which one could only taste to the full when one was alone: town-bred women, on these occasions, were apt to be anxious and peevish. But this time, as luck had it, the chosen lane improved instead of deteriorating. After four or five miles of steering by faith rather than by sight, the sense of direction on which he prided himself (and which his family laughed at) was vindicated; for the car escaped from the long green tunnel on to the brow of a gravelly upland, a patch of common scattered with flagrant gorse-bloom, whose almond scent hung on the milk-warm air.

On his right the echeloned line of the Clents now rolled away westward. Before, and perhaps six hundred feet below him, stretched the mid-Worcestershire plain, its wave-like contours so foreshortened that its whole expanse, dimly misted by summer air, lay outspread like a time-frayed tapestry in which the dark hues of woodland and hedgerow were merged so insensibly into the higher lights of meadows as yet unmown and still paler fields where hay lay in silver swathes or had already been carted, that the whole appeared as one tissue of softly-graded greens. Only amid the near middle-distance, at the foot of the slope, where, here and there, a tall-chimneyed farmhouse of red and black half-timber gathered round it a group of barn and orchard and shining duck-pond, could any detail of pattern be discerned. Beyond these, for more than twenty miles into the south, stretched a deep green mystery unmarred by any trace of human habitation or handicraft.

Mr. Lucton sprawled on the tussocky turf and gazed down on it. He could have stayed there, wrapped in dreamy sun-drugged contemplation, till sunset. Perhaps he actually did fall asleep for a moment; for it was with a shock of surprise that he suddenly realized that his stomach, having digested its midday burden, was uncomfortably empty, and recalled as desirable his original plan of supping in one of the villages under Bredon Hill, whose form, now that the sun was waning, appeared far away on the southern horizon as a long blue cloud in the shape of a well-strung bow. So he rose from the ground and re-started the Pearce-Tregaron's engine—so perfectly balanced that it fired at the turn of the switch—and, crossing the gravelly brow, drifted down into Worcestershire.

"Drifted" was hardly the word. "Sailed" or "glided" was nearer the truth of this swift, deliberate progress. Though he still kept to the narrow lanes, the car's speed—so much greater than its silence suggested—did not alarm him. Even if those brakes did pull to the left, they were so smooth and powerful in action that he felt he could trust them. What was more, his doze on the hill-top had freshened him. All his senses seemed sharper than usual; and the stimulus of the air that swept past his face produced in his brain a state of masterful activity and conscious well-being. It seemed to him, too, as if the whole countryside shared in this shaking-off of his afternoon lethargy. The very character of the landscape's lighting had changed; for now the descending sun threw longer shadows, producing heightened effects of chiaroscuro, in which light and shade assumed more positive values—in which the tarnished ivory of hawthorn-bloom gleamed more white and the pale green of unfolding filigrees of fern seemed more piercing.

How green this land was, and how full of hope was its greenness! How sweet, too, the rushing air that swept past his nostrils; now a breath of hedge-roses or honeysuckle, now the waft of a hayfield. He would have been content, Mr. Lucton told himself, to go on for the rest of his life in this way, his mind just so deeply absorbed by the process of driving as to forbid its dwelling on any time but the swiftly-passing moment; his senses assailed by a series of flashes of the most astonishing forms and colours, the most ravishing scents!

If he were to go on at this rate—for, in spite of their twisting, these lanes were empty and he must have been averaging "forty" —he would have passed through this unknown belt of deserted country, of which, it would seem, he was the only enjoyer, before he had appreciated it to the full. So he slowed down to what, for the Pearce-Tregaron, was a mere idling amble of twenty-five miles an hour, and discovered, when once the rate had been checked, that the air which at speed had seemed so exhilarating had become close. It was so hot that he felt the need of slipping off his thick Harris coat. An odd stillness possessed it; every hawthorn-twig, every bracken-frond stood motionless. Not a single bird sang; and even the one sound he heard, the gentle swish of his tyres over the gritty roadway, seemed pressed down, as it were, by the weight of a sky that, though it was cloudless, had the heaviness of late July. The whole earth wore an air of suspension, of hushed expectancy.

"There must be thunder about," Mr. Lucton thought. "I'd better push on, or I shall be caught in a storm. Now what a damned nuisance!"

Even on the rising ground which now faced him, and which the big car took, at a touch of the throttle, with gathering speed, the air grew lighter. When the car surged over the crest he could see the reason for this oppressiveness. The bow of Bredon Hill, now rising full in front of him, appeared no longer an unsubstantial cloud, but a solid barrier. To the west the serrated shapes of the Malverns, sharp-cut as inky cardboard, and on the east, the level Cotswold escarpment, equally threatening, enclosed a gigantic amphitheatre sunk in the shadow of a low curtain of tattered thunder-cloud which, even as he gazed at it, appeared to be advancing towards him, blotting out the light of the foreground with increasing, malignant speed, while already the middle distance was blurred by diagonal blue-black columns of falling cloudburst.

"If I'm lucky, I may pass between them," Mr. Lucton thought. "That tower on the left must be Pershore Abbey, but I've no time to look at it. Shall I put up the hood? No, there's no time to lose. I must take my chance."

He depressed his foot, and the car leapt forward with a sudden release of energy. He had reached a main road now, and the very smoothness of the surface was an invitation to speed. The speedometer-needle moved forward without any encouragement: to his gentle pressure on the pedal it responded with a jump of ten miles an hour to sixty-five.

"My stars, what acceleration!" Mr. Lucton thought.

It seemed to his animistic mind as if the car, no less than himself, was eager to escape from the threatened deluge, actually enjoying, as he did, the fun of racing the storm which now moved across his path with increasing rapidity. Lightning ripped the black sky on his right like a whip-lash; the rumble of thunder which followed immediately was almost inaudible through the curtain of rushing air. Then one raindrop, as big as a table-spoonful, spattered the windscreen, and another, simultaneously, splashed in his eye, and a second later the full force of the deluge broke on him, soaking his shirt to the skin before, using one arm at a time, he could wriggle into his coat. A fierce fusillade of rain and hail commingled drummed down on the steaming bonnet; it danced back from the tarmac in a mist of broken water, waist-high, and so dense that, even if he had been able to keep his eyes open, he could not have seen twenty yards in front of him.

"If I could only get this damned hood up!" Mr. Lucton thought. And why not try? The mechanism for raising the hood was one of the "extras" with which, regardless of expense, the new car had been equipped. All one had to do, in theory, was to wind one geared handle which raised the sidescreen, and another that brought the hood's front edge within reach of the clips on the windscreen in front. With such perfect self-centring steering, a single hand could be trusted to steady the wheel. Mr. Lucton turned the handle. The hood raised itself obediently and came forward over his head. The rain beat on the top of it viciously and no longer blinded him.

"I ought to have done that before," Mr. Lucton thought. "What a topping gadget! Worth every penny I paid for it. Now, when once I've got these clips fixed . . ."

With one hand on the steering-wheel and an anxious eye on the road ahead he succeeded in fixing one clip. As he did so the windscreen went dim with his own breath and the steam from his body was condensed on its inner surface by the chill of the rain.

"I can't see," he thought. "The storm's beaten me after all. I shall have to slow down."

He lifted his foot from the pedal and leant forward to wipe the mist from the screen with his sleeve. On the road, a few yards in front of him, the clear patch momentarily revealed a dip filled by a barrier of water pouring across it from a choked ditch to join the river. There was no means of guessing how deep the impediment was. Though he had slowed down to "forty," he knew that, if he plunged through it, he would be in for a hell of a splash and, quite possibly, for a broken spring. Before he could see he was on it; the screen clouded again, and again he was sightless. He leant forward to wipe it, at the same moment instinctively ramming on the brakes. But the car did not stop. In the blinding splash of the puddle it seemed to shudder, then leap into the air. As it descended, the steering-wheel was wrenched from his fingers.

Though he tried to right it two-handed, it would not obey him. There raced through his mind the memory of the ill-balanced brake that pulled to the left. He was swerving now to the left in a front-wheel skid that he could not correct: at the mercy of two tons of metal hurled sideways through space by a velocity of forty-odd miles an hour. There was a flash on the left of white railings, a sound of splintering wood. The car slithered downhill on its side and the screech of torn metal was added to the splinter of wood as the wings were carried away. The off-wheels left the ground. As the body rose and heeled over, Mr. Lucton wrenched open the door and threw himself out. He landed face-downward in a patch of willow-herb, and slewed round just in time to see the new Pearce-Tregaron roll down the steep bank and turn over twice before disappearing beneath a fountain of spray.

Mr. Lucton gazed at this strange phenomenon with curiosity rather than any other emotion. Where, a moment before, he had watched the car's final plunge, there was nothing now to be seen but a busy seething of bubbles, as though the river boiled, and a slow-spreading oil-patch; but the bubbling soon ceased and the oil-patch drifted down-stream, leaving nothing whatever to show where the car was sunk beneath that surface of turbid water still thrashed by rain.

He continued to gaze at the spot with a puzzled, detached curiosity—almost as though the whole incident had been produced for his entertainment in the course of a dream cinema-show in which the operator had only to touch a reversing-switch and the Pearce-Tregaron would perform, in a backward direction, the same evolutions, at the end of which he would find himself back on the driving-seat, leaning forward to wipe the mist off the windscreen with his sleeve. The scene had been flashed on his retina so rapidly, the part he had taken in it had been played with so little volition, that for a few dazed moments he couldn't convince himself that anything so monstrously violent had actually happened. Then, all of a sudden, a fit of giddiness seized him; his head swam; the scene became blurred; the bank on which he had thrown himself appeared to be slipping away from him, and he found himself clutching wildly at the stems of the rose-bay lest he should fall and be lost in the blackness that surged in on his brain. He supposed he was fainting—for the first time since the day when he had been blown-up by a shell-burst before Kut—the two moments, so widely divided in time, overlapped and were mingled. Perhaps the booming of thunder overhead suggested gunfire; but indeed, he had neither the desire nor the power to separate them. The blackness enveloped him and he knew no more. . . .

PART TWO

THE COUNTRY OF STRANGE ADVENTURES

(I)

SCHIZOPHRENIA

A WILLOW-WREN sang. His sweet, pure, mounting note, with its tender climax and dying fall, was the first sound to pierce the penumbra of Mr. Lucton's consciousness. The song of birds was familiar to his waking ears; his Alvaston garden echoed at dawn with the clamour of blackbirds and thrushes which, Muriel complained, awakened her at an unearthly hour. For a moment, entranced by that limpid fountain-jet of sound and its falling droplets, Mr. Lucton's hazy mind accepted the song as proof that he was awakening from a dreamless sleep in his own bed at home, and that the time was early morning. He had not opened his eyes; and so far as the quality of the light was concerned, his illusion was pardonable. While he had lain there unconscious on the bank of the river, the storm had rolled on overhead and was now venting its fury a dozen miles away on the asparagus-beds of the Vale of Evesham; and the low beams of the setting sun that slanted over his eyelids shone, like those of sunrise, through an air that had been cooled and refreshed not by darkness but by rain.

It was only when he turned over to bury his head in the softness of the familiar pillow, and, stretched out one hand to pull up the coverlet (for he felt chilly) that his fingers encountered, instead of the linen they expected, the cold stems of crushed rose-bay among which he was lying. At this contact, as in the memory of a bad dream disquietingly prolonged into the half-light of waking, Mr. Lucton became aware of his true situation and the series of swift incidents that had precipitated him into it.

When he did at last come to himself and sat up blinking at the sunlight and rubbing his eyes, he still found it hard to believe he wasn't dreaming, though the line of splintered white railings through which the car had skidded, the hurricane-track of its wild career down the sloping bank, and a twinge of pain in his right arm, which he had stretched out to break his fall, convinced him that what he remembered was something more than a nightmare. The last and the most convincing evidence for this was the fact that the car in which he had been sitting when the dream began had vanished: it would have taken more than a dream, he decided, to spirit two tons of metal away!

"My God . . . that's done it!" he thought. "That hasn't half done it!"

Sitting there on the bank and rubbing his sore arm which, since he could move his fingers, he supposed wasn't broken, Mr. Lucton proceeded to take stock of his position. Being at heart a timid romantic, he had always schooled himself to behave in emergency as a stolid man of action, immune from any excesses of emotional disturbance; and this habit served him well now. Oddly enough, the shock of the accident had cleared his mind in much the same way as the breaking of the storm had cleared the air. He surveyed the scene and recalled the details of the catastrophe with cool clarity. Oddly, again, he was no longer hungry or thirsty. When he had rummaged in his sodden coat-pocket for his oil-silk tobacco-pouch and contrived, at the fourth attempt, to light his pipe from the sputter of a damp match, he felt himself unusually competent to deal with the situation.

First of all, lamentable though this might be, his new, two-thousand-pound Pearce-Tregaron was gone. There was nothing to be done about that. Often enough he had hopefully wrestled with the iron obstinacy of a car that had died on him and refused to start; but this car was far beyond starting. It lay drowned and invisible in heaven knew how many feet of black mud, and could only (if ever) be raised by a powerful salvage plant; even if it were lifted and landed, it would have to be taken to pieces and reassembled. That was that. Mr. Lucton faced the fact with laudable stoicism. As a business man he had always believed in cutting his losses; and his ability to cut a loss so monstrous as this without flinching had a certain magnificence which made him think well of himself. He could imagine the hysteria he would have had to face if his wife had been with him. That she wasn't, was one item he could place on the credit side of unevenly-balanced luck.

Secondly, he realized that he was at least forty miles from North Bromwich, and five or six, as he reckoned it, from any town or village. If he wished to return home that night he could only do so by walking to the nearest of these and hiring a car, or by telephoning to Alvaston for one of the boys to drive down and fetch him. Neither of these courses appealed to him. He knew that a call for help would be considered a nuisance. Wasn't it just like the clumsy old fool, his family would say, to get himself into a mess of this kind and have to be dragged out of it? Serve him right—that was how Muriel would put it—for his selfishness in buying a car that nobody but himself could drive! Furthermore, apart from his dislike of being laughed at, scolded, or patronized, he remembered that at this hour it would be no use telephoning to Alvaston. The whole family, Fowler had told him, were "out to dinner", and he himself had urged Fowler to take an evening off. In all probability his call would be answered by the housemaid who had retrieved the parcel containing his Harris suit. She would certainly bungle the message, and could not deliver it, in any case, until the rest of the family came home—perhaps in the small hours.

Should he walk to some town—say Pershore—and hire a car at a garage to drive him home? That would cost him a fiver. He didn't mind the expense. A man who had just lost two thousand pounds in five seconds couldn't boggle at that. But such a journey would be equally uncomfortable and humiliating, and might even be dangerous—for by now the declining sun had left the river, and he was becoming aware of the chill of his storm-sodden clothes. He remembered anxiously, having heard somebody say at the club that men of his years, in the prime of middle age, were particularly liable to be snuffed out with pneumonia; and, once having avoided death by drowning, he had no intention of slinking home quietly to die in his bed.

He felt far more anxious not to die than he had felt that

morning. Indeed, it was one of the oddest results of this remarkable adventure that, sitting there on the bank and shivering a little as he puffed at his pipe, he was aware of a quite unusual zest for life.

The accident had shaken him out of his brooding self, dislodged him from the safe rut in which he was running. He had skidded in more ways than one; the stimulus of that hazardous escape had made life seem doubly precious. Indeed, soaked and bruised as he was, he was actually enjoying himself more than he had done for months, and at that moment the thought of returning to North Bromwich, or relapsing into the rut out of which he had slipped, revolted him.

"Supposing I didn't go back?" he asked himself.

He smiled at the very extravagance of such an idea, and yet couldn't help remembering that this was the second time in the last few hours the question had formed itself in his mind. "Supposing I never went back?" Extravagant? Yes, but wasn't it just about time he did do something extravagant, if only to assert his rights as an individual? That bold phrase was all very fine and large; it might be applicable, perhaps, to a man who had the energy, the adaptability of youth to sustain him. "But you, Owen Lucton," his prudence warned him, "are middle-aged; you have made your bed and must lie in it. You're a family man"—was he *not?*—"a respectable citizen, a prospective Lord Mayor, with a knighthood in sight"—and wouldn't that just suit Muriel? "Men of your kind," the argument went on, "don't do things like that." (No, because we haven't the guts: that's the proper answer.) "And, what's more, the idea isn't practicable: you know perfectly well that you couldn't carry it off: the sheer complications—financial, domestic and the rest—would be too much for you. The fact that you're considering such hair-raising possibilities, even as a joke, merely shows that this shock has temporarily unbalanced you. For heaven's sake try to be reasonable, or you'll suddenly wake up and find yourself stark, staring mad. It's clear you are not quite yourself."

Mr. Lucton sat quietly laughing at himself. This was undeniably true. He still felt a trifle giddy and, considering the gravity of the disaster, unreasonably elated. He was, he admitted, outside of his normal self, in a delicious state of what was called ecstasy, the privileged condition of lunatics, lovers and poets. Or rather, perhaps, the effect of the shock had been to emphasize an already existing division between two conflicting sides of his nature—what was the word for it? Schizophrenia?—with the result that the side which had been rigidly and consciously bound to the other for so many years had now broken loose like the kernel of a split chestnut and was insisting on the right to a separate existence, while a third Owen Lucton, the one who sat there smiling, was permitted to enjoy the contest without engaging in it or deciding which of the other two was the genuine article. Let the debate continue!

It continued vehemently, his emancipated self (as Mr. Lucton thought of it) protesting against every practical objection his conventionalized self deployed. Weren't the newspapers, to say nothing of the radio appeals, full of cases of "lost memory"—stories of missing men who vanished and often were never found?

Yes, indeed. But had the new Mr. Lucton noticed that, apart from an occasional absconding solicitor, prominent citizens were never involved in these disappearances? In other words (the point had been made before), in reputable circles such things were not done. The publicity in which men of substance lived, the very fact of their faces being well known to so many people, made it almost impossible, even if they lost their memories, to succeed in losing themselves. More people in the world knew Tom Fool than Tom Fool knew. When once the fugitive's clothes and personal appearance were described, the hunt was up; a cloud of witnesses would testify to every step he had made, until he was tracked down and brought back and publicly humiliated. Then Tom Fool would deserve his name!

That was all very well, the new Mr. Lucton parried, but wait a moment. As for his personal appearance, there was nothing distinctive about it: the ordinary blue-eyed Saxon of medium height and indeterminate colouring was the commonest physical type; on the streets of North Bromwich he could meet his double a dozen times in a day. As for clothes: why, if he had planned such a disappearance deliberately, he couldn't have laid his plans more cunningly! He was wearing a suit which, for all the world would ever know, was already lost in the Alvaston parish rummage-sale. The only living soul who could possibly guess what had happened to it was the second housemaid; and she, by the time the alarm had spread, would already be back in her home and well out of hearing. Anything else?

A man who wanted to disappear, the old Mr. Lucton returned sardonically, would hardly set out in a brand-new Pearce-Tregaron: not only a car which nobody who knew anything about motoring could fail to notice, but also one which was unique in the style of its bodywork. A hundred envious, interested eyes must have watched it stealing through the crowded afternoon traffic of the Halesby Road.

But exactly! If such evidence transpired it would all agree that the car, when last seen, was rapidly travelling westward—while he, the new Mr. Lucton, had come to life forty miles to the south, where the police were hardly likely to look for him. And as for the car: where was it, and who could trace it? It was *spurlos versunken*, as the Boche used to say.

Ah, no. Not so *spurlos* as all that. Pray observe these shattered white railings, the skid-marks on the road, the track where the wings had ploughed up the slope before the car turned over. Anyone passing the spot would see there had been a smash and wonder how it had ended.

And supposing he did? This was a turbid stream at the best of times. In a few days the car would certainly be coated with mud. Was the curious stranger likely to start dredging the river in search of it? That wasn't his business. If the owner of the car thought it worth recovering, he would surely have reported the accident and set about the expensive and arduous job of salvage himself. If there really was a car there, and he didn't report it, it might be taken for granted that it was nothing but an old crock that he was thankful to see the end of. In any case nothing was likely to be fished up for weeks or even months, by which time the story of the vanished accountant would have been forgotten.

The fact remained that there was only one Pearce-Tregaron of that kind in existence. If it were discovered it would soon be identified.

Well, damn it, one couldn't essay an adventure of that kind without leaving some traces. The main drawback to murder had always been the disposal of the victim. One must take a risk occasionally. Nothing dare, nothing win!

Still, even if you faced your risks and got away with it, it was no use pretending that the moral issue would not also have to be faced. A decent man (if he still had the nerve to call himself that after playing with such ideas) had no right to evade his domestic and financial responsibilities—in other words to embarrass his family and his firm.

To this pleading the new Mr. Lucton responded with some irritation. As for his family, they had all of them shown pretty pointedly, that, apart from his function of universal provider, they could manage without him quite easily. Indeed, they had done so. Their ways were no longer his, and their income, anyway, was assured. They would be able to go on their way without having their style cramped by his old-fashioned prejudices. That also "went for" the firm—as Leith, with his beastly Hollywood jargon, would put it. Even the faithless Miss Jenkins—the morning's wound still smarted—had clearly begun to regard that hard-headed young man as the dominant brain in it.

There was no need to waste tears on Leith. The business was sound, and nothing could stop its development. As for the "scandal", if that were the word, neither the firm nor the family would be any the worse for it. A cynic might even say they would benefit by the publicity. There was nothing discreditable in a fellow losing his memory. People who didn't know the facts of the case would feel they had to be kind to them. An orgy of sympathy!

Well, the devil's advocate replied, since it appears that you're lost to all domestic decency and devoid of moral sense, let me put one more question: If you still persist in playing with this moonshine madness, may I ask what you're going to live on?

That was a poser, and no mistake! It brought the giddy new

Mr. Lucton up short—so violently that for a moment the three discrete personalities into which he had been shaken cohered in the dubious whole of their original, a chilly middle-aged dreamer sitting alone on the river-bank. This crest-fallen gentleman shook his head hopelessly, and knocked out his pipe with a rueful gesture that signified the end of an entrancing dream.

"Yes, that puts the lid on it," he thought, as he pulled himself up on the uninjured arm and rose, turning his back on the river. He stood there for a moment, crushed but resigned, and thrust his chilly hands into his trouser pockets. The right hand encountered a handful of silver and copper, the change which the steward had handed him that morning in the club. The left closed on a bulky packet whose existence, at the moment, he couldn't account for. He fished it out wonderingly and stared at it. His thick neck went red. It was the envelope of bank-notes the odious Mr. Hogget had handed him in payment for the sale of the old house in King's Road: two thousand four hundred and twenty-six pounds. Two hundred a year. . . . Just a trifle more, in fact, than the income on which he had lived happily in his early married life.

This discovery had the effect of disintegrating his newly-restored personality. Out of this turbulence the transformed Mr. Lucton rose triumphantly.

"Two thousand four hundred and twenty-six. . . . By heaven, I'll do it!" he cried.

Even as he spoke these rash words, he realized that unless he persisted in putting them into practice and refused the voices of convention and prudence a hearing his determination might fail. He wished he could perform some symbolical act, equivalent to the burning of boats or the crossing of a Rubicon, which would commit him irretrievably to the madness on which he had decided. There was none of which he could think. The first thing he could do was obviously to remove any personal traces that might connect him with the accident; so he searched the bank systematically and was rewarded, at the last moment, by discovering a soft felt hat, with gilt initials inside, which, if he had left it, would certainly have betrayed him: that was a bit of good luck, he told himself, or at least a welcome sign that he had all his wits about him and wasn't so dazed as he felt. The next was to remove himself, as quickly as possible, from the scene of his transformation; so, with shaking limbs, he proceeded to climb up the bank and regain the road. As he reached the broken railings and began to pull them into line again in such a way as to make the breach less noticeable, some mysterious extension of normal consciousness warned him that he wasn't alone.

A shiver of guilty apprehensiveness ran down his spine. There was no sound but the persistent falling note of the willow-wren and the subdued murmur of water trickling away from the puddle in the road. His eyes searched the surroundings carefully without finding anything until, of a sudden, a trailing bramble stirred in the hedgerow opposite, and they became aware of the cause of the movement and the source of his uneasiness.

It was a man, a small, gnomish figure, huddled in the hedge. He wore a tattered overcoat, green with age and buttoned high at the neck, above which a bristling beard and a tousle of wispy hair framed a face in which the only features discernible were a pair of small hedgehog eyes and a clay pipe stuck like an Aunt Sally's in a toothless, nut-cracker mouth. The creature grinned sardonically at Mr. Lucton, but neither moved nor spoke. There was something malignant in its scrutiny and its continued silence which, to Mr. Lucton's mind, could have only one significance: the secret on which he had plumed himself was no longer a secret; those small, evil eyes had witnessed the accident; his plan of escape was still-born. His first impulse was one of disappointed fury.

"What the devil are you grinning at me like that for?" he shouted. "What do you want?"

"I ain't grinning at nobody, guv'nor," the gnome whined in reply. "It's me ruddy teeth being gone that makes me look like I do. It ain't no fault of mine. All I want is a fill of tobacco and the price of a pint."

"What are you doing here, anyway?" Mr. Lucton persisted.

"My Gor, if a poor beggar can't sit down in the hedge for a

minute to ease his boots without being dropped on, it's a ruddy poor look-out for all of us." He spat in the ditch. "A free country? I don't think! Anyone'ld think you was a copper," he added contemptuously. "Leastways, you behave like one."

"Well, how long have you been there?" Mr. Lucton asked, with anxiety.

"That's my business, too," the tramp answered sullenly. "But if you want to know, I've only sat down here this instant, when you come up the bank. Just to ease me feet, like I've told you—and you'ld know what that meant if your boots was like mine and your poor feet had been on the road since eleven o'clock this morning—to say nothing of being soaked through and three hours' walk to get to the Union at Tewkesbury. If it comes to that, what d'you reckon you'm doing to them railings?"

Mr. Lucton sighed with relief. His chilled spirits warmed rapidly. He felt kindly instead of hostile towards this pitiful human flotsam. Still, the question had to be answered and suspicions allayed. He unfolded his pouch and gave the creature, whose grimy claws grasped it eagerly, a lavish fist of tobacco. Then he spoke off-handedly—and, as he felt, unconvincingly.

"Just having a look at them. Seems to me as if somebody has given them a devil of a biff. I can't see any skid-marks, though."

The hedgehog eyes glinted out of their thicket with diabolical hatred.

"Whoever it was, I wish he'd a'skidded down the bank and been drownded. It's them lorries. Blasted murderers, that's what I call 'em. Think the whole road belongs to 'em. Tear the ruddy clothes off your back and then turn round and laugh at you. If I had my way, I'ld drown the whole lot of 'em, bost me if I wouldn't." He resumed his cringing whine: "What about that there pint, guv'nor? It's a week since I tasted a drop."

Mr. Lucton was doubtful about that. He took out his handful of change and selected a half-crown. The poor devil could drink himself stupid on that to-night, and pay for a bed if he couldn't stagger to a barn.

"Well, one thing I'll say," the tramp grinned, "and that is:

you're a toff. Here's good luck!" He pouched the coin in his toothless mouth like a monkey. "Now I reckon I'll get my boots on."

Mr. Lucton did not stay to witness this revolting ceremony. Now that he had satisfied himself that his secret was still his own, he was anxious to free himself from this embarrassing company. He smiled, nodded and waved his hand, and walked rapidly round the turn out of sight.

(II)

WARMEST WELCOME

THE village was all he had hoped for. He approached it over a narrow bridge that spanned the stream an hour's walk below the point where the Pearce-Tregaron lay sunken.

Mr. Lucton did not know the village's name, and had no wish to know it. It was sufficient for him to know that he had come within sight of a place of rest and refreshment, both of which he was prepared to enjoy; for, in spite of his fatigue, he felt astonishingly young and alive and lightened in spirit. It was almost as if the sudden loss of his newest and proudest possession had produced a similar effect to the loosening of Christian's burden in the *Pilgrim's Progress*. That loss had symbolized the shedding of every kind of material preoccupation, with the result that the atmosphere of his walk through the delicious air of that summer evening, at an hour when the birds had grown drowsy and the shapes of the hills appeared to be composing themselves for sleep, had a quality nearer to that of legend or fable than to that of everyday life.

No doubt the aftermath of unusual nervous excitement, to say nothing of what to a man of his age had been a considerable nervous shock, combined with the fact that he had neither eaten nor drunk for eight hours to enhance this impression of unreality. As he paused on the brow beyond the bridge to gaze at it, this nameless village revealed, in addition to a heart-subduing quietude and simplicity, a substance so tenuous that it might well have been a mirage. Once granted that it existed, there was nothing either death-like or sinister about it. On the contrary, the dim, straggling street was full of signs of a warm and friendly life: smoke rising straight from a dozen cottage chimneys; the voices of children which echoed in the deepening dusk; swallows (or were they bats?) darting under the eaves of thatch and circling the church tower; a colony of agitated rooks that seemed loth to alight on their nests in the elms that guarded the green; a late cuckoo, distantly calling with the cracked note of June. More than this: in the roadway that twisted between cottages of Cotswold stone and luminous half-timber, several slow rustic human shapes were to be seen—an old man, hobbling home on a stick; a woman, wearing a sun-bonnet, carrying buckets of milk or water attached to a yoke. He could hear their footfalls more distinctly than he could see their figures. That, perhaps, explained the village's mysterious enchantment: the extreme stillness of an air so thin that the most minute sounds —such as the squeak of the bats (they were not swallows, it seemed, after all)—could be heard without any straining of the ears to catch them.

"I hope to goodness there's a passable pub," Mr. Lucton thought, his mouth suddenly watering and his stomach proclaiming its emptiness at the mere prospect of food.

Assuredly there was a pub: a long white-washed building with a hanging armorial signboard, an inviting open door, and a line of lamplit casements whose light threw on the roadway the shadows of trim geraniums planted in window-boxes. The scent of these, and an equally alluring odour of cider and beer combined with shag tobacco, excited Mr. Lucton's nostrils as he hesitated momentarily under the latticed porch—hesitated because, simultaneously, he heard from within a babel of talk and realized that the bar-parlour was full.

In ordinary circumstances he would have welcomed this sound. At this moment, however, he felt oddly shy and vulnerable. Apart from his encounter with the tramp, this was the first time he had been threatened, in his new incarnation, with the impact of curious eyes. He was a stranger, and therefore would be subject to scrutiny in a confined space; he was about to perform a new part without any opportunity for rehearsal, and felt himself incapable of playing it consistently and convincingly. Amid the easy friendliness of this village bar-parlour, he would have to establish himself as what he was not, and deal with a number of innocent questions for which he must improvise answers. If he opened his mouth, he would probably contradict himself: if he kept it shut, he would become an object of the attention and suspicion he was anxious to avoid.

But there was another force, even stronger than these inhibitions, which impelled him to enter. As he stood there wavering, he became aware that he was not merely ravenously hungry, but mortally tired. His legs ached and trembled, his head swam with giddiness. Leith had spoken the truth when he warned him that he didn't take enough exercise. "Unless I sit down and get something inside me," he thought, "I shall simply collapse. So here goes!"

He turned into the bar. It was warm and thick with tobacco-smoke, and so light that it blinded him. The interior of the pub was as neatly kept as the outside: full of polished brass and pewter; the shelves ranged with shining bottles brightly labelled; the counter arrayed with clean glasses set in rows as precisely "dressed" as a detachment of guards on parade. Behind it he saw an opulent, well-preserved woman, with prominent blue eyes, a rigid brass-coloured toupet, and three rows of imitation pearls draped on the bosom of a white silk blouse. She was laughing immoderately and winking at one of the customers she was serving; but that didn't prevent her seeing Mr. Lucton the moment he put his head inside the bar-parlour door.

"Service, Charlie!" she cried, with shrill brightness, in a voice as brazen as her hair.

A man turned from another group of customers and came briskly towards Mr. Lucton: a tall, middle-aged man, with a high bald forehead, purple cheeks and a sandy moustache each end of which was twisted into a skewer and darkened with wax. He was in shirt-sleeves and carried a tray of empty glasses. Over one forearm was draped a white towel that gave him a business-like air. He stood at attention. "An old regular N.C.O.," Mr. Lucton thought. "Gone to seed a bit, more's the pity. But still a fine fellow. You always know where you are with a man like that."

"Good evening, sir. What can I do for you?"

Mr. Lucton murmured something about bread, cheese and beer

"Pint of bitter, Florrie, and a cut of the new Double

Gloucester," the landlord bawled in a barrack-square voice. "We're a full house to-night, sir," he added apologetically. "If you'ld like me to bring it to the sitting-room, just over the passage there, you'ld find it more quiet."

"Oh, don't trouble to do that," Mr. Lucton said hurriedly. So far none of the company had taken any notice of him, and he felt that if he were segregated in this obvious manner they probably would.

"O.K., sir. Just as you like. You can squeeze in at the table over there with those other four gentlemen. I shan't be a tick."

He bustled away, while Mr. Lucton walked rather uncertainly to the other end of the room, where a group of four men made a place for him at the end of a shiny bench with a table in front of it. His companions were by no means of the type he would have expected to find in a country pub. Though their foreheads were fiery with sunburn, the rest of their faces had the pasty complexion of townsmen. All four wore billycock hats and black Sunday clothes, and their sombre faces suggested that they must have come from a funeral. On the table in front of each stood an empty tankard. Though they made way for Mr. Lucton, none of them spoke to him. They continued to contemplate their tankards with a solemn air, so morosely that Mr. Lucton felt it incumbent on himself to make the first move.

"A nice day," he said cheerfully.

"Glad you think so," his neighbour said sullenly. "Too much thunder about for my liking. 'Ad any luck?"

Mr. Lucton laughed in spite of himself. What could he say? It would be difficult to explain that he had just lost a two-thousand-pound car and, possibly, found a new life.

"Luck?" he said. "I don't understand."

"You'ld understand if you'd 'ad the same luck as me and my mates 'ere. Eight ruddy hours without so much as a bite."

At this point Mr. Lucton perceived for the first time that each of his sombre companions was equipped with a bundle of sticks, resembling, except for the brush, a chimney-sweep's outfit, together with a wicker basket and a stone gallon-jar tucked between his feet under the bench.

"Ah, I see what you mean. You've been fishing."

"That's right. Small 'Eath Piscatorial Society. Coarse fishermen, that's what we are, boss, or what we used to be. Eight hours on the bank and not so much as a bite, if you call that fishing. You may say, like I did just now, it's the thunder what done it; but that's only part of it. Fishing's not what it used to be twenty years ago. What do you say, 'Erbert?"

"It's gone off and it's going off worse, Jim. No two ways about that. Getting worse every year. As a working man's sport, I reckon it's just about finished."

"I'm sorry to hear that," Mr. Lucton said. "Any way of accounting for it?"

"Well, look at the way beer's gone up," his neighbour replied indignantly. "That's what killed it to start with."

"And look at the swipes you get for double the cost," his companion added, draining the dregs of his tankard. "Tap-water bewitched: that's about all it is."

"No complaints about my beer, I hope, gentlemen?" With a flourish the landlord planked down Mr. Lucton's pint with half the top of a cottage loaf and a substantial wedge of cheese. "There you are, sir. Now you can judge for yourself. Flower's best, and an extra good cask in the pink of condition."

To Mr. Lucton's dry throat it was a draught of nectar. He immediately felt better pleased with himself and his company.

"Seems all right to me—to begin with," he said. "The trouble is that your tankards don't hold enough. If these gentlemen here would join me in another, they might change their minds."

They didn't mind if they did. "Four pints, Florrie," the landlord shouted as he whipped up the empties.

Mr. Lucton fell-to. He found the rough fare delicious: the crusty loaf neither too new nor too white, the Double Gloucester more appetizing for a faint bitterness, and creamy in spite of its solid consistency. One might do worse, he thought contentedly, than settle down for the night in such a comfortable inn. There was no hurry to make a decision in any case. No hurry for anything. As the full tankards appeared and his guests made a hole in each of them, they caught the infection of his zest, forgot the day's disappointments, and became communicative. The invincible hopefulness of the fisherman's temperament asserted itself; they discussed their plans for the morrow, their last day on the river. Mr. Lucton's immediate neighbour, who appeared to be the head of the party, produced three tobacco-tins in which he proudly displayed the baits he intended to use next morning; red brandling-worms wriggling in moss, swollen grains of stewed wheat, and revolting honey-coloured maggots which he described as "gentles", and said he produced at home from fly-blown bullock's liver.

"Them's the only thing about fishing," he said, "as my missus can't abide. Dirty, stinking things, she calls them; but, Lord bless your soul, it's only a matter of habit the same as everything else. These 'ere gentles are so well scoured and 'olesome you could make your dinner off of them and be none the worse."

Mr. Lucton was feeling slightly the worse for the mere sight of them; but his neighbour was so full of innocent enthusiasm for these horrors that, in spite of his qualms, he felt it would be unkind to protest.

"Them's the bait for to-morrow, thunder or no thunder, 'Erbert," the fisherman said. "And what's more, I know where I can land as good a basket of roach with them as you ever seen."

"Where's that, Jim?" the other asked eagerly.

"Go on, 'Erbert; of course, you know where I mean as well as I do. That swim where I grassed the 'alf-pound chub last August. Look 'ere: you cross the bridge, as if you was going to Pairshore, see?—and after a goodish step—about three mile, I reckon, you come to a place where the river runs close to the road. There's a steep bank with a length of white railings along the top of it . . ."

Mr. Lucton went hot and then cold. This was dangerous ground. What was more, inspired by his second pint, the fisherman was now talking so loudly that the group of men standing in front of the bar had begun to listen. One of them spoke in a high, brazen voice: a gawky young farmer with a blond face blistered by haymaking:

"You mean Pritchett's Pool, mister. That's where you mean: Pritchett's Pool."

"I know nothing about Pritchett's Pool. I know nothing about the name of it; but there's a line of white railings, just like I said."

"That's right. Painted white they are; the Council done it so you can see them night-time. That's an awkward bit of road. There's a dip, and water lies in it. Why, I damn near went through them myself one night just a year ago after Pershore Fair. Straight I did. It's the water lying there."

"It wasn't no water, Harry, as made you do that!" one of the others chuckled, a fat little red-faced man with small, lecherous eyes. "I seed you that night. *And* I saw the bird you'd got sat on the pillion."

"Never you mind who I'd got sat on the pillion. You're a one to talk, George. Never do any courtin' yourself, I suppose? You ought for to be shamed on yourself, a man of your age with a wife and family."

The fat little man laughed silently, shaking his paunch.

"Well, if you 'ad gone in, Harry, you wouldn't have been the first. I reckon you know why it's called Pritchett's Pool?"

"I know nothing except that that's the name it goes by."

"Well, I'll tell you then. It happened before you was born, when I was a lad. Mr. Harber, who had The Tack then . . ."

"Ay, that meadow on the far side is part of my land."

"That's just what I'm telling you, if so be you won't interrupt. Mr. Harber, he had a labourer called Pritchett. A bit wild, like some whose names I won't mention, but a darned good hand with horses and a first-class ploughman. Well, that wasn't a meadow in those days like it is now. Mr. Harber, he bust it up for a bean-field, from what I remember. Ay, I reckon 'twas Seville beans . . ."

"You'd better be getting a move on, George," the young man warned him. "It's just on closing time."

"This is my story, not yours, Harry. It's all right. Four minutes to go. Give Mr. Wilder another pint, Mrs. Walters, to keep him quiet. Well, this chap Pritchett was ploughing that there field with a single-furrow Oliver digger, and just when he come to the headland a fox jumped out of the hedge. Pritchett had a stick in his hand and took a wallop at the darned fox, and instead of hitting the fox, he caught the old horse, who was ploughing asleep, like an old horse do, a hell of a swipe on . . . well, you can guess where, Mrs. Walters—so as the old horse just give one spring in the air and landed first go in the river."

"You don't say so!" said Mrs. Walters. "Well, really, I never!"

"I do say so, ma'am; and what's more, he never come up, nor yet did the plough."

"Don't tell me horses can't swim," the young farmer said scornfully.

"This one couldn't, not with the plough and all behind him. I reckon it must have got caught on the bottom."

"Go on, George, it can't be all that deep!"

"I don't know how deep it is, Harry; but that's what happened. And that's why it's called Pritchett's Hole. Harber give the poor beggar the sack. He worked for me afterwards."

An old man, huddled in the corner, lifted his voice:

"That's true enough, Mr. Baker. And I can tell you there be deeper holes in the Avon nor that. There was one E'esham way as a steam-roller once went into. Not a steam-roller, rightly speaking: it was one of them fair-ingins. I seed him myself when they hauled him out, none the worse for it neither."

"Well, in that case, I reckon I'll have a go for to drag up that plough. I could do with an Oliver digger myself. Will you lend me a hand, George?" the young farmer said.

"Not me. I've no time to waste. That's just the kind of ruddy fool thing you would do, Harry. That plough'll have rusted away to nothing by now. Cost you more than it's worth, in any case."

"Well, my hay's all in, thanks be, and I could do with a bit of a lark. You never know what you might find in a hole like that."

Mr. Lucton shivered at the awful truth of the observation. All through this protracted recital he had been sitting on the edge of his seat anxiously hoping that something might turn the course of the conversation from this perilous subject. As the tale, which had been scaring enough in its innocent beginnings, wound relentlessly to the very heart of his secret, he had felt an urgent desire to bolt. When the young farmer actually expressed the intention of dragging the pool, his nerve forsook him completely. This was no place for him. If his way had been unimpeded and he could have managed to escape without being noticed, he would have tried to make a dash for it. At last relief came. Mrs. Walters, glancing at the clock, cried: "Time, gentlemen, please!" Mr. Lucton, squeezing himself out of the narrow space in which he was wedged, made a bee-line for the doorway. He was nearly through when the landlord caught him by his bruised arm.

" 'Ere, 'ere! None of that, now!" he said in a thick voice from which all the politeness had vanished. "Thought you'd get away with it, did you, my beauty? I know that game."

Mr. Lucton wriggled. "Let go of my arm," he gasped. "What's the matter? What do you want?"

"What do I want? I like that! I want the money you owe me. Six pints and one portion of bread and cheese. Three and sixpence. That's what I want."

Mr. Lucton, recovering from his surprise, apologized. He was thankful to find it was nothing more serious than that.

"I say, I'm awfully sorry. I'd forgotten all about it."

"Forgotten, 'ad you?" The landlord was quite unappeased: he had been taking surreptitious nips regularly throughout the evening; now his purple face wore an ugly look, his spiked moustache appeared to bristle ferociously. "I know your kind," he said. "One of these days you'll forget all about it once too often and find yourself given in charge, like you ought to be. Don't you think I'm as soft as all that; I've had my eye on you: I seem all along you was looking for a chance to slip out on the sly."

Mr. Lucton bowed to the torrent. "Look here, I assure you . . ." he began.

"I don't want any more of your lip. I want my money, see?"

"You shall have it at once, if you'll kindly let go of my arm," Mr. Lucton said mildly.

The landlord released the bruised arm unwillingly. Mr. Lucton dived into his right-hand trouser pocket, discovered it was empty: the handful of change must have slipped through a hole in it, unless he had unwittingly transferred it to the other side after giving the tramp his half-crown. He explored the left-hand pocket. That, too, was empty. As the landlord watched this vain search his purple face hardened; his lips curled in an ugly leer that said: "I thought as much."

"Better have one more go," he said, "for the sake of appearances, afore I call the policeman. I don't mind telling you I misliked the look of you from the first, the way you slunk in."

Mr. Lucton flared up. Who was this half-sodden innkeeper to talk like that to a prominent business man, the leader of his profession in the second city of the Empire, a prospective Lord Mayor?

"There's no need to be insolent, my good man," he said firmly. "What I happen to look like is no concern of yours. I'll thank you to mind your own business."

"That's what I'm doing," the landlord maintained—not entirely without reason. "All I want is my money."

Mr. Lucton's hand nervously examined the right-hand breast-pocket of his coat. His fingers trembled under the fellow's vindictive scrutiny. This also was empty. His face grew hot with confusion. There was only one pocket left, and here, to his infinite relief, he discovered not only the envelope containing his fortune, but also a driving licence, and a blue pocket cheque-book on which the eyes of the landlord fastened immediately.

"I'm not taking no cheques, if that's what you're after," he said.

Mr. Lucton made no answer. He was wondering how he could manage to extract a single small note from the bulging envelope without revealing the rest of its contents to those suspicious eyes. He tried to divert the landlord's attention by asking him a question.

"How much do you say I owe you?"

"You know that as well as I do. Three and sixpence."

The man's eyes were still concentrated on the envelope. As Mr. Lucton cautiously extracted a Treasury note, a folded hundred-pound bank-note slipped to the floor. Both dived for it simultaneously, but the landlord got there first. He picked up the note and gazed at it with goggling eyes. Mr. Lucton snatched it away from him, only hoping he hadn't seen the figures in the corner, and handed him the other.

"If you'll give me sixteen and sixpence," he said.

The man took the note without a word. He retreated behind the bar and opened the till with a rattle. Then he called his wife. "Come here, 'alf a mo', Florrie." Mr. Lucton heard him speaking in a hoarse, urgent whisper. The woman nodded and hurried out through the door at the back of the bar.

"My change, please," Mr. Lucton demanded haughtily, feeling more sure of himself. "I happen to be in a hurry."

"I'll bet you are," the landlord replied malignantly. "You'll get your change all in good time, and maybe something more. But you needn't think I've finished with you, not by a long way. That there note I picked up was one for a hundred pounds, and I seed a lot more of the same colour in that there envelope. What I want to know, cocky, is how a chap like you comes to be carrying all that brass and where you've got it from. There's only one place where you see notes like that—and that's in a bank, unless they happen to have been stolen out of one, as I reckon these must have been."

"You've no right," Mr. Lucton blustered . . .

"That's for me to decide. I know what I'm going to do: I'm keeping you here till you've satisfied the policeman. He won't be long: I've sent my missus after him. You can take a seat, if you like. 'Ere's your change, if you want it. Three and six from a quid: that leaves sixteen shillings and sixpence."

He spilt a handful of silver on the counter, and moved simultaneously towards the other end of it, where a hinged flap, folded backward, left a gap through which those behind it could enter the bar-parlour. His purpose was evident: to cut off his victim's line of retreat to the door and the street. No doubt he was counting on Mr. Lucton's stopping to pick up his change. If so, he soon saw his mistake. Mr. Lucton was off the mark like a flash. The bar was between them, and, as he reached the end of it, he had just enough time to slam down the hinged flap and gain the split second he needed to make his escape.

"'Ere, 'ere, you can't do that!" the innkeeper bellowed.

It was all very well to say that: Mr. Lucton had done it. In a moment he was out in the street and running faster than he had ever run since the war, with the landlord pounding hot on his heels. Both were middle-aged men and both were out of condition; but Mr. Lucton had the advantage of having only drunk two pints, whereas the other had been steadily soaking not merely throughout the evening, but ever since he had got his discharge from the army. Mr. Lucton had turned right-handed—not for any particular reason: the faculty of organized thought had forsaken him in his panic. He ran straight down the village street, past the church, past the green, until he suddenly saw in front of him, and running towards him, two sinister figures: the innkeeper's wife, her white silk blouse gleaming in the dusk, and another more ponderous shape, that of a helmeted policeman. He pulled up with a jerk and turned in his tracks. He was now between two fires; for the landlord, though losing ground, was still pounding along in pursuit.

"Now I'm for it," he thought. And yet, oddly enough, his mind had become clearer. He was no longer driven by mere panic. As he turned there flashed into his mind the half-humorous memory of a remote, an almost forgotten incarnation of himself, in which he, Owen Lucton, a slim, steel-sinewed young man, had played stand-off half for the North Bromwich Rugby Football Club. In his prime he had been mildly well known for the trickiness of his feet, a baffling body-swerve and a savage hand-off. This was no moment for the display of such refined manœuvres, even if he could have achieved them without spraining his ankle or cricking his back; but if he wasn't still a match for this slow-witted, fuddled opponent, he would deserve to be caught and hauled back ignominiously. The landlord stood in his path with straddled legs, waving his arms like a man driving sheep to market. Mr. Lucton feinted to throw him off his balance, pretending to swerve to the right, then, changing his step, leapt clear of the outstretched arm and went pelting away down the street, out of the village, over the bridge.

The footsteps and shouting grew faint behind him, but still he did not stop running. His breath came less laboriously now; it seemed as if he were actually getting a "second wind". And he laughed as he ran; for, when once that unreasoning confusion of panic was over, he saw how ridiculous his anxiety had been. Even if he hadn't bolted, if he had obediently waited for the policeman to come, it would have been perfectly easy for him to establish his identity and explain himself. He had obviously behaved like a fool.

Yet, now that he came to look back upon the escapade, he knew he had enjoyed himself. It was a primitive, physical triumph: for the first time since the war he had proved the superiority of his wits and his limbs. After twenty years of smug and submissive respectability, he, Owen Lucton—whom the policemen on duty in Sackville Row saluted and the Chief Constable frequently lunched with in the Constitutional Club—had run from the powers of the Law like a pickpocket and thereby satisfied some suppressed, mysterious craving for adventurous action. The situation, of course, was ridiculous; yet the contrast between the breathless, bedraggled figure he was at this moment and that which, less than ten hours before (was it possible?), had dozed off the effects of an imprudent luncheon in the central shrine of Midland respectability, excited in him not merely his sense of the ridiculous but a less reasonable—and even more satisfying—exultation.

"If I go back to-morrow," he thought, "nobody can say I haven't had a run for my money."

"But I'm damned if I'll go back to-morrow," he told himself boastfully—with the monitory reservation, on the part of his more prudent self, that this remained to be seen.

(III)

TIBBERTON'S FARM

THAT night Mr. Lucton slept in a barn. He had walked on, without any clear idea of his direction except that the road led away from that hateful village, until his legs refused to carry him any farther. At this point he had played with the idea of sleeping under a haycock. After all, it was midsummer, and though he was unused to country life, he recalled there were romantic precedents for this in pastoral poetry and in folk-song. In practice, these traditional delights were overrated. Not only did he find the hay abominably prickly: he also discovered that the haycock he had selected for trial was steaming with moisture. A late-rising moon kept him awake in spite of his tiredness; it bathed the whole visible world in a cold, silvery light, and revealed the fact that the field in which he was lying was spread knee-deep in a milk-white coverlet of mist that accounted for the sensation of cold which he had assured himself must be imaginary.

Of late years, though his family assured him his health was excellent, he had become secretly nervous and fussy about it —a man with only twenty more years to live couldn't afford to be careless—and now, in addition to the dangers of pneumonia or rheumatic fever, he remembered an old wives' tale about the baleful effects of moonlight: how, at the best, it might paralyse one's face and, at the worst, affect one's reason. Moonstruck: that was the word. By normal standards of behaviour his actions during the last four hours had been sufficiently eccentric and uncontrolled to suggest that he was already a borderline case, and to persuade him not to take any unnecessary risks with his reason. So, after a shivering, restless hour, he forsook his haycock and discovered, in the corner of the field, a friendly barn.

So far as comfort went, that wasn't much better. Dry straw,

he found, was even more prickly than hay. It got in his ears and his hair and clung to his Harris tweeds. He was also quickly convinced that the barn was not uninhabited. The stacked bundles of straw were lively with rustlings and scratchings and scamperings which he put down to rats. Mr. Lucton had a profound antipathy to rats; but by this time he was so weary that not even this could keep him awake. The barn's pleasant warmth dispelled the aching cold from his limbs; its musty air had a somnolent quality, suggestive of hops, and, within a few moments, without knowing it, he had fallen asleep.

When he woke, the sun was high in the sky and the thin nocturnal mist had vanished from the fields. No sooner had he opened his eyes than he was wide awake, and not merely awake but as thrillingly alert and alive as though, during that dreamless sleep, he had actually grown younger. Even his tongue and palate felt cleaner than usual: a state which he attributed to the fact that, for the first time in twenty years, he had gone to sleep on a relatively empty stomach unvitiated by a couple of after-dinner cigars. Though his limbs were slightly stiff from unwonted strains and exertions, there was even in them a feeling of ease and lightness, as though the very blood that ran through them had been cleansed of accumulated impurities, and a similar lightness, a sense of resilience and well-being, enlivened his mind.

"I feel like a different man," Mr. Lucton told himself, "a new man, as the saying goes; and, heavens, what a day!"

Its promise was certainly superb. He brushed the straw from his clothes and stepped out of the barn into the sunshine. The hay-field was still deserted; but from over the hedge, in the next, he heard the clatter of a rake dragging swathes into rows and the distant voice of a carter encouraging his horses. They were sweet, midsummer sounds, in tune with the broken call of a flying cuckoo and the fine note of bees and other winged insects already at work in the tarnished hawthorn bloom and in the creamy plumes of meadowsweet foaming along the unmown headland. Sight, smell and hearing—every sense Mr. Lucton possessed—appeared to partake in the effects of that astonishing lustration, to have achieved a new sensitivity, an unusual acuteness. Never in all his life (or, at any rate, since his boyhood) had mown hay and hedgerows smelt sweeter, the face of the earth appeared more lovely, more friendly and more familiar. Though he was still, as it seemed, in the heart of the Severn Valley (as, indeed, he must have been, since he had not crossed the great river), the hills that embraced it were still in evidence: the dome of Bredon, from whose feet he had fled overnight, now sunk in the distance, and before him, the line of the Malverns, no longer inkily threatening, but enormous shapes soft with the bloom of smooth turf or swathed in the piercing green of young bracken, as clear in their detail of form and enamelled brilliance of colour (though displayed against a gentler, mistier blue) as those miniature landscapes which shine through windows in portraits of the Italian renaissance. "An air of eternal spring," Mr. Lucton thought; and the phrase seemed to him not contradictory, since an English midsummer still breathes the magic of spring.

Only one thing was lacking to complete the sensation of physical and spiritual cleanliness. His chin had grown stubbly with a twenty-four-hour growth of beard, the skin of his face was still sticky with sweat, and his hands had not been washed since he left North Bromwich. He felt an urgent desire to complete his inward purification by a wash and a shave. A shave was out of the question, and the ditch from which his trampling released a sharp odour of horse-mint showed no more than a trickle of water; yet that trickle led him at last down the slope of the field towards a swampy patch, pale with more meadowsweet and tussocks of thin reeds, and a file of pollarded willows; and here, in the dip, he found what he sought, a small stream unhurriedly pursuing the line of the hedge, flowing into a shallow pool where a bridge of logs crossed it, carrying a farm road that led to another field.

Mr. Lucton knelt on the bridge and looked down into the pool; the sun, too, beat down on it. It was so still that its surface mirrored his leaning figure—such an unkempt apparition that it was no wonder, he thought, the landlord had taken him for a bilker!—so clear that he could distinguish the tremulous shape of a fingerling trout, its head pointing up-stream, and see, etched on the tawny-sanded bottom, as in a Japanese print, the shadows of a single straggling trailer of briar and a fugitive wren which flickered past it. Even the gauzy anatomy of a dipping dragon-fly's wing was so reflected. The still water looked so cool and inviting that, but for its shallowness, he would have been tempted to undress and lie down in it; but, in addition to being bulky, Mr. Lucton was modest; and the voice he had heard in the next field, if only a carter's, warned him that haymakers were near. So he contented himself with stripping to the waist, scrubbing his hands with wet sand, and sousing his head in the pool. The water ran into his eyes and ears; sparkling droplets hung on his eyelashes and spangled his moustache. Then, selecting a shallower runnel, farther up-stream, he lowered his head again and drank a long draught of water, the most sweet, the most limpid, it seemed to him, that ever had passed his lips.

He was drying his face, for lack of a towel, with his shirt, when a creak of dry axles and a sound of plodding hooves surprised him. He slipped the bundled shirt over his head as quickly as he could, and emerged to see the shape of a great blue wain with vermilion wheels approaching the bridge from the other side of the hedge.

"Steady, now, boys," a rustic voice said, as the shaggy feet of the leader pounded on the bridge with a hollow note. "Come up, then. Take it easy: there's naught to be scared on."

Mr. Lucton watched the empty wagon roll forward into the sun. The horses were led by a thick-set young man with a broad, humorous Saxon face, a sprig of meadowsweet in his teeth, and blue eyes narrowed to the sun. His blond hair was sun-bleached, and the skin of his face, like that of his golden-downy forearms and massive throat, was tanned brick-red as the sand in the bed of the brook. Earthen, too, was the hue of his cord breeches and leggings beneath a snowy shirt, so that, as he advanced, his whole figure, as that of the team-leader, a chestnut with a bunch of flaming poppies stuck in his head-stall, seemed suffused by warm light. Behind him, clinging grimly with both hands to the forward rack of the lumbering wain, stood two little girls in print pinafores and sun-bonnets, whose solemn faces resembled those of a couple of kittens in a cage. When he saw Mr. Lucton, the young man jerked his head sideways in friendly salutation; his face broke into a charming smile.

"Having a swill?" he said. "You'm lucky. It looks like being a fair scorcher. Looking out for a job? If you be, us can give you one."

"What kind of a job?" Mr. Lucton asked.

The young man's eyes widened reproachfully at such a display of ignorance.

"Why, there be only one job now: haymakin'. Fifteen acres we've got to get in by to-night. I don't trust this weather. Like as not 'twill breed tempest."

"Yes, I'll gladly give you a hand for what it's worth," Mr. Lucton said.

"A bob an hour. That's what it's worth if so be you put your back into it. But we don't want no passengers, mind. And there's another field to be carted to-morrow if the thunder keeps off; so that'll be two full days."

Mr. Lucton's first instinct was to say that he didn't want to be paid; but the young farmer was so simple and earnest that he felt it would be unkind to complicate matters by any argument.

"All right then, jump up behind. Come on then!"

The chestnut tossed his plume of poppies and obeyed with a jerk that dragged Mr. Lucton forward unceremoniously. By an acrobatic feat that astonished himself he managed to scramble up on the floor of the wagon where the two solemn little girls, though he smiled at them, gazed at him with curious eyes. No doubt, as he reflected, he did look a trifle odd with his pale townsman's face and the wet hair draggling over it; an odd fish, at any time, to come out of their private brook!

The wagon went jolting and swaying across the grain of the linchet-ridges into the field in which Mr. Lucton had heard the horse-rake at work, then swerved towards a corner sheltered by a clump of elms, in whose shade two distinct groups sat eating breakfast. One was a family party, consisting of an elderly man with a square-cut beard, who wore a wide-brimmed straw-hat with a black band on it, a severe-looking woman of the same age, in a black dress, high at the neck and covered by a white apron, and another, much younger woman, who might have been their daughter, nursing a baby on her lap. The other group was composed of four men, two old, one middle-aged and one a lad of eighteen, all, obviously, labourers.

"Lift them kids down, will you?" Mr. Lucton's friend said. He smiled at the grey-bearded man. "I've brought you another hand, Dad."

The old man nodded. "That's good, Ted. The more the better."

Mr. Lucton swung the little girls down from the tail of the wagon. He liked handling these warm little creatures: theirs was the age, he thought, when children were most enchanting; he would have liked to kiss them before he set them down. They accepted his help as a matter of course, without thanks, and ran to the younger woman, who, Mr. Lucton supposed, was their mother.

"You'd better chum up with your mates over there," the young farmer said, jerking his head towards the group of labourers.

"Has he had any breakfast, Ted?" the old woman asked shrewdly. There was no personal solicitude for Mr. Lucton in the enquiry: it was the question of a manager who liked everything in order. The young man laughed:

"I don't know, Mother. Had your breakfast?" he asked Mr. Lucton, who shook his head.

"Well, there's plenty here," the old woman said. "Take this, Lucy, and give it to the man."

The elder of the two little girls advanced, holding in both hands a hunk of bread cut in two to enclose a slab of boiled bacon and a lettuce as big as a cabbage. Mr. Lucton sat down beside the four labourers. They took no notice of him. As a casual worker and a stranger, he was evidently beneath their notice, and, in any case, their mouths were so full and their jaws so active that they could not have spoken. Their silence was less embarrassing than his own inability to deal with the bacon sandwich, which was far too big to go into his mouth. Each of the other men was armed with a horn-handled clasp-knife, with which he sliced chunks of bread and bacon together, balancing the cut morsel mouthwards between knife-blade and thumb, and finally flicking it in with an accuracy which, even if he had possessed a knife, Mr. Lucton could not have emulated. The old man surveyed his bungling efforts to handle his bread and bacon with curiosity rather than contempt.

"Where's your knife?" he said.

"I'm afraid I haven't got one," Mr. Lucton confessed.

"You ain't got no knife? I suppose you mean you've a'lost 'en?"

"No, I've never had one."

"Never 'ad no knife," the old man repeated incredulously. "Then 'ow did you ever manage to ate your vittles?" he asked triumphantly.

The question was difficult to answer without involving explanations, and appeared to be regarded as a poser which had shown Mr. Lucton a liar. The two elder men smiled, and the youngest, who had bolted his breakfast before the rest, and was now lying flat on his back, let out an unbecoming roar of laughter which made Mr. Lucton think he was probably a mental defective, the unfortunate result of in-breeding in this remote rural district. The old man was no better pleased.

"There's no call to bust out with a beller like that, Jim Barley," he said severely, "not when ladies be nigh. That's ignorance, that is; and at your age you'd ought to know better." He swallowed his last mouthful of food and washed it down with a draught from a miniature cask without spilling a drop. Then he thrust his knife into the turf and wiped its edge tenderly. "Now this knife I got 'ere," he explained to Mr. Lucton, "I've had en since I was a lad, belike before you was born, when I started workin' for Mr. Tibberton's father. That's the sort you should get, if so be as you want to ate decent. He be whetted that sharp you could slice a cat's whiskers unbeknownst to him; and whether it be for stringin' up rabbits or cutting a ram-lamb or ateing your dinner, he can't be bate. Four shillin' I give for him. Ay, I bought him in North Bromwich, I did, the time I took the old master's bull to the Cattle Show, Bingley 'All, and won the gold medal."

"I shall have to look out for one like it," Mr. Lucton said seriously. "I come from North Bromwich myself."

The old man regarded him pityingly. "I might a' knowed it. Out of a job?"

"No . . . well, not exactly. I'm taking a holiday."

The old man grunted disparagingly. "Holidays . . . holidays! They do talk about naught but holidays nowadays. Holidays with pay. That's all the go with the young 'uns. Now I've never had no holidays in my life, with pay or without it, exceptin' the time I broke the big bone in my leg with a fracture, and that well-nigh druv me off my 'ead, by the time I come to the end of it. What's the use of holidays? That's what I want to know. A man's place is at home in his garden when he bain't at work. What's he going to do if he's naught to put his hand to? Except what the devil finds for him. You answer me that, Jim Barley!"

The grey-bearded man approached.

"Come on, you fellows, come on. Time to get a move on."

Mr. Lucton found himself with a hay-fork in his hands. The whole family had turned-to. Even the young mother had put her baby to sleep in the shade, where the old sheep-dog sat with his tongue out, keeping guard over it. They followed the empty wagon to the far end of a line of cocks, and the menfolk started pitching hay into the wagon, while the women, and even the two children, busy with rakes, scraped together the scattered wisps that fell, so that none of the precious stuff should be lost. On the top of the wagon, uplifted high like the sun's charioteer, a flaming Phaethon, Ted Tibberton stood spearing the flying forkfuls in mid-air, cunningly caught them and sifted and strewed them with quick turns of the wrist, and trampled them firmly on the bottom of the wagon.

Mr. Lucton found this novel exercise superbly exhilarating. It involved every muscle in arms and loins and torso. He had discarded his coat and his collar and turned up his shirt-sleeves;

his body rejoiced in an unaccustomed freedom from the restrictions of civilized clothing, almost as if it had suddenly been freed and come to life. The men worked in silence, but his ears were full of pleasant sound: the soft swish of the hay through the air, Ted Tibberton's muffled stamping, the jingle of harness as the patient horses tossed their heads or switched their tails to dislodge the flies. The sense of unburdened ease that accompanies a mechanical task in which no effort of thought is involved, spread over his mind a soft glow of contentment. The rhythmical labour engrossed it completely. Such reminders of ordinary experience as entered it were as remote and detached as the high-sailing cumulus which, now that the heat of day was increasing, wandered slowly across the sky yet cast no shadows. Even the thought of what, but for the astonishing chain of events in which he had been carried along, he might have been doing at that moment: a vision of himself throttled by a starched collar, irritably dictating business letters to Miss Jenkins or fighting Leith's uncomfortable efficiency in the stuffy office above the rattle of traffic in Sackville Row, could not jolt his mind out of its content by rousing the pangs of a guilty conscience or the sense of evaded responsibility. North Bromwich, thank heaven, was far away, too far away to seem real. The only true realities were this sun-drenched hayfield, the soft air that quivered with heat, the clean blood that coursed with such splendid vigour through his limbs.

It was pretty hard work. From the first he had thrown himself into it with an abandon that was imprudent in a man of his age and figure. It was not only hard but endless. Fifteen acres to lead! No sooner was one haycock triumphantly dealt with than another presented itself. He noticed with envy that not only the half-wit, Jim Barley, who was an animal bred to such toil, and the two younger labourers, but also the old farmer and the ancient man with the knife were wearing better than himself. They performed the double task of forking and pitching with a third part of the effort it cost him, and apparently without taking aim or thought: the separate muscular movements were so co-ordinated that, in practice, they became one, like a good golfer's swing, with the result that whereas Mr. Lucton went off with a speed and a vigour which made the others look half-hearted and listless, by the middle of the morning his pace and his strength were beginning to flag, while the little old man, with his skinny nut-brown forearms, was still swinging his fork and pitching hay with the same ease and accuracy as when he had started. Mr. Lucton leant on his fork and breathed heavily; the pulses in his temples were thudding like steam-hammers, his scorched face streamed with runnels of sweat, and his mouth was dry with the dust of hay. He thought wistfully of the old man's little keg of cider.

"It's a hot job," he gasped.

"Hot enough for them that don't know how to do it," the elder Tibberton said, without breaking the rhythm of his work. "I'm sure it's a new job to you. If you'd been brought up to it, like these chaps here, or my boy Ted, you'ld know it's a case of more haste less speed, as the saying is. Gently does it. Put less beef into it and you'll save a gallon of sweat. 'Tis the same with milking or hoeing or scything or anything else on a farm: you gain naught by hurryin', only by keepin' on steady. Isn't that so, Aaron?"

"Ay, slow and sure, Master John—and that be more nor ever when you be pressed for time. Slow and sure. The last shall be first, as it says in the Bible."

"We'll knock off at the end of this row," Mr. Tibberton said.

It was easier, as he said, when one put less beef into it. By the time they were nearing the end of the row Mr. Lucton was beginning to get the knack; and with the discovery of the complicated movement's secret there came to him a sense and a pride of physical mastery: the fork was no longer a clumsy implement, detached from himself, but a mere prolongation of the series of muscles extending from toe and calf through loins, back and shoulder to the blistered fingers that grasped it; its movements were just as much an extension of thought and will as a pen that transcribes the words a brain has assembled. There was something soothing as well as satisfying in this measured rhythm; it composed his mind to the sort of slow meditation to which it was inclined but which, in the swift chop and change of a busy professional life, it had never been allowed to achieve. "Slow and sure . . ." This was the prescription on which Nature had probably made him. "You gain naught by hurrying." That, again, was true in his case. He had been hurrying all his life, and what had he gained—what could anyone gain save money, position, which were no gain at all, but merely an incentive to make more, as ambitions widened, committing one to even more frenzied exertions and greater restlessness until, at last, some wretched strained organ gave way and one died and was soon forgotten. "If I could go on like this for the rest of my life," he thought, "I might be able to think things out for myself and find out what it's all about or, at any rate, have a shot at it . . ."

None the less, he felt more than thankful when the long day closed and the last wagon-load rolled slowly homeward over the brook to the Tibberton's farm. To Mr. Lucton's eyes the scene of that tired returning appeared strangely beautiful: the big meadow, cleared of its haycocks now, lay naked and luminous in a mild light that seemed nearer the moon's light than the sun's; the black bars of the elms' long shadows that crossed it intensified its pallor; and in the midst of this wide expanse which their labours had cleared, the procession of haymakers (of whom he was one) straggling slowly homeward with forks and rakes over their shoulders, seemed oddly pathetic and humble, yet mildly triumphant too, and rich in the satisfaction of a day's work well done.

He walked by the side of old Tibberton, and after a while the two little girls, who had conquered their shyness, ran up to join them. One took her grandfather's hand, the other Mr. Lucton's; and this compliment made him proud and softened his heart, for it gave him the feeling that he wasn't, after all, so much of a stranger to this family life of theirs which had seemed to him so desirable and so unattainable; that he had been accepted as part of it. The old man, too, was friendly. At first he had been naturally cautious of this man whom his son had picked up out of the hedge; but Mr. Lucton's willingness had impressed him favourably and he had soon recognized him as belonging to a grade of society above that of the casual labourer, and spoke with him now as an equal.

"Do you want your day's money to-night," he said, "or will you put in another day with the hay to-morrow?"

"I don't want any money at all, to tell you the truth," Mr. Lucton laughed. "I'm afraid I've not been of much use; but I've enjoyed every minute, and it's done me a power of good."

"Well, you're not over-handy with a hay-fork as yet, I must admit; but you're a trier, I will say that for you; you've earned your day's pay and you'll earn it even better to-morrow. If you like to stay on, I dare say as Mother can find you a bed."

Mr. Lucton thanked him. He was so exhausted already that his legs found it hard to keep up with this wiry old man and the tireless children, and he wilted at the thought of having to plod on until he found an inn; he felt more like trudging back to his barn and flopping down on the straw like a tired dog. He was not only fagged, but also, strange though it might seem, a trifle lonely; for he was used to the company of his fellow-beings and had been touched and warmed by the acceptance implicit in the confiding grasp of the small hand that had taken possession of his. He liked this family party. They were, it seemed to him, what a family should be: united in the pursuit of a common interest, one so near to the simplicities for which he hungered and withal so dignified. He would like to identify himself for a time with this sane and serious life.

"Hi, Mother," the old man called, "can you give our friend here a bed?"

"Of course I can, Father," she said with a smile, "and welcome."

"Come to think of it, I don't even know your name," the old man chuckled.

Mr. Lucton hesitated.

"My name's Owen," he answered truthfully.

"That's a Welsh name, isn't it? Well, now we know where we are. Come along, Mr. Owen."

They approached the farmhouse. It was not a beautiful building: a rectangular block of red-brick late Georgian architecture, without any particular graces, surrounded by numerous farm buildings rather the worse for wear. The only feature of any distinction was a dovecote, detached from the rest and evidently older, from beneath whose high-pitched roof, as the haymakers drew near, a flight of fantails fluttered out like white petals blown suddenly upward on a gust of wind.

"Them there birds," old Tibberton said proudly, "they've always been here as long as I can remember. You'll hear them a-cooin' in the morning as soon as it's light. Our dovecote be famous. Time and again we get gentlemen coming here to take drawings and photographs off it. But the thing we've got I like best," he went on enthusiastically, "is that jargonelle pear tree climbing over the end of the house. He must be the biggest-and oldest in Worcestershire, by what I reckon. He can't be much younger nor the house. My grandfather, who came to the Grange in the year of the Battle of Waterloo, told my father 'twas just the same size when first he saw it. Bears every year, too, he does, and wonderful sweet and tasty. We've picked up to thirty bushel of fruit off that one old tree in a season. It be the warmth of the wall that favours it, and the roots going down into what they say was a moat running round the old farm that stood here afore this one was built."

Yes, that, Mr. Lucton reflected, was what gave this group of buildings, which were not otherwise distinguished in any way, its peculiar air of comfort and homeliness: the colour of its brickwork. Though there was no longer any sunset light in the west, it continued to glow with a warmth that suggested a gradual release of sunshine absorbed and garnered not merely during that summer day, but throughout the hundred and fifty summers the house had experienced. It had something in keeping too, he felt, with the ripe hue of a healthy old age, the token of clean and comely living, which he had remarked in the wrinkled cheeks of his host. It was the house of a man who was both old and contented, he told himself.

"Step in, then, and make yourself at home," old Tibberton said. "If you want a swill, you'll find a pump at the back, and soap and a towel on the sink in the scullery."

The interior appeared to owe more of its atmosphere to Mrs. Tibberton. It was gratefully cool and airy, yet vaguely permeated by an aroma that called to mind that of a beeswaxed chest of drawers where clean linen had been folded in lavender. Outside the living-room window, indeed, there was a lavender hedge. But another, and more elusive element in its air was the faintly acid odour of buttermilk which rose into it from the lower level of Mrs. Tibberton's dairy. Ted's young wife and the children were already laying the table. As Mr. Lucton entered, she looked up with a friendly smile, and he smiled back at her.

"Can I give you a hand?" he said.

"No thank you. These little mischiefs, they know where everything is, though they're that excited they're more of a hindrance than a help. They're not used to having strangers about, you see."

Mr. Lucton went out to the back, where he found an iron pump with a sandstone trough beneath it. He pumped, and the cold spring-water squelched over his head, quenching the fire in his sun-blistered face. A familiar phrase came to his mind. Living water . . . yes, living water. In North Bromwich one turned on a tap, hot or cold, and took water for granted. Even though it came, as one knew, from the buzzard-haunted source of the Garon River in the uplands of Wales, that North Bromwich water had sluggishly travelled eighty-odd miles through pipes and culverts and lain stagnant in reservoirs, while this precious liquid, more limpid for its very hardness, had been pumped up by his own exertions from the icy springs of the earth. So cold, so clear! There would never be any water so satisfying as this in Muriel's black-mirrored bathroom, not even if she scented it (as she certainly would) with pine-needles, sandalwood, attar of roses, lilac, and every other synthetic aniline perfume distilled in Germany!

Returning, refreshed, to the living-room, he found the whole Tibberton family already at table, firmly established on a set of horsehair-seated mahogany chairs—two of which had been heightened with hassocks for Ted's little girls. The light of an oil-lamp, with a globe of red-and-white-patterned glass, intensified the blueness of the dusky sky framed by the open window. It illuminated old Tibberton's square-bearded face at the head of the table, enhancing its rugged architecture; it sparkled on an array of plated cups and ewers and other prizes, the tokens of his agricultural prowess, which, highly polished, like everything else in the house, were proudly displayed on the massive sideboard behind him. Up till now, Mr. Lucton had scarcely realized how handsome the old man was. There was something superbly patriarchal about him that emanated not only from his beard, but from all his confident presence. He sat there at the head of the table, assured in his dignity as master of the household, whetting his carving-knife over a magnificent round of cold beef, the mere sight of which made Mr. Lucton's mouth water.

"Come along, Mr. Owen," he said. "Draw up beside mother. I don't mind betting you've earned a good appetite; and I can tell you this beef here is worth it. No joint ever comes into this house but what's my own feeding, and this beast was a beauty."

Mr. Lucton took his seat at Mrs. Tibberton's right hand, between her and Ted's wife. He found the old lady, with whom, so far, he had hardly exchanged a word, more intimidating than her husband. She had taken off her white apron and sun-bonnet and now appeared as a study in grey and black, a wisp of a woman, with a back as straight as a larch, her face pale and her features clear-cut as a carving of ivory, her fine eyes, which were actually grey, turned black by lamplight.

It was these eyes which, handsome as they undoubtedly were, Mr. Lucton found disconcerting. They had the coldness and keenness of a hawk's and, scarcely appearing to move, observed everything that took place at the supper-table, with a more particular concentration on himself. Beneath their calm, silent scrutiny, which was neither kindly nor hostile, Mr. Lucton felt like some curious insect being examined under a microscope, an object of pure scientific research. He had the feeling that every movement he made, every word he spoke was being weighed, and usually found wanting, by the intelligence that brooded behind those black eyes of hers. Her gaze was so searching, so paralysing and so disarming, it made the falsity of his position and everything about him appear so evident, that he found it difficult not to escape from his embarrassment by a public confession, declaring that his name wasn't Owen but Owen Lucton, that he wasn't what he had pretended to be, a decent man on a country holiday, but a fugitive from the ties of family life, a clumsy liar, and just possibly a suspect in the eyes of the law.

He felt sure that this shrewd old woman had already divined all this and despised him for it; he felt even more certain that, for all her silence and unobtrusiveness and her husband's patriarchal air, she was, in fact, the ruler of this household; that her cool brain and tireless energy of body and spirit were the mainspring which kept it running as the smooth, speckless piece of well-oiled mechanism that it was. He saw that not merely her husband but Ted and his mute, subdued wife and the two grandchildren whose spirits appeared to have been quelled from the moment when they were hoisted up on their hassocks, were subject to her control. In her presence Mr. Lucton himself began to feel like a naughty child who had been telling lies—as indeed he had! He noticed not only the old lady's eyes, but also her hands. They were bony and hardened by use, the wedding-ring on her finger worn thin and bright by long years of devoted domestic toil; but the sight of them, in his mood of recurrent guilt and panic, frightened him almost as much as her eyes, and took away his appetite.

It was Ted, his first friend and patron, who, lumbering up from the cellar on his noisy hobnails, provided a diversion from this intolerable scrutiny by planking down on the table in front of him a glass jug full to the lip with a greenish amber liquid.

"Try a glass of that, Mr. Owen," he said. "You'll find it goes down well after a day of haymaking. It'll make a new man of you."

"Ay, you must try our perry, Mr. Owen," the old man encouraged him. "'Tis a thing we've always been proud of here at the Grange. Naught in it but wild pears—choke-pears, we call 'em—the same as you see on the Worcestershire coat-of-arms, what they gave to old Queen Elizabeth when she came this way. We keep it in sherry-casks for seven month and never broach it till the next year's pear-blossom's broke. This'll be the new barrel that Ted's just tapped. Now, what do you think of it?"

Mr. Lucton thought it was excellent—so excellent that he emptied his glass and refilled it.

"It's stronger than what you might think," the old woman said warningly.

Mr. Lucton didn't mind how strong it was; at the moment he felt he could do with a little Dutch courage or courage of any kind; and Mr. Tibberton's newly-tapped perry, pale and dry, with the ferruginous after-taste of a hock and lightly-aerated like Vouvray, was an inspiring drink. It loosened the old man's tongue as well as Ted's and his own, and increased their confidence to a point at which even Mr. Lucton was no longer conscious of Mrs. Tibberton's disapproval, though he felt it even more necessary than before to keep a guard on his lips for fear of his tongue betraying him.

The three men sat on, talking and smoking, while the table was cleared and the children, after saying good night, were packed off to bed. Their talk was of the things that appeared to compose this uncomplicated life. The preoccupations of the outer world—wars and rumours of wars, the stock-market, political conflicts—did not enter this green oasis of the red marls, or affect it except in so far as their remote repercussions swayed prices of cattle or foodstuffs or labour. They were even proud, it seemed, of this isolation.

"Folks laugh at me," old Tibberton boasted, "when they hear me say I've never set foot inside of one of these cinemas. There's two big 'uns I see every time I go to market in Worcester, but if what they shows inside is anything like the pictures they put up outside, they're welcome to keep them so far as I'm concerned. It beats me, the way folk chucks good money away on going to them places—ay, and working-chaps too. It's the same with the wireless."

Ted laughed. "Father's always stood out against having the wireless. He's got a reg'lar bee in his bonnet about that."

"Ay, and you've got a lot of johnny-robbins in your head, too, Ted. If I'd let you have your way and fix up your wireless, like as not the farm 'ld have been struck by lightning yesterday."

"Well, no other house, so far as I know, was struck. What I say is, the wireless is convenient; it gives you the fat-stock prices right on the nail, like, and it tells you what the weather's going to be."

"If you want to know what the weather's a-going to be, I can tell you that by taking a squint at the fox on top of the dove-cote to see where the wind is, and the look of the sky and the smell of the air. That's a matter of experience. When you come to be my age——"

"Yes, Dad, that's all right; but then there's the news as well."

"The news! Hark at him! Isn't there enough to think about without worriting your head over the news? What does it matter to you, Ted, whether you hear what's happened a day later or earlier? You can't alter it, can you? If you did the same as I do and waited sensible until the end of the week, you could get all your blessed news from *Berrow's Journal*, the paper your father and grandfather and great-grandfather before you has always took in. By that time it don't matter much, one way or the other. All you want to know, practically speaking, 'll come to you sooner or later by word of mouth. Old Aaron's as good as any newspaper, I reckon. To tell you the truth, Mr. Owen, the older I gets the better it suits me to stay at home. If it wasn't for the markets I doubt if I should go to Worcester more nor once in six months. And why should I? We've got everything here a man can want: food and drink—have another glass?—and firing in winter."

"It's the same with the telephone," he went on. "Ted here claims we ought to have it put in; but when should I use it?"

"Lots of times, Dad—like when you wanted the vet in a hurry. It's not as if we had a car."

"Ay, that's an old story of Ted's. I reckon as keeping motor-cars 'll be the ruin of more than half the farmers hereabouts.

Before they came in, a farmer might drive to market once a week. Now, Monday, it's Worcester or Gloucester and Tuesday it's Bromsberrow and Wednesday it's Hereford or Tewkesbury—to say nothing of North Bromwich Smithfield every other day; and all them poor fools go flitterin' about from the beginning of the week to the end of it, to say nothing of taking the missus a ride on Sundays. They never sets eyes on their farms. So what happens? I know the answer."

"Well, a motor-bike, then," Ted mildly urged.

"Them murderous boxes-of-tricks? You've got that idea in your head off your friend Harry Wilder. That's a pal of my lad's, Mr. Owen, who lives at a farm called The Tack, t'other side of the river. More time to waste than sense: his dad ought to have tied up the money he left him. Too much whisky and pillion-ridin'. One of these days he'll dash his silly brains out against a stone wall. No . . . we don't want no motor-bikes here, Ted. We don't want nothing, I tell you, beyond what we got."

Mr. Lucton was thrilled by this picture of a self-contained, self-sufficient isolation. It just suited his book. In a place like this, he told himself, where nobody bothered about anyone's business but his own, he might remain in complete obscurity for as long as he liked. Though he was at present, thanks to the perry (Ted had brought up another quart of it from the cellar), content to sit smoking and listening to this agricultural talk, which was not merely soothing but had the attraction of novelty, the time might come, no doubt, when his rested mind would feel the need of fare less monotonous; but that, after all, need not be so difficult to arrange; he could get all the books and newspapers he needed by post, and settle down to the quiet, contemplative life he had always desired.

What times he could have, with all the great books he had wanted to read and had never had time to begin, with the interests of the farm, that changed with every season, to distract his mind with their novelty; with unlimited fresh air and just as much exercise as he needed to keep his liver in order, and, when simpler diversions appealed to him, the company of Ted's nice little girls, who were real children, not precocious, acquisitive monkeys! Supposing that, after a day or two, the Tibbertons and he came to know and understand each other better, why shouldn't he propose himself to them as a paying guest? There was plenty of space in the house to allow him a couple of rooms of his own. They might be glad of the money, and he could afford to pay them generously.

By the time he had swallowed his third pint Mr. Lucton found it hard not to broach this scheme there and then; but the old man and his son were already thinking of the morrow's labour and anxious to go to bed. It was only when he found himself rather uncertainly groping his way upstairs behind Ted with a candle in his hand, that he recalled the monitory vision of Mrs. Tibberton. He felt sure she was listening, lowered his voice, and proceeded on tiptoe.

For the second night in succession he could not get to sleep. That was no fault of the room they had given him. It was evidently one of the best in the house, and spacious, as it needs must have been to house the gigantic feather-bedded four-poster, in which he could imagine generations of Tibbertons having been begotten and born and probably having died. Perhaps what kept him awake was sheer tiredness, or too much perry, or the fact that the ample Georgian windows were entirely uncurtained—with the result that whenever he opened his eyes from an uneasy doze, he was certain, so bright was the midsummer sky, that dawn must be breaking. Perhaps, again, it was the sheer silence that kept him awake: though Alvaston was generally considered quiet, no city night was ever so silent as this. When, a little later, the moon rose, the sounds which its light awakened were of a kind so unfamiliar that he could not help listening to them: the thin, quarrelsome bark of a vixen calling up her cubs, the crow of a cock that had mistaken moonrise for daybreak, the tremulous whinny of brown owls which seemed to be hunting the bats that circled the dovecote. And with the true dawn, when the broken-voiced cuckoo had started the brief June chorus, the fantails, against which Mr. Tibberton had warned him, began their muttered love-song. It was then, unexpectedly, that he fell asleep, to be wakened within a few moments, as it seemed to him, by Ted's cheery voice advising him that it was time to be moving and that they must get to work as soon as the dew had gone from the grass.

Mr. Lucton sighed. "I certainly drank far too much of that perry," he thought.

He sat up in bed and immediately became aware of a stiffness involving every muscle of his body from forearm to toe.

"No doubt I shall be able to shift it," he told himself, "as soon as I'm dressed and get going. If I can't I shall look a damned fool and no mistake."

He crawled painfully to the window. He had no idea what time it was, for his wrist-watch had stopped—perhaps he had forgotten to wind it; but he saw that the horses had already been harnessed to the wagon and that a group of labourers, including old Aaron and the oafish Jim Barley, were standing, as patiently as the horses, waiting for orders.

He dressed with discomfort—it was almost as much as he could do to fasten his bootlaces—and hobbled downstairs. Old Tibberton greeted him cheerily.

"The hills be neither too clear nor too mistified," he announced, "and that means another dry day—whatever the wireless tells you. Only twelve more acres to carry. We should do that easy."

"I doubt if I shall be of much use," Mr. Lucton said gingerly—it hurt him even to speak. "I'm as stiff as a gatepost."

The old man laughed: "Well, that's no matter," he said, "what's more, I can't say I'm surprised, the way you plugged into it yesterday, not being used to it. But we'll find you a job all right. You can take turns with old Glen looking after Ted's baby."

It was rather humiliating, Mr. Lucton thought, but by no means unpleasant, to be turned into a nursemaid on such a sweltering day. He lolled on a heap of hay in the shade of one of the venerable pear-trees from which Mr. Tibberton's perry came, watching the slow figures of the haymakers crawling from row to row. Ted's baby, as its mother promised, was as good as gold. His only cause for anxiety was the attitude of his joint-guardian, the sheep-dog Glen, a collie with a matted coat and one milky wall-eye, too old to make friends with a stranger, which snarled jealously at him whenever he moved a finger.

"Glen 'll be all right," Ted told him, "so long as you take no notice of him. He's cracked on that kid."

So Mr. Lucton lay still as a hare in its form; and after a while, so somnolent was the still air, he and Glen and the baby all fell asleep.

About noon the sound of voices and laughter awakened him; the haymakers had knocked off for their dinner-hour, and Ted's wife was unpacking a clothes-basket full of food at his elbow. Ted himself unharnessed his horses from the wagon and left them to graze in the hedge where the labourers were sitting. He came back to the family-party rocking with laughter.

"Old Aaron has got a fine story," he said. "It seems they had some rare fun in the village the other evening: a reg'lar man-hunt."

Old Tibberton laughed. "What was I telling you, Mr. Owen? We never be short of news when old Aaron's about. What was it, then, Ted?"

"Well, it seems that some criminal, like, dropped into Charley Walter's pub, about an hour before closing-time. Charley never liked the look of his face from the moment he first came in. There's no flies on Charley; been too long in the army for that! Decently dressed and well-spoken, he was, but a tough-looking customer. Still, as Charley said, you get all sorts in a public. Well, this chap settles down to his supper and orders regardless. Charley cut him a prime pork chop off the joint they'd had Sunday."

"And I bet it *was* prime," Mr. Tibberton put in proudly. "That was the porker we sold Hollies last week!"

"That's right. Charley noticed this here chap was pretty flush with his money, ordering four lots of drinks all round and the like; but when closing-time come, Charley sees him making a dash for the door without paying and only just stops him getting away with it—and that took some doing, by all accounts, for the beggar was as strong as a bull. Forgot all about it, he said but Charley knew better and stood over him, having no nonsense, till he forked out his cash. Sixteen shillings and ninepence he owed."

Mr. Lucton became momentarily and uncomfortably aware of the fact that old Mrs. Tibberton's dark eyes were fixed on him.

"It wasn't you, Mr. Owen, by any chance, was it?" she said in a calm, clear voice.

The whole company burst out laughing at this excellent joke, even the children laughed, without knowing why.

"Well, really . . ." Mr. Lucton said.

"Go on, Mother! Didn't I tell you this chap was a tough-looking customer? What's more, it turns out he was a reg'lar criminal—a bank-robber!"

"How could Charley Walters or anyone else know that?"

"I'll tell you. When he opens his wallet to stump up, 'twas cram full of thousand-pound bank-notes, dozens of 'em."

"Thousand-pound bank-notes! There's no such thing," the old man laughed. "Only fives and tens, Ted. Isn't that so, Mr. Owen?"

"Well, that's what Charley Walters see'd, anyway," Ted went on without giving Mr. Lucton time to answer, "and when he see'd that, he knew where he was, and sent Mrs. Walters running after Constable Parker, while he kept this chap talking like. But the beggar must have suspected what he was after. Afore Charley could say 'knife', he ups with a chair, and if Charley hadn't been quick it'ld 'ave been murder as well as robbery. Pretty near broke his arm as it was. Then off up the road this chap runs like a blooming hare—slap into the constable. He gives poor Parker such a damn great wallop on the jaw . . ."

"That'll do, Ted. We don't want any public-house language here," Mrs. Tibberton said.

"Sorry, Mother. What was I saying?"

"You know what you said."

"Ay, that's it. Such an almighty wallop as lifted him up in the air—fifteen stone on him, mind!—so he came down in the road like a sack of potatoes."

"Well, that don't sound like you, Mr. Owen, anyway," old Tibberton said.

"A'ter that he turns round and goes for Charley Walters. Six foot two, he was; but Charley stood up to him and gave as good as he got, waiting for Parker to come round, like, until this chap—Charley swears he must 'a been an all-in wrestler—cotched hold of his legs and threw him and got clear away."

"Which way did he go, then?"

"Back over the bridge, 'cross the river."

"Well, I never did hear such a tale," old Tibberton chuckled. "That's better nor any wireless or cinema, that is. It only goes to show, don't it?"

"It shows you can't be too careful with strangers, Father," the old woman said malignantly. "That's all it shows."

They went on with their meal; but for Owen Lucton, the memory of this highly-coloured account of his exploits threw a shadow on all the rest of that sunny afternoon. This place, on which he had begun to count as the most obscure of refuges, was too near the scene for his liking. Could there be any doubt that old Aaron, the purveyor of news, would talk of the stranger at the Grange in the village that evening? The next thing would be an exploratory visit from Constable Parker. Inquiries, explanations. . . . And then? The risk was too great: he must manage to get away as unobtrusively as possible. To-morrow morning, perhaps, when his stiffness had worn off.

By seven o'clock the remainder of the hay had been carried and ricked. Mr. Lucton felt oddly melancholy as they sat down to supper. Though he had been with them less than thirty-six hours, he liked the Tibbertons—with the exception of the old lady, whom he feared, perhaps unreasonably—and had looked forward to settling down with them for a while. Not even the perry, of which he drank freely, could lift his spirits: the decree of exile from paradise had already been promulgated.

As they were ending this disconsolate meal, he heard, from the yard outside, the sputter of a motor-bicycle.

"That'll be Harry Wilder, Ted," the old man said grimly. "I wonder what he's up to now: no good, I'll be bound."

The cyclist strutted his machine and approached the open window. Ted advanced to meet him. Mr. Lucton, fading skilfully into the dark background, heard a high brassy voice:

"Hi, Ted, are you in there? Got all your hay in? Are you game for a lark? You know Pritchett's Hole, at the bottom of that field of ours that goes down to the river? Well, George Baker tells me there's a single-furrow Oliver digger-plough at the bottom of it. Been there years. And I thought if you could get off one evening next week we might have a shot at dragging the river and getting it out. You see . . ."

His words faded away. Mr. Lucton spoke to his host in an unnatural, choked whisper.

"Think I'll take a bit of a turn, Mr. Tibberton, and see if I can work off this stiffness."

"Ay, you might do worse. What about a stroll in the garden?"

Mr. Lucton did not reply. By the time the old man had reached the end of his leisurely sentence he was gone. Out of the back door he went, past his pump of living water. He climbed over a gate with an agility that was remarkable considering his stiffness, crossed a single field rapidly, hugging the hedge, and came out on the road. Then, remembering the speed of the motor-bicycle, he began to run.

(IV)

TRANSFORMATION SCENE

MR. LUCTON had run due west for the best part of a mile before it occurred to him that he had really no need to be running at all. As soon as he recovered his nerve sufficiently to use his wits, he perceived that this road was smaller and therefore probably much less frequented than the one by which he had arrived at the Tibbertons' farm. It was more of a drove than a road; so little used that the grass verges had overgrown it except for two parallel sets of wheel-tracks; and, after a while, these too petered out, leading into a field where another isolated barn reminded him of the one in which he had slept two nights before.

But this time he was not tempted to halt and take shelter. His most urgent desire at this moment was to put as great a distance as possible between himself and that accursed village. Furthermore, having dozed through the greater part of the day, he wasn't sleepy, and his watch told him that he could count on at least four more hours of daylight. Nor yet was he tired: apart from an uncomfortable rigidity about the neck and shoulders, his stiffness had disappeared; his legs, loosened by running, were good for as many miles as the light would allow him.

The drove, after the point where the cart-tracks left it, made easy walking. It was paved with springy turf close-cropped by rabbits—at every turn their white scuts scattered before him with a lazy reluctance which showed how unused they were to human invasions—and this turf was not merely soft but vividly green, for the depth of the track encouraged the infiltration of water while the rampant hedgerows shielded it from the sun and prevented evaporation. It must have been many years, Mr. Lucton thought, since these hedges had been laid and heathered. Though the heat of the last two days had finished the may, whose spent petals lay drifted like snow or spread in milky sheets, it had brought the more frequent elder-bloom to its full magnificence. Its high-lifted panicles filled the drove with a sickly scent, and combined with the umbels of cow-parsnip, ready to break, to fill the green tunnel with a luminosity resembling that of moonlight.

It would have been hard to imagine any retreat more secure or secret than this, as was proved by the abundance of shy creatures that made it their refuge. Mr. Lucton saw not only the half-tame rabbits, but a red squirrel that sat up on his haunches to stare, and a white-waistcoated stoat that paused in his hunting to peer at him: other outlaws, too: screaming jays and magpies; a sparrow-hawk skimming the tall hedge, and once a white owl, moonlight-pale as elder-bloom, planing silently as a ghost before him down the green drove.

It was still light when at last he heard the thunder of heavy traffic and reached a main road running south, as he guessed, from Worcester to Gloucester. Lorries and cars were travelling along it in opposite directions so continuously and at such an alarming speed that he was forced to wait several moments to find a safe crossing, and when he ventured at last he had to jump for his life as a big grey saloon sailed silently round the corner and swerved to avoid him. It was, as he saw from the attachment of the spare-wheel behind, a Pearce-Tregaron, and as he turned to curse it, his imprecations dissolved in a wry smile at the thought of how nearly the potential murderer resembled his former self.

"That was a pretty close shave," the driver would be joking as he swept on his way. "These damned pedestrians have no more road-sense than poultry!"

He had talked like that often enough himself; but now, for the first time since the main-roads became shambles, he himself was a poor damned pedestrian, which was no joke, and cursing the very qualities of silence and speed in which he had gloried. There was something, perhaps, to be said for a motorless world.

He came to an iron bridge spanning a sullen river. On the farther bank rose a church with a graceful campanile of crumbling sandstone. Its silhouette was so unexpected that it immediately stirred Mr. Lucton's imagination, and attracted him to the notion of staying there for the night. The whole scene appeared to him oddly foreign: the slow river resembling some southern stream, Loire or Garonne (why had he never seen either?); the church tower with its alien symmetry suggested Italy. One might almost expect to find on the other side a stone-paved *place* or *piazza*, with canopied café-terraces and tall stuccoed houses with green shutters surrounding it, a gaily-coloured crowd (like the chorus in "Carmen", which he *had* seen), and in the midst a gendarme or a cloaked carabineer with a sword and a three-cornered hat.

What he did see, in fact, was a small, rather gloomy country town. Its main street was almost deserted; indeed, the only human figure visible was that of a helmeted policeman. He stood there as though guarding the approach to the bridge, and appeared to be concentrating all his attention on Mr. Lucton's advance.

Mr. Lucton quailed at the sight. He had become, during the last twenty-four hours, a member of a class to which a policeman's helmet is a signal of danger. He hesitated. New terrors assailed him. Supposing that, by this time, his description, as that of the suspected bank-robber, had been circulated throughout the whole area controlled by the Worcestershire constabulary? Supposing that this man had been posted there on purpose, as part of a widely-flung cordon? There was no question of avoiding his scrutiny. This constable was a tall, athletic young man, much more difficult for him to outpace than the well-fed village policeman. If he halted midway on the bridge and affected to look at the view, he would probably be suspected of trying to get rid of his booty by throwing it in the river; if he turned and went back, his action would seem even more suspicious: he envisaged a chase in which he would certainly be overtaken. His only reasonable course of action was to march straight on.

He advanced with an unconvincing air of nonchalance and a thudding heart, hoping that the dusk would conceal the details of his ruffianly appearance. The policeman continued to regard him with keen attention. It would not be a bad idea, Mr. Lucton thought, to show his unconcern by whistling; but when he pursed his dry lips not even a feeble squeak issued from them. He felt that his tiredness was making him walk unsteadily, and tried, without much success, to control the movement of his legs. He came so close that he could see the policeman's features; the stalwart young man was chewing gum, after the fashion of his kind, and the jaw that chewed was full of determination. As Mr. Lucton veered to the right to avoid him, the policeman's glance slewed round, like the beam of a searchlight. "If I say nothing," he thought, "he'll think I'm trying to slink past him: if I speak, he may start asking questions." These doubts were fantastic, he told himself; he had nothing to fear. He remembered, encouragingly, the constable who had saluted him in Sackville Row.

"Good night, officer," he said.

At the sound of a cultured voice the man stiffened himself automatically; his hand came up to a salute.

"Good night, sir," he said.

It was over. Within a few yards of the end of the bridge there was a providential turn to the right, a road following the river. He had no idea where it led, but grasped gratefully at its immediate offer of obscurity. It was in fact the main road to Malvern: through the gathering dusk he could see the lights of the hillside town strung out in a glittering chaplet. Though he knew it was a town of no great size, he had no doubt that a watering-place would contain a number of hotels, in one of which he could find a bath and a bed and restore his appearance to some semblance of decency; he had long since been disillusioned of the idea that remoteness implied security; indeed, now that he came to consider the matter, he remembered that convicts who escaped from jail invariably did their best to get to London.

So he went on his way. He found it a very long way. For more than an hour that jewelled chaplet winked at him from the flanks of the hills, yet seemed hardly more approachable than the stars which spangled the sky. He passed several hamlets that tempted his tired feet to diverge; the lengths of level tarmac seemed endless, their surface as unyielding as naked granite. He was thankful, although the collarwork tried him, when the road began to climb, and brought him, panting, but triumphant, into the centre of Malvern at the moment when the abbey clock struck half-past nine.

On the terraced road that clung to the face of the hills, he saw a number of gloomy buildings that announced themselves as Private Hotels or Boarding Houses; but all of these wore a deserted, forbidding aspect; the lowered blinds and closed doors repelled him; he could foresee himself being coldly received by superior landladies in black satin dresses and reduced circumstances, whose eyes would regard his dishevelled figure—and, even more, his lack of luggage—with disapproval and suspicion equal to Mrs. Tibberton's. If he could have got a shave and tidied himself, he might more easily have faced them; but that was impossible; all the shops, including the barber's, were shut with an air of finality which suggested that they would never re-open. The whole town appeared to be locked in a catalepsy.

The middling type of public-house was obviously the thing for a man of his questionable appearance; but Malvern, it seemed, was far too respectable to support—or at any rate to display—such inferior kinds of hostelry; and in any case, his experience of public-houses had not been fortunate. At the point where he felt his legs could not carry him another yard, he found himself abreast of a largish building which looked like a Commercial Hotel and whose signboard described it as the D'Abitot Arms. It was clearly more frequented and less refined than the others he had passed. A number of shabby motor-cars and two motor-bicycles were parked outside it. Through its open windows he could see a brightly-lit, crowded bar-parlour, and hear raucous laughter and voices loudened by liquor.

"If I can find the hall-porter or someone of that kind," Mr. Lucton thought, "I may be able to slip in and get to bed without being noticed."

He crossed the road cautiously and peered into the hall of the hotel. As he stood on the step, wondering if he should ring the bell, the door of the bar swung open violently to release a departing guest, emitting, at the same moment, a flood of excited talk on the surface of which Mr. Lucton recognized with horror the tones of one brazen voice.

"So he swipes at the fox and misses him," he heard, "and caught the poor old horse a hell of a wallop— and the next thing he knew, the whole ruddy caboosh, plough and all, was at the bottom of the river! Ay, a good plough, too; single-furrow Oliver digger . . ."

Mr. Lucton turned, colliding with the fat man who had just left the bar.

" 'Ere, look where you're going, can't you, you clumsy beggar? What's more, I should like to know what you're doing, snoopin' in 'ere!"

Mr. Lucton made no attempt to satisfy his fuddled curiosity. As he fled his coat caught in the handle-bar of Harry Wilder's motor-bicycle and brought it down with a crash. He turned into a precipitous byway and staggered on and up till he found himself in a thicket of bracken on the face of the hills.

This was the third night on which Mr. Lucton had not slept, and the worst of the three. He was now a thousand feet above sea-level and miserably cold; and in the middle of the night the weather belied Mr. Tibberton's predictions by breaking in a pelter of drenching rain. When day came at last, mist lay on the hills so densely that Mr. Lucton could not see ten yards in any direction. Sitting up disconsolately in his nest of wet bracken, he remembered that it was from here, on a morning of May, that Langland, the father of English poetry, had conceived the vision of Piers Plowman and seen the field full of folk; but Mr. Lucton's mood was far removed from poetry; his only immediate desire was to get warmth into his limbs and the remains of stiffness out of them. He walked to and fro on the hill-tops, stamping his feet and threshing his arms, until the sun appeared as a disc of platinum and the shape of the Abbey tower defined itself in thinning mist.

He slipped downward into the town, which seemed hardly awake, and made straight for a barber's shop which he had noticed the night before, demanding a shave and a haircut. The barber, a sad-looking man, with a few wisps of orange-coloured hair over a bald domed cranium, appeared. He had not quite finished his breakfast, and continued to masticate the last morsels sleepily as he set to work. He was not, like most barbers, inclined to be conversational, and gloomily handed his untimely customer a morning paper to keep him quiet. Mr. Lucton, his arms embarrassed by the white overall, opened it eagerly. It was the *North Bromwich Courier*, his usual breakfast-time reading, so he knew his way about it. He turned to the page which was usually devoted to local news, and scanned every headline with fluttering anxiety, expecting, at every moment, to see his own name stare at him in leaded type. There was not a sign of it, there or anywhere else—nor even any allusion to what had happened at the village inn.

Though relieved, he was also surprised and felt vaguely hurt. In a way it seemed to him a reflection on his own importance that the leading North Bromwich newspaper should neglect to record such an important event as the disappearance of one of the city's most conspicuous figures—a prospective Lord Mayor. He relinquished the paper with a sigh.

"That's better," the barber broke silence, simultaneously swallowing the last, elusive fragment of his breakfast and regaining his speech. "If you'ld keep your head still a moment I might be able to make a decent job of it. As far as the paper goes, it's a waste of time reading it. Nothing but talk: Hitler this, and Göring that, and Mussolini the other! I'm dead sick of the lot of them. What are they, after all? Why, nothing but foreigners! If I had my way I wouldn't pay them the compliment of printing the rubbish they talk. Either drop it or call their bluff: that's what I should do if I were the Government, and give us tradesmen a chance. The 'ead forward a trifle, please, sir. H'm . . . Getting a bit thin on the top."

"I'm not thin on the top. I'm bald," Mr. Lucton growled.

"Well, it shows up your age, sir, don't it? It's all very well to say a gentleman's as old as he feels; but the 'air does tell a tale, there's no getting beyond it. A dry scalp: that's your trouble.

Now I've got an 'air-lotion here, which my brother-in-law, who's a certified chemist, puts up for me. On the lines of honey and flowers. I can't pretend to perform any miracles like the advertisements; but this I will guarantee: if you use this stuff, with a little moderate friction like, every morning, you won't lose another 'air." He held up a flask of viscous orange liquid. "If you'd started using this a couple of years ago . . ."

Mr. Lucton said gruffly that he detested all hair-lotions—particularly scented ones.

"Well, that only shows, as I say," the barber answered reproachfully. "You needn't suppose I'm trying to push anything off on you. I'm not much of a salesman and never was. But the 'air, in a manner of speaking, has always been my passion; and when I see a fine head like yours going to waste, if you'll pardon the phrase, for the want of a little daily friction and oil at the roots—well, it makes me feel down-hearted, and that's the truth. Four shillings a bottle, that's all it costs; and once tried, you'll never regret it. See for yourself, now!"

With an expansive gesture he picked up the flask and, before Mr. Lucton, pinioned by towels, could protest, poured what seemed like half its contents over his scalp, enveloping him forthwith in a highly-scented aura resembling that of a cheap perfumery or the pavement of Piccadilly by moonlight.

"Damn it all, you mustn't do that!" Mr. Lucton cried—too late, for already the noxious drippings had reached his ears and the nape of his neck. Though he knew it would make no difference—unless, indeed, it spread the foul scent further—he rubbed his head with a towel snatched from the hand of the barber, who listened to his muttered curses with an air of injured dignity.

"Whatever I done, I done with the best of intentions."

"Take your damned intentions to hell!" Mr. Lucton said.

The barber ostentatiously closed the door that led to the living-room at the back of the shop.

"Whatever I done," he repeated, "there's no call to create, nor use foul language and blasphemy in a Christian 'ouse. As I'm thankful to say this 'ouse is," he added with satisfaction.

"Well, it doesn't smell like one anyway," Mr. Lucton began. "It smells like . . ." He thought better of saying what kind of house it smelt like. He paid the man hurriedly and, still fuming, stumped out of the shop. There must surely be something wrong with his luck, he decided. Wherever he went, some petty disaster pursued him. He looked ruefully at the lining of the hat he had crammed on his head: the leather band and the silk in the crown were both tainted. "I shall stink like a badger for a week," he told himself; and the thought of the hunted beast which the stock phrase suggested brought another, fantastic, admittedly, yet revealing the foolish preoccupations that smouldered in his mind. "If they set bloodhounds after me now," he thought, "their job would be easy!"

Yet already, in spite of the pervasive effluvium which made him a marked man, Mr. Lucton was beginning to feel better for his haircut and shave. It was, for one thing, a superb morning. The sun shone brilliantly. The mist had vanished from the hills and the green plain beneath, yet had left in the air a hint of mountain freshness. When he paused for a moment in front of an empty show-case backed by mirrors, he perceived that he was no longer the ruffianly figure of the last two days, but a sunburnt and not unprepossessing middle-aged gentleman, in a Harris suit which had—at least originally—been well-cut, at whom not even a suspicious policeman would look twice.

Thus fortified, and somewhat consoled, he sat down on a public seat in the sun and tried to collect his thoughts. At his feet, beyond the tower of the Abbey, the land fell precipitously to the wide plain, already hazed with heat, with the island dome of Bredon Hill in the midst and the dim cliffs of Cotswold beyond. The sheer magnitude and serenity of this prospect had a soothing effect, and enabled him to see life in better proportion and even to recognize the elements of the ridiculous in his own situation and behaviour.

For the first time since the accident he felt able to laugh at himself. As he sat there, enjoying this reasonable mood, a red two-decker motor-bus rolled up and emptied itself of its passengers at the terminus. It had come, as he saw, from North

Bromwich, and having turned, would shortly set out on its homeward journey. It offered him, in short, the simplest solution of all his remaining doubts. If he chose to mount it now and pay a modest fare, he could find himself, in a couple of hours, deposited within three minutes' walk of his office, where the routine of morning work would be in full swing.

Yet the more easy the immediate prospect of doing this seemed, the more its remoter implications repelled him. It would imply explanations which his indolence—or perhaps his moral cowardice—shrank from; it would imply a climb-down, a defeat, which his newly-asserted obstinacy could not easily stomach; it would imply the end of what, at that moment, was just beginning to seem a delightful adventure—the last of the kind he was ever likely to have in his life. Furthermore, he flatly didn't want to go home. It was the attitude, no doubt, of a naughty child, but, considering how well he had behaved for half a century, he felt he was entitled to it. Even a savage dog, they said, was allowed his first bite!

The one-sided debate was finally closed by the conductor ringing his bell and the red double-decker bus rolling away and out of sight on its homeward journey. At once Mr. Lucton's dreamy mind became businesslike. He realized that, now that the die was cast, he was ill-equipped for the indefinite adventure on which he had decided. First he entered a chemist's shop in which the effluvium he carried with him was made less noticeable, and his self-consciousness assuaged, by a blunderbuss charge of chemical and cosmetic odours. He bought lavishly: a sponge, soap, tooth-brush nail-brush and nail-scissors, a shaving-brush and a kind of safety-razor for which, stimulated by advertisements, his soul had been yearning for years. That was a good beginning. Next, he remembered an outfitter's he had seen on the same side of the street. His most urgent needs were a clean shirt, and some pyjamas to sleep in; but as he went in search of them his attention was caught and held by a bookseller's window.

It was one of Mr. Lucton's inveterate weaknesses that, however busy or pressed for time he might be, he could never pass a second-hand bookshop. Muriel had always complained that all his coat pockets were distended and ruined by his habit of stuffing them with unreadable books which he bought, as it were, by accident.

This Malvern bookshop was not particularly inviting, its windows dressed with children's gift-books and annuals; but amid their florid covers Mr. Lucton perceived a single row of a series of classical reprints in which he felt sure he could find one or two old favourites. He examined them eagerly and found them disappointing. The majority were works he knew well, or had tried to read and found boring. After a hurried glance, he selected four shillings' worth: the two volumes of Malory's *Morte d'Arthur*, which he already possessed, and slipped them, unwrapped, into the pockets of his Harris coat.

Then, still in an extravagant mood, he went on to the outfitter's and purchased a suit of salmon-pink silk pyjamas, two pairs of lovat socks and half a dozen handkerchiefs.

"Anything more you require to-day, sir?" the young assistant said brightly.

Mr. Lucton looked at his growing bulk of parcels.

"Well, I really want something to slip over the shoulder and put all this stuff in," he said. "Some sort of wallet or haversack—you know what I mean."

"That depends what you want it for, sir. If it's just the matter of a picnic . . ."

"I'm thinking of going on a walking-tour," Mr. Lucton boldly declared.

"Oh well, in that case, what you want, of course, is a rucksack. Nothing like them for walking-tours. We've got them in several lines and various sizes. Now this is the Norwegian style. It's the most expensive—run you into about thirty shillings—but they're remarkably comfortable to the shoulders and, as you might say, commodious. I've used one myself on my last summer holiday. Walked all over North Wales. The canvas is guaranteed rot-proof and the leather chrome-tanned. Three outside pockets, too; it's astonishing how much you can carry in them."

"Let me try it on," Mr. Lucton said.

It was certainly comfortable, and the webbing bands, when the rucksack was loaded, would have the effect of correcting the stoop in the shoulders of which Leith had irritatingly warned him.

"Yes, I think that will do nicely," he said.

"And now, what about shorts, sir?" the young man went on persuasively.

Mr. Lucton laughed. He had never worn shorts since his days in Mesopotamia.

"Well, I hardly think for a man of my age and figure . . ."

"Oh, that's where I'm sure you're making a big mistake, sir. There's one customer of ours, General Sir Hamilton Blagdon-Rouse, who's eighty if he's a day, and always wears them when he goes walking on the hills; and, speaking for myself, you've no idea of the comfort and freedom."

Mr. Lucton wavered. He thought of his thin motorist's shanks, of his bony knees which would need a month of sunshine to bronze their pallor. Yet there was one thing certainly to be said in favour of shorts: as a disguise they could not be bettered; nobody of his acquaintance could possibly associate him with such unconventional attire. What was more, if his trousers got wet, he had nothing to change into. In any case, before he could make up his mind, the young man had whipped out a tape-measure and slipped it under his jacket and round his waist.

"Forty-four. That's a bit of a problem, sir," he admitted. "Wait a mo', though: I'm almost certain I've got one pair of outsizes in fawn corduroy. Go lovely with your brown coat, sir, if I may say so. Yes, here they are. The waist-measurement's perfect, but if you'ld like to try them on . . ."

Mr. Lucton found himself the possessor not only of a pair of fawn corduroy shorts, but also of another of hand-knit stockings which matched his suit. He stuffed all these purchases, together with the chemist's parcel, into the rucksack and was astonished by the lightness of the load.

"Now, what do I owe you?" he asked.

The young man totted up the figures. "Three pounds nineteen and six, if you please, sir."

Mr. Lucton searched in his envelope and carefully extracted one of the nine ten-pound notes. It would be a good thing, he thought, to provide himself with some smaller currency.

"If you'll kindly change this," he said.

As he spoke, some hidden, protective instinct warned him of imminent danger. He realized with quick horror that the cashier who had handed those notes to Mr. Hogget would almost certainly have taken a record of their serial numbers.

"Of course, sir. That's all right. If you'll just sign your name on the back," the assistant said.

Mr. Lucton laughed uneasily, and blushed to his perfumed scalp.

"How stupid of me!" he said. "I needn't have troubled you. I've plenty of Treasury notes here."

"No trouble at all, sir, if you want change."

Mr. Lucton paid him hurriedly and left the shop. He could have sworn—though, of course, he might have imagined it—that the face of the pleasant young man had looked puzzled, his eyes doubtful, when he had changed his mind. If he had not imagined this, it became clear that Malvern was no place for him. The old, unreasoning panic returned. He was "on the run" again.

And there, as he reached the pavement, he saw the perfect means of escape: another red motor-bus, labelled Hereford, which, at that very moment, was gliding away from the terminus, gathering speed in low gear, preparing to cross the hills. Mr. Lucton ran after it and just managed to swing himself aboard. The conductor glared at him.

"You shouldn't have done that," he said, "taking risks—a man of your age! Safety First! You'd ought to know better."

The bus took a corner and gave a lurch that sent Mr. Lucton staggering very nearly into the lap of a blowzy female who sat, hedged in by baskets and brown-paper parcels, clutching the hands of two children, one on either side of her. On the opposite seat an elderly couple, whom he took for a farmer and his wife, showed strong disapproval of his involuntary antics.

"I'm awfully sorry," he panted. "I beg your pardon."

The fat woman, on whom he had nearly sat, sniffed "Granted," pulling the small girl towards her and away from him, as though she felt the child needed protection. "You come and sit here, Elsie, along with our Albert," she said, "and mind you be'ave, the two of you." Mr. Lucton sank down panting next to the farmer—a grizzled man who leant on a blackthorn set between his knees and appeared to be sunk in depths of despondency—then took off his hat and mopped his sweating forehead. The two children surveyed him with furtive attention, while they giggled and whispered together.

"He's hot, ain't he, Mum?" the little boy sniggered.

"Sh . . . h!" the fat woman said. "You sit quiet like you've been told. 'Aven't I told you again and again it's rude to be personal. Now 'old your 'ush, or I'll send you 'ome to your dad."

Mr. Lucton smiled benevolently, just to show that he didn't mind; but the devilish child went on:

"What's that funny bag 'e's got, Mum?"

"It isn't a bag: it's one of them things 'ikers carry." She turned to the farmer's wife for sympathy. "Questions, questions, nothing but questions from morning to night. There's no stopping him: it's enough to drive you crazy."

The other woman bridled. She was a prim, spare woman, with small, acid features and scanty grey hair twisted viciously into a bun beneath a black bonnet.

"If you can't make them behave, you've only yourself to blame for it. It's all a matter of rearing. You've got to be firm with them from the first, and if once you show yourself weak they take advantage, the same as a dog."

The blowzy woman shook her head helplessly.

"If you 'ad six like this, and the eldest one only ten."

"I've had nine—*and* lost two," the old woman said contemptuously. "*I* know all about it. Once let them make little nuisances of themselves and you might just as well give up. They're ruined for life."

The small boy took courage from this prophecy.

"What's 'ikers, Mum?"

"What's what?"

"You said 'ikers carry them things what's he a-carrying of."

"Bless me, so I did! Only see what a memory 'e's got! 'Ikers is folk that goes walking all over the place for amusement. That's the last time I'm going to answer you, Albert. So 'old your 'ush and be said."

The grizzled man broke silence, glaring at Mr. Lucton.

"If that was all they done," he said bitterly, "there'd be no complaint. What I say is, this hiking ought to be put down by law—what with leaving gates open for cattle to stray through and breaking down hedges and trampling the crops and lighting fires anent haystacks. Ignorant, that's what they are!"

The small boy returned to the attack:

"Mum!" His mother took no notice of him. "Mum!" he persisted more loudly, "what's that funny smell?"

The fat woman sniffed. "It's the flowers in the 'edge and the 'ayfields."

The little girl spoke for the first time:

"It never," she said venomously. "It's *'Im.*"

She pointed a grubby finger at Mr. Lucton. Now the conductor and all five passengers were sniffing in unison. The old couple exchanged glances full of disgust. He began to feel so unpopular, so much of a pariah, that, a moment later, when the bus reached the crown of the hills, he rose preparing to get off.

" 'Ere, you can't get off 'ere," the conductor said offensively. "This is non-stop—no halt before Ledbury."

"I'll get off where I damned well please," Mr. Lucton shouted angrily above the rumbling of the bus's body and the grinding of gears. "What's the full fare to the first stop?"

"It's a bob to Ledbury."

Mr. Lucton gave him a shilling and pushed his way past him. As the bus gathered speed downhill, he took a flying leap and landed, with more luck than judgment, on his knees on the grass-grown verge that fringed the road. The conductor leant out of the back and shook his fist at him.

(v)

SIR OWEN WENT WEST . . .

It was an extraordinary thing, Mr. Lucton reflected, that wherever he went and however innocently he behaved he seemed compelled by fate to be thrust into unwelcome prominence; to become a centre of disturbance and the victim of violent activity. He shouldn't, of course, he admitted, have lost his temper. It would have served him right if he'd sprained a wrist or gravelled his knees. What he really wanted, he now discovered, was food. In the excitement of getting his haircut and shave and making his purchases he had forgotten that he had eaten nothing since his ample supper at the Tibbertons' yesterday evening.

That deficiency was eagerly remedied. At the highest point of the road, where the bus had ground over the crest, he had noticed a trestled table set with bottles of mineral-water warming in the sun and a signboard announcing "Refreshments". He had only a few yards to walk back before he was able to provide himself with an unconventional breakfast of ham-sandwiches and lukewarm ginger-beer. It was a schoolboy's breakfast, he told himself, yet not wholly inappropriate, for his mood was that of a boy on a holiday. When he had eaten, he lit a pipe and sat down on the short mountain turf to consider his plans for the immediate future.

Since his last survey, they had been complicated by several new problems. The first—that of his perfume-impregnated hat—was a small, private irritation which he dealt with by burying the beastly thing in a gorse-bush after carefully scratching away the gilt paper initials with his new nail-scissors. The second was more serious. The scene in the outfitter's had brought home to him the unpleasant fact that the greater part of the sum on which he had counted for his independence was not negotiable. Out of the two thousand four hundred and twenty-six pounds, only thirty-one had been given him in Treasury notes which could be passed without scrutiny. He counted them over anxiously, and found that, in three days, he had already broken into six of them. That left only twenty-five: less than a quarter of what he normally spent in a month on the upkeep of Alvaston Grange! How long could a man live on twenty-five pounds?

Mr. Lucton dismissed the question firmly, telling himself that sufficient unto the day were the evils thereof and that he wasn't, in any case, going to worry about money until he had to. And sufficient, surely unto this moment was the prospect of illimitable freedom and mystery which now lay at his feet: the green foot-hills of the Malverns rolling away into Herefordshire, and beyond them, deep blue beneath a sunny sky flecked with high-sailing cumulus, all the tumbled hills of the Marches of Gwent and Radnor. Which, of all these blue mysteries, should he choose for his voyaging?

He was in no hurry to choose. Indeed, anything so positive as a choice seemed out of tune with his present state of blest relaxation. He would go, he thought, when and whither the spirit moved him, and accept whatever his luck brought him—it was surely due for a change—with interest and without complaint. At the moment the spirit hardly moved him at all; he was content to be alive in the sun and the sweet hill air and digest his schoolboy breakfast. The day was yet young.

He rolled over on his back and took out of his pocket the first book that came to his hand. It was proper food for a romantic imagination: the first volume of the *Morte d'Arthur*. He opened it idly and read:

Now, said Sir Marhaus, we will not depart so lightly, for I will bring you through the forest; and rode day by day well a seven days or they found any adventure. At last they came into a great forest, that was named the country and forest of Arroy and the country of strange adventures. . . .

"The forest of Arroy and the country of strange adventures," Mr. Lucton thought. . . . But who were "*they*"? He read on:

In this country, said Sir Marhaus, came never knight syne it was christened, but found strange adventures, and so they rode and came into a deep valley full of stones, and thereby they saw a fair stream of water; above thereby was the head of the stream, a fair fountain, and three damosels sitting thereby. And then they rode to them and either saluted other, and the eldest had a garland of gold about her head, and she was three score winters of age or more, and her hair was white under the garland. The second damosel was thirty winters of age, with a circlet of gold about her head. The third was but fifteen years of age, and a garland of flowers about her head.

When these knights had so beheld them, they asked them the cause why they sat at that fountain? We be here, said the damosels, for this cause: if we may see any errant knights, to teach them unto strange adventures; and ye be three knights that seeken adventures, and we be three damosels, and therefore each one of you must choose one of us . . .

This is well said, said Sir Marhaus: now shall each of us choose a damosel. I shall tell you, said Sir Uwaine . . .

Mr. Lucton stopped. Uwaine? That must be the same as Owen. He laughed, but read on more eagerly. He was anxious to know the fate that befell his namesake:

I shall tell you, said Sir Uwaine, I am the youngest and most weakest of you both, therefore I will have the eldest damosel, for she hath seen much, and can help me when I have need, for I have most need of help of you both . . .

"Wise man," Mr. Lucton thought. "Showed his sense. That's what I should have said—or would I? What about Balzac's Woman of Thirty? Let's see what happened, anyway."

Then every damosel took her knight by the reins of his bridle, and brought him to the three ways, and there was their oath made to meet at the fountain that day twelve-month an they were living, and so they kissed and departed, and every each knight set his lady behind him. And Sir Uwaine took the way that lay west, and Sir Marhaus took the way that lay south, and Sir Gawaine took the way that lay north. Now we will begin with Sir Gawaine . . .

"Oh no, we won't," Mr. Lucton thought. "Sir Uwaine's the man for me."

He turned over the nine pages that dealt with Marhaus and Gawaine until he saw his own name once more at the head of a page:

Now turn we unto Sir Uwaine (the chapter began with a phrase that was like a tucket of trumpets—whatever a tucket might be!) *that rode westward with his damosel of three score winters of age. And she brought him there as was a tournament nigh the March of Wales—*

"The March of Wales," Mr. Lucton thought. The phrase was an incantation. Those words had always excited him with their fine open vowels suggesting . . . What did they suggest? he asked himself dreamily. Old pomps and chivalries. And wildness—always wildness! The great, gone names of Mortimer and Clare and Bohun, the last Lords Marcher. A bunch of damned gangsters, no doubt; but what did it matter if they bore names of such mournful splendour? "The March of Wales . . ." Repeating the words for the mere relish of their sound, he forgot the story that had brought them into his head. He was exalted and drunk with them. "The March of Wales. . . . Of course, that's where I'm going—though as for the white-haired damosel of sixty winters and more . . ." He chuckled to himself as he stuffed the book back in his pocket. "That's another kettle of fish. Thank the Lord, I've finished with women, old, young or middle-aged."

He had not, after all, so completely finished with them that he failed to notice one who, at that moment, flashed across his vision on the road beneath the bank on which he was standing. She was young—somewhere, he guessed, between eighteen and twenty-two. She wore a shortish skirt which looked as if it were made of heathery Harris tweed, like the suit he was wearing, and an almond-green riding-shirt, open at the neck; on her shoulders she carried a rucksack of pale green canvas, in her hand a walking-stick. What caught Mr. Lucton's attention and held it was not so much the kind or hue of her clothes, nor even the shape of her body, which was tallish and slim, as her colouring—that combination of honey hair with dark eyebrows and, probably, hazel eyes, which, although it wasn't his wife's, had always had power to enrapture him—that and a lovely ease of movement, lithe and fluent, which, together with the line of her forehead and wind-swept hair, gave to her progress an impression of swiftness: not an Amazon swiftness, but that of a Dryad, soft and fleet and virginal.

She was not, alas—though what could that matter?—alone. Beside her there walked a young man, well-made, a little taller and older than herself. He was as dark as she was fair, with a fine-featured, thin-lipped face—the face of an intellectual, Mr. Lucton thought—but whereas her face radiated the joy of swift movement and health and physical perfection, his was compressed and a trifle sombre, as though, in spite of such adorable company, dark thought shadowed it. As she walked she smiled with lips slightly parted. When she reached Mr. Lucton's level the smile turned on him and dazzled him, so that he was forced to smile back at her—though he knew that his smile was wasted, and hers not for him, but merely an unconscious expression of her abundant joy in life and movement, as impartial and impersonal in its benevolence as that of the sun itself.

The vision passed swiftly and left him oddly shaken, though he would have found it difficult to describe the quality of the emotion it raised in him—like the wave of a speed-boat, it seemed to him, spreading and breaking on the shore of his mind. As the wasted smile died on his lips and the couple swung out of sight, he began to wonder what was the true nature of this quick exultation, this bewildering softness, this pang that troubled his heart? There was nothing gross in it; of that he could frankly acquit himself; no desire to possess what he knew was unattainable. Rather, perhaps, that odd mixture of joy and piercing melancholy with which the sight of youth in all its fugitive beauty affects those who have lost it for ever: desire, indeed, yet desire of a rarefied kind, the longing for an impossible spiritual identity with the creature desired, a yearning to breathe and recover, if only for one moment, the perfume of youth.

Mr. Lucton shook his head sadly and sighed. She was gone, gone irrecoverably as the magic of spring. And that scowling young man—too young, too prodigal of happiness, too self-centred (judging by his looks) to realize the privilege of the sweetness he squandered—had gone with her. He would walk by her side, with his brooding face, through this miracle of summer loveliness. Were they married or were they lovers? Perhaps, though that hardly seemed likely, brother and sister. He would never know now: the only thing he knew and felt with a deepening indignation was that her companion wasn't worthy of her.

"If I only had that young fool's chances!" he thought. But he knew in his heart, still softened and pained, that if he had the chances he wouldn't be capable of making anything of them: he would be tongue-tied and dazzled and tremulous, or heavy-footed and vaguely paternal, damn it—as unable to keep up with her lightness of spirit as with her lightness of foot. Only a few moments ago he had been pluming himself on this feeling of youthfulness. It was no use codding himself. In spite of the handsome façade of expensive dentures, his smile had been toothless; the skin of his neck was wrinkled and lax; he was losing his hair and his figure; he had reached that stage at which, in the life of the wild, he would have been driven away from the herd: a despised and shabby old bull. Crabbed age and youth! They couldn't go together even on a walking-tour.

Despite these painful reflections, the stimulus of the encounter had roused Mr. Lucton from his after-breakfast lethargy and now set him on his way. He went west, like Sir Uwaine. Though he couldn't pretend to be quite so lissome and sprightly as the vanished young couple, he was delighted to find that, on such a morning as this, he was still capable of considerable physical zest. It must be remembered, of course, that he was going downhill and that the force of gravitation, exerting itself favourably on all his twelve stone four, made walking effortless. A spirited line of poetry sang through his mind. "*Afoot and light-hearted*," he thought, "*I take to the open road.*"

Down and down he went, with long, swinging strides that stretched every muscle, into a greener land and a milder air, between rippling acres of sea-green corn and huge hop-yards, strung with a criss-cross of twine resembling a gigantic cat's cradle, up which tendrilled hop-bines were already spiring and climbing clockwise with an energy so violent that one could almost feel them growing. The very earth in this valley seemed to radiate an intrinsic heat in addition to throwing back the glare of the sky. It was coloured a hot Indian red stained with streaks of darker crimson or brighter vermilion, and was so caked and cracked or powdered that it was hard to imagine whence the hop-bines drew their lustre and sappy strength, or the butterfly-haunted verges their luxuriance.

Mr. Lucton, having neither roots nor hidden sources of moisture, felt the heat more than they. As he dropped into it, the closed air of the valley had the heat of a brick-kiln. It grew steadily drier and hotter as the sun climbed the sky. Even on the level he felt his stride shortening, his pace beginning to flag; and when he came to a rising gradient every new step was an effort: his scalp tingled; sweat dripped from his temples over his cheeks and ran down the back of his neck. After all, he decided, there was nothing to be gained by pretending he was young or in good condition, and no point in exhausting himself; so he unshouldered his rucksack and sank down with relief by the roadside, amid the tall grasses and restless butterflies, to relax and, if possible, to "cool off".

He closed his eyelids to shield his eyes from the glare, mitigating his sense of physical defeat with the thought that he still had the greater and better part of the day in front of him; that nothing but the ingrained habit of years of slavery to the clock pricked his conscience and made him feel guilty of laziness; that, for all it mattered, he might just as well stay where he was until a breeze freshened the air and the sky grew cooler. As he sat there, his urgent heartbeats slowing to normal and the runnels of sweat evaporating, his ears became aware of a rhythmical, crunching sound that gradually grew louder. Reopening his dazzled eyes, he perceived that the long stretch of road over which he had plodded alone was no longer empty. Out of the middle distance, still quivering with heat, a human figure advanced.

It was not, Mr. Lucton decided at a glance, an attractive figure compared with that of the vanished dryad, being that of a little bare-headed man in a khaki shirt and shorts whose skimpy cut emphasized the shape of a pair of bow-legs which should have deterred their owner from wearing any such a garment. At a distance the most notable thing about this apparition was the air of almost ferocious haste and intensity with which it advanced. As the rapid footsteps grew nearer and louder and his face became visible, this impression of deadly earnestness was increased. His head, several sizes too big for the narrow shoulders and fringed with red hair turning grey which encircled a pallid tonsure, was supported on a scraggy throat, with a large Adam's-apple, that appeared to be thrust forward with every step in a manner suggesting either that he was short-sighted (an idea supported by his large, round, iron-rimmed spectacles) or else that the weight of the enormous rucksack suspended from his thin shoulders so displaced his centre of gravity that, but for this eager attitude, he would have been pulled over backwards. As he approached he appeared to be looking neither to left nor right, regardless of anything but the road in front of him; but when he reached Mr. Lucton's level, his pace unslackened, he plumped himself down without hesitation beside him and hurriedly extracted from the patch-pocket of his shirt a silver watch and a watch-like pedometer.

"Four miles and five furlongs in fifty-five minutes," he exclaimed triumphantly. "That's going, that was!"

Mr. Lucton grunted reluctant agreement. He disliked the intrusion and the intruder's familiarity. This was doubtless one of those hikers against whom the farmer on the bus had inveighed. He was inclined to agree. Innocent though this specimen of the breed might be—and nothing could have been more naïve than the little monster's enthusiasm and quick assumption of friendliness—he had no wish for his company. The creature was out of tune with this placid landscape; his appearance revolted him. There was something indecent, he felt, in the almost feminine whiteness of the fellow's knees and his skinny thighs. He was conscious, too, in spite of himself, of the social gap that separates people who habitually ride in motor-cars from those who clutter the highway on foot—forgetting, momentarily, that this was the category into which he himself had descended. It was the realization of this intolerance on his part that shamed him into continuing a conversation he would far rather have closed.

"A pretty hot day for record-breaking," he said.

"You're telling *me!*" said the hiker. "But 'eat . . . After all, what is it? It's grand for the system and blood-pressure to have a good old muck-sweat. Purifies the blood, as they say. What's more, kid, if you'd been as starved of sunshine as I have for more than eleven months, you'ld be glorying in the heat, not begrudging it. Cooped up in a ruddy office! I tell you what: in the place where I come from, Wednesford that is, you don't hardly ever see genuine sunshine from one year's end to another. And if you got it on the first day of your 'oliday like this, you'ld make the most of it, I reckon, the same as I do. I only wish it would last for another fortnight. That's straight."

There was no need for him to tell Mr. Lucton where he came from. He had recognized at once the familiar Black Country accent and intonation—of which, indeed, though he did not know it, his own speech was not wholly innocent. To his ears, in this alien setting, there was even something soothing and homely about it. It awakened, unreasonably, the vague nostalgia which an exile feels when he hears his own tongue in a foreign land, and, at the same time, made him feel guilty of being standoffish. The very grotesqueness of this odd little figure, bald-headed and straggly-moustached like himself, combined with its disarming enthusiasm and complete unself-consciousness, made him feel churlish. Here, in fact, was another prisoner, escaped, like himself, from the glooms of an industrial civilization, yet, unlike himself, condemned to return to it within a couple of weeks at the most. He remembered, guiltily again, how often he had been irritated by the departure of useful members of his office staff on their annual fortnight's holiday. Until now he had never realized how much this unique brief respite meant to them; their ardours of anticipation, their ecstasy of release. He was learning a number of things that had never before occurred to him, and felt that some sign of sympathy was demanded, if he could find anything to say. There was no need to search for it.

"And as for 'eat," his companion went on blithely, "why, that's all a matter of clothing. Once you get into shorts and a shirt that's well open at the neck—none of your throttling collar-and-tie nonsense!—you'ld never believe the difference it makes. As I always says to Em, it takes years off your age in a jiffy. As soon as I get me shorts on, I tell her, I feel I could jump over the moon, as the saying is."

"Isn't that rucksack of yours a trifle heavy?" Mr. Lucton suggested.

"Well, there now. It is and it isn't, if you see what I mean. When once it's strapped over your shoulders you don't feel you're carrying anything. It's all a matter of balance. Companionable, too. To tell you the honest, kid, I shouldn't feel I was off on a holiday without it—not after all these years. It isn't light I admit. But then, as I say, if you're going to be independent you've got to be prepared for anything. And that's what I am." He chuckled. "Like to see what's inside it?"

He proceeded, without Mr. Lucton's encouragement, to turn out the rucksack's bulging contents on the grass. It seemed unlikely that he would ever get them in again. They comprised a ground-sheet, an oiled-silk poncho, a flashlight, a compass, an aneroid barometer, a vest-pocket Kodak, a spool of adhesive plaster, a portable tent, a collection of shaving-tackle; tins containing vaseline, health-salts, biscuits, cocoa and insect-powder; a grey alpaca jacket with stockings stuffed into the pockets; a pair of folding slippers with tablets of soap in the toes; a tin cooker, designed to be heated by solid methylated spirit and packed tight with Kodak films, sticks of chocolate and soup-cubes; two hand-books, on British Birds and Wayside Flowers; a pocket New Testament, and finally a bundle of dog-eared ordnance maps.

"There you are," he said proudly; "and when it's empty you can use the rucksack as a waterproof seat. Neat, isn't it?"

That was hardly the word Mr. Lucton would have used to describe this dizzying confusion. As he surveyed it his mind went back instinctively to the White Knight.

"Where's your mouse-trap?" he asked.

The little man goggled at him through the enormous spectacle lenses which magnified his mild eyes into an aspect of perpetual surprise.

"What's that you say? Mouse-trap?" he asked, with portentous gravity.

Mr. Lucton smiled. "I'm sorry. That was only my little joke."

"Joking, were you?" The tone was reproachful. "I can tell you, there's nothing to joke about," he went on defiantly. "When you've been on this job as long as I have, you'll find out that you can't afford leaving anything to chance. I've been caught out too often for that!"

He began to repack the collection with a methodical grimness and an air which suggested that his most intimate feelings had been hurt. His damped enthusiasm was so pathetic to witness that Mr. Lucton felt it his duty to make amends.

"Please forget what I said," he told him. "I didn't mean to be critical. You know more about it than I do, of course. How long have you been . . . er . . . hiking?"

The little man frowned.

"That isn't a word I like to hear. Too undignified, and too many nasty jokes made about it. Call it Rambling. The Ramblers' Association: that's what I belong to. Here's my membership ticket. See for yourself."

Mr. Lucton examined the card, and learnt that the stranger's name was Hubert Hopkins and that he lived (poor devil!) at 86, Dulston Road, Wednesford.

"It's a fine show, our Association," the little man went on gravely, "and if ever you thought of taking up rambling seriously—we don't want any triflers, mind!—you ought to belong to it. Reduced railway fares and the loan of maps, and full lists of decent, moderate accommodation where a chap can turn in for the night and be sure of a welcome and know he's not going to be rooked for his B. and B.—bed and breakfast, that is—all for half a dollar a year. You may talk about your A.A. or your C.T.C., but I reckon the Ramblers give better value for money. I was one of the earliest members myself, came in on the ground floor," he added proudly, "and never regretted it."

"I can see you're an old hand at the game," Mr. Lucton flattered him. "As I asked just now: How long have you been . . . rambling?"

"Oh, ah . . . so you did. Well, that's a long story, that is. You know my name now. Bert Hopkins . . ."

"And mine's Owen." This time the word came quite easily.

"Owen. Right. Now we know where we are, then. Well, you see, Mr. Owen, it started like this. I'm a Black Country chap: you can judge that from the address. Wednesford born and bred. Never lived nowhere else. You know Wednesford?"

"I can't say I've ever been there."

"Well, you wouldn't go there, not except in the way of business. It's nothing to look at, you know; but with me, as you might say, it's home; and the Wednesford folk—though they aren't much to look at either—their heart's in the right place and no mistake, though they may be a bit rough and ready. Now when I was a kid . . ."

It looked, indeed, like being a lengthy story. Mr. Lucton regretted his question, but knew he would have to listen. It began with Bert Hopkins's grandparents, parents, and a selection of uncles and aunts; it passed on through his boyhood at an elementary school to the great occasion when he had entered the offices of the Wednesford Amalgamated Ironworks as a junior clerk, and the even more triumphant day when he had led "the wife" (or alternatively "Em") down the aisle of the United Methodists chapel.

"And a better woman never stepped," he averred, "though, my God, she can be aggravating, and always was, when she's a mind to. Of course, after a time, a chap learns to make allowances. You mustn't forget her feet."

"Her feet?" Mr. Lucton echoed bewilderedly.

Bert Hopkins shook his head darkly.

"Corns . . ." he said. "Hard and soft. Incurable. The fortune we've spent over twenty years, mind, on cutting and paints and plasters: you'ld never credit it! And all gone down the drain, as you might say. And now, since she's started to put on weight, it's the arches give way."

"How very unfortunate!"

"Well, there you are! Like everything else, it is and it isn't. Aggravating she is, bless her heart, as only a woman *can* be; and yet, if it wasn't for her corns and her arches I shouldn't be here. You see, it's like this," he went on confidentially, "when first we was married, or as soon as the brass would run to it, Em used to take rooms every year at the seaside for a week or ten days. That's her idea of a holiday: to sit on the beach all day in a deck-chair and watch the kids playing around—we've none of our own—or listen to the band and the pier-rots. I don't blame her, mind you. It takes all sorts to make a world, to coin a phrase. But me . . . well, I've always been active by nature; I like to be on the move; and sitting about like that without any exercise and eating too much, the way you do at the seaside, always tells on my liver, and what's the result? Why, words! And when it comes to words, well, you know as well as I do that no man is a match for his missus: once start on that game and you might just as well jack up from the first like I always have done. Anything for peace in the home: that's been my motto . . ."

Mr. Lucton ardently agreed. He knew all about it.

"And then come my illness: what's called the yellow jaundice. I'd never been ill—not to say properly bad—before; but this was a knock-out. Went all through me the yellow did, from the whites of my eyes to my toe-nails; and everything all round went yellow too—I felt that downright miserable I didn't care whether I lived or died, and that touchy and savage you'd never hardly believe it. I was in bed for a fortnight before it worked out, and when I came round, like, another two weeks on the box. I'd tipped the club doctor the wink, as it was the seaside what done it, and he done me a good turn by telling Em what I wanted was exercise. 'He's the type that can't do without it, Mrs. Hopkins,' he told her, 'and I shan't let him go back to work till he's walked this here yellow clean out of the system.' That's what he said, and that's how it begun. . . . Yes, that's how it begun. . . .

"You see—though it's a nice little place and I've nothing against it—there's no walks, properly speaking, round Wednesford: it's all collieries and brickworks and such-like—nothing to see and no air to breathe, if you know what I mean. So, the last week, I took the steam-tram out to Dulston and walked up beyond Sedgebury. I'd never been there before: Sedgebury's not much to look at either; but when you get there, on the top of the ridge, it's astonishing what you can see: miles and miles of fields and woods—real country, you know. When the wind's in the west, and all the smoke's blowing away from you, you can look right down into Shropshire and clean over Wales. I didn't know what I was seeing, being that ignorant, until I went to the library and looked it up on a map. Never thought of maps either, till then. Now Em says I'm cracked on them—names of villages and all that—and I reckon I am; they're as good as a book to me. When I'd worked it all out I used to take the tram regular and sit on the top there and gaze at those ruddy hills until I forgot where I was. Longing, like. You know what I mean?"

"Yes, yes." Mr. Lucton knew well what he meant. As he listened to the naïve confession his heart had been warming towards this odd little man who so readily poured out his soul to him. Beneath the unsympathetic and even grotesque exterior he recognized a kindred spirit, the sharer of emotions and aspirations similar to his own, yet so much less easily attainable. How he must have fought for them! "Yes, yes," he repeated. "Go on . . ."

"I somehow reckoned you might, though I can't say why. Well, all through that year I kept on hankerin', as you might say. Bought a couple of maps of me own and kept them in a drawer at the office: used to read them dinner-time—if read's the right word. Then, when summer come round, I had to pull up my socks like: I knew all the time there was going to be trouble with Em"—he shook his head—"and there wasn't 'alf, I can tell you. You see, she'd wrote off, as she usually did, for lodgings

—got all the addresses out of the newspaper—and one evening she says: 'What d'you think about Skegness this year, Bert? They say the East Coast's more bracing and you want setting-up.' So I started off gently: 'I can't say I fancy Skegness, Em,' I said. 'Surely you don't want to go back to Criccieth,' she says, 'not after last year? It's all right for me, but you know it didn't suit you.' I told her I didn't fancy Criccieth either. 'Well, you are a hard one to please,' she says, 'and no mistake! Of course, if you like, I could write to that Mrs. Jones at Weston, but I don't call that sea, rightly speaking, though the rooms was all right, I admit. Remember the clotted cream?'

"Well . . . I knew I'd got to spit it out sooner or later, so I told her straight I was fed up with seaside holidays. 'I don't want to cop the yellow jaundice again,' I told her. 'The doctor says I want exercise for the liver, and I'm going to follow his orders,' I says. 'And can't you get all the exercise you want at the seaside,' she says, 'walking up and down the parade?' Quite nasty, her tone was. 'Well, look here, it's like this, Em,' I says. 'I've been thinking this over ever since I was ill, and I reckon a man of my age knows what's best for him. I'm going a walking-tour.'

"That put the fat in the fire, I don't mind telling you. 'Oh, you're going a walking-tour, are you, Hubert, and what about *me?*' 'Well, you can come too: there's nothing against it,' I told her. 'Nothing against it, isn't there? And what about my poor feet? You 'adnt thought about them, I suppose? No, you 'adn't—what's more, you wouldn't!' After that she blew up good and proper, like I'd expected. 'You may call it a walking-tour if you like, but I know your game. Hiking, that's what you're after, going tramping all over the country along with a lot of brazen young hussies in shorts, and laying about in the open, and no questions asked about sleeping accommodation. After twenty years of respectable married life, a man of your age! You get into shorts, then, Hubert Hopkins, and see how they'll laugh at you! If I'd seen those legs of yours before I'd married you, I should have thought more than twice about it myself. But you're like all the rest, I suppose. When a woman gets over forty, no matter how faithful she's been and washed and cooked and darned and slaved through all the best years of her life and worn her fingers to the bone, a man starts looking round for something fluffy and foolish. You can't kid me when you talk about hiking, Hubert. Free love, or whatever they call it, though I've got a better name for it, that's what you're after! Just to think that it comes to this!' And then she turns on the water-taps."

"That was awkward," Mr. Lucton agreed. "And what did you do about it?"

"Well, what *can* you do? When once they start crying like that it's no use reasoning with them or being soft either. Give them an inch, as the saying is. No, I stuck to my point, the same as I'd made up my mind to. 'Look here, Em,' I says, 'you know perfectly well, or ought to by now, I'm past all that in the ordinary way of speaking. I'm not out after any birds. All I want is fresh air and exercise, the same as the doctor told me; just to go mooching round, like, and seeing a bit of variety—not sitting down in one place. Why not give it a trial?' I says. 'There's no need to overdo it. Five or six miles a day, going quiet and easy. That wouldn't hurt you,' I told her. But Em wouldn't have it. 'Five or six miles a day!' she says, 'you're just talking silly. If you don't know me better than that after twenty years, well, I reckon you ought to. If you're going hiking, Hubert, then you're going alone,' she says. 'That remains to be seen,' I told her," the little man chuckled. "Yes, I had the last word for once---and that doesn't mean, mind you, Em isn't a perfect wife."

"So you went after all?"

"You bet—and don't I remember it! It's like everything else, you know, there's no time like the first. Em took her sister Maggie to Scarborough and paid all expenses. Spent a good bit more than she need 've done, too; but, things being as they was, I couldn't begrudge it. It was worth every penny and more. Yes, that was my very first ramble, starting at Bewdley and right through Werewood and up into Shropshire. It rained most of the time, that I will say, and I wasn't so well prepared for everything as I am in these days. They watched for the weather reports in the newspaper, the two of them, and laughed when they read as how rain was spreading from the west. 'Now Bert's going to cop it!' they said; but, Lord bless your soul, they could laugh till they bust their stays and welcome, so far as I was concerned. Nothing made any difference to me. It was like—well, like I was 'called', if you take my meaning. All those places I'd seen on the map in the dinner-hour, all those names I knew come to life. Far Forest and Clows Top, Neen Savage and Cleobury Mortimer, and Abdon Burf and Corvedale and Caer Caradoc . . ."

The words, as he murmured them in his flat Wednesford accent, acquired, Mr. Lucton felt, a haunting beauty that was rich and new: even so might a man have spoken the names of women he had loved in the spring of youth and never forgotten; and, as he spoke them, the eyes of Bert Hopkins, magnified behind their round spectacle lenses, grew strangely tender, excusing himself and pleading for Mr. Lucton's comprehension of an emotion which most people—even Em and her sister Maggie—would certainly have considered "soft". But Mr. Lucton found no difficulty in comprehending it. For him, as for Bert, those village names were poetry, the unwritten poetry of the inarticulate made even more tender and more magical by their sharing of a common emotion as yet unexpressed. *Lost bliss, to thee no more communicable* . . . That was Milton, surely?

He said quietly:

"Have you ever read *The Shropshire Lad*, Mr. Hopkins?"

"No, I can't say I have. Never heard of it. I've never been much of a one for reading; hardly bought a book in my life. These here are my books"—he pointed to the dog-eared maps. "When I first took up rambling, you know," he went on confidentially, "I used to trace all the roads I'd walked over with red ink from the office and go over them again, as it were, when I sat at home by the fire of a winter evening. If you cast your eye over those maps, I'm ready to bet you'ld be surprised at the amount of ground I've covered during the ten years I've been at it. Never went the same way twice: I made that a rule, so that the first impression's the one I carry in my mind and go back to.

But now I've changed all that. Never look at a map any more——in fact, I don't know why I go on carrying them about with me. Just 'abit, I reckon. No, I set out with some place in my mind that I've never been to, and go on, trusting to luck, till I get there. Sometimes I never get there at all—I mean summat or other turns up that leads me away from it and I find myself somewhere else at the end of the fortnight. But what does it matter? I say. That's the best part of it, never knowing what's going to happen. Just hark at me, how I run on!" he ended, with an apologetic laugh.

"And where are you aiming for this time?" Mr. Lucton enquired.

Bert Hopkins gazed at him questioningly, as though he were not quite sure that he hadn't allowed his enthusiasm to run away with him and make him ridiculous in the eyes of a stranger.

"Do you mean you really want to know? You're not kidding?"

"Not a bit. You've made me curious."

"All right, then. Just come along with me a few steps. When we get to the top of this hill, with any luck, I reckon I'll be able to show you." He helped Mr. Lucton on with his rucksack. "My word, this is a beauty," he said; "but the straps are too long; if you shorten them a bit you'll find it rides easier. As I told you before, it's all a matter of balance. If it's wrong it tells on you uphill. How's that now?"

Relapsing into the speech of his youth, Mr. Lucton said it was champion. Bert Hopkins glanced at the dial of his pedometer—"Just to check up, like"—and they set off together in silence, steadily climbing the gradient. This was a strange encounter, Mr. Lucton told himself, and anyone who saw them together—the soft, portly, middle-aged business man and this odd little Black Country clerk with his bow-legs, his sloping shoulders, his bulging pack, and the air of fierce concentration that emanated from his determined gait and his goggled eyes—must have found them the most unexpected of combinations. There was still in the back of his mind, a class-conscious inhibition of the kind that is commoner among the bourgeoisie than the aristocracy. He could not, for instance, imagine himself striding along Sackville Row under his office windows in Bert Hopkins's company. But then he would not, in any case, have walked along Sackville Row hatless and sweating and shouldering a rucksack. This new vision of himself was, in fact, a symbol of his emancipation. And he had begun to like his companion. Not only did he like him: he was also feeling a trifle ashamed of the superior scorn and distaste he had felt for him on his first appearance. When it came to essentials, to the deeper things of the spirit, Bert Hopkins was nearer to him than the familiar acquaintances (he had no intimate friends) who shared with him the privileges and amenities of his club in North Bromwich. Their obvious inequality in culture and social status seemed somehow of little importance now that they walked side by side, their steps keeping time, over this vast corrugation of the earth that had mothered both of them, beneath the wide sky. It was even easier, he found, to walk thus, in company, than alone. His companion, more waywise than he, knew how to conserve his energies and adjust his pace to the unequal demands of the road. The air, too, grew thinner and cooler as they climbed the long slope. When they came to the top of it and halted, seeing before them the green contours of domed hills and dark woodlands rolling away fold on fold to spill themselves wave-like against the mountain barriers of the Silurian March, he was surprised to find himself neither breathless nor uncomfortably hot.

"There it is," Bert Hopkins said quietly. "That's what I'm aiming for. D'you see that sharp peak on the left? That's the Holy Mountain, I reckon, though how it came by the name I don't know; and behind that again, and a good bit higher, there's a long, level ridge, with a hump sticking up in the middle, which dips down at the end like a rubbish-tip or one of our Black Country spoil-heaps. Well, that hump on the top, according to the map, is the highest point, Pen Savaddan; and I mean to get up on it and see what's beyond it before I've finished. But that isn't why I'm going there, mind. I've made that there mountain my object because one of our members, a Rambler that is, once happened to mention that the valleys inside that mountain are the quietest and rummest places he's ever been in. There's two or three valleys, by what he said, and a river runs out of each of them; and by one of these rivers—Dulas Fechan's its name—there's the ancient ruins of an Abbey called . . . let me see . . . No, I don't recollect what it's called; but the point of it is this here Abbey, or what is left of it, 's been turned into a pub—not ruinous, mind, but still a bit on the stiff side compared with cottage lodgings, he says, but he didn't mind going a bust for a couple of nights, and no more do I, just once in a while, when there's no other way of seeing a place that is different from anything else I've ever heard on."

"It looks a goodish distance away," Mr. Lucton said.

"Something round about forty-five miles, I should say. Call it a couple of days' steady walking. If you've the time and nothing better to do, you might come along with me. Share and share alike as far as expenses goes. It's nice to have company on the road," he added shyly, "and two's company, as they say."

"I'm afraid I should never keep up with you, Mr. . . . er . . . Hopkins."

"Oh, I shan't overwalk you. I'm getting too old for that, kid. When you saw me timing myself just now I was loosening up, like. And if it's all the same to you, you might drop that 'mister'. I'm called Bert, short for Hubert, among pals and fellow-ramblers. We don't hold with surnames on the road."

"Very sensible, too. Of course, I'll be glad to come with you, Bert."

"That's O.K. by me, then. What's your first name, by the way?"

"It's . . . it's Owen," Mr. Lucton said, with a laugh.

"Owen Owen? Well, that's a knock-out, that is! I reckon your dad must have been hard up for imagination."

"So am I, if it comes to that," Mr. Lucton thought. But it would have been difficult to lie in any case, he told himself, to anyone with eyes so disarmingly ingenuous, so good and so kindly as those which beamed at him now from behind Bert Hopkins's spectacle lenses.

(VI)

FOREST OF 'ARRY

BERT had spoken truly: it was nice to have company on the road. His company, in fact, was as entertaining as his enthusiasm (which Mr. Lucton had been prepared to find a bore) was infectious. It was a lesson for Mr. Lucton merely to see the enormous zest which this queer little man was apparently able to extract from the drabbest of circumstances, a lesson, and also something of a reproach to his own discontent with a life which, compared with Bert's, was incredibly easy and spacious and rich in neglected opportunity. For Bert Hopkins, living on three pounds a week with a crotchety wife in a back street of Wednesford, was obviously a happier (and in some ways a freer) man than himself—for all the privileges of station and wealth and security which he had been able to take for granted through the greater part of his life. It was, Mr. Lucton supposed, a matter of "values", and he began to suspect that the values which he and his family had come to accept were radically false.

As Bert Hopkins had promised him, they "took it easy", averaging no more than three miles an hour, and occasionally dallying in the shade for a while to break the monotony of steady walking. The weather continued peerless, though there were signs that foretold the end of the heat-wave: a cool sea-borne breeze from the south-west awakening to drive before it fleeces of cumulus which a stronger wind, in the upper sky, caught and carded into silvery mares'-tails.

"The glass is still high," Bert said, "but that's maybe only the wind. By the time we get under the mountains I reckon we may have a regular drencher, and when it rains there, there's nothing half-hearted about it."

Mr. Lucton assented lazily. The warning did not disturb him or quell the contented buoyancy of his spirits. He was beginning, in fact, to enjoy the benefits of three days of plain living and regular exercise. And what could be more delightful than to move on, without any sense of hurry or fatigue, through this wide green world made magical by the wash of limpid Atlantic air?

The country through which they passed was neither exciting nor yet particularly beautiful. It was one of hop-yards, of tidy red-brick farms with cowled oast-houses; of infrequent, tawny streams and elm-bordered meadows where white-faced Hereford cattle placidly browsed. On most of the farms the haymaking was over; the roadside hedges were tufted with wisps of grass scratched from passing loads. Few men could be seen in the fields; the land seemed deserted, deep-sunk in the midsummer lethargy that marks the brief period of suspension between the labour of haymaking and the later harvest of the hops and grain and the crushing of cider fruit already setting in millions on the gnarled orchard-boughs. The only active elements visible in the landscape were their own slow-moving figures; the only sound that broke its brooding silence—for not a bird sang—was that of their measured steps; yet, beneath the semblance of languor, Owen Lucton was always aware of a vital energy continuously stirring: of the sap that rose through the hop-bines into every glossy leaf and questing tendril, through the stalks of the corn into the grain that swelled milkily in its ears: a rich flow that lacked, perhaps, spring's most turbulent vitality, yet was none the less constant and strong; and it seemed to him, as he thought of these things, that his own body was permeated by a similar essence; that, though he was no longer young, the tide of life still flowed through it with a mature persistence. For him, as for all these green things, this was high summer, the season of full content and early fruition: the prime of life, as men called it. He felt proud and happy to be alive, and surrendered himself, without question, to the joy of mere living.

So the long miles, the smooth contours of pastures and darkening woodland, rolled away behind them. From time to time, as they breasted a rise, the shape of the mountain massif that was their goal—that level ridge, broken only by the eminence called Pen Savaddan, falling away to the plains with the proud stoop of a bird of prey—rose before them, black as a thunder-cloud, and always seeming higher, until its dark magnificence dominated and filled the whole of the west.

"There you are! That's your Mynydd Savaddan," Bert Hopkins said.

"It looks only a few miles away."

"That's because of the size of it, and the air being that clear in these parts. A sign of rain, too, I tell you: we're going to cop it. When it comes, I reckon I shall have to lend you my ground-sheet to keep your shoulders dry. You can joke about me carrying mouse-traps and that till Christmas, but it's a ruddy good thing for you, kid, I'm prepared like I am. I can smell the rain now."

He sniffed like a terrier. But still the rain did not come. Indeed, as afternoon lengthened, the sky cleared of cloud; the breeze dropped, and the air in the valleys, every one of which seemed deeper and moister and more leafy than the last, grew heavy—as though the panting trees, whose growth they encouraged, had drunk all the virtue out of it.

They took tea at a farm-house in the bottom of one of these valleys, not one of the substantial buildings of staring red brick whose size and solidity proclaimed the wealth of some prosperous hop-grower, but a humbler dwelling built of shaly stone with a sagging roof of slabs green with moss and golden with lichen.

"It's the last grub you're likely to swallow this day, kid," Bert said, "so you'd better stoke up."

Mr. Lucton took his advice. With a schoolboy's appetite he devoured two boiled eggs, so fresh from the nest that the whites would hardly set, and several platefuls of home-made bread thickly spread with pale ice-cold butter, faintly acid with whey. There was damson jam, too, of a superb, a Tyrian purple, with the richness of autumn in it, and with it three steaming cupfuls of strong black tea—very different from Muriel's delicate smoky Lapsang—a combination which, under ordinary conditions, would have given him heartburn for the next twenty-four hours.

The farmer's wife charged them a shilling apiece for this spread, and the cool whey-sour butter was so delicious that, for a moment, Mr. Lucton wondered if it wouldn't be possible for her to post him a couple of pounds of it every week to Alvaston Grange for his private consumption instead of the anæmic grease the Alvaston grocers supplied—until, of a sudden, he remembered that he was quite probably never going back to North Bromwich again.

They sat for half an hour, digesting their meal, in the farmhouse kitchen beneath rafters decorated with sides of home-cured bacon and noble hams which, for all his repletion, made him wish he had asked for a rasher with his eggs. Never had the reek of his after-tea pipe smelt so delicious: even the Woodbine which Bert cautiously produced from a crumpled green packet had an ambrosial savour. He would gladly, indeed, have begged for a bed for the night; but Bert, who had checked the readings of his battery of instruments, was stronger-minded.

"We've only done thirteen miles and three hundred yards since this morning," he said, "and the glass is beginning to fall."

"Damn you and your ruddy pedometer!" Mr. Lucton said.

But he knew he would have to give way to the expert's guidance. In the technics of walking-tours he admitted that Bert was his master.

"You're not foot-sore nor nothing like that, partner?"

"Not a bit. I'm good for another ten miles," Mr. Lucton boasted, though, in fact, one of his heels had been rubbed to a blister, and the soles of his feet felt as numb as if they had been bastinadoed. And, indeed, these minor discomforts were negligible when he set them against the general sense of physical well-being which made even fatigue a luxury.

"That was the best meal I've ever tasted in my life," he reflected, "and this day is about the best I have ever had. This was just what I wanted." He could think with scorn and without regret of the drowned Pearce-Tregaron. "A damned good riddance," he told himself. "I don't mind if I never sit in a motor-car again."

Even so, at the end of another couple of hours, he would

have been glad of a lift in one. It was not so much his blistered heel and his pounded soles that troubled him as an increasing numbness in the unloosened muscles of the calf, hard-tried by the unending series of steep climbs and descents—for they had been walking, as it were, across the grain of the land, and every yard of the way downhill was a torment. What was worse, they now seemed to have entered a wilder and lonelier country in which no human habitation was visible. In spite of his sumptuous tea, his stomach, as much a slave to habit as himself, complained that it had passed its accustomed dinner-time, and he was even more thirsty than hungry. If only, on this abandoned by-road, there might be such a thing as a pub! He suffered from tantalizing memories of Mr. Tibberton's straw-coloured perry and the prime-conditioned brew he had drunk in that accursed village inn.

"Couldn't I do with a quart of either," he thought. "No, by Jove . . . half a gallon!"

And there, at the bottom of the hill more precipitous than any that had taxed his complaining muscles before, where a bridge spanned a noisy river, Mr. Lucton saw a collection of buildings, a hamlet, rather than a village the first glimpse of which lightened his spirits instantly. On the farther bank rose a conical hill, its flanks overgrown with brushwood and tall forest trees, above whose motionless tops there emerged the keep of a ruined castle. It was a scene to satisfy the most romantic of minds, but what stirred him more deeply was the signboard that hung above the door of the largest of the buildings and announced its identity as "The Grosmont Arms". The sight made his dry mouth water.

"Well, thank God we've got somewhere at last," he said, with a sigh. "I was beginning to think we'ld have to sleep out. What about a pint to begin with?"

"You can have your pint, all in good time and welcome," Bert said. "Drink's not in my line. I'm T.T. Always have been, from birth. But if you think we're going to sleep in that there hotel, you've made a mistake, partner. I know all about them places. Look down their noses, they do, at anyone who don't turn up in a motor-car; charge you half a crown for a bit of cold beef and pickles and soapy potatoes, and five bob for your bed and breakfast. I've had some: I know. But there's one or two snug-looking little cottages over the other side of the road, and I'll eat my 'at—or would if I 'ad one—that I'll find a good lodge for a shilling a head in one of them."

"How d'you know they'll be willing to take us in?"

"I don't—and *they* don't neither. But I tell you, they're going to. You leave it to me, partner, and see if I don't pull it off."

Mr. Lucton, succumbing to an attack of unconquerable shyness at this projected invasion of some innocent cottager's privacy, retired to the pub, where he drank the pint he had promised himself. Any beer would have tasted excellent in the circumstances, and this draught was home-brewed, as the landlord's daughter proudly informed him, from Herefordshire hops and local malt and river water. "Dad says it's the water that makes our beer so good," she told him; and Mr. Lucton, inspired by the generous stuff on an empty stomach, was tempted to say that the water was excellent for other things too—complexions, for instance; for this child's—she could not have been more than sixteen, though she showed the self-possession of a woman—had the authentic West Country brilliance: its hues of a ripe nectarine combined with black hair and brows and deep violet eyes. A Welsh type, he reflected—and indeed this valley could not be far from the border. In the Middle Ages, no doubt, that ruined castle had commanded a ford, at the point where the stone bridge was built, and in it the Norman Grosmonts, whose arms the inn bore, had been set by some Marcher Lord, Clare, Bohun or Mortimer (the names still clanged like armour in his mind) to keep an eye on the Welsh and hold the line of the river, or to ride out armed cap-à-pie on a punitive expedition into the mountains. And this child, his roused imagination ran on, was doubtless the ultimate fruit of one of these ancient forays, descendant of some white-armed captive with her skin and hair and her eyes. There was something a little wild about her beauty, something foreign in the lilt of her speech and in the liquidity of its consonants, particularly of the 'r's and the 'l's. This inn was decidedly a good place to stay in. He hoped in his heart that Bert would fail in his quest.

As he debated on the advisability of ordering another tankard, a tap on the window disturbed him. Bert was standing outside and beckoning.

"Come inside," Mr. Lucton shouted; but Bert shook his head and held his ground obstinately; so Mr. Lucton grudgingly paid his score, with a quite unnecessary tip, and joined him.

"All fixed up," Bert said. "A couple of bob for the two of us. She was glad of it, too: a widow with an old-age pension. She's making the bed up now in the front room over the river. Everything spick and span, and as clean as any new pin."

"The bed?" Mr. Lucton gasped. "D'you mean she's only got one?"

"Why, what do you think? It's a cottage, not a pallis."

"Well, you know," Mr. Lucton began; but he could not continue: Bert's spectacled eyes were so glowing with innocent triumph. After all, he supposed, he would have to put up with sleeping double: a habit he had relinquished more than fifteen years ago on the day when Muriel had decreed that sleeping single was not only more modern, but also more hygienic, and sold their old-fashioned brass bedstead, with the loose knobs, to a buyer of scrap-metal. Since then he had been accustomed to privacy, and the thought of sharing a bed with anyone filled him with horror. Bert was a good little chap and all that; but he certainly wouldn't have chosen him as a bedfellow. Now at the Grosmont Arms. . . .

The old woman apparently took this unnatural proceeding as a matter of course.

"It's a lovely bed," she told them, as she wished them good night, "and I know that it's comfortable: my poor husband and me slept in it till he died, poor dear soul, and we laid him out. And a face that calm you'ld have said he was an angel already."

Mr. Lucton, with difficulty, banished this macabre picture from his mind. It was rapidly growing dark as they groped their way up the narrow, creaking staircase, which smelt faintly of cheese and apples and immemorial staleness. It seemed doubtful that the windows of the front room had ever been opened since the old man died. When Bert prised the casements free, dragging tenacious runners of ivy along with them, a gust of fresh air wandered in, like an eager ghost that had been waiting to enter, and with it the roar of the river racing over a stickle. The draught blew the flame of their single candle side-ways.

"Now this lodge is what I call champion," Bert Hopkins proclaimed, with enthusiasm. "Running water to listen to and plenty of fresh air."

Well, that was something to be said for it, Mr. Lucton thought gloomily, but there wasn't much else.

He unpacked his rucksack and spread his new salmon-pink silk pyjamas over the foot of the bed.

"Crikey, you ain't 'arf posh, are you?" Bert exclaimed, with a voice in which scorn and reluctant awe were mingled. "Who'ld have thought of bringing things like them on a ramble?"

"What's wrong with them?" Mr. Lucton asked testily. "What do *you* wear, anyway?"

"Well, naturally, when I'm at home I wear a nightshirt. When I'm walking I wear the same as I've worn during the day, like anyone else would."

The prospect of spending the night with him appeared more than ever unpleasant to Mr. Lucton; for the moment, however, his chief preoccupation was the state of his right heel, where a broken blister had stuck to the sock. Bert Hopkins, even more grotesque than before as he stood bare-legged in his crumpled shirt, surveyed the damage with professional interest.

"There you are!" he said. "That's where me and my mouse-traps come in." It was evident that the joke still rankled. "What you want now is to strap your heel up with ad'esive plaster. You've got to be prepared, like I told you. 'Ere you are, then."

Mr. Lucton accepted the spool of plaster gratefully. By the time he had made a botched job of the strapping, Bert was already in bed.

"You blow out the candle, partner," he said.

Mr. Lucton did so, put on his pyjamas, and joined him. Fortunately the width of the bedstead was ample, and by wrigg-ling down into the substance of the feather-bed he was able to isolate himself in a sort of private compartment. But, for all his fatigue, he knew that he could not sleep. The roar of the river, rising and falling with every breath of air, made a restless background to Bert's snores, which produced a volume of sound out of all proportion to his diminutive size. Then the old woman on the other side of the thin partition began to snore antiphonally, and a mouse—or mice—started to scratch in the wainscot. Next, his skin began to itch in a dozen different places. That might possibly be due, he told himself, to the unfamiliar coarseness of the sheets; but his anxious mind suggested an explanation more horrible: that the bed in which the old couple had slept was infested with fleas. His wakeful imagination exaggerated this dread until he felt himself itching from head to foot. The most reasonable course would have been to re-light the candle and investigate for himself; but the knowledge that this would have meant awakening his bed-fellow from a profound sleep deterred him. He thought longingly of the tin of insect-powder in Bert's rucksack. As he lay miserably awake, hour after hour, the high spirits on which he had been congratulating himself gradually evaporated.

This was the fourth night in succession, since his adventure began, on which he had only been able to snatch a few hours of broken sleep, and his normal requirement and habit was to take no less than seven. The only thing he could do was to lie there, itching, and wait for the dawn.

He must have slept finally; for when he opened his eyes the room was full of pale sunlight and Bert was already up and skipping about with an irritating and most unseemly energy.

"I ought by rights to have woke you an hour ago," he said brightly, but you were snoozing that heavy I hadn't the 'eart. Nine hours to the tick! That's the right way to sleep. What I call a first-rate night."

"You speak for yourself," Mr. Lucton said crossly. "There were fleas in the bed and I hardly slept a wink. What time is it?"

"Seven o'clock, and the glass going up again. As for fleas, you must have imagined it: none never bit *me*. It's time to get on the road again, too; the best part of the day. And look 'ere:

I see you've a pair of shorts in your rucksack. You put them on, right away, and you'll feel twice as spry as what you did yesterday. Come on, now!"

At the moment Mr. Lucton felt anything but spry. When he had obediently put on his shorts, he crawled downstairs, blear-eyed and irritable, and gulped a cup of tea the old woman made for them: a turbid brew which had evidently been stewing and thickening on the hob for a couple of hours. Its astringency revolted his delicate stomach; but Bert smacked his lips over it.

"That's the stuff to start the day on, Grandma!" he said with offensive exuberance. "A beautiful bed you gave us, too. I shall tell all my pals about it if they happen to be coming this way, I can promise you that. So long, then, and good luck to you!"

He set off at a swinging pace which Mr. Lucton's sore heel, for all its plaster, made it hard for him to emulate. The river roared sullenly below them; its valley lay shrouded in white mist (which, Bert cheerfully said, was only for heat), but which chilled Mr. Lucton's white knees and made him feel pitiably unprotected and naked, until suddenly, as they emerged from the woods that clung to the castle's mound, the sun smote on his back and warmed his frozen spirits. In this generous light things didn't look so black after all, and by the time they paused for breakfast on the thick slices of bread and butter the old woman had cut and a stick of chocolate from Bert's rucksack, washed down with a draught of cool water from a wayside runnel, they began to look even brighter, and his abominable night was forgotten.

The remnants of morning mist still hung on the flanks of the hills and lay tangled among the dark woods like torn fleeces, gave the landscape an air of mystery, magnifying the shapes of its mountain contours, enhancing its wildness and solitude. This was a very different world, Mr. Lucton thought, from the rich Worcestershire plain—or even the homely Malverns. It was hard to believe that, even now, he was less than two hours away, at the pace of the Pearce-Tregaron, from the heart of North Bromwich. It had an atmosphere—that was the only word—of other-worldliness, belonging to the realm of imagination rather than that of everyday life. "A still, strange world . . ." he thought. Yes, that was it: "*A still strange land, unvext by sun or stars, where Lancelot rides clanking through the haze* . . ." and, with this, he was back in the pages of Malory, himself no longer Owen Lucton in his new shorts, but the armoured Sir Uwaine, approaching the Forest of Arroy—though with what knightly figure he could identify his perky companion was a matter more difficult to determine, and as for the damosels . . .

"Day-dreamin' again!" Bert said. "You'm a rummy cove, partner. A penny for your thoughts."

Mr. Lucton laughed. "I was wondering," he said, "if there was any place-name in this part of the world like Arroy. The Forest of Arroy."

Bert shook his head: "That's a new one on me. The only forest I know to hereabouts is the Forest of Dean, and we've left that behind a good bit to the south. Not that there mayn't be some such name: I can't set out to know everything; and there's plenty of woods on the hills between here and the mountain. Look at that lot in front of us."

Over the convolution that faced them next, the dense woodland surged toward them like a long, dark wave, with a broken crest, spilling over the slope to spend itself in a ragged fringe where it reached the valley, and ceasing suddenly like a stayed lava-flow.

"There's nothing so big as that marked on the map, not that I can remember," Bert said dubiously. "But what might be noticeable round our way—in the Midlands, I mean—wouldn't hardly count for nothing in these wild parts. It may be your Forest of 'Arry, or whatever you call it, for all I know." He consulted his compass: "It looks like we'll have to go through them woods any how."

At the point where it met the edge of the woods in the valley bottom, the road took a sudden swerve to the left, as though it were scared, and even turned back on its course for a while to skirt them.

"I don't like this 'ere," Bert said. "The direction's all wrong. If the road goes right round this forest of yours it'll lose us a couple of miles at the best; so I reckon we'd better go through it."

There was a rickety gate, shagged with pale incrustations of moss, and beyond it some signs of an over-grown path twisting between the clumps of coppice-wood that had sprung up where, long since, forest trees had been felled; the green floor lay closely set with rosettes of primrose-leaves and the glossy spikes of vanished bluebells—a magical place it must be in spring, Mr. Lucton thought. Bert climbed the gate, the top-bar collapsed like tinder beneath him. While he sprawled there, Mr. Lucton stepped over the remains of it and found himself faced with a notice-board which had once been painted white: "*Notice!*" he read. "*All unauthorized persons found in these woods will be prosecuted. Beware of mantraps! By order.*"

The board didn't specify whose the orders were; but to Mr. Lucton's law-abiding mind the words were intimidating.

"We can't go through here, Bert," he said. "D'you see that notice-board?"

Bert, flustered by his fall, flared up like a Very light.

"'Oo can't go through where?" he sputtered. "Is this a free country or isn't it? I know my rights, and I go where I ruddy well please when I want to. Got that straight, partner?"

"Well, look at the notice."

"Notice be jiggered! Mantraps!" He spat disdainfully. "If any mantrap goes catching me, the owner will have to pay for it in a court of law. Besides, there ain't none. That's put up to scare fools that have neither courage nor sense. I'm a Rambler, I am. Come on!"

Mr. Lucton followed him doubtfully. Quite apart from any question of meeting mantraps, which were surely forbidden by law, the steep path was infested with briars and brambles whose trailers tore maliciously at his naked knees, and he found it difficult to make headway. Bert, on the other hand, seemed to make nothing of these impediments. He went on and up like a goat, with a new, ferocious energy, inspired, no doubt, by his social indignation.

Mr. Lucton went cursing and stumbling after him, and joined

him, panting, his knees smothered with blood, a little way up the slope where the tree-felling had ceased and the deep woods began.

"You'll find it better going from now on," Bert said. "Them brambles won't grow under oak, nor anything else. We shall make good time now, provided we stick to the path."

"That's all very well; but where is your path?" Mr. Lucton asked pertinently.

At that point, indeed, there was hardly any sign of it. The whole forest was floored with a matting of fallen leaves, the death of innumerable years. Nut-brown and russet and golden the dense carpet stretched before and around them. Only here and there a vast ant-heap of twigs broke its continuity.

"Well, first of all, I 'appen to 'ave a sense of direction. Get that?" Bert answered defiantly. Mr. Lucton had noticed that in moments of anger or stress his 'h's dropped as inevitably as leaves in autumn. "And, secondly, being prepared, like what you ain't, I 'appen to 'ave a compass 'andy, stowed away in me 'aver-sack. Get that, too?"

Mr. Lucton decided it would be only prudent to get it. Bert's eyes, behind their round glasses, blazed with momentary pugnacity.

"Well, then, don't stand there looking like a funeral," he said. "Come on, then. Mantraps! I like that! What are you laughing at now?"

Mr. Lucton was chuckling to himself, in fact, over the memory of that characteristic perversion of the high-sounding, mysterious word Arroy into the everyday name of 'Arry, but thought it more tactful, regarding Bert's touchy mood, to conceal the source of his private amusement.

"Nothing worth mentioning," he said. "You lead on, Bert."

He led on. It was a mystery to Mr. Lucton that anyone, however richly endowed with instincts, could possibly steer his way with confidence through that multitude of identical trees. If the suspected path had ever existed it had certainly left no traces; but, for all that, Bert Hopkins apparently had no doubts as to his direction. He walked on, threading his rapid way without the least hesitation, and Mr. Lucton followed blindly, neither attempting to think for himself nor questioning his companion's judgment.

It was a ghostly progress. Their footfalls made no sound but the faintest of stealthy rustling; and although by now the sun must surely have been full overhead, no direct beams penetrated the coverlet of dark leaves intertwined overhead. The only light that enlivened these forest glooms proceeded miraculously from below: a pallid illumination diffused from the russet carpet, more in keeping with winter, Mr. Lucton thought, than with a mid-summer noon. What impressed him most about these great woods was their utter silence. No jay screamed, no wood-pigeon murmured. Such life as there was in them appeared to be concentrated, inaudible and invisible, in the leafy crowns uplifted high in the sun.

Beneath, all was still and death-like. Less like death, perhaps, Mr. Lucton thought, than death's dream-haunted borderland, the timeless, twilight serenity of extreme old age; for surely this Forest of Arroy (if such it were—and his fancy had greedily accepted its identity) was old beyond any imagining; just so, dim and silent and trackless, it must have lain in the days when Sir Uwaine rode through it, seeking adventures. "But now there are no more adventures to be found, more's the pity," Mr. Lucton thought, "and, what's more, we don't appear to be getting anywhere."

"Look here, are you sure you're right, Bert?" he shouted.

His voice sounded oddly feeble and toneless. There were no echoes; its vibrations seemed to be damped by the felting of leaves below, the matted branches above.

"What d'you mean: 'sure I'm right'?"

"Well, we've been in these ruddy monotonous woods the best part of an hour. That's nearly four miles, and there's no sign of our getting out of them. It's my belief we're just going round in circles. Why not have a look at your compass?"

"You don't trust me. That's it, is it? All right, here you are. You can see where you are for yourself. He tossed Mr. Lucton the compass contemptuously.

"Well, it looks to me as if we're going due north, and we ought to be steering west. You say we've no time to lose."

"Give it here," Bert said savagely. Mr. Lucton handed the compass back again.

"All right, 'ave it your own way. If you're so knowledgeable as all that," he added grimly, "you'd better take the lead."

"Don't be a damned fool, man," Mr. Lucton laughed. "I only . . ."

"Oh, so that's what it's come to now! I'm a damn fool, am I? If you thought we was going wrong, why didn't you say so before? You're not bound to foller me, are you? You got out of bed the wrong side this morning. That's what's wrong with you."

"I wish I'd never got into the blasted bed," Mr. Lucton said. "Now, come on, Bert. Be sensible."

The little man resumed his lead reluctantly. His very back betrayed his offended dignity. His walk had lost its swagger. They were both of them irritated, in fact, by the sense of so much lost time and labour, oppressed by the woodland's vast monotony and its devitalized air. The cushion of deep leaves, which gave no purchase, was as tiring to the legs as snow. At the end of another half-hour a slight hardening of the yielding carpet suggested the existence of a track which, at some recent time, must have been trodden. Bert's spirits rose immediately.

"There you are!" he called back. "We're on the path after all. Now we shan't be long, kid!"

He resumed his jaunty gait and began to whistle, though, as Mr. Lucton forbore to remind him, they weren't out of the wood yet. Still, wherever it led, a path was a path, likely, sooner or later, to lead to some human habitation, and any sort of escape was better than none. Soon the wood began to grow thinner. Rays of brilliant sunshine surprisingly penetrated the green roof. The trees thinned to a sunlit clearing scattered with hutches for rearing pheasants. There was also a pole-trap, and near it a wire, slung between two larch-poles, displayed a gamekeeper's mortuary of sun-shrivelled corpses: jays and magpies and stoats and kestrels and owls and one wide-winged buzzard. As they advanced, the living birds shrilled with alarm or the anticipation of food, and Bert Hopkins hesitated.

"Better go easy here," he whispered. "You never know . . ."

But his warning came too late. Already other sharp ears had caught the sound. A bearded man, in cord breeches and gaiters, appeared, with a gun in his hands, and stood in their path.

"What do you chaps reckon you're doing here?" he asked threateningly.

"Just taking a quiet walk, Mister, like anyone else," Bert replied with a dangerous mildness.

"Don't you know you're trespassing? Didn't you see the notice?"

"Ah, I saw the notice all right. Nicely worded it was. 'Beware of mantraps' an' all. That's a fine joke, that is. I had a good laugh off it. Made illegal, they was, in the year 1827."

"Not so much of your jokes! You admit that you've seen the notice, and you know you've no right to be in these woods after being warned. You can understand English. It says: 'Trespassers will be prosecuted,' and that's what it means."

"All right then. What are you going to do about it?"

"I shall want your names and addresses, the two of you."

Mr. Lucton shuddered. In addition to his native horror of any infringement of the law, there rose in his mind the fear of having to disclose his identity, with its chain of disastrous consequences. If he gave a false name and address, it would be even worse. That was probably another indictable offence, and even more serious. Was the fellow bribeable? Should he offer a tip? He looked towards Bert for guidance. But Bert was still smiling.

"Want our names and addresses, do you? Just fancy! That's awkward ain't it? 'Ow are you going to get them? That's what I want to know."

"You're ruddy well going to give them. None of this nonsense, my lad!"

"And supposin' I won't . . . what then? That's an awkward one, as I told you. Talkin' of trespass . . ."

"I've had enough talk. Come on, now." The keeper looked

ugly. He put down his gun and spat on his hands. "I know you hikers. Disturbing my birds in the breeding-season. I've had just about enough of it."

"Now keep your 'air on, Tarzan, and mind you don't lose that beard either. It's no use your shouting your 'ead off at me that way. My pal 'ere's a lawyer, he is, and if you're too ruddy ignorant of the law to know your own job—like you show by setting up pole-traps and shootin' buzzards, a bird that's protected, mind—I'll tell you what trespassing means. There ain't no such things in law as trespass, not without damage. You show me the damage I've done; then I'll talk about names and addresses. Not before, though: I tell you that straight. So now, what about it?"

The keeper scowled at him.

"You know a lot, don't you?" he sneered. "But remember one thing: you've been warned off this land, and if I catch you along here again I can have you run in. Now hop it, the pair of you, and get out of my woods."

Bert laughed in his face:

"Get out of your woods? Why that's just what my pal and me have been trying our hardest to do for the last two hours! I don't care if I never set eyes on your woods again in my life, and the sooner we're out of them the better I'll be pleased."

"All right, then. You go past that shed there. There's a path runs downhill behind it. A private path, mind, and remember I don't want to see you again."

"That's mutual, that is. First time I've agreed with you. And if I was you, I should take down that pole-trap and burn that poor ruddy buzzard before it's reported, see? What's more, next time you're planning to make yourself unpleasant, you find out where you stand, before you start threatening. What you want . . ."

"The first thing I want is no more of your lip," the keeper broke in angrily.

"Then be'ave yourself better next time," Bert Hopkins said.

The encounter, which, in its first stages, had so deeply perturbed Mr. Lucton, had restored his companion's spirits. The old swagger returned to his walk; his face was flushed with victory and his voice was excited.

"Those beggars are all the same," he said. "They need telling a thing or two."

"Well, I didn't much like it. He looked as if he might have turned nasty."

"Oh, that's nothing," Bert chuckled. "I know how to deal with gamekeepers. Had plenty of practice. As a matter of fact, I never reckon I've had a proper holiday unless I've run into a bit of a scrap and told one of them ignorant beggars where they get off. I've read up the law of trespass, and they can't catch me out. I know what my rights and theirs are, and I reckon it's my duty, as a citizen like, to stand up for them. And I'll tell you something else: I should never have gone through them woods at all if I hadn't come ack over tock at the foot of that notice-board. Mantraps . . . !"

"Well, we're out of them anyway now," Mr. Lucton said thankfully. "Where are we?"

There wasn't much doubt. They had entered the road at a point a few hundred yards beyond the gate over which they had left it. Bert took out his watch and looked at it ruefully.

"Five o'clock. That's two hours lost, damn it, and four more to go. Well, that can't be helped: we may get to the Abbey soon after sunset."

"That's late to turn up. Supposing we can't get a bed there? What shall we do then?"

Mr. Lucton remembered his four nights of broken sleep.

"Well, in that case we shall have to sleep out, partner. That's what. It's all in the game."

An increasingly strenuous game, Mr. Lucton thought—though, indeed, a night in the heather could hardly be worse than the abominable bed of last night. He was determined, whatever happened, to sleep by himself.

"Come on then," he said, "we've got to make up for lost time."

Bert shot off like an arrow. Mr. Lucton trudged solemnly behind him, resenting the fact that his comrade's mischievous pugnacity had forced him to climb the hill twice. On this gritty country road the pull seemed even harder than over the leaf-padded path. By now he had lost his morning vigour and freshness, and the plaster on his sore heel was beginning to ruckle.

Yet, in spite of fatigue and pain—or, perhaps, even because these discomforts absorbed his conscious mind and allowed his subconscious a looser rein, that evening's grinding trudge of more than four hours was to remain in his memory more vividly than any period that had preceded it—with the possible exception of certain remembered moments during Aylmer's futile advance on Kut-el-Imara in 1916. It was an odd comparison of small thing with great; yet something of the same exaltation, the same unreality, marked both these journeys—with the difference that whereas in Mesopotamia the dreadful monotony of the dun landscape and the feeling of enormous toil without progression had deadened his senses, in this new case it seemed to him as if they had never been more receptive or more acutely alive and awake.

From the brow where the great woods ended he had stepped into a new world: one entirely different in time no less than in space. Though, for all he knew, he might still be in homely Herefordshire, such arbitrary distinctions as county boundaries had no longer any validity. It was the spiritual geography of the region that had suddenly changed. In that respect, this was neither England nor Wales. It was a no-man's-land of the spirit: that debatable zone of the Silurian March which, for those men of mixed blood and divided racial instincts who can feel its influence, is still one of the strangest, the loveliest, the most poignantly-haunted parts of the British Isles—a land whose ghostly and delicate moods have found their only expression in the words of great Silurists, such as Vaughan and Traherne and, later, but unmistakably, Arthur Machen, all of whom have sprung from the same enchanted soil.

It was beyond Mr. Lucton's power to express or even to analyse what he felt. He only knew that this revelation of beauty and strangeness was a unique and, in some ways, a rather frightening experience—frightening because though, like Bert, he "had his rights", he was not quite sure that this country accepted him. It was so old, so watchful, so wary, so densely inhabited by influences (ghosts, if you will) which, if they did not actually resent it, were critically aware of his intrusion. The solemnity of these great domed hills that lay quiet as sleeping monsters (but were they indeed asleep?) beneath the shadow of the mountain barrier, which grew blacker and blacker; the stillness of these rock-strewn fields, with their ruined stone walls, within which the barren orchards of black yew and wind-writhen thorn and spreading thickets of brake attested the long-abandoned conflict between man's hopefulness and the insurgent wild; the secrecy of the valley-bottoms, clogged with alder and bramble, beneath which hidden water flowed silently or moved with malicious chuckles and whispers—all these elements contributed to the feeling, deep in his heart, that this was land where the newcomer, man, was regarded with resentful and even hostile eyes; that these valleys and hills were still the jealously-guarded stronghold of ancient and potent influences that had always defied his intrusion.

No doubt human beings still dwelt there and persisted on sufferance; but the few white-washed farmsteads he saw on the flanks of the hills looked blanched and pitiful, as though they were beleaguered, and he had a feeling that the men who contrived to inhabit them must surely be unlike himself, the survivors of an older, more savage race whom time had inured through generations to this life of perpetual warfare, and who had finally accepted an uneasy truce or compromise.

One such he saw: a hirsute, subhuman figure whose pale blue eyes gazed at him fearfully, as it seemed, from beneath a bundle of lichened branches which he was carrying home on his bowed back. Mr. Lucton wished him good evening, but the man gave no answer, continuing to peer at him from time to time with those frightened blue eyes as he vanished silently into the thicket of alder. It was a subtly disturbing encounter. As he went on his way Mr. Lucton realized what the ancients had meant when they spoke of panic fear. This was the realm of Pan, the last refuge of natural forces old and unknown, which still had power, in moments of ecstasy or spiritual disarmament, to clutch with cold fingers at the heart of civilized man. He was thankful, and yet in a way disappointed, when, without any warning, he found himself suddenly emerging on a macadamized road, and saw Bert, who had outstripped him by more than a mile, impatiently waiting for him at the foot of a petrol-pump.

"I thought you were never coming," Bert said reproachfully. "If you want a drink there's a spout over there in the hedge. Lovely water, as cold as ice. I've had a good swill in it."

"What about snatching a hurried cup of tea in one of these cottages?"

"No time for that, partner. Lost too much time in them woods. The light's beginning to fail, and we've six more miles, as I reckon, in front of us. We don't want to get there in the dark."

"All right. Carry on then," Mr. Lucton said wearily; "but remember, I can't manage your pace. That's a rum bit of country we've just been through."

"Rum? It's pretty hard going, if that's what you mean." (There was nothing of the mystic about Bert.) "And it's nice and lonely, though I can't say I'ld fancy living there."

Mr. Lucton shivered: "Live there? I should damned well think not!"

(VII)

THE ABBEY

IT was almost twilight when they entered the jaws of the Dulas valley between two bracken-covered domes that guarded the pass. Now that they had reached its feet, the black bulk of the imminent mountains was no longer visible. The foothills that hid them from view on either hand had a gentle, pastoral aspect, and the white farms that glimmered on their slopes looked neither isolated nor beleaguered. A leat rippled beside the road. From the tunnel of alders below, the water of the Dulas river sang a companionable song with no hint of the strange or sinister. The whole valley, in fact, was musical with moving water that gurgled and chuckled in ditches or drummed into moss-grown cups of stone with a tinkling sound, and the whisper of wind-stirred birches and aspens was watery too.

It was only when Mr. Lucton paused for a breather and looked backwards, that he became aware of a huge green limb which, outstretched behind them as they walked side by side, had already gathered them to the mountain's heart, shutting them off from the outer world with such an air of finality that it was difficult to believe it still existed. That was one of the characteristics, Bert's friend had told him, of the valley of Dulas Fawr: not merely its physical isolation, but its almost complete independence of the life that went on outside it. Its inhabitants were a self-contained, self-supporting community. On the lush fields of the valley's alluvium they grew their corn and fed their well-liking cattle; on the steep slopes they pastured their nimble sheep; on the heathered tops, under the sky, roamed their droves of wild ponies. Very few owned motor-cars; for the metalled road did not penetrate more than nine miles into the sandstone massif, and in their winter, which lasted for seven months of the year, many farms in the upper part of the valley were unapproachable. They were a race apart, Bert's friend had said, neither Welsh nor English, though most of them spoke both languages, but a friendly folk none the less—since, in that small space, there was hardly room for serious quarrelling—and generous in spite of their sharpness in driving a bargain. They lived to themselves and within their own interests. Beyond the level of the inn, the valley's penultimate outpost of civilization, where there was a post-office, but neither telegraph nor telephone, there was hardly a farm in the valley that "took in" a daily paper.

"Believe it or not," Bert said, "when my pal come here, there wasn't even a wireless set at the Abbey. They'd got one, he said, but it was mostly out of order. It was a job to remember to take in the battery to change at Aberdulas on Fridays, and nobody cared. Why should they? That's what I call peace—no wireless."

Yes, peace: that was it, Mr. Lucton thought: a settled peace—not that sense of a perpetual veiled and silent combat which had frozen his marrow and filled him with strange disquietude a few hours earlier. This valley, for all its wildness, was kind; even the shapes of the mountains were friendly. "And what a refuge!" he told himself. "A place where they don't read newspapers or listen to wireless. I might settle down here till the end of the summer," he thought, "and nobody be the wiser! It's a fine bit of luck, my coming here: the first I've had."

Yet even as he played with the idea of "settling down" and losing his identity, he couldn't help remembering how unsuccessful his previous attempts at doing either had been. He had little faith in the luck that he welcomed. There was no peace for the wicked, they said (if indeed he was wicked), and the fact that even now they were approaching an inn, a public place where, for all its remoteness, anyone of the myriad inhabitants of North Bromwich who knew him by sight might turn up unexpectedly, made him shrink from what faced him.

"It would be just my luck," he reflected ruefully, "if I ran slap into somebody."

For the moment he was able to put these fears behind him. Even in that fading light he could not but observe the green valley's astounding beauty, some new aspect of which was revealed by every turn of the road. At times they walked blind, with resinous plantations of fir or larch on their left, and on the right a wooded bank falling precipitously to the river. Yet even these shadowed passages had their reward, for, at the end of each of them, they emerged into a slowly-deepening dusk, midway between fading daylight and nascent starshine, in which the crests of the high barriers that hemmed them in, now magnified beyond belief, stood out sharply defined, as though cut by the point of a graving-tool, against a sky still transfused by light that had vanished from the earth. Then, unexpectedly, the valley doubled its width, spreading out into a basin of pale green bounded by walls even more precipitous; and in the midst of this open space—like some singular work of art for which a collector has chosen the perfect setting—a group of stone masonry, which included a massive tower and the Gothic arches of a ruined nave, took their breath with a sudden surprise and wonder that made them halt simultaneously and left them both speechless. Bert was the first to recover his tongue.

"There it is," he whispered excitedly, "the same as I told you! Honest, kid, it's got no right to be there, a thing like that, miles and miles away from anywhere! I've seen a good many things in my time; but this ruddy old ruin, I reckon it beats the lot. And to think that we're going to sleep there to-night! No matter how much it costs, partner, I'ld rather do that than spend the night in Buckingham Palace or Windsor Castle. What do *you* say?"

Mr. Lucton laughed. "I don't care a damn where I sleep as long as I get a bed to myself," he said.

Like many frustrated romantics, in moments of deep emotion such as this, it was his instinct to mask his true feelings with affected cynicism. Bert stared at him incredulously.

"Well, you are a knockout and no mistake, partner!" he said. "Made of stone, you must be, not 'uman flesh and blood."

Little light was now left below, and the sky above their heads was rapidly darkening to a clear indigo as they climbed the last lap and turned into the Abbey's grass-grown courtyard. At close quarters, the great grey ruin was even more impressive than it had seemed in its first revelation. The square south tower rose above them; the roofless nave of the great church seemed more majestic for its emptiness, more solemn for its desolation. A string of washing, hung out to dry, served to emphasize rather than to diminish the ruin's remoteness from the sphere of man's everyday life. Even in death those time-worn, crumbling stones asserted the permanence of the aspirations which had devotedly contrived this calculated loveliness. It was, Mr. Lucton thought, a benignant beauty, shedding peace and serenity on those who walked in its shadow: the persistent influence of an Act of Faith.

In the kitchen of the inn, a long chamber with a groined roof, resembling a cathedral's crypt, the landlady greeted them with a smile. She was a comely, soft-voiced woman of middle age, unhurried and placid. The stone-flagged crypt, which was clearly not only a kitchen, but also the public-bar and the family's living-room, reflected the orderliness of a calm and capable mind.

"Well, you are rather late," she said, "and I'm afraid I can't give you dinner, because we've just finished the washing-up; but there is a room empty—the one at the top of the tower, if you two gentlemen don't mind sharing a bed."

"Oh, that's nothing. We're used to that, aren't we, partner?" Bert answered cheerfully.

Mr. Lucton sighed. It was the one thing he could never get used to; but he supposed he would have to put up with it. There was some consolation, at any rate, in finding himself in such comfortable surroundings and pleasant company. Undeterred by the disapproval in Bert Hopkins's eyes, he ordered a tankard of beer and drank it luxuriously, while the landlady's daughter disappeared up a spiral staircase set in the wall, carrying a tray with a second jugful of beer and one of water, with bread and butter and home-made Caerphilly cheese, to the room where the other guests of the inn, who had dined, were assembled.

By the time he had finished his drink and emerged from the kitchen with Bert, who had watched him impatiently, night had fallen. Only a grey luminosity defined the brim of the mountain basin, against whose darker background the tower and the arches of the nave stood out sharply defined. They groped their way along the uneven flagging of the path, and mounted a flight of stone steps guarded by wooden rails draped with fishermen's waders and brogues. At the top of the steps they came to a narrow passage, where, on a long oak refectory table, they discerned the shapes of a collection of rods, reels, and fly-boxes, together with a number of canvas bags and rucksacks resembling their own.

"Better dump our gear with the rest here, partner," Bert said. "That looks like the custom of the 'ouse. We can pick it up later on when we go to bed. Which way do we go now?"

A chink of light showed from beneath a door on the right-hand side of the passage.

"I expect it's in there. You go first," Mr. Lucton said nervously.

It was a ticklish entrance. At that moment he was expecting—though by no means prepared—to find himself confronted by some familiar North Bromwich face—so many of his business acquaintances were fishermen—which would put an end to his hopes. As they entered the long low room—Bert announcing their arrival with a perky chuck of the head and a brisk "Good evening, everybody"—he scrutinized the company eagerly in search of this messenger of doom. His heart bounded with sheer relief when he saw not a single face that he knew. . . . Or, at least, none that mattered. It leapt again, more inexplicably, when he found himself gazing into the hazel eyes of the girl who had passed him, and made him feel so confoundedly old, on the westward slope of the Malverns.

Bert plumped himself down at the end of the table in front of the loaded supper-tray, then pulled out his pedometer.

"Twenty-three miles six furlongs," he boasted. "Not much wrong with that, is there?"

Nobody took advantage of this conversational gambit. The company—apart from Mr. Lucton's young woman, and her gloomy young man, who looked even more intense and no better pleased with himself than before—was entirely composed of trout-fishermen of the leisured class who frequent obscure mountain valleys and lake-sides from early April until the beginning of October, and regard every inn that they patronize as a preserve in which the presence of visitors who do not fish—or even of authentic fishermen unknown to them—must not be encouraged. The members of this particular batch were mostly middle-aged men, accustomed to take plenty of exercise in the open air, to "do themselves well", and to spend the time which they did not devote to their sport in talking about it. Each entrenched behind a private bottle of whisky on which his initials were scrawled, they continued to describe and discuss the details of their day's fortunes as though these were the only matters of importance in the world. They talked of flies—pheasant tails, Tup's Indispensables and coch-y-bonddhus; of difficult switch-casts under bushes; of the peculiar vices prevalent among the trout in the Dulas—the gravest of which was a reasonable "dourness" in taking an artificial fly. One of their number, a scraggy veteran in a clerical collar who "knew every stone in the river", having fished it pertinaciously (and jealously, Mr. Lucton guessed) for more than forty years, took the head of the table as a sort of self-appointed chairman to whose judgments the younger members tacitly deferred. He had a long, narrow, thin-lipped face, with a jutting nose, hooked like that of a bird of prey. A cruel, malicious, jealous face, Mr. Lucton thought. Another, a stout, rubicund gentleman, with the air of a sulky child, sat gloomily silent, having apparently suffered that day the most crushing misfortune of his life, in the loss of a heavier fish than had ever before been lost in the Dulas. When once they had satisfied themselves (and this was not difficult) that neither Mr. Lucton nor Bert was a potential claimant to a beat on the limited water, they took no more notice of them than of the young couple who had chosen for themselves an inconspicuous seat on a sofa in a corner, far removed from the light.

Mr. Lucton was not altogether sorry that Bert's naïve overture had been turned down. The less he was noticed, the better he would be pleased, and the "shop" the fishermen talked seemed to him even more boring than that of golfers, with which he was daily surfeited at his club. He did hope, however, that Bert's rich Black Country accent had not equally queered his pitch with the couple on the sofa. Though he knew his own attitude was snobbish and indefensible and that it was unworthy to wish to dissociate himself from this innocent companion, he would have felt much more comfortable if he could have found some way to dissuade Bert from continually talking with his mouth full "at" the group round the head of the table, from brandishing chunks of Caerphilly cheese on his knife, and washing down with a gulp of water every mouthful that bulged his cheeks.

Not that either of the young people appeared to be taking notice of him, or even of one another. They were sitting at opposite ends of the shabby sofa: the boy pretending to read a book of what looked like poetry; the girl listlessly staring in front of her with troubled eyes. Mr. Lucton found it even more difficult than before to diagnose their relationship. He had already instinctively dismissed the theory that they were brother and sister: their physical types seemed too completely divergent. Nor was it reasonable to suppose them a honeymoon couple. Past observation and personal experience alike suggested that, had they been newly married, he would have noticed some furtive look or gesture or smile that betrayed their state. Nor, at this moment, had he any grounds on which to conclude that they were lovers. The division between them was palpably more than the negative width of the sofa. He was aware of a positive separation that amounted to antagonism. He had no objection to that: he had decided, long ago, that the young man was a gloomy, self-centred, nasty bit of work, entirely unsuited to his lovely companion—more than that; a dank, sodden wet-blanket on her glowing vitality, a check on her buoyancy, a chain on her freedom. Mr. Lucton grew hot with indignation at the fellow's melancholy half-heartedness. If they were brother and sister, he might be polite to her; if they were lovers who had quarrelled he ought, at least, to recognize her existence; if they were a honeymoon couple, by this hour they should have been in bed.

These sour, so-called intellectuals! The fellow wanted kicking. Mr. Lucton felt he could gladly have supplied the necessary correction.

And the girl had changed. She was no longer the swift dryad, the incarnation of youth and physical delight, who had flashed, so lightly and brilliantly, across his vision on the Malvern slopes and vanished, leaving that odd ache in his heart behind her. She looked shrunken, subdued—as well she might!—and pitiably unprotected. Her cheeks were pale; her honey-coloured hair had lost its lustre. Her eyes—yes, indeed, they were hazel as he had guessed—had the vacant look of sheer misery. Though they were gazing in Mr. Lucton's direction and saw, no doubt, Bert's deplorable table-manners, they appeared to take nothing in; and once, when she closed them and sighed, Mr. Lucton thought he saw her soft lips tremble as though tears were at hand.

The sight was almost intolerable. He felt it his duty as a man of the world, as a father of grown-up daughters, to offer his help and protection to this exquisite child, to provide the advice and the tender appreciation which her sullen companion, glowering over his book, seemed unable or unwilling to give. But whatever he dared to do—and it was easier to will than to act—he dreaded Bert butting in, as he almost certainly would do, with his naïvely blundering loquacity. This delicate situation was none of Bert's business; his intervention would brush the bloom from it; it could only be handled, he felt, if handled at all, by a fatherly man, a man of unusual tact and sensibility, such as himself, in conditions of intimacy and quietude; and, at the moment, there seemed not the faintest chance of either, for Bert had so much to say and to eat that in all probability the poor child would have vanished upstairs with her detestable young man before he had swilled down his last mouthful.

In the meantime, as was his romantic wont, Mr. Lucton imagined a tender scene and the probable course of its dialogue. He would try to fix her attention and say "Good evening" in the most cultured voice he could command as an offset to Bert's uncouthness. No doubt the young man would glare at him. But that couldn't be helped. She could hardly refuse to reply to a polite salutation, spoken in accents which showed that it came from a man of breeding. Then he would say: "This isn't the first time I've seen you, you know," unobtrusively bringing his chair a little nearer her and of the sofa. "You passed me a couple of days ago, just west of the Malverns. You probably didn't notice me; but of course" (significantly) "I recognized you at once when I saw you to-night."

At this point the imagined dialogue met with a hitch. She might, quite improbably, murmur: "Of course I remember you, too," or, more likely, stymie him with a dim, disinterested "Really?"—neither of which replies would provide a promising gambit for the next moves Mr. Lucton's fervid imagination suggested: a further approximation; the touch of a fatherly hand, and a persuasive whisper: "My poor child, what's the matter, and why don't you tell me all about it? I'm an old man. I shall understand"—all of which, he was forced to admit, would be quite impracticable so long as her glowering companion remained within sight and earshot. Perhaps, disagreeable as that might be, it would be better to approach the young man first, with a cheery, but not too familiar, comment on the weather, and the hope that they had had an enjoyable walk. That, of course, considering their two faces, would have been a mockery, and the young man's aspect did not encourage cheeriness of any kind.

It was obvious that he must find a new opening. But what? While he debated the question, which seemed hard to answer, Bert supplied an unsentimental diversion, by vulgarly smacking his lips and suppressing a loud eructation as he lit his last Woodbine.

"That's a champion blow-out, that was!" he breathed in a husky voice. "Time we hit the hay, I reckon. Coming up, partner?"

Mr. Lucton blushed. He resented this description of himself. But for the accidents of the road he would never have been Bert's partner. He felt like disowning him.

"No, I think I'll just smoke another pipe," he said, in accents of studied refinement.

"That's O.K. by me, partner. All I want to know *is*, which side of the bed you'ld sooner doss. Take your choice. It's all one to me."

"It's all the same to me, too," Mr. Lucton said. "As a matter of fact, I shall probably stay down here and sleep on a sofa."

Bert Hopkins flared up:

"H'm . . . Chummy, ain't you? Don't fancy my company. Is that it?"

"No, no." Mr. Lucton filled his pipe nervously. "I'm all right. You just leave me alone."

"You bet I will, if that's the 'umour you're in. Let sleeping dogs lie, for fear of getting snapped at. Well, here goes then." He picked up a candlestick. "Good night, all."

By this time Mr. Lucton knew that the attention of the whole room was focused on him. The red-faced fisherman had stopped dead in his fifth recital of the manner in which the monster trout had snagged itself and escaped his landing-net. Even the black-browed youth had looked up from his book and relaxed his lips in the ghost of a scornful smile. The hook-nosed old man at the head of the table broke the embarrassing silence.

"Not a sound was heard," he intoned. "It must be twenty to ten."

"That's all right," said the red-faced fisherman. "We shall get the Regional News at ten o'clock." He fumbled lazily for his watch.

"Why on earth you fellows want to worry about news in a place like this," the old man snarled, "is a thing that beats me. And as for carting one of those beastly things about with me. . . . Why, forty years ago, when first I came to Llandewi . . ."

"No, it isn't, by Jove! Why did nobody notice the time? Losing that blessed fish put me off. It's nearly a quarter-past. There you are! We shall probably get nothing but announcements or football results."

"No more news of that fish of yours, anyway, Jones, thank goodness!" the wag of the party laughed.

The red-faced man dived on all fours in front of the piano and retrieved a small portable wireless-set, which he set on the table. He switched on, and fiddled with the tuning-knob in the imperfect light. An anguished squeal resembling that of a pig in its death-agony filled the air.

"That's Hamburg," somebody whispered.

"Sounds more like Whipsnade."

"Where the devil is Midland Regional?" the red-faced man muttered. "It's not marked on the dial. Two hundred and ninety something, I think: not far from Hilversum. There you are: I've got it!" he cried triumphantly, and stood back beaming with pride.

"*And that*," a suburban voice proclaimed smugly, "*is the end of the news.*"

". . . which will keep quite well till to-morrow morning," the old man mimicked, "and nobody any the better or worse for having missed it. Turn the beastly thing off and put it away, Jones."

"*And here*," the announcer's standardized voice continued, "*is a police message that has just come in. The name of the person it refers to is Lucton . . . Owen Lucton. Missing from his home in Alvaston, North Bromwich, since last Wednesday, Owen Lucton. Age fifty-one, but looks older; medium height; inclined to be stout; rather bald, with greyish hair and military moustache. He will probably be wearing a black town jacket, waistcoat with white slip and striped cashmere trousers.*"

"Sounds to me like a shop-walker."

"*It is thought that this man*," the suave voice ran on, "*may have lost his memory. He left home driving a grey Pearce-Tregaron car, Number OXH 943 . . .*"

"The devil he did! That ought to be easy to spot."

"*Will anyone having information as to this man's whereabouts please communicate with the Chief Constable of North Bromwich. Telephone Central 0555. The next part of the programme follows almost immediately.*"

"Well, that's that! Anyone here answering to that description?" the old man said.

"None except the gentleman who's just gone upstairs," the wag put in slyly. "He came from North Bromwich all right. And you come from that way, too, Jones, don't you?" he went on. "Do you drive a Pearce-Tregaron, by any chance? Living a double life. That's what it is, my boy, but we've got you now."

The man with the red face grinned. "Drive a Pearce-Tregaron? No, I wish I did. The chap must be rolling. What did he say the name was? I missed it."

"Lucton. Owen Lucton. D'you know him?"

"Well, I can't say I do. I know the name well enough. Rather out of my line of life—stockbroker or something of that kind. But that Lucton isn't the kind of chap who'd be doing a bunk unless he'd got into hot water—embezzlement, you know, or something of that kind."

"You never know in these cases," the old man said cannily. "Lost memory . . . that's an old story. I say '*Cherchez la femme.*' An expensive sport, that, Jones. Much better stick to trout-fishing." He pointed at Mr. Lucton. "What about *you*, sir? The description fits you all right when I come to think of it."

Mr. Lucton jumped at the unexpected challenge. Ever since he had heard the fateful syllables of his own name he had been lost in a turmoil of blind terror and panic. It was frightening to think that even in this remote Eden the vibrations of that accusing voice could reach him over the ether. His first instinct had been an overwhleming desire to take flight, to hide himself, like Adam and Eve in the Garden. Only the quick inhibition of what was left of his reason had warned him that this would be equal to a confession. So, with difficulty, he had forced himself to stay where he was, going hot and cold alternately and clenching his pipe in his teeth to keep them from chattering. Now the old parson's stern (though probably jocular) demand compelled him to speak. His mind clutched at Bert—whose companionship, a few minutes before, he had been longing to repudiate—as the only plausible evidence in his favour.

"Are you speaking to me, sir?" he stammered, producing, at the same time, a laugh which sounded, to his own ears, singularly hollow and unconvincing. "Well, really . . . Is that a joke, sir? You see, I and my friend, who's just gone upstairs, have been on a walking tour, so of course . . . er . . ."

Mr. Lucton licked his trembling lips and dried up; but there was no need for him to finish his sentence. The other fishermen had finished their laugh at the older man's extravagant joke, and had already forgotten him. He was conscious of no further interest in himself except on the part of the sombre young man in the sofa corner, whose dark eyes still watched him with a cold, quizzical scrutiny. They were extraordinarily penetrating, those eyes, and remarkably intelligent. Beneath their concentrated gaze, Mr. Lucton felt naked and unprotected. No secrets were hid from them. They had missed, he felt, not a single symptom of his suppressed agitation: his quick flushings and palings; the tremor of his hands and of the hot pipe clenched in his teeth; the volumes of smoke he had puffed from it in his nervousness. He was looking at Mr. Lucton now with a faint, sinister smile on his finely-carved lips—a knowing smile that frayed the last shreds of his precarious composure. The strain was intolerable.

Mr. Lucton rose from his chair with a calculated leisureliness, which he felt only too transparent, and knocked out his pipe in the empty grate. Then he turned back unsteadily and opened a door on the left which led, he discovered to his embarrassment, into a dark cupboard used for storing bacon.

"The way out's over there," the young man said in a melodious voice. It was the first time he had spoken. His tones were full of amusement and mockery.

"Thanks, thanks," Mr. Lucton murmured, with a wan smile. "I thought I'd just take a stroll and look at the moonlight."

"There *is* no moon," the young man observed brutally.

"Well, well. Fancy that. It's a lovely night, anyway," Mr. Lucton said.

Nobody answered him. At last! He had reached the passage. He stood there, trembling in the dark, thinking desperately. He must get away somehow—and quickly: there was no question about that. Complications presented themselves. First of all, Bert Hopkins, who, by this time, no doubt, lay peacefully snoring on his back. Let sleeping dogs lie—as Bert himself had remarked. But supposing, to-morrow morning, Bert woke up to find he was gone and that the bill was unpaid? That wouldn't be fair on the poor little blighter who, for all his pepperiness, was a decent fellow. No . . . Before he left the Abbey that bill must be paid in some unobtrusive manner. Mr. Lucton groped on the refectory table for his rucksack: the stiffness of the unused straps and the canvas, made it easy to identify. Then, slipping it over his shoulders, he made his way gingerly down the steps and tiptoed along the flagged path till he reached the kitchen.

The stone-arched chamber was empty of casual customers, for it was now long past closing-time, and the members of the family had gone to bed, with the exception of the landlady, who, now that work was over, had allowed herself to relax, for the first free moment of the day, in an arm-chair by the side of the sinking fire. Once more Mr. Lucton was struck by the serenity of this hard-working woman's face. Sitting there, half asleep, with eyes closed and hands folded on her lap, on her benevolent face the smile of a marble Demeter, she was unaware of his stealthy approach until he had reached her, and came to her business-like self with a start.

"Oh, dear, dear," she said. "I must have dropped off. Have you lost your way, sir? The Abbey's a terrible place for people losing their way and popping out unexpectedly. You see, the stone spiral stairs go right through the tower from the top to the bottom."

"No, it isn't that," Mr. Lucton whispered apologetically. "I don't like to trouble you, but I want to get off very early to-morrow morning, and I'ld rather pay the bill to-night if you'll let me."

"Oh, you needn't have worried about that, sir. I expect I shall be up before you. This is a farm-house as well as an inn, and cows have to be milked. And what about breakfast?"

"I'm afraid I shan't be able to wait for that," Mr. Lucton said hurriedly. "If you could cut me a couple of sandwiches"—he saw her face fall—"or just give me a handful of biscuits and a bit of cheese, I shall be quite happy."

"Well, that would be easier," she admitted. "You see, everything else has been put away in the larder. Do you want the bill for both of you gentlemen?"

"Yes, please."

It was a shame to disturb her like this, Mr. Lucton thought, as she moved slowly towards a paper-littered desk in the corner.

"My daughter usually looks after this part of the business," she said as she searched for a bill-head. "Let me see . . . I don't think you told me your name?"

"Make it out to . . . Mr. Hopkins."

He lowered his voice as he spoke. Outside, in the court-yard, he heard two of the fishermen, who had decided to take the air, discussing the direction of the wind and the prospects of weather. In the stillness of night their voices echoed back from the ruined walls, then died away. The landlady handed him his bill. It was, by his standards, extremely moderate: he smiled to think how scared Bert had been of this modest expenditure. Well, he wouldn't have to pay: that at least was one atonement, Mr. Lucton thought, for his own appalling snobbishness. Now for money. . . . Once more the envelope of bank-notes eluded him. He experienced some moments of terror before he found it, at last, in the hip-pocket at the back of his shorts. He paid the bill, thanked the landlady and made for the door.

"You're forgetting your biscuits and cheese, sir."

Again he was forced to wait while she found the tin and buttered them and cut slices of cheese. She was tired, no doubt, and he had no right to hurry her; but, as he watched, the leisurely process got on his nerves.

"I'm sure that's enough," he protested.

"You wait till to-morrow morning before you say that, sir. This mountain air gives you an appetite. There, now . . . That ought to do. If you had such a thing as a thermos . . ."

He hadn't, Mr. Lucton confessed.

"Would you like them packed in your rucksack?"

"No, I'm sure they'll go into my pocket all right. Good night, and thank you."

"Thank *you*, sir. I hope we shall have the pleasure of seeing you again when we're not quite so crowded. You needn't go round by the yard: you can get to the top of the tower by the stone stairs if you like, though our visitors do generally get themselves smothered in whitewash, they're so dreadfully narrow."

"No, I think it's safer outside," Mr. Lucton said. "I can see my way well: it's bright starlight."

When he had reached the end of the flagged path, he looked back cautiously and made a diagonal dash for the gate that led out of the court-yard. An owl, swooping down from the ivy that draped the tower, supplied him with an appropriate farewell to Llandewi, a derisive halloo that was like a cat-call. "Gone away . . . gone away . . . gone aw-a-ay!" it screamed after him.

(VIII)

THE DRIVE

THIS time there was no fear of immediate pursuit, and therefore, thank heaven, no hurry. Mr. Lucton actually felt less rattled than sore at the maliciousness with which Fate, by a series of ridiculous coincidences, had contrived to keep him on the move. "Like some boy tormenting a wretched grasshopper," he thought. "No sooner do I settle for a moment than the shadow of a finger comes up on my tail and off I have to skip again!"

He was sorry to leave Llandewi. The benignant beauty of the ruin, which he had gaped at with awe but barely had time to appreciate, and the simple kindliness of the folk who kept the inn, had made him look forward to hanging on there for a day or two and making plans for the future.

In all his life he had seen no surroundings that seemed better suited for the soothing of jangled nerves, the calming of turbulent emotions, the solving of vexatious problems in an atmosphere of true tranquillity. There was another cause for regret. He had wanted—unreasonably, no doubt—to speak to that girl; to find out the cause of her distress and "do something" about it. He knew he had neither the right nor the qualifications for this; but that did not console him. From the moment when, a few days before, that entrancing, fugitive vision had first troubled his heart, it had never wholly left him. The fact that they had hardly exchanged a glance and never a word made no difference to his feeling that, strangers and different though they might be, they were destined to meet again; that, in some mysterious way, their lives were interconnected; that each had something essential to give to the other; that the mere persistence of her image in his mind had an undeniable and hopeful significance.

These assumptions were fantastic, of course. In any case, the events of the last two hours had rudely revealed their fragility. He would probably never set eyes again on the face and form that had enraptured him. Yet, even now, he could not dismiss them from his thoughts. Her image abode with him and recurred, for all his resignation, with the poignancy of a dream remembered on waking.

The sense of frustration, of emptiness, of something decreed yet unfulfilled, accompanied him on this new stage on his flight and distracted his mind from the practical needs of the moment. Now that the news of his disappearance and a more or less accurate description of his person had been picked up by every wireless antenna in the British Isles and others far beyond them, the dread of pursuit and imminent discovery which, until now, had been vague, became urgent and definite. He had never before appreciated the searching vindictiveness of wireless. Now that Droitwich had spoken, his name had gone out into all lands and had been registered, consciously or unconsciously, in millions of idle minds. He could imagine the raised eyebrows of his friends and business acquaintances discussing this titbit of news at home in North Bromwich. He could hear myriads of anonymous listeners—from the uttermost crofts of the Hebrides to Australian sheep stations, from storm-tossed trawlers at sea and the cars of mobile police to hunters' camps in the heart of Africa—repeating in various accents the fateful syllables. Owen Lucton . . . Owen Lucton . . . Owen Lucton. . . . The whisper circled the world. He was now, in the fullest sense, a fugitive. His friend the Chief Constable of North Bromwich had sent the word forth. From this moment the hands of all law-abiding men were against him. The hunt was up.

Where should he go now? Though starlight still illumined the stones of the Abbey and the valley pastures, the flanks of the mountain rose black and impenetrable on either side. Before he could "take to the heather", as other romantic outlaws had done before him, he would have to surmount or evade incalculable obstacles—gateless hedges, dense tangles of woodland, treacherous morasses—which, in the dark, would obstruct him with a series of checks and pitfalls. Before daybreak, at least, it was unlikely that any hostile observer would be abroad. Until the light came he would be reasonably safe if he followed the valley road up to the point where, as Bert had told him, it ceased to exist or petered out into pony-tracks crossing the sheep-walks.

It was not so much a road, indeed, as a narrrow gully, meandering deep-sunken between grassy banks topped with dark hedges of holly entwined with honeysuckle which could be smelt but not seen. Its uncertain course, varied by steep rising pitches and descents that appeared to be bottomless, followed, roughly, the contours of the invisible mountain. In the main it was certainly climbing: so much Mr. Lucton could guess from the increasing coolness of the air and from a sense of renewed vitality and exhilaration.

For, in spite of his twenty-three-mile walk, he was not conscious of any fatigue and felt oddly light-hearted. There was one anxious moment, indeed, when the ordeal of passing a farm where the sheep-dogs, aroused by his cautious footfalls, broke out into a fury of barking, made his heart beat fast—as he crouched in the hedge, a man poked out his head from a bedroom window and cursed them in a strange tongue which he took to be Welsh—and another, a little later, when a fox startled him by darting out of the hedgerow under his nose. The fox appeared to be less disturbed by the incident than he; for when it had ambled on for a few yards, a grey shadow in the starlight, it turned round, with one forepaw uplifted, and gazed back at him, with interest rather than anxiety, and then trotted forward again. After this the beast continued to keep him company, running on and then halting and turning to look, as though it were making allowances for a slow-footed companion whom it would be sorry to lose. This behaviour was not merely very odd, Mr. Lucton thought, but rather exciting. His romantic fancy, which by this time was getting to work again, began to speculate whether this ghost-like creature might be not just an ordinary fox but a were-fox supernaturally "sent" to guide him (or to lead him astray) or, alternatively, whether some instinct might have revealed to it that he was no enemy, but, like itself, a shy, hunted fugitive worthy of sympathy.

Whatever the fox may have thought of him, if it thought at all, it decided after a mile or so that it had had enough of him, and vanished through a glat in the hedge as silently as it had arrived. Mr. Lucton was sorry to lose the creature's company, but soon saw why it had left him. At the bottom of the hill, within forty yards of the glat, he came suddenly on a little collection of sleeping cottages and, on the other side of a narrow bridge spanning the Dulas, a small building that looked like a church or chapel and a humble graveyard shadowed by aged yews. The hamlet, it seemed, marked the end of the mountain road which, at this point, forked into two unmetalled tracks. He chose the one that bore to the right, and crossed the river.

Now the going grew rougher. The road, its twistings still defined by straggling hedges whose branches met overhead, resembled the dry bed of a torrent, loose pebbles alternating with diagonal shelves of water-worn sandstone. It was rising abruptly, too, as he could tell by the strain on his legs and his labouring heart which compelled him, from time to time, to halt and take breath. It was probably rather stupid, he thought, to go on like this until he exhausted himself; but there seemed to be no spot in that tar-black tunnel in which he could comfortably spend the rest of the night, and no gate or gap in the hedge through which he could escape and find a bed in the bracken. So he climbed on and on, frequently slipping on the loose stones and stumbling over the ledges, spurred to needless exertion by a sense of suffocation, a desperate desire to break out, at all costs, into the open.

He must, in the course of this struggle, have risen four or five hundred feet; for when the imprisoning hedges ceased and he emerged from their shelter, he found himself perched high up on a sheer mountainside not far beneath the summits which, like a gigantic horse-shoe, embraced the head-waters of the Dulas. The air was thin and still and icily cold. The stars shivered with a frosty radiance. He had never, he thought, seen any night sky so superbly canopied since the far-off days of his service in Mesopotamia; yet its magnificence, as well as the magnitude of the mountains which rolled away on every hand to lose themselves in the darkness, was oppressive rather than inspiriting: they emphasized, almost too cruelly, his own loneliness, his own insignificance. Though he was so tired and cold that he would gladly have lain down where he was, he felt an urgent need for some kind of protection or shelter.

At the moment none offered itself but an occasional shallow depression scooped in the turf to shield ewes from wind or snow in the season of lambing. At this height the bracken grew sparsely; the slopes of the mountain were covered by tussocks of sour grass with peaty crevasses between them; so Mr. Lucton was forced to trudge on, if only to keep himself warm, until he saw, on the right of the track, to his relief and surprise, what looked like a group of farm buildings. He approached them warily, remembering the dogs which had barked at him in the lower valley, and was delighted to find that the cottage was deserted and falling to ruin. The barn, though its door had been snatched away by the wind, was in better condition; and here, in an air that smelt strongly of sheep, he laid himself down on a pile of last year's bracken.

He had no idea what time it was—in the discomfort of the previous night's lodging he had forgotten to wind his watch—but whatever hour it might be, he felt no inclination to sleep. Rather guiltily, remembering the inflammable nature of his bed, he lit a pipe to soothe his nerves and surrendered himself to reflection.

First of all, he tried to recall the precise wording of the wireless Police Message and its description of himself. *Age: fifty-one, but looks older*. He could see Leith's critical candour in that. *Medium height; inclined to be stout*. It was, alas, undeniable—though he felt he must have lost a couple of stone during the last few days. *Rather bald, with greyish hair and a military moustache*. The last detail, fortunately removable, was most likely to betray him. He might, of course, grow a beard; but that would take time, and he resented the idea of making himself look even older. His best course, he decided, was to shave off his moustache as soon as it became light. It was lucky that he had supplied himself with shaving-tackle, though the growth would be difficult to remove unless he first clipped it. As for his clothing: that was a most satisfactory disguise. It was evident—and typical of his laziness—that Fowler had neither noticed the fact that the parcel addressed to the rummage sale had been tampered with nor that the black business coat and cashmere trousers were hanging in the wardrobe—while the housemaid, the only witness of the substitution, had gone to her home in Dorset. Would she have listened to the wireless that night? By ten o'clock, unless she were courting in the lanes, she would probably be fast asleep; and it was doubtful, in any case, that West Country folk would think of "tuning-in" to the Midland Regional programme. Things were not so bad as they might have been. With this final consoling reflection Mr. Lucton burrowed into his bed of bracken and fell asleep.

This was his best night since the day he left home. He had no means of knowing what time it was when he woke; but on the tops of the mountains the sun was already shining out of a blue sky, and the rolling prospect whose lonely vastness had crushed and dispirited him overnight seemed no longer threatening. In an air so bright and exhilarating as this it would have been hard not to feel buoyant. When he had eaten part of his packet of biscuits and cheese, he shouldered his rucksack and went in search of water for shaving. He found it, not far from his barn: a gin-clear runnel, stained by peat to the colour of brown sherry, tinkling into a mossy pool surrounded by pale rosettes of butterwort. On the rock near-by, a small brown bird, a meadow-pipit, apparently the only living creature in that high sanctuary, flitted to and fro with quick, metallic chirpings.

Mr. Lucton slipped off his rucksack and undid the straps. From the moment he touched them, he felt that something was wrong—as, indeed, it was. The rucksack was not his. It contained a soiled shirt and a not so clean pair of pyjamas; a silk tie, with diagonal stripes of claret, dark blue and gold; a set (thank heaven!) of shaving tackle; a notebook in which lines of verse had been scribbled, and a book called *New Poems* by a writer unknown to him—Alistair Shiel.

He surveyed the strange contents of the rucksack lugubriously.

It was easy to see how he had come by it, for in its shape, its size and its newness, it was almost identical with his own, and in the hurried confusion of his departure he had picked it up without thinking. On the whole, its owner had had the better of the exchange: he had always regretted buying those pink pyjamas. In any case, it was now irreparable. He felt inclined to regard it as a rather good joke.

It seemed less of a joke when he came to examine its implications. To begin with, since the rucksack contained its owner's pyjamas, it was reasonable to suppose that its absence had been discovered before he went to bed. No doubt the tired landlady would have been sent toiling up to the top of the tower in search of it—only to discover that Mr. Lucton had vanished and find Bert sleeping alone. He could imagine the whole train of alarms and questions and speculations. Why had he vanished, and whither? One of those knowing fishermen was bound to associate his disappearance with the police message which their joking had underlined. By this time they would probably have attempted to communicate with the police. He thanked heaven that the telephone line did not run up the valley.

But that was not all, nor even the worst. Recalling the contents of his own rucksack, which would certainly have been carefully examined, he remembered among them the one remaining piece of evidence of identity; the pair of Harris trousers which he had stowed away when he took to shorts. Did his tailor inscribe his customers' names on the labels he sewed in their trousers? Was the tailor's name stamped on the buttons? He could not remember. A moment later it occurred to him that his Harris suit had actually been made by a country tailor in Oban, an old man with a thin white beard, who would hardly have been likely to indulge in such luxuries as buttons of his own, and was probably dead by now. This comforted him a little until he remembered that the rucksack also contained a pair of worn socks. Were these marked with woven initials or laundry labels? He thought it unlikely, but could not say.

In any case, this ridiculous incident had made his position more precarious. The sooner he escaped from the neighbourhood of Llandewi the better. There was no time to waste. It was easy enough to shave his cheeks and chin; the cold mountain water was so soft; but the task of removing his moustache was painful as well as difficult. The blade of the safety-razor had been designed for lighter work: the process was like setting a lawn-mower to reap a cornfield, and by the time he had cleared the last stubble he knew by the taste of blood—for the pool made an inadequate mirror—that he had sliced his lip deeply. That couldn't be helped. From the little he was able to see of his reflection he felt satisfied that none of his casual acquaintances could possibly recognize him.

The most urgent necessity now was to get away from the mountain. The valley road, no doubt, would be closed, as would every other recognizable track, including the one on which he had been travelling. Apart from the embarrassing lack of cover, his best plan was obviously to keep to the open moorland, to cross the great horse-shoe of horizon that now enclosed him and drop down into the plains. His instinct, as it had been from the beginning of his flight, was to press westward—a course which gave him now the immediate advantage of having the sun behind him. He recrossed the road and began to climb, but had covered no more than forty yards of the upward slope before a sight met his eyes that made him drop to his knees. He saw, silhouetted against the bright sky above the rim of the mountain, a scattered file of five stationary horsemen who appeared to be patrolling the crest. Keeping as close to the ground as he could, he crept down again and turned eastward with the purpose of crossing the upper part of the valley and gaining the ridge on the other side of it.

This was even more difficult going than the steep slope; for the bottom of the basin was filled with the bog in which the Dulas rose: alternations of peaty crevasses and patches of sogging moss strewn with snowy drifts of cotton-grass which, when he had floundered knee-deep into one of them, he knew to be even more treacherous. Stooping low and keeping his eyes on his feet, he held on this difficult course, until, lifting them suddenly, he saw that the ridge for which he had been aiming was occupied by another and slightly larger company of horsemen moving slowly along the crest to left and right.

There was left to him, it appeared, only one direction of possible escape: due northward towards the ridge which formed the horse-shoe's concavity. His only doubt was whether his floundering progress could bring him to the crest before the two detachments joined forces. There was just a chance, he felt, that neither had yet seen him, for those on the western limb were still stationary. It was a hope that began to fade rapidly when a hurried glance showed him that these, too, were on the move. Still, thanks to his good night's sleep, he was fairly fresh, and the violent exercise of the last four days had brought him into good condition; so he plunged on and on, avoiding the crevasses and patches of bog as carefully as he could, though not without mishaps. It would be a close race, and he knew it; but the horsemen still moved in such a leisurely manner—he supposed the tussocky ground compelled the horses to walk—that for the moment he seemed to be gaining on them.

By the end of a quarter of an hour of desperate struggling he judged himself to be within a few minutes of the top, and the gap between the converging patrols still lay open so widely that he felt he could afford to allow himself a short "breather". He crouched, with no more than his head above ground, in the bottom of a crevasse which resembled one of the shallow trenches his battalion had dug during the march on Kut. It was odd how all his movements this morning—and even his state of tense apprehensiveness—reminded him of the war: if he had had a rifle, he thought, he could easily have taken a long-range pot at the hostile silhouettes on the eastern skyline, while any new enemy coming up over the ridge on the north would have made an easy target. Two hundred yards, he judged the range, with no need to make any allowance for the wind. Say two hundred and twenty. In spite of the appalling surface he ought to be able to manage that dash for the gap in three minutes at the most. Three minutes . . . He breathed deeply and braced himself for it; then cautiously levered himself up out of the trench and went over the top.

But no sooner had he straightened his legs than he was forced to drop down again; for, at that moment, the heads and bodies of three more mounted men bobbed over the ridge full in front of him. That, no doubt, was what the other detachments had been waiting for. Now the hostile circle was closed. He knew he was finished.

Perhaps not quite finished, he told himself. Supposing—and there was always the chance—he hadn't been spotted, he might still lie doggo without being discovered while the horsemen, advancing fanwise, swept down the valley. In that wilderness of bog and cracked peat they couldn't search every cranny. He crawled back into his trench and crouched miserably waiting for the triumphant view-halloo and the humiliating surrender.

Huddled there, his clothes blackened with splashes of peat and sodden to the thighs, and still, against hope, vaguely hopeful, Mr. Lucton was forced to confess a grudging admiration for the swift efficiency of the police who, at a few hours' notice, had apparently mobilized half the farmers of the mountain to join in their man-hunt. As a North Bromwich man, he could not help feeling a paradoxical civic pride in this achievement: that was one up for the hardware city.

What troubled him more than the prospect of being captured was the probable sequel. Though the Police Message had politely mentioned loss of memory as the cause of his flight, he supposed he was likely to be treated as a lunatic. He remembered a novel he had read in his youth—was it one of Charles Reade's?—in which the minds of sane men had been broken by the use of strait-jackets and solitary confinement and all sorts of monstrous cruelties. There was also a recent American film he had been dragged out to see by Muriel, in which a charming young man, as rational as himself, had been imprisoned and found it hard to establish his sanity in a court of law.

These examples filled Mr. Lucton with dread. Though he believed himself as sane as the Chief Constable and even saner than most of his conventional North Bromwich colleagues and rivals, he despaired of ever being able to prove it. The more candid he was, the less chance he would have of being believed.

He could see himself spending the rest of his natural life, a sane—an unusually sane—man, among the inmates of what was now euphemistically called a Mental Hospital, but was, none the less, an Asylum. That would be a heavy price to pay for five days of freedom!

In the meantime there was nothing to do but await his fate and hope for the best. The uncomfortable moments dragged by without anything happening. Then, at last, his alert ears caught approaching hoof-beats. From the sound, he judged that there must be a greater number of pursuers than he had imagined, and their advance was oddly irregular: long moments of silence alternating with swift bursts of movement that sounded like a stampede. The hoof-beats grew nearer and nearer. Mr. Lucton lay flat on his back in the bottom of the trench, holding his breath for fear that the sound of it might be heard. They were right on the top of him now. He closed his eyes and waited. A thudding of hooves and a snort on the very brink of his trench compelled him to open them. He raised himself and found himself looking up into the shaggy face of a wild mountain pony, which swerved away violently when he moved, whinnying shrilly and sending a spatter of peat into his face. Then the sound of a fierce stampede began again. Mr. Lucton, cautiously lifting his head to the top of his crevasse, saw twenty or thirty others streaming away down the valley, wildly tossing their shaggy manes and tails and floundering in the bog as they went. In the middle distance the narrowing arc of mounted men advanced, slowly, relentlessly, urging the herded drove before them. Sheep-dogs trotted obediently at their heels. The truth burst on his mind abruptly. The spectacle which had filled him with terror was not a man-hunt, but a pony-drive!

His first feeling was one of astonishment rather than relief. Then the comical aspect of his discovery struck him and he burst out laughing. He crawled out of his hiding-place to watch the fun. What a moment before had seemed a grim situation had become an unusual and charming experience which he wouldn't have missed for anything. It was a pretty sight, with an attractive element of wildness, to see the drove of thirty or forty ponies strung out down the valley, pausing sometimes to crop tufts of grass, as though they had nothing to fear, and then, with one accord, taking alarm and breaking into a furious gallop. There were several stallions among them, like the wild-eyed black which had stamped and snorted on the edge of his trench, but the greater part were mares, with mouse-coloured foals, no more than a few months old, trotting timidly at their side. Even the farmers taking part in the drive looked less formidable at close quarters than they had appeared gigantically silhouetted against the sky. They were most of them small, rugged, bearded men who rode with a slouching seat, long stirruped, and in the colour of their clothes and their general air of shagginess resembled their mounts. The last straggler of the cavalcade, an ancient white-bearded man on a sturdy grey, raised his stick as he passed, and shouted some salutation, which sounded friendly, in Welsh.

Mr. Lucton waved back. This imaginary peril was over, at any rate; but that didn't mean he was free from the threat of pursuit. For the moment, the sense of immediate relief had masked all his other preoccupations; but now he must follow his original plan of escape with the handicap of more than an hour of lost time. He did not find it easy to set about it. The emotional and physical strain had unnerved him; his heart was still racing tumultuously; he felt oddly light-headed.

Distrusting his powers of scaling the greater barriers on either hand, he decided to make for the nearer and lower crest over which the last horseman had appeared. From this (remembering the shape he had seen from the woodland which he still thought of as the Forest of Arroy) he imagined that the mountains would fall abruptly to the Wye Valley and offer a swift, if somewhat exacting, descent to the plain.

He approached the crest with eager expectations of the great view that awaited him. From that point, which could hardly be less than two thousand feet above sea-level, he might hope to command all the mountainous confusion of mid-Wales: that welter of huge, mysterious hills, the wildest in Britain, which he had often wistfully gazed on when he was a boy. It seemed odd to him, and encouraging as a sign of spiritual youth, that even in the midst of his present anxieties he could still feel this thrill of boyish excitement in a moment for which he had been longing for forty years. He must hurry, he thought, for the peerless morning blue was clouding over and the sun had already gone in.

And when, panting, he reached the crest, there was little to see: nothing, indeed, but the northern buttresses of the mountain, black in shadow, falling precipitously to foot-hills swathed in dark woods. Since dawn, a colder air moving from the north-west had blanketed all the low-lying land in a sea-white mist. Rolling wave on wave, it had already impinged on the woodlands. Now, meeting the warm flank of the mountain, it was thrown, or sucked up by rising currents of air, into vast billows and flying sheets of vapour that resembled spindrift snatched from the crests of a silent surf.

It was the association of this enormous assault with utter silence which made it impressive and even terrible for all its beauty. Before Mr. Lucton realized what was happening, the surges of mist had overspread the whole mountain, concealing not merely the falling escarpment and the dark chasm at his feet, but the series of prominent summits on which he had counted as landmarks. Even the ridge he had crossed a few moments before was now lost to him; though it was still light, he was as utterly blinded by the enveloping whiteness as if it had been pitch-dark. The mist condensed in fine globules on his eyebrows and eyelashes and on the wool of his rough tweed coat; and the odd thing about it was that although, judging by the area it had encroached on while he stood watching its progress, the white tide must have been floating at an enormous speed, it appeared, as soon as it reached him, to become stationary; not the faintest breath of wind fanned it; not a blade of the tufted grass at his feet was swayed by it as it passed. The stillness seemed to him contradictory and even uncanny, until it came to him that this Atlantic current of moisture-laden air had been scooped up into the sky by the concave face of the mountain, and that he himself was wrapped in the heart of a cloud that was being born about him as he stood.

Whatever the explanation of the phenomenon might be, one of its results was obvious: nobody in his senses would set out that day to search for him on the mountain. Another—for it cut both ways—was that it would be equally hard for him to continue his flight. Mr. Lucton rebelled against this difficulty. Though unskilled in mountain-craft, he had always prided himself on his bump of direction and was ready to trust to it. From the glimpse he had caught of the disappearing landscape, he believed his memory still carried an accurate picture of the lie of the land. As he watched it, he had stood facing north-west, and, since then, he believed he had not changed his position. For his greater encouragement he remembered noticing a downward path, little more than a sheep-track, which had appeared to cross the flank of the mountain diagonally in the direction of a wooded gully six or seven hundred feet below him.

He decided to attempt the descent. It wasn't easy; for the sheep-path proved to be much steeper and narrower than he had imagined, with abrupt drops over which he stepped before he was even aware of them, since it was impossible to see more than two or three feet ahead. The fourth of these deposited him in a moss-covered runnel which soaked the seat of his shorts and his shirt-tail. When he had recovered from the jar to his spine and the wetting and picked himself up, he began to feel doubtful if the path he was following were the one he had chosen. At that point, indeed, it split into three of equal size and steepness, and he found it difficult to decide which of these he should take. The one he finally chose proceeded perversely to change its mind (as a damned sheep-track *would*, he thought) and turned back on itself, uphill, in what he imagined to be the direction of Llandewi—the last place in the world he wanted to reach. Its whole behaviour was so irresponsible, Mr. Lucton reflected, that there was little likelihood of its holding on this dangerous course. Sooner or later, in all probability, it would turn downhill again, as, in fact, after more than half a mile of aimless meandering, it did—so decidedly that he was forced to cling to bushes of heather to check his descent.

Then, suddenly, the track gave up the ghost altogether, losing itself on a shelving platform devoid of vegetation and covered with screes. Mr. Lucton, still hopeful that after this interruption it would continue, decided to prospect. The sloping shelf was so steep, and the screes were so loose, that he thought it prudent not to conduct these investigations on his feet for fear of slipping. Squatting down like an ape, he propelled himself forward with his hands, his legs stretched out in front of him. He moved cautiously, no more than a few inches at a time. In the direction he had chosen the rock soon shelved more gradually than he had expected; its surface, though shiny with condensation, was no longer made treacherous by loose screes. He was wondering, in fact, whether it mightn't be safe to abandon this undignified method of progress, when, all of a sudden, his advancing feet encountered no support, and he found himself sitting on a ledge with the lower part of his legs dangling free.

Mr. Lucton shivered. There might be no need for alarm: he had more than once taken a toss over a shallow ledge of this kind. Though he couldn't touch bottom, there was no reason, he felt, why he shouldn't lower himself carefully in the hope of finding it. Yet the density of the mist, which at this point was so thick that he couldn't even distinguish the shape of his toes, deterred him from any rash experiment. After a moment's meditation, he picked up a fragment of sandstone and dropped it gently into the milky void, listening attentively for the sound of an impact at the end of its fall. No sound came. Perhaps it had lodged in a bush of heather. Groping behind him he discovered a larger fragment of rock, the size of his doubled fists, and cast it more violently. For a few moments, again, he was puzzled by hearing nothing. Then there came from below—from far below—a remote splintering sound followed by another and yet another. Two huge birds—he supposed they were ravens—came soaring out of the mist with raucous cries. He could feel the rush of air from invisible wings as they beat above him. He realized, with a thrill of horror, that he was sitting nonchalantly on the edge of a precipice.

The first phrase that took shape in his mind was "My God!"

In the second he thanked goodness that Muriel wasn't there. "She would have said it was all my fault," he told himself, laughing feebly.

Though he laughed, he was almost too scared to lift his feet out of the abyss in which they were dangling, and his retreat, on all fours, was even less dignified than his ape-like approach. When he had regained the heather at the head of the screes, he was almost too exhausted by the mingled emotions of terror and relief to think consecutively. The two birds swooped down in turn, so close that for a moment he saw them. If they were angry, he thought, they would probably make for his eyes. He rolled over on his face, protecting his head with his hands, and heard no more of them. Lying there, in the wet heather, he realized that the Providence which protects fools had actually saved him from a particularly brutal form of death by violence. On one thing he was quite determined: he was making no more experiments; he was not going to move another inch in any direction until the mist lifted; he would cling to that spot even if he had to stay there till he starved, he told himself.

It took a long time to lift. In spite of the cold and discomfort of his sloping bed, he must have fallen asleep. When he woke, it was certainly lighter. There was even a suspicion of bleared sunlight in the air above his head, and he could see the whole length of the scree-strewn slope to the edge of the precipice. Then a stronger gust of wind tore the thinning curtain to tatters, and rising to his feet, he saw through the gap it opened the full horror of the position from which he had escaped. From the ledge over which his legs had dangled, the cliff fell away in an almost perpendicular drop of four hundred feet. On either side the sheer precipice extended farther than he could see. It seemed clear that, on this eastern face of the mountain at least, there was no possibility of his reaching the plain.

He was anxious, in any case, to remove himself from his present position. Safe though he was, the proximity of that ghastly drop still gave him the shivers. So he turned his back on it and scrambled, as best he could, up the heathery slope, then turned north-west again in the hope of regaining the point from which he had started. The mist was still patchy, thinning at times to clear windows through which he could see vignettes of the wooded foot-hills and sunlit plain, momentarily startling in their beauty and vividness, then fading, and finally vanishing as the impalpable veil swept over them. For long periods, having learnt his lesson, he decided it was more prudent to halt, pushing on again as soon as he could see a few yards in front of him. Thus, after an hour or more of rough walking, he reached what he judged from the short bursts of sunshine to be the northern escarpment and prepared to descend it.

This time he was not trusting to any wayward sheep-track. However difficult it might be, he was determined, barring precipices, to go straight downward; and for a time this new plan worked reasonably well. Indeed, after a few hundred feet, the surface improved, heather giving place to sparse bracken through which he could pick his way without fear of sudden collapses. And then, to his surprise and delight, he saw beneath him a road—or at least a wheel-marked cart-track—pursuing a diagonal course which climbed on his left to the deserted summits and sank on his right to the plain.

"That's more like it," he thought exultantly. "I should have been on it three hours ago if I hadn't been so damned clever. Can't think how I came to miss it. Now, thank heaven, it's full steam ahead!"

He was encouraged, again, by the frequent appearance of sheep, which, he supposed, denoted his nearness to some farm in the foot-hills. They loomed out of the mist before him as big as ponies, then scampered away—all but one, a monstrous ram with dewy fleece, which stood his ground, angrily stamping, and lowered his horns as though he were preparing to charge. Mr. Lucton didn't like the look of him; but at the last moment the beast changed its mind and ran away after its ewes; and, a moment later, rounding a curve in the track, he saw in front of him something even more surprising: a solitary human figure, wearing a rucksack, the sight of which brought his heart into his mouth. It was a young woman, wearing a green blouse and a tawny Harris skirt. It was She . . .

(IX)

THE YOUNG DAMOSEL

MR. LUCTON paused in his stride and gazed at her with an uneasy, defensive smile, not knowing what to say. She looked small and pathetic and lonely sitting there in her mist-bedewed tweeds, her hair, too, bedraggled with dew, her features pale and compressed. She returned his gaze without interest or surprise, then, at last, smiled faintly.

"So it's only you," she said. "I heard footsteps. I thought it was Alistair."

"Your friend?"

"Yes. You've shaved off your moustache and cut yourself."

"I'm not used to safety-razors," Mr. Lucton apologized, "and I think the blade must have been an old one too."

"I'm sure it was, if it was Alistair's. I suppose it *was* you who stole his rucksack last night?"

"I picked it up by mistake in the dark, if that's what you mean. I'ld much rather have my own, as a matter of fact. Was he very much upset?"

"I should think he was! What he worried about most was his wretched notebook. You'ld have thought at least it was Leonardo's or Beethoven's," she added bitterly. Her lips quivered slightly as she spoke.

"I'm terribly sorry," Mr. Lucton said. "Of course, if I'd known. . . . You see, the whole thing was just an unfortunate accident. I don't *want* your friend's rucksack, you know. In fact, I'ld be much obliged if you'ld take it and give it back to him with my apologies."

She shook her head. "It's no good your giving it to me. I don't suppose I shall see him again—at least I hope not."

"I'm sorry . . ." Mr. Lucton repeated; but she changed the subject abruptly.

"I suppose you shaved off your moustache," she said, "because you're the man? That wireless message, I mean."

The directness of the question took Mr. Lucton aback. He hesitated.

"Well, what if I am?"

"So Alistair was right after all. He watched you, you know, while the message was being read. He's awfully observant: I'll say that for him. All that part about having lost your memory . . ."

"No. That's quite all right, thank you. I remember seeing you and your friend four days ago, just this side of the Malverns. How's that for memory?"

"I remember seeing you, too. But you weren't wearing shorts. there was one thing in the message that puzzled me . . ."

"What?"

"The Pearce-Tregaron. Did you pinch it?"

Mr. Lucton laughed out loud. "You still think I'm a thief? Of course not. It was my own. A brand-new one too."

She regarded him quizzically. "Now that makes another difficulty—or rather, two."

"Let me try to clear them up."

"Well . . . what have you done with it? The Pearce-Tregaron, I mean?"

"I left it at the bottom of a river. You probably won't believe me . . ."

"Yes, I do, though it does sound a trifle original. It's hardly the sort of thing you'ld expect from . . ."

"Go on. Say 'a man in his senses'," Mr. Lucton broke in. "But I assure you, I'm perfectly sane."

"That's one comfort, anyway."

"And what is your second difficulty?"

"Well, if you're *that* sort of person—the owner of a car like that, I mean—what on earth were you doing with that little man?"

"Bert Hopkins? Of course, that must have looked odd. But you mustn't judge by externals; he's the salt of the earth. He picked me up—or I picked him up—on the day when first I saw you. We've kept company ever since; and jolly good company he was, too. Anything else?"

"I don't want to appear inquisitive or be too . . . well . . . personal; but I really should like to know what it's all about. You don't look as if you'd done anything desperate or violent; but you must have done something, mustn't you? or else they wouldn't be after you—you wouldn't have bolted in a hurry like that, and you wouldn't have shaved off your moustache. That's what makes me wonder . . ."

Mr. Lucton nodded. "Look here, if I tell you the truth, do you think you'll believe me?"

She looked at him so solemnly, so searchingly, that he blushed.

"Yes, I'm sure I'll believe you."

"It's a secret between you and me."

"Of course. After all, nobody's listening."

"Do you mind if I sit down a little nearer, and light my pipe?"

"You've a match? Thank heaven for that! Alistair borrowed my matches last night and forgot to return them as usual. I've been dying for a cigarette."

She took a case from the pocket of her skirt, a delicate, expensive thing of platinum with a jewelled initial "D" on the front of it. There were four cigarettes inside it, with cotton-wool filter-tips.

"Won't you have one?" she said. "They're Turkish."

"Thanks. I'ld rather smoke my pipe." He struck a match for her. His hand trembled as he held it.

"You're shaky, aren't you?" she said solicitously. "I think I'd better take it, if you don't mind. Hurry up, though: we mustn't waste matches."

As she took the match from him her fingers touched his; they were small and shapely, yet capable—astonishingly delicate compared with his blunt, peat-mired hands. This brief contact made Mr. Lucton even more tremulous—that and the sound of her voice, the exquisite precision of her speech in which every syllable seemed as clean-cut as a diamond. They were all of a piece with the rest of her, with the refinement of body and spirit, the limpidity, the frankness which he had divined, in a flash of bitter-sweet apprehension, when she had swung past, her hair flying in the wind, on that Malvern hill-side. Once again he felt in his heart that obscure commotion, that strange yearning, that aching aspiration, which had made this child's very presence a delight and a torment.

"Oh, that's better," she said, with a sigh of content. "Now tell me all about it—that is, if you want to."

There was nothing he wanted to do more. He leapt at this, the first opportunity for confession that had come his way for longer than he could remember. If he had possessed any sort of safety-valve—a friend with whom he could have blown off steam occasionally—he need never have reached this dangerous state of compression. But he had no friends—one didn't make them in business, and those of his youth had been either submerged by marriage, like himself, or wiped out by the war. Come to that, he wasn't at all sure that a man friend, however intimate, could have satisfied his need. Human nature—his nature, at any rate—demanded a confidant of the opposite sex. That was where Muriel had failed him. No doubt he had failed Muriel too; but that was beside the point. He found this unreserved opening of the heart a ticklish business, requiring all sorts of unexpected circumstances: first, odd though this seemed, that the recipient of his confidences should be a stranger, and, again, that the confession should be made at a particular moment and in the right surroundings. Here every condition was satisfied. He was alone, in that cloud-enwrapped solitude on the roof of the world, with the companion whom he would have chosen.

So, sitting on the damp ledge of rock beside her, Mr. Lucton began—shyly at first, and with difficulty—for he had lost the habit of intimate speech and expressed himself awkwardly—but later, thawed by a silence that was more encouraging than words, with increasing freedom and fluency. He told her of his suburban boyhood, the long dreams of youth, the ardours of first love and marriage, the struggles and triumphs of early manhood. He told her of how he had served in the war, expressing, for the first time, that unique sense of personal heroism which had made him feel like a paladin and had ended in disillusion.

"That was before you were born," he said, "yet it seems like yesterday. In spite of everything one suffered, you know—and at times it was damnable—I can't help looking back on those days with a sort of romantic regret for them. One didn't fear death, for one thing; it was too familiar. And one didn't fear growing old. One lived every moment, intensely, on—how shall I put it?—a different plane of existence. When the war stopped, it felt just like being let down with a bump on to a new kind of world—and not a particularly pleasant one. You young people have never known any other, so you can't possibly imagine what that meant to us. Whether we happened to be blown up or not, we're all cases of shell-shock: more or less wounded men."

She nodded. "I think I know what you feel. My father's a bit like you. He was a regular soldier, of course. That meant that he'd lost his job, and he's never found another. But please go on . . ."

Mr. Lucton told her of the breach between himself and Muriel, and how, gradually, it had involved his children as well.

"On the surface we're what you'ld call a happy family. We have plenty of fun of a sort, and we more or less understand one another. If an outsider attacked any one of us the others would all rally round. That's only natural, isn't it? A troop of baboons would behave in exactly the same way. And yet, somehow, I always feel there's something between me and the rest of them—an invisible barrier, like those rays jewellers use for protecting their show-cases from burglars. Once you've passed it, although you can't see it, off goes the alarm, and you step back in a hurry and rather ashamed of yourself. I've consoled myself often by thinking that it's nothing but the difference between middle age and youth: that—what shall I say?—we're working on different wave-lengths. But that can't be it. If it were, I should feel the same when I'm talking to you as I do when I'm talking to Dorothy, my younger daughter. And I don't. Not a bit."

"No . . . I don't think it's altogether that," she said gravely. "But go on."

"Where was I? Ah, yes, the end of the war. A different world, but one had to make the best of it, and I don't think I failed entirely."

He told her, not without pride, of his growing fortunes. He couldn't help boasting a little about his financial success, though, even as he spoke, he had an uneasy feeling that talking about money did not impress her. He was anxious, however candid, to make the best of himself, always watching her face—not merely because its beauty and innocent gravity ravished him, but because her features (and, above all, her eyes) so clearly mirrored her unspoken thoughts . . . "like a mountain tarn ruffled by passing breezes," he told himself. Sometimes she smiled faintly—as when he told her of his interview with the purchaser of his old house. But the smile was rather one of compassion for himself than of amusement at Mr. Hogget's gaucheries. All through this prolonged narration he was encouraged and warmed by the certainty that, for once, his emotions and motives—however small, unimportant, or even childishly ridiculous—were being acknowledged with a deeper understanding and sympathy than he had ever hoped for. From the first his heart had assured him that this would be so, yet the actuality moved him, none the less. In that high and misty solitude a miracle had removed his loneliness.

So he came to the scene by the river: the moment of emancipation in which his eyes had been opened to the astonishing fact that the things for which he had toiled and lived were vain and unprofitable. He told her how he had sat, half-dazed by his fall, on the river-bank; how he had wrestled in thought with the devil's (or the angel's?) advocate; how, in an access of sublime (or base) irresponsibility, he had left his past drowned in the Pearce-Tregaron and set forth on the highly-coloured series of adventures which had carried him in its climax to this desolate spot on the flank of Mynydd Savaddan.

"What d'you think of it all?" he demanded.

She laughed; delightfully, Mr. Lucton thought.

"Well, you haven't lost your memory, anyway."

"I told you I hadn't. Of course, I've been talking too much. I never talk to anybody. But that's not what I mean. What d'you think of *me?* That's what I want to know. Am I mad or sane—I assure you I haven't the least idea which—or . . . well . . . am I just a romantic old fool who ought really to be ashamed of himself?"

She hesitated, facing him gravely. Then her eyes smiled.

"You're romantic, most certainly," she said, "and perhaps a bit of a fool—but rather a nice one, I think."

Mr. Lucton, tremulous with adoration, lamely disowned the compliment and her tactful suppression of his second adjective.

"Do you know," she went on, "when I saw you come round the corner out of the mist, I was simply scared stiff?"

"Of *me?* My dear child!"

"Well, wasn't that reasonable? A man wanted by the police? When they say 'loss of memory' it generally means something worse. For all I knew, you were an escaped lunatic or even a criminal; and you really did look pretty terrifying, you know, with that cut on your lip and black to the waist with peat."

"But you're not scared of me now," he pleaded, "and you're not going to give me away?"

"Of course not. I'm glad you turned up. These damned mountain mists are bad enough, anyway. It's a bit clearer now, so I ought to be getting on."

"Where are you going?" Mr. Lucton asked humbly.

"Home. Over there into Radnorshire. If it weren't for the mist you could see the mountain just beyond where we live. It's called Forest Fawr."

"I know. That's where the North Bromwich water comes from. There's a house—a house under the water. I've always wanted to see it."

"I suppose you've read that book. Well, you can't see much of it now: just a bit of the garden wall when the lake runs low. How right you were when you called yourself romantic!"

"But . . ." He hesitated. "That must be thirty or forty miles away. You can't possibly get there to-night."

"I shan't try to. There must be some farms on this side of the mountain, and I'm certain of finding shelter for the night. Welsh people are beautifully hospitable when you know how to deal with them, as I do. I couldn't walk much farther, anyway," she went on, with a sigh. "I've been wandering over the mountains all night as it is."

"Alone?"

"Yes . . . That couldn't be helped. I didn't mind it. But I'm fearfully hungry."

"Good Lord, what a fool I am! But why didn't you tell me before? I've plenty of biscuits and cheese." He produced the remains of the grease-paper packet and spread it out on the rock between them. "It's horribly sodden and smashed, I'm afraid," he added apologetically.

"But it's food! Oh dear, and I haven't tasted anything but water since dinner last night." Her eyes were greedy.

"Then for heaven's sake eat what there is. You must be starving."

She restrained her hand in mid-air.

"But what about you?"

"I'm all right. I had lots this morning," Mr. Lucton lied cheerfully. " 'Inclined to be stout', as the police message said. Time I started slimming."

She looked at him searchingly. "Oh no, that's not good enough. 'Share alike, partner,' as your little friend would have said."

He laughed. "Very well, then. Ladies first."

Methodically, she divided the biscuits and cheese into mathematical halves. Mr. Lucton watched her eating with fascination. The child was obviously famished and fell on the food with a schoolroom appetite. By the time Mr. Lucton had started to eat, her share had vanished.

"Do have a bit more," he pleaded. "I've far more than I want."

She shook her head firmly. "No, no. I couldn't possibly. You've saved my life: I feel a new woman already." She rose and held out her hand. "Good-bye, and thank you," she said.

Mr. Lucton blushed.

"Would you mind very much," he faltered, "if I went a little way with you?"

"Of course not. The point is: where are you going?"

"Heaven knows. I'm just going on, that's all. I've never known where I was going since I left home. But wherever I do go," he added gloomily, "I'm bound to run into trouble. I don't want to land you in any of my complications."

She laughed with a gaiety that brought back to his mind his first vision of her.

"No, I've complications enough of my own," she said, "but I'm not afraid of yours. Come along then, partner."

If she had been wandering over the mountains all night, she seemed none the worse for it. She was as light on her feet and as agile as a mountain pony. "The miraculous resilience of youth," Mr. Lucton thought, plodding on beside her. Yet this was the greater miracle, he told himself: that he, Owen Lucton, bald and old and fugitive, was at this moment actually taking the place of the unpleasant young man whom, a few days before, he had envied so fiercely. No matter how brief the experience might be, he had attained the height of his hopeless desire and been granted full compensation for all he had suffered.

For a while they walked on in silence. Though he had opened his heart to her, she did not seem in the least inclined to give her own confidences in return. Indeed, now that he was actually with her, the tender scene which he had imagined, under the emboldening influence of the Llandewi beer, seemed less practicable than ever. He knew nothing whatever about her, save that she was hurt and unhappy and lovely and that her home was in Radnorshire, under the shadow of Forest Fawr. The fact that she had been wandering over the mountain all night without her young man, implied a predicament more serious than a mere lovers' quarrel. He wanted to help, to console—or at least to advise her. And she had no intention of letting him. She was more unapproachable at this moment which seemed made for intimacy than in the inn overnight. It was ridiculous, he told himself, that he, a benevolent man of the world with the best of motives, should be intimidated by a mere child. He should have been able to break through this reserve, to demand explanations. But he couldn't. He was too shy.

And, with every step, he reflected bitterly, this enchanting episode was drawing nearer to its end. He tried to prolong it by slackening his pace, but she only went on like the wind. They were now within easy reach of the first belt of woodland which, although they could as yet see no sign of habitation, probably sheltered a farm. In a few more minutes they would be saying good-bye. She paused for a moment.

"I wonder," she said, "if it's worth my while keeping to the road any longer? I think I ought really to make a short cut, dropping down to those trees; there's almost certain to be a farm below them."

"I shouldn't, if I were you," Mr. Lucton dissuaded her. "These distances are terribly deceptive. Those trees look quite near; but they're probably four hundred feet beneath us. The slope's pretty steep, and you might easily get into difficulties."

Playing for time, he explained what had happened to him that morning when he had found himself with his legs dangling over the precipice.

"Oh yes, I know all about that," she said impatiently. "But the mist is quite thin; you can see a long way in front of you now."

"Still, there's always the risk," Mr. Lucton urged, "of your turning an ankle or something in a scramble like that."

"Risk?" She laughed. "I love to take risks. I believe in taking them!"

"Well, if you go," he said obstinately, "I shall insist on coming with you, as far as the edge of those woods, at any rate."

"All right. Come along then," she said. "Just as far as the woods."

He had been right: the descent was more difficult than she had imagined. After a few minutes of scrambling downward they came to the edge of another scree or landslide. Mr. Lucton shook his head in a way that said: "What did I tell you?"

"We shall have to get round this," she said cheerfully.

It made him dizzy to watch her rapidly skirting the precipice while he cautiously picked his way fifty yards behind her. He only wished his feet were as sure and his nerves as good as hers.

"Come along. Hurry up, if you're coming, partner!" she called back. "I believe this damned mist's beginning to thicken again."

It was true. Even as she was speaking her voice became faint. The small beckoning figure in front of him grew cloudy, then vanished. By the time he caught up with her, the milky stuff was so dense that he nearly fell over her.

"Damn and blast!" she said. "That's done it. You were right after all. My luck's out. I suppose we're here for the night."

Mr. Lucton's heart lifted triumphantly. He forbore to explain that his luck, for a change, was in.

"We shall just have to make the best of it," he said with affected melancholy.

They sat down together in silence. It was clear that she had nothing to say, or nothing she thought worth saying. When he spoke, she answered him shortly and without enthusiasm. The atmosphere of delicious intimacy on which he had flattered himself had gone. He began to feel she was finding him a bore and his company an infliction. Mr. Lucton rebelled against this. After all, she was merely behaving like a sulky child. A family man like himself, with grown-up sons and daughters, ought not to put up with her sulks. They found themselves in the same boat—or rather marooned on the same misty island through her childish caprice. He refused to be intimidated by her silence. He had a right to insist on a certain degree of politeness, even if he were forced to take a high hand.

"Look here," he said. "We seem to have got ourselves into a mess, through no fault of mine. We're probably here for the night, as you say; but we've got to put up with each other's company, haven't we? And it's no use sulking."

"I'm not sulking," she answered wearily. "This isn't exactly fun, is it? Do you want me to be . . . chatty?"

"No. I want you . . ." He found it hard to say what he wanted. "I want you to treat me as if I were a human being like yourself, not as if I were a nuisance. You know all about me. I've kept nothing back. I'm quite harmless. Talk of 'share and share alike!' I really think you might give me a little bit in return. Why, I don't even know who you are!"

"I really don't see why you should want to."

"Well, I do," Mr. Lucton said forcibly.

"Oh, don't let us quarrel," she said reproachfully. "I'm so sick of quarrelling."

"Exactly. I'd guessed that already."

"Confession for confession? Is that what you want?"

"I think it would do you no harm. It might even do you good."

"Well, perhaps you're right, partner. My name's Diana Powys. Rather a pretty name, don't you think?"

Mr. Lucton thought it enchanting. "It suits you," he said.

"My father's Lord Clun—you've probably never heard of him—a retired soldier who loses most of the money he's got pretending to be a farmer. We've a beastly house near Belgrave Square, which I loathe, and another I love in Radnorshire, called Glan Irvon. Aged nineteen, but looks older," she mimicked the announcer's voice, "inclined to be thin. Hair—what shall we say?—bedraggled. Complexion fair and passable—though I've never yet sold my photograph to advertise face-cream. Eyes hazel, they tell me . . ."

"I know all about *them*," Mr. Lucton said. "I want to know about *you*."

"Well, I'm telling you as fast as I can. Amusements, walking—if you call this amusing. Religion—not much to speak of. Politics—Communist."

Mr. Lucton laughed. "Now you're pulling my leg."

"Honest to goodness I'm not. All thinking people are Communists. At Oxford, anyway, I'm an undergraduate—please don't say 'ette'—at St. Katherine's. At least last week I was. I've probably been sent down by now."

Mr. Lucton remembered his Tennyson. Princess Ida. "*And sweet girl graduates . . .*" How did it go? He smiled. This picture hardly fitted the Victorian frame.

"And your friend?"

"H'm. I thought you'ld be coming to that before long. His name's Alistair Shiel. He's an undergraduate, too, at the House—that is, Christ Church; but he'll probably soon get an All Souls' Fellowship. He's a poet, you know."

"So I gather," Mr. Lucton said grimly. "It's a new name to me. Of course, I'm old-fashioned . . ."

"And proud of it. Aren't you just proud! He isn't recognized yet as a *major* poet, of course, like Shelley or Auden or Milton or Cecil Day Lewis. But he is terribly good. He's only published one volume, and the poor dear had to pay for the production of that."

"Why?" Mr. Lucton enquired.

"Well, you know what publishers are. Just shopkeepers, playing for safety. Of course, it was very 'left', and above stupid people's heads. Nobody bought it except a few of our friends, and most of those expected Alistair to make them a present of it."

"These shopkeepers," Mr. Lucton thought, "apparently know their business." He said: "Why was that? I mean, why didn't it sell?"

"All geniuses have to go through a period of neglect," she replied sententiously, "especially those who write for the proletariate. And the English hate irony anyway. Alistair really *is* good. He's a brilliant reviewer, too. You should see how he slashes up pernicious reactionaries like Shaw and Wells and all the popular novelists!"

"Has he written any novels himself?" Mr. Lucton asked.

"Oh no. He thinks it an inferior form of art, but he's going to . . . with his tongue more or less in his cheek."

"His slashing reviews won't make him very popular in the literary world, I imagine," Mr. Lucton suggested.

"Oh, you don't understand. He doesn't care about popularity. He wants to make himself *felt*. In Russia his work would be subsidized."

"I see . . ." Mr. Lucton said. "Yes, I see. You're a staunch supporter."

"Of course. He's a Comrade. It's a lovely word, *Tovarich*."

"You're not . . . secretly married by any chance?" Mr. Lucton said timidly.

"Good God, no! *Married?* Marriage is an unhealthy bourgeois convention."

"Well, of course I *am* a bourgeois; so it seems to me a natural and laudable state."

"By your own account, you haven't made much of a job of it," she said mischievously. "Anyway, no intelligent people believe in it any longer. And poets should never marry, as Alistair says."

"He would!" Mr. Lucton thought angrily. "I suppose," he said, "this young man's in love with you?"

"Well, isn't that 'natural and laudable'?"

"Entirely," Mr. Lucton agreed with conviction. "And you . . . You're in love with him?"

She hesitated. "I don't know. That's the devil of it. That's why I've landed myself in this mess. I'm a coward by nature. My mind isn't my own. I'm full of the most despicable and degrading inhibitions. I expect I really ought to go and be psycho-analysed, as Alistair says."

"Oh, I shouldn't waste time on that if I were you," Mr. Lucton said seriously. "If you asked me my candid opinion, I should say you were exceptionally healthy."

"You don't know me, you see. Nobody does but myself. That's the miserable part of it. Do let's change the subject. It isn't interesting, anyway."

"I find it enormously interesting. And I'll tell you one thing for certain: if you were in love, you wouldn't have any doubts about it."

She shook her head.

"It's not so simple as that. To begin with, Alistair and I have a great deal in common. Our beliefs, for instance. We've seen a great deal of one another; and I find him physically attractive . . ."

Mr. Lucton shuddered, but held his peace.

"But there are some things about him I don't like," she went on. "I'm afraid he's a little bit selfish, and no genuine communist ought to be that. Then he's hard in patches. Do you know what I mean? Like nougat. Of course he's Scotch, and Scotsmen are different from us. In their sense of humour, and things like that. And he's a poet, too . . ."

"I should have thought . . ." Mr. Lucton began.

"Don't you believe it! I'm certain all great poets are hard. They jolly well have to be, or the world would just crush them."

"H'm . . . I wish I could help you," Mr. Lucton said. "I'm not . . . what's the word? . . . intellectual; but I've had a good deal of experience in . . . er . . . matters of this kind."

She looked up and smiled. Mr. Lucton forgave the contempt implicit in that smile for its dazzling beauty. He was overwhelmed with compassion and tenderness. It was monstrous that this sombre, conceited young man should have caused her a moment's unhappiness.

"Why did you run away from Llandewi?" he asked her bluntly. "You might just as well tell me."

There came a long pause.

"All right, then. I'll tell you," she said. She shivered. "It's growing colder: the sun must have set, and the mist seems thicker than ever. Have you any idea what time it is?"

"Not the faintest. I forgot to wind up my watch last night."

"And I lent mine to Alistair. What a bore! Not that it matters anyway."

"Won't you have my coat? I'm quite warm."

"And as romantic as ever! Oh no, that won't do. Is there anything . . ." She hesitated . . . "in Alistair's rucksack?"

"Of course. What was I thinking of?"

He opened the rucksack and turned out its contents, displaying the soiled shirt and the grey flannel trousers.

"These trousers will be perfect," she said, as she draped them round her shoulders. She laughed. "What an example of poetic irony . . . or poetic justice! If I were you, I should wrap myself up in that shirt."

Mr. Lucton declined. He disliked being beholden to that young man for anything. Every word she had spoken of him as yet had confirmed his original opinion, and no doubt there was more to come.

"Well, here goes," she said, with a heavy sigh. "It began about three months ago. I've a cousin at Christ Church, quite a nice boy, who's a blue; and Alistair's good at cricket."

"That's the first decent thing I've heard about him," Mr. Lucton thought. All through his life he would have given his eyes to be "good at cricket".

"I first met him in Anthony's rooms," she went on. "All Anthony's friends were quite distressingly hearty—not a bit my kind, although we were cousins—and Alistair, somehow, didn't fit in a bit more than I did. They ate meringues and drank beer and talked about nothing but cricket. You know: Fowler's match and body-line bowling and googlies. So Alistair and I just gravitated into a corner, like two shipwrecked sailors. In fact just like you and me. We found we'd read the same books and thought the same about most things; and, of course, we were both terribly impressed by meeting anyone like ourselves in a place that reeked of bat-oil and buckskin boots and pads, like a cricket-pavilion.

"After that . . . well, it just seemed inevitable. Alistair lent me books about Russia and Communism and the coming World Revolution and Modern Poetry and *Lady Chatterley's Lover*. We met every day. We used to go for long walks and lie talking and reading aloud for hours in a punt on the Cherwell. And, of course, from the very first, he wrote poems about me—not actually so much about *me*, you know, as about proletarian conditions in Clydeside and the East End of London. I got dragged in for the sake of ironical contrast, because my father happened to be a lord. I suppose he wanted to make me ashamed of all that sort of thing, though it really wasn't my fault.

"Poor Anthony was furious with me. He said I'd gone and ruined Oxford cricket by snaffling their best bowler in the middle of the season, and begged me to make Alistair play. But he only laughed at me. He'd wanted to get his blue because he knew it would help him into a good job as a schoolmaster. Now that he'd got it, it didn't matter. Besides, since then he'd decided

H

to make a career in Literature and Politics, and he much preferred spending his time with me because I was his Inspiration. Not as a Laura or Beatrice or anything of that kind, you know—he was terrified of old-fashioned sentiment—but because I irritated him, like the speck of sand that irritates an oyster into making a pearl.

"Of course, I was tremendously flattered. I was in a bad patch at the time. The family had always fought against my going to Oxford, and when I got my way I fancied myself as no end of a rebel. But St. Katherine's wasn't a bit rebellious: it was just deadly tame—full of rather dowdy young women with sentimental attachments and no other idea in their heads but getting a good degree and settling down as school-marms. Meeting Alistair was like opening a window in a stuffy room. It made life exciting and stimulating. We used to go to meetings in dim little houses at Cowley, and once he took me up to Headquarters in London. Some of the people we met looked pretty awful, you know; but they were all so alive compared with the deadness of Oxford, and they were so utterly in earnest that things like accents and clothes simply didn't count. And it was so grand to think that we were all Comrades in one great Movement—not just lonely, self-centred individuals. Do you know what I mean?"

Mr. Lucton couldn't honestly say that he did, but dared not seem unsympathetic for fear of cutting short her confession.

"Well, it went on like this for a month or two," she went on. "I was terribly happy—though I can't say that Alistair was: that's not in his nature, anyway, and he says that it's criminal for anyone to be happy in a world so full of injustice and misery. He thinks it's one's duty not to be satisfied. In the end, he wasn't even satisfied with me."

"Then all I can say is: he's damned hard to please," Mr. Lucton growled.

"No, no, you don't understand. He was still in love with me. The trouble was that his being in love with me distracted him and got between him and his work. At first it had made the poetry simply pour out of him. He said he had never felt so marvellously rich in ideas; but now the springs had dried up. He said I tormented him."

"Why?"

"Because we weren't lovers in the proper sense of the word, and he knew he would never be any good till we had been."

Mr. Lucton had known this was coming. Suppressing his fury, he encouraged her to go on.

"Well, what did you say?" he asked tensely.

"I didn't know what to say. You see, I realized that in theory he was perfectly right. I believed in companionate marriage. We were both of us communists and I knew it was our duty to keep nothing back, to share everything; but . . . well, I suppose in practice I wasn't sufficiently advanced. I saw I was being stupid and mean and ungenerous, but I just couldn't face it. Though I knew that his work and the cause had a right to come first, I felt . . . I felt I didn't know him well enough. It was rather like that story of Balzac's about a man and a leopard. *A Passion in the Desert*, I think it was called."

"I don't know the story. All I want to know is what happened."

"Oh, the man who made friends with the leopard and played with it had to kill it."

"I don't mean that. I mean what happened to *you*."

"Well, naturally, I had an awful time with him. I put up with that because I thought being furious might make him write again. But it didn't. He only looked more and more pathetic—so nervous and haggard and drawn! So, at last we agreed that it simply couldn't go on, and that we'ld have to come to a compromise. So we decided we'ld go on a walking-tour in my own country. He'd always been scornful about it and said that it couldn't hold a candle to Scotland, and I wanted to show him how wild and lovely it was. And I thought . . . well, I thought the exercise might be good for both of us, and that by the time we'd been together for four or five days I should know him better and be able to see things more clearly. Alistair said he knew it would be no good unless I slept with him; but

I'd made up my mind, and so he had to give in. He was really quite good about it."

Mr. Lucton sighed with relief.

"That was last Wednesday?"

"Thursday . . . Yes, Thursday. It was wonderful starting out from Oxford that morning. We took a bus first to Witney, and then walked up on to the Cotswolds—long stretches of stone-walled road with the sweetest of air blowing over them, drenched with white clover, and the sky so palpitating with larks that you felt your heart lifted. Of course, Alistair turned up his nose at it. He likes everything on the grand scale, like the pass of Glencoe with great clouds swirling over Ben Nevis and the ghosts of the Macdonalds wailing in the wind. I told him he looked like a Highland steer, with his hair blown over his eyes. Oh, a perfect day!

"We stayed that night with a friend of his who's bought a delicious Costwold-stone cottage and writes novels about the awful conditions of miners in Durham. He lives with a Russian woman who once saw Lenin, much older than himself and rather terrifying. I'm afraid they're not very happy; but, as Alistair says, good writers never are, and the poor man has to put up with the oddest sort of housekeeping—they're the kind of people who live out of paper-bags, you know, just having a snack when they feel like it. There was only one bed in the house, and I had to share it with Tatiana, while Alistair slept on a sofa and his friend on the floor. I'm afraid that description sounds spiteful. I should hate to be that, because they were hospitable. In fact, they invited us to stay for as long as we liked."

"But you didn't."

"We did! We went off next morning before Tatiana was up, without any breakfast, worse luck! I'm not used to sleeping with anybody, and Tatiana kept on grinding her teeth and muttering in Russian, while the two men never stopped talking all night and prowling about downstairs. She wanted us to wait for her to get up; but we really hadn't the time to spare, so they came out to wish us good-bye and went back to bed again.

"The next two nights were so warm and lovely that we

decided to sleep out in hayfields. It wasn't as romantic as it sounds—well, *you* know all about it. I couldn't sleep properly because Alistair was so restless" (that was not, Mr. Lucton thought, entirely surprising) "and the moonlight kept me awake, and then the birds. Alistair would go on chanting dirges in Gaelic, which is Greek to me, and reciting poems by his communist friends, which are terribly thrilling, of course, when someone's explained to you what they're about, but hard to understand when they haven't and you happen to be half asleep. You see, they're not like ordinary conventional poetry," she went on earnestly. "They're much more stark and subtle. It's the suggestions of words, their overtones not their sounds, that really matter, if you know what I mean . . ."

"I don't," Mr. Lucton said flatly. "All I ask of a poem is that it shall be comprehensible and beautiful."

"But that's where you're so wrong. They *mustn't* be beautiful! The whorish trappings of rhyme, as Alistair calls them, only distract your mind from the sociological truth, and smooth rhythms lull you to sleep. The poet's job is to make you sit up and keep you awake and indignant."

"Well, that's quite beyond me, I'm afraid."

"Some of their poems are rather beyond me, too," she admitted. "Sometimes when I ask Alistair to explain one he gets quite angry. He says they can't be explained; even the writers can't explain them. They're meant to explain themselves, like music, you know; and if they don't express anything to you—well, that's your misfortune."

Mr. Lucton sighed.

"All right, that brings us to Sunday morning."

"Yes. That was the worst day of all. I woke up with a headache, through not having slept for three nights. I felt so rotten I didn't want to talk; so Alistair thought I was sulking on purpose, and went up in smoke. That was the worst row we'd ever had: it made me feel what a failure the whole thing was and wish we'd never tried it; but when the eruption was over he was so pathetically humble that I felt I'd treated him badly, and tried to make up for it by pretending I hadn't minded. When I told him I simply must have a good night's sleep in a comfortable bed at Llandewi, he agreed at once. I think he was a bit excited by seeing our mountains, though, of course, he said they weren't a patch on his own, and nobody could possibly help being impressed by Llandewi, could they?

"Of course, he was difficult when he found the inn crowded with fishermen, because he loathes and despises all kinds of sport; but I managed to calm him and took him away to walk up and down the nave between those lovely arches. He had to admit the ruins were beautiful, in spite of hating them because they'd been built by priests and reminded him of General Franco. Then, after we'd strolled about for a bit, he told me what he'd done."

"What had he done?"

"Booked a double room for us. I told him he'ld have to change it at once; but he said that would be giving the whole show away and making a fool of him, and, anyway, the room he'd booked was the last one available—which, of course, wasn't true. By this time I was really angry. I said: Well, *I* wasn't going to be made a fool of, anyway, and that he'ld have to sleep on the sofa downstairs. And he said that would only make it worse, because he'd given our names as Mr. and Mrs. Smith and spoken of me as his wife. It wasn't so much what he'd done as the sly way he'd done it that made me furious. If he slept in that room, I was going to sleep on the mountain.

After that, he turned really dramatic and nasty and went for me bald-headed: said I was a cold-blooded little bitch of an *allumeuse*, with a dirty mind full of rotten bourgeois prudery, who'd been deliberately leading him on for a couple of months, that I hadn't the courage of a louse, and he'd had enough of it. He said we'd come to the Parting of the Ways—just imagine Alistair using a cliché like that!—and that I'd got to choose, once and for all; and I told him I had. He said if I let him down he'ld drown himself in the Dulas; and I laughed and told him it wasn't deep enough. Then the maid came out in the middle of all this and said dinner was ready; and, though I felt like death, I was so hungry that I had to go in . . .

"It was a marvellous dinner, too; but I couldn't eat, nor could Alistair. When it was over, we sat miles apart on that sofa. I could feel, all the time, he thought I was going to give in. After you'd got up and gone out, he said, in a shaky kind of voice, that he'd better fetch our rucksacks. Then he discovered that you'd taken his and left him yours, and hurried off to complain to the landlady. And that gave me the chance I'd been waiting for. I slipped out and ran like a hare—and here I am. I mean, here we are. Isn't life horrible?"

Mr. Lucton was silent. He filled his pipe and lit it.

"Well, haven't you anything to say?" she asked, with a disappointed petulance.

"I've plenty to say. But I don't suppose you'll like it."

"Go on, if you want to," she said. "You can't hurt me."

"All right. First of all: I do like you, and I don't like your young man; but I think you're a couple of silly children, and if you were mine, which thank God you aren't, I should want to give the pair of you a damned good smacking. If you've got yourself into a mess, you've yourselves to blame for it. As for life being horrible: that's nonsense. You know nothing about it. You've been playing at living instead of getting on with it—wrapping yourselves up in a lot of high-flown, half-baked theories that have no connection with normal life, as you'll find it when you decide to grow up."

"Oh, you don't understand!"

"All right. I don't understand. That's another cliché. But I've never had much use for people who are misunderstood. It's part of our job to make ourselves understood. If we don't, we're failures. I know what that feels like. I've been a failure myself. I shouldn't be here if I weren't. But there's nothing for you to worry about. You're nineteen—nothing more than a child—with all your life in front of you. You're beautiful and healthy and honest as well as young. You've got everything in your favour . . ."

Mr. Lucton paused, half expecting a tornado to break; but she did not speak.

"As for this young man of yours," he went on, "I don't like

his type, as I've told you. I don't blame him for being a communist. I fancied myself as a Fabian socialist when I was his age. When you see the world full of miseries and inequalities and feel that everything's wrong, you're shocked, and you naturally want to do something about it. You see yourself in a minority of a good many millions to one in a mess that looks so hopeless that the only reasonable thing seems to be to smash up the lot. You'd probably smash up yourself as well as a few million of other innocent folk in the process. It gives you a jolly, heroic feeling to cock a snook at conventions just because they are conventions. You know you're right, and the other ninety-nine out of every hundred are wrong. Very well, you may be right. But that doesn't get you anywhere. Now I'm a business man . . ."

"Oh, Lord!"

"All right. You may laugh if you like; but everyone has to learn by his own experience; and I've learnt that in business, as in every other kind of life, there's nothing to be gained by bitterness. It just turns you sour, and doesn't help you or anyone else. The only thing that does is kindness and sympathy. Call it Love, if you like. *The greatest of these is Charity*. That's a good working rule. I'm not much of a Christian myself, but whatever you may say about Him, Christ wasn't bitter, and He didn't despise people."

"But . . . you see . . ." she began, "we don't . . ."

"Just let me finish my sermon. Preaching's not much in my line; but I've got a bit more for you. You set so much store on frankness in matters of this kind that I'm going to be frank. Well, I think you treated that boy abominably. Brilliant, lovely creatures like you have no right to go gaily and innocently floating about, exciting normal young men: sleeping out in hayfields on warm moonlight nights, coldly discussing your nice little theories of Free Love and Companionate Marriage and what not. Just think of the strain deliberately combining—what was it Shaw called it?—the maximum of provocation with the minimum of opportunity! No wonder the poor lad got rattled! St. Anthony wasn't in it! And all through your silly, conceited, highbrow ignorance in imagining that physical love was a matter governed by theories instead of by flesh and blood. Before you started playing that game you ought to have found out something about the rules of it, and conducted your love-making in the ordinary civilized way. You went asking for what you damned near got, my girl—though I'm glad you didn't get it. That's because I'm a sentimentalist. I'll give you that. Now you know what I think of both of you, bless your hearts! You'd better let go and say what you think of me. It may do you good."

She was silent for a moment.

"I'll give you full marks for frankness, partner," she said; "and there may be something in what you say. I hadn't thought of that part of it—Alistair's, I mean. You see, at Oxford . . ."

"Oh yes, that reminds me . . ." Mr. Lucton broke in. "I've always been told that Oxford's the home of Lost Causes. That's one consolation. Don't you think it's just about time we both of us tried to get some sleep?"

"If we can." She shivered. "It's so cold. Can I have that shirt of Alistair's?"

"Of course. Here it is; but I'm afraid it won't give much warmth. If you're sensible you'll just snuggle up to me." He laughed apologetically. "You know, people 'inclined to be stout' have useful reserves of animal heat."

She drew near, and he put his arm round her. Her body was small and childlike and cold; her hands were icy, too. This combination of pitiful qualities melted his heart.

"You poor child," he said brokenly; "you've had a rough time. But it's over. Lie close to me and get warm and forget about it."

She obeyed, with an affecting submissiveness. "Like a kid . . ." Mr. Lucton thought sentimentally. "God bless my soul, that's all she is: a tired, unhappy child who's burnt her fingers. And I've made it worse by being so rough with her. I'm a heartless brute. She must hate me like hell."

Then, suddenly, her body was shaken. She was crying. Mr. Lucton's broad breast sustained the convulsive impacts.

"Go on. That'll do you a world of good," he muttered encouragingly. "Don't mind me!"

At the moment she was past minding anything or anybody. Silent tears ran down her cheeks and on to his hand, until, at last, the shuddering ceased. She lay mute and still in his fatherly arms, and soon her slow, regular breathing assured him that she slept.

Mr. Lucton, too, in spite of cold and hunger, was ready for sleep. He felt like a final pipe to compose his nerves, but dared not light one for fear of awakening her.

"To-morrow morning," he thought, "I must put this right and persuade her there's nothing she need be tragic about."

As he fell asleep he conceived, as was his wont, a new scene of surpassing paternal tenderness, out of which he came very well as a paragon of kindly wisdom. Thanks to his close embrace, her body was warmer now. It seemed to be giving back the heat he had given it. He drew a deep sigh, closed his eyes, and went to sleep with a smile on his lips.

When he awoke, with the dawn, she was gone; but, before she went, she had carefully spread the shirt and the grey flannel trousers over his shoulder. As he removed these, a pencil-scribbled paper fell on the heather beside him. Mr. Lucton examined it in search of a message and found one.

Thanks for the animal heat and the sermon, it read. It was signed with initials: *D.P. Comunist.* Yes—the word was written with one '*m*'. . . .

(x)

DOUBTFUL AUTHENTICITY

THE mists, too, had vanished. The sun came rolling up out of England into a crystalline sky, illuminating the plain beneath and the mountain masses to westward with a light too powerful and revealing for any element of mystery to resist. These clear beams had an equally clarifying influence on Mr. Lucton's waking mind. At the moment when he was falling asleep it had reached the verge of becoming maudlin, and ready to indulge in those dangerous excesses of feeling to which it was prone. Now he saw this romantic encounter and its affecting sequels unclouded by any mists of sentiment. He was glad the experience had come his way, but not altogether sorry, for his own peace of mind, that it was over. He found life sufficiently complicated without the addition of emotional distractions of that kind.

He was touched, none the less, by the thoughtfulness which had led her to spread the shirt and the trousers over him while he still slept.

"A nice-natured child," he mused, "in spite of all the nonsensical theories with which they've stuffed her poor little head. She'll get over that before long. She's had one good lesson, at any rate. Now she'll probably fall in love, in the ordinary way, with a decent young man of her own class, and marry and settle down into a charming mother. The sooner the better," Mr. Lucton thought grimly. "Girls like her are a public danger. But some day, perhaps," his fancy ran on, "she'll remember the night when she slept on the top of a mountain and cried in the arms of a middle-aged business man who'd just given her the dressing-down of her life. She'll smile at the memory, and her husband will ask what she's smiling at; and she'll say: 'Nothing really, darling'—as innocent as be damned. Well, well . . ."

His mind returned from these speculations to matters more

practical. A new day had begun, "a fine hunting day"; and no doubt the hunters would soon be "out" again. He imagined the new description which, passed on from the inn at Llandewi, would be substituted for the old one broadcast by the police. So far as his physical characteristics went, there was nothing more to alter now that his moustache was gone. As for his clothes: by now shorts would have taken the place of the striped cashmere trousers mentioned in the Police Message. So the shorts must go. They were noticeably stained with peat in any case, and he wasn't sorry to see the last of them when he trampled them deep in a hole that looked like a badger-sett, for he knew he would feel safer with his pale knees covered than naked.

He didn't much like the look of Alistair's flannel trousers. They were cut with a poetic license, much too wide for his taste (though not, alas, for his waistline) and at least three inches too long for his legs. Even in this matter, however, he felt he had had the better of the exchange; for whereas he could reduce their redundant length by turning up the bottoms two or three times, the unfortunate poet, wearing Harris trousers clear of his ankles, would look like the pictures of Smike in the original editions of *Nicholas Nickleby*. He doubted if Alistair's sense of humour would rise to the joke. His own shirt, thank heaven, was still wearable, and the club tie of red, blue and gold—which he borrowed without hesitation—would distract any careless eye from the shabbiness of the old Harris coat. He was satisfied, in fact, that his appearance, thus transformed, would resemble the picture he had presented at Llandewi as little as the first description the police had circulated.

He felt different, too. The subconscious encouragement given by this change of clothes was astonishing. It was equivalent to a new incarnation which involved not only his person, but also his mind. Believing that he no longer looked like a fugitive, he no longer felt like one: it was heartening, for instance, to find that the prospect of entering a pub did not terrify him. For a long time, indeed, he had no opportunity of putting this newly-found brazenness to the test. The lost track, which he regained without much difficulty, meandered down-hill for several miles before he reached a hamlet consisting of a group of farm buildings and two or three scattered cottages, one of which proved to be an inn. If he had insisted on keeping to the wheel-tracks, instead of making that rash short-cut overnight, they would have been able to sleep in comfort with a roof over their heads. On the whole, he was glad they hadn't. The adventure, odd though it had been, had left with him a curiously intimate flavour or perfume of its own which he would always remember tenderly.

And the inn, stark and primitive though it had appeared, was a marvel. Mr. Lucton could hardly believe his eyes or his nose when, entering a long, low room with a low ceiling festooned with hams and sides of bacon and a floor of newly scrubbed sandstone flags, he saw that the farther end of it was occupied by an oak table burdened with food that made his mouth water: enormous crusty loaves that still smelt of the oven; a golden ham and a huge round of beef from which the top slice had been cut, disclosing a surface of appetizing redness; bowls of crisp lettuce garnished with spring onions; plates of pale mountain butter, and, trestled on either side, two twenty-eight-gallon casks which, he guessed, contained beer and cider. In the present state of his stomach, which, but for a handful of biscuits and cheese, had been empty for thirty-six hours, the sight of this gargantuan embarrassment of riches, this glutton's paradise, was overwhelming. A dark, bird-like little woman, with cheeks red as a polished Worcester Pearmain, appeared in a scullery doorway and peeped at him with black eyes, her head on one side.

"Good morning," he said. "Could you possibly give me some breakfast?"

Amid such abundance the question seemed ridiculous; but her face became anxious and hopeless.

"I don't know as how I can manage," she fluted in a high singsong. "We do be expecting company. I've only this moment finished setting the table, and I couldn't clear it and start all over again."

"What company are you expecting?" Mr. Lucton asked.

"They do be holding the rent audit. There'll be Mr. Meredith, the agent, and his lordship's tenants riding in from all over the mountains. If it had been any other day, sir . . ."

"Couldn't you just let me have a slice of that beef?" Mr. Lucton pleaded. "It looks delicious, and cooked to a turn," he added, "if I may say so."

She glowed at the compliment.

"Yes, isn't it a beautiful round? Mr. Meredith, he always says you can't beat our beef. Mr. Maddy, the Pentre's, feeding, it is." She contemplated the masterpiece lovingly. "Killed Wednesday, but it'ld be a sin to start cutting into it, wouldn't it? before Mr. Meredith's seen it."

Mr. Lucton could not agree. If he had been hungry before, he felt famished now. He remembered the story he had once read in a popular "outline" of science of a Russian physiologist's experiments on dogs: how, stimulated by the sight and smell of raw meat, gastric juice had poured into the victims' empty stomachs. He was suffering from the effects of a smiliar reflex. A "gnawing" hunger: that was the word! It was all he could do to restrain himself from sweeping the landlady aside and falling on the food like a dog himself. He could understand now why hunger bred violence and revolutions.

"If you could put up with ham and eggs," the little woman said tentatively, "and wouldn't mind eating it in the kitchen, I dare say . . ."

Mr. Lucton leapt at the offer. He followed her into the kitchen and watched with gloating eyes while, darting here and there with robin-like movements, she cut a thick slab from a ham that hung from the rafters and set it sizzling in the pan.

"Would three eggs be enough?" she asked.

Mr. Lucton laughed. "I shan't know till I've eaten them."

"My, you have got an appetite, haven't you?" she exclaimed.

He was on the point of boasting that he hadn't eaten anything since Sunday evening, when he realized how completely he was allowing the animal instinct of hunger to disarm him—"like hunted antelopes," he reflected, "which flock down to drink from a waterhole in the bush at night, forgetting that their natural enemies may be prowling and on the watch". He became even more aware of the gravity of this threatened imprudence when he heard, on the road outside the inn, a clatter of ponies' hoofs, and saw through the kitchen window a wild-looking group of bearded farmers, resembling the pictures he remembered of a Boer commando, who had ridden in for the rent-audit. They were talking rapidly in Welsh, and though he could not understand what they said, his apprehensive mind jumped to the conclusion that they were discussing the news, already diffused by wireless, that the object of Sunday night's police message had been "spotted" in the Dulas Valley and was probably still hiding in the mountain. He recognized one of them, the most talkative of the lot, as the white-bearded man on the grey who had waved him good morning from the tail of the pony-drive.

"Here they come," the landlady said excitedly. "You see that old gentleman over there with the white beard? That's Mr. Maddy, the Pentre, the same as fed that lovely bit of beef there. A wonderful man for his age, he is, and that highly respected by the gentry, they've made him a magistrate. And the young fellow just behind him—that's Evan, his son, who got married to Gladys Morgan, Bryntirion, last sheep-shearing. They do be looking for a christening, indeed, at the Pentre next month, I'm hearing. My, what am I doing, chattering away like this?"

Mr. Lucton abandoned his last egg. His appetite had vanished. He hurriedly demanded his bill. The little woman looked puzzled.

"Would a shilling be asking too much?" she said anxiously.

With the clatter of more hoof-beats in his ears, Mr. Lucton thanked her and paid. He made straight for the back door of the in.

"That way only leads down the garden," she said.

Mr. Lucton vaguely indicated an urgent imaginary physical necessity. She smiled and nodded in token of understanding.

"You'll find it at the bottom of the garden," she said, then hurried to meet her guests.

He had to force his way through gaps in three hedges before he rejoined the lane. Providentially, he found it empty: a deep-cut tunnel, as rough underfoot as a water-course, heavily shadowed by hazels, and so steep that he had no doubt but that it led to the plain. By this time he had recovered his composure. Serene and well-fed—though he could have done with that third egg—he was able, at last, to appreciate the quality of the morning air and the beauty of his surroundings. Behind him, the mass of Mynydd Savaddan rose blacker and more sheer than ever, shutting off the lower sky; the dark, raven-haunted darens and screes of its northern escarpment frowned above him. Looking back from this point he was aware, as never before, of the mountain's magnificence. It seemed a pity that he was now being forced to leave unexplored that shape which had so often fascinated him as he gazed at it, eighty miles away, from the edge of the Midland plateau; and his thoughts turned kindly, and a little enviously, to Bert, who, at this moment, no doubt, was setting out grimly to scale the eminence of Pen Savaddan. He would probably never see Bert or the mountain again; and that seemed a pity—for he owed him an apology for the melodrama into which the poor little man had been dragged, and the mountain, however savagely it had used him, had at least provided him with the only kind of romantic experience which one could expect in advanced middle age.

Hurrying forward and downward, he turned his back on the mountain and all its memories. The road, which was one of a multitudinous network formed by the action of water rather than the intention of man, ran capriciously, now skirting patches of crubby sheep-walk or open moorland golden with broom, now plunging deep into ravines clogged with thickets of hazel beneath which, even in this dry season, the companionable voice of running water could be heard. All these falling streams, he supposed, were hurrying toward the Wye, of whose green valley, quivering with heat, he sometimes caught glimpses far beneath him. But amid those lofty foot-hills it seemed as though the summer he had left behind him in Worcestershire had hardly begun. Here the scanty hay was unmown, and the hedgerow briars, of a deeper rose than those he had lately seen flowering, were still in bud. It seemed, he was glad to find, a singularly lonely country. In all his downward walk of more than two hours, he only encountered one human being—and this solitary looked to him rather less than human: a shaggy, low-browed man driving sheep to a shearing-fold near a farm whose ivy-wreathed skeleton suggested that it had been long deserted.

Here curiosity overcame his prudence. Following the hot-smelling flock to the fold, he watched the sheep cast and stood listening to the silky whisper of the shears as they swiftly severed the tangled fleeces—so close that the creatures' skins, shining through, gave to the nap of wool that was left an appearance of creamy velvet flushed with the pink of a flamingo's breast. None of the shearers deigned to notice him: these border Welsh seemed a taciturn, incurious race, absorbed in their delicate craft, or perhaps unwilling to air their English. He could easily have wasted an hour there watching them, hypnotized by the whisper of the deft shears, and wondering how this farm, so superbly placed, commanding not only the mountain but also the broad Wye Valley and the moors of Radnor beyond, had come to be deserted. Attached to the ruined farm-house stood a massive tower, surrounded by the remains of a moat, which, long ago, he imagined must have been the keep of a castle. Its interior, like that of the farm-house, was overgrown with nettles. The problem puzzled him so much that he ventured to ask one of the shearers the name of the place.

"Trecastel," the man answered shortly, and went on with his work.

Trecastel. . . . A lovely name, and oddly familiar, though he could not remember where or when he had heard it. The syllables rang in his mind as he went on his way, like a musical phrase which obstinately rises from the deep well of memory, but cannot be traced. Their echo, mingling with the ceaseless murmur of water, still kept him company until, without any warning, the steep lane ended, slipping, as unobtrusively as if it wished to avoid being noticed, into a metalled roadway, running east and west, the first token of which was the swish of a motor-car, flashing past the outlet of the green tunnel and making Mr. Lucton jump with surprise—and rather more than surprise, for he saw it was occupied by two mobile policemen.

At this sight, he pulled his vagrant wits together. Prospecting, with caution, he perceived that he had reached the outskirts of a small town with hilly streets grouped about another castle. In a place of that modest size, where everyone's business was everyone else's, he could be sure that the presence of a stranger would be noticed immediately; so he shied away from it like a nervous horse, feeling painfully conspicuous as he passed in front of a row of hideous "council houses" with a sinister rigging of wireless aerials behind them. At their front doors women stood shaking out mats and gossiping, and his conscience told him that several of these regarded him curiously. He was thankful when he had passed them—and even more so when he found himself caught up in a crowd that surged round the entrance of a field where a market was about to be held. The roadway was blocked by a welter of bewildered sheep which had just been discharged from lorries or driven in from their pastures. Men were shouting and stamping and waving their arms and dogs were barking, while a worried policeman held up the traffic to allow the poor limping beasts to be scared into their pens; but neither he nor anyone else had a glance to spare for Mr. Lucton.

It took him five minutes to thread his way through this dusty confusion of men and animals. He emerged from it with the increased confidence of a hunted animal whose track and scent have been obliterated and washed away by a stream. On the mountain, lovely as it was, the depths of his mind had been troubled not only by the aloofness or actual hostility of a wild region unfriendly to man, but also by the sense of isolation—of being the only quarry likely to attract the hunter's attention. On this relatively populous road he felt safer. Among so many wayfarers nobody had any reason to question his presence or right to challenge it. He had returned to the ways of ordinary civilization and the sheltering ubiquity of his fellow-men. The very character of the country-side protested against violence. It was smooth and rich and settled. Its inhabitants were too deeply absorbed in their own busy avocations and too contented to worry their heads about anyone else. It had an atmosphere of "live and let live", so bland and friendly that, for the first time since the day when he fled from Tibberton's farm, Mr. Lucton felt encouraged to relax or to suppress his underlying apprehensiveness, to be persuaded that he had nothing to fear, to surrender himself to its warm, sweet air and its placid beauty as though this were the first day of an innocent holiday, to walk without watching his step.

He had still not the faintest idea where he was or whither he was going. He didn't much care; but the problem of making a decision presented itself when he came to a cross-roads in front of an inn, where a finger-post told him that the main road ran to Brecon. Though he knew nothing about Brecon, its name did not attract him. It sounded harsh and mountainous, and during the last two days he had had enough of Wild Wales. Mountains doubtless had their romantic aspects; but, for the moment at least, he wouldn't mind if he never set foot on one again. He was in need of peace, not excitement. He wanted to sleep in a comfortable bed; to loaf and invite his soul, to "stay put", if such things were possible. This green valley, with its fat farms and fields of placidly browsing Herefords, with their great heads and albino eyelids, suited him.

So, instead of the high-road to Brecon, he chose the other, which led to a wide bridge spanning the Wye: he liked the idea of putting a river between himself and the mountains. A schoolboy, carrying a satchel, came bounding over the bridge and whistled as gaily as any blackbird as he skipped along. How ruddy and well fed, Mr. Lucton thought, were the children of this high valley, and what a grand thing it was to come home hungry from school to dinner at the age of thirteen! He smiled with instinctive benevolence as he asked the boy where the road led after crossing the river. The answer came in an eager burst of the same lilting speech as that of the bird-like woman at the inn.

"Well, left, it is going up the river to Boughrood and Erwood, and right it is going down to Felindre and Clyro and Norton Lacey."

He was off again, skipping and whistling, before Mr. Lucton could thank him.

"Felindre and Clyro and Norton Lacey," he thought. "What musical names! That's the road for me;" but, before he had crossed the bridge, his attention was caught by the sight of a fisherman standing waist-deep in the tail of a stickle below it and casting his fly athwart a current that tautened the line and swept it down-stream across a deep pool.

Mr. Lucton paused to watch. His mind, temporarily (if unreasonably) freed from its former anxieties, was particularly sensitive to all kinds of beauty that day. It was delightful to see the curve of the wet line flash in the sun, as the man made his backward cast, and straighten itself to shoot forward again like a thing alive. Lovely, too, was the sound of water brushing the piles of the bridge, roaring over the stones of the stickle into the silence of the pool's quiet depths of dark jade, and then finding a deeper voice in a run of greater strength and lesser turbulence, whose curves of unbroken water shone in the sun like a serpent of living bronze.

It was odd, he thought, how, wherever he went, he seemed to meet fishermen. Though he had never engaged in this sport—or any other, for that matter—there was evidently a lot to be said for it. It was lonely. One didn't have to listen to people talking just because they had nothing else to do, or because they liked to hear their own voices. All the fishermen heard, indeed, was the sweetest, the most enchanting of sounds: the noise of running water amid surroundings that, of their nature, were far from the haunts of men. If one were tired, or the fish wouldn't take a fly, one could sit on the bank and smoke a reflective pipe and watch the life of the river: dimpling trout in unreachable eddies under the bushes, yellow wagtails and whinnying curlews and water-ouzels bobbing their white breasts—and, perhaps the electric streak of a kingfisher. It didn't matter if it rained; for, a fisherman's meat being another man's poison, he could enjoy foul weather for his sport's sake, and fair for his fellow-men's or his own. Nor—comforting thought!—was the advance of age an impediment: that hard-bitten, hook-nosed parson, the doyen of the company at Llandewi, must have been seventy at least.

"I've a good mind to 'take up' this fly-fishing," Mr. Lucton murmured to himself, forgetting momentarily that he would never, in his new condition of life, be able to afford it. "The ideal recreation for a contemplative man, and a cast-iron alibi. Nothing violent or excessive about it. Just a mildly absorbing pastime without any serious excitement . . ."

He spoke too soon. Before he had finished his sentence, he found himself hurrying to the end of the bridge and excitedly scrambling down the side of the ramp to the river-bank. The fisherman had let out a sudden whoop of triumph, the reel an agonized screech; he stood with his rod bent nearly double, lightly checking the line, while, forty yards below, a silvery shape churned the water and then leapt clear to flash into the sun. Excitement? Mr. Lucton had never seen a salmon before save when it was lying limp on a fishmonger's slab; and never imagined one capable of such fierce resistance to capture. Three great rushes it made: the first two to the apron of the pool, where it leapt twice, head and tail, in a desperate attempt to reach the rough water below: in the third, it streaked rapidly up-stream to the bridge, where the current was against it. Mr. Lucton could see the arrowy body flash past him under the bank as the reel whirred again: a second later it broke water under the alders on the opposite side. He watched the unequal struggle breathlessly: unequal, because it seemed to him that the tenuous cast and the delicate rod, still bent double, could not be expected to hold—much less to subdue—a creature so swift and sinewy, fighting for life in its native element. Twice more the salmon ran and leapt. Each time the fisherman lowered his rod and the line fell slack, and each time Mr. Lucton thought the fish had freed itself—until the rod bent again and the tightened line stripped the water, and he drew a breath of relief.

The salmon had sounded now, and sulked at the bottom of the pool. The taut line trembled, scattering bright droplets. He could imagine the silent, unrelenting struggle under the water: the silver body wedged in a crevice of rock; the busy fins thrashing the water; the strong tail finding purchase and used as a lever. Yet that part of the fight was invisible: its only index the quivering line, the bowed rod, the fisherman's tense wrists and forearms continually strained to support it.

Mr. Lucton could almost feel that strain in his own arms' muscles and sinews. The fisherman's struggle was his. Some primitive instinct, hitherto unperceived, had fiercely enlisted his sympathies on the side of his brother man. If the cast broke now or were frayed and cut by a rock or caught in a snag, he felt he would almost weep with disappointment.

But the fish was beginning to tire. Mr. Lucton saw the line slacken and the fisherman reeling-in rapidly. For one moment the salmon showed itself, drifting languidly, half on its side, into a patch of foam fringing an eddy a few yards below where he stood. It was a magnificent monster—far bigger than he had imagined, and seemed to be floating into the bank. It was so near that an unthinking desire to take part in the victory, to seize the line, pull the victim ashore, overwhelmed him. He was after it, scrambling down the bank on his hands and knees. An angry bellow startled him.

"What the devil d'you think you're doing, damn you? Get back, sir, get back!"

At the same moment the water of the eddy boiled beneath him. An arrowy wake streaked over the surface of the pool as the salmon made one more furious dash for liberty. The fisherman shouted as the reel sang again.

"Keep away from the bank, for God's sake. I'm bringing him in; but he's not killed yet by a long way."

Mr. Lucton retreated in shame, while the fisherman, in his soaked body-waders, moved cautiously in towards the bank, one hand clutching the reel to keep the line tight, the other sounding the depth with a wading-staff topped by a wicked-looking gaff. He was an old man with a fierce, swarthy, heavily-wrinkled face and a bristly white beard above a clerical collar which, because of his highly unclerical language, gave Mr. Lucton a shock. It was evident that the struggle had tired him, for he was breathing heavily—so tired that the effort he felt in lifting his sodden legs and brogued feet was communicable. The hand that held the rod trembled as he reeled-in the line, bringing the beaten fish nearer and nearer. Mr. Lucton watched its reluctant approach inch by inch through an eternity of anxiousness. The old man grasped his gaff firmly and stretched out his arm. As he did so, the fish gave a lazy swirl and wallowed away out of reach into the froth of the eddy. The old man was swearing under his breath. He tested the depth of the water in front of him, but the staff failed to touch bottom. He looked at the steep bank above him and shook his head. Then he looked at Mr. Lucton.

"Hi, you, sir!" he said. "Have you ever gaffed a salmon?"

Mr. Lucton shook his head. The noise of the stickle made it seem useless to speak.

"Well, I can't get at the fish from here; and the water's too deep in front of me—it shelves to six feet. I don't want to hand-line him in, because the cast is an old one and can't be trusted—I know I ought never to have fished with it. I can't climb up the bank here, holding my rod, and keep in touch with him—and I don't want to give him time to recover, either. Now from just below where you are you could easily reach him. Mind having a shot at it?"

Mr. Lucton signified his willingness.

"Well . . . You take the gaff—here it is—and lean over the bank. Don't show yourself any more than you need, and don't let your shadow fall on him. Then you slip the gaff into the water quietly—on the far side of him, understand!—until the point's underneath his belly. Then pull it up sharply and haul him out in one movement. Don't be afraid of it. Sharp and strong. You'll probably find he's heavier than you think. Fifteen pounds, I should say, and fresh-run. Now then, have you got that clear? All right: fire away, then!"

Mr. Lucton swarmed on his stomach to the undercut edge of the bank. Below him the big fish listlessly floated, showing a white flank. Its small eye regarded him blankly as if it were already dead; but now and again the gill-lids opened and shut convulsively, revealing the scarlet gills, dark for lack of oxygen. His nervous hand trembled as he lowered the gaff into the water beyond it. He heard the old man's whisper: "That's right.

Gently does it. Get the gaff right under. Now . . . Pull!"

Mr. Lucton pulled upward with all his might. Perhaps the refraction of the water misled him; perhaps, in an excess of caution, he had miscalculated the angle of his gaff. Whatever the cause may have been, the hook grazed the silvery body without penetrating it and the gaff came away. With a last effort the wounded fish rolled over like a floating log and began to move away.

"Don't touch him," the old man shouted. "Leave him to me!"

But already Mr. Lucton had lost his head. In his frantic anxiety he was making wild grabs with the gaff at the retreating body. With the last, which just missed its head, the broken cast came away, and the fish, with a bewildered wallow, reached the swirl on the edge of the eddy and floated down-stream.

Mr. Lucton, still brandishing the gaff, ran along the bank, hoping to stop it before it was caught by the current. As he ran, he heard behind him an angry shout:

"You double-damned, mutton-fisted oaf!"

The old parson had turned his back on him and was splashing his way up-stream to the shallow water. His back affirmed eloquently that he had no more to say. He had even forgotten his gaff.

Mr. Lucton, ruddy with shame, ran after him. "You're forgetting this, sir," he called; but the old man did not hear him. Mr. Lucton pursued him and overhauled him as he stepped ashore.

"I'm most awfully sorry, sir."

The old man slewed round and put a hand to his ear. "What's that? What's that?" he said. "I'm a trifle deaf."

Mr. Lucton repeated, more loudly: "I'm awfully sorry"; but still, it appeared, the fisherman could not hear what he said.

"What's that you say? Awful? Awful isn't the word," he snarled. "Mutton-fisted: that's what you are." Then the wrinkled old face, which had been red with anger, broke into a charming smile, and the bright blue eyes, under their bushy white eyebrows, smiled too. "Look here, sir," he said. "I apologize. A parson's no business to swear in any case, but the circumstances were extenuating. Heat of the moment. Well, I suppose I deserve what I got for forgetting my cloth. But that was a beautiful summer fish, as clean as a new pin. In this state of the water it was a hundred to one against my hooking him. That's the beauty of the greased line. You see, when gaffing a fish . . ."

As he paused, Mr. Lucton noticed that the blue eyes were set on his face with a curious, earnest fixity—and, even so, not quite on his face, but a trifle below it. Then his lips broke into a smile again.

"By Jove," he cried. "I believe you're the very man we've been looking for!"

Mr. Lucton paled and went cold. His first impulse was to throw down the gaff and take to his heels, in the certainty that the old parson, impeded by his waders, could not overtake him. As he hesitated a wiry hand was clapped on his shoulder.

"That tie's Authentic; isn't it?"

Though it wasn't his own, Mr. Lucton had at least no reason to doubt its authenticity. He stammered a few confused words to that effect; but the deaf man did not hear them.

"My eldest boy used to play for the Authentics about nineteen-two," he went on. "He's in India now: Woods and Forests. You're about his age. Peter Marlow's the name. Remember him?" Mr. Lucton shook his head. "No? Well, that doesn't matter. The point is: what are you? Batsman or bowler?"

Mr. Lucton, though longing to be both, was forced to shout that he wasn't much good at either. The old man caught the last word.

"Splendid . . . splendid!" he chuckled. "An all-rounder, eh? That's just what we want. Now if you'll give me a hand getting off these waders, my boy, I'll explain. I'm all right when I'm on my feet: it's the bending that catches me. Thanks . . . thanks. Now, where was I? Ah yes: this afternoon's match. It's a kind of little festival we hold every year as soon as the haymaking's over: my team against one of my neighbour's, Jack

Harrowby, the Vicar of Norton Lacey, who played for Cambridge with me in eighteen eighty-three. Nothing elaborate about it: it's really just village cricket; but that, to my mind's the most enjoyable kind. What?"

Mr. Lucton nodded vigorously.

"But to-day my curate, who happens to be our stand-by, is down with lumbago—ridiculous in a man of his age—and so we're one man short. So if you'ld like a game and can spare the time, you might help us out."

Mr. Lucton said he would like nothing better, but that, unfortunately . . .

"Splendid . . . splendid! I was sure you'ld be game, my boy," the old man roared. "I knew any old cricketer would jump at it."

There was, apparently, nothing more to be done about it. It would have been cruel, Mr. Lucton felt, to refuse, and unpardonable to damp this old heart's charming enthusiasm.

"Come along, then," the parson said. "I'll drive you home and we'll have some luncheon. It might have been grilled salmon steak with the cream in it if you'd been a bit handier with that gaff; but I think my housekeeper can give you a nice dish of trout all the same. And I hooked the brute, anyway, with the water dead-low and gin-clear. That's the beauty of the greased line and the lightly-dressed fly—I'd put up a Blue Charm, by the way. If you've never tried that technique, my boy, you ought to begin. It's most fascinatin' . . . Well, here's the car. Perhaps you wouldn't mind crankin' her up while I work the throttle? She's sometimes a bit temperamental in startin'."

Mr. Lucton surveyed the car with distaste. It was a Morris two-seater, approximately twenty years old, he judged, by the narrow, domed radiator. The engine was not merely temperamental, but vicious, back-firing, with a contemptuous spitting of smoke that smelt of burnt oil, when he pulled it over.

"That's all right. She usually does that," the old parson said. "Needs a bit of humourin'. Growin' old, like myself."

"If you'ld retard the ignition a bit," Mr. Lucton suggested, rubbing a sore wrist.

"What's that you're saying?"

"The ignition. *Retard.*" Mr. Lucton shouted.

"Yes, yes. I know it's hard. Try again. She's all right. She'll come round in a moment."

Mr. Lucton sighed and gave in. At the seventh pull, the engine started up with the sputtering roar of a tractor. It was clear that the silencer was either adrift or broken, though the old man was far too deaf to have noticed the noise.

He let in the clutch with the throttle full open. The car lurched over the verge and cleared the gutter with a bump and rattle that drowned the machine-gun stutter of the open exhaust. Mr. Lucton was used to fast driving and liked it; in the Pearce-Tregaron he counted on averaging "fifty"; but never before, in all his experience of motoring, had he felt so unsafe as now, at the Morris's maximum speed of "twenty-five". This old man was, without exception, the worst driver he had ever known, crashing his gears whenever he changed them—as he had to do for even the mildest of gradients—without any change of engine-speed; ramming-on his brakes without warning, so that the rear-wheels waltzed across the road; bumping the verge on the opposite side when he shot on again; charging every hump-backed bridge or culvert (of which there were many) like a steeple-chaser taking Becher's at Aintree, and cutting every corner (of which there were even more) without any check of speed and with so few inches to spare that he seemed to have calculated how closely it could be done without overturning.

Round one of these corners, a right-angled bend, Mr. Lucton saw himself on the point of being thrown over the heads of a team of horses dragging a hay-wagon. He hung on with one hand to the rattling door of the car, with the other to the back of the seat, awaiting the shock with closed eyes. In spite of this anchorage he felt his body thrown forward and the rear-wheels sliding from under him, as the car, with a jolt, a shudder and a shrieking of brakes, came to rest with its radiator under the leader's nose.

The driver seemed quite unmoved by this miraculous escape. He put his hand to his ear.

"I fancy I've stalled that engine," he said. "Just give it another pull up."

"It was lucky you did stall the engine," Mr. Lucton thought.

"Put the lever in neutral first," he warned him. The old man only laughed and nodded his head encouragingly, so Mr. Lucton took the precaution of doing it for him, at which he laughed even more loudly.

The carter in charge of the team appeared, and pulled his horse aside to allow Mr. Lucton to get to work with the crank. He was a tall young man, with an honest face, burnt brick-red, and kindly blue eyes.

"Hullo, Harry," the parson bawled. "What are you doing here? I hope that's the last load. All right for this afternoon?"

The young man nodded violently, with a broad smile.

"That was bloody near *his* last load, too," he murmured to Mr. Lucton. "What am I doing here? I like that? That old beggar's a terror. It'll be manslaughter one of these days."

The engine started again, with a roar which scared the horses so much that he had to clutch at the leader's bridle.

"All right, sir. Go on!" Mr. Lucton shouted.

As the car shaved the wagon, overhanging wisps of hay swept the old man's face.

"That was a near shave . . . what?" he said. "These country folk have no road-sense. But that's a nice boy, Harry Kington: not much brains, but a safe pair of hands—best slip-fielder we've got. Christened him and his father before him. Oh yes, I know all these people, and they know me."

Mr. Lucton felt he wouldn't mind betting they did, if they often met him on the road. He had prided himself on his nerves, but this old fellow's utter disregard for danger continued to shake them. He supposed that, at such a great age, the thought of sudden death might have become so familiar as to have lost all its terrors; but he, being only middle-aged, preferred to live, and it was an enormous relief to him when, after four or five miles of purgatory, the car swept on two wheels into a gravelled drive and pulled up, with a bubbling radiator, in front of a small, high-gabled house with a porch wreathed in honey-suckle.

"Here we are," the old man said. "This is my Rectory, and there's my church, and there's my cricket-ground." He pointed proudly to a flat field with a large square of close-cut sward roped-off in the middle of it. "The out-field's a bit rough, but the wicket's not bad, though a bit on the sporting side. It oughtn't to be bad: I've looked after that turf for forty-nine years. I never knew the day when it wouldn't take spin. Now you can get a wash before luncheon while I go and change. When you've finished, you can go into the study and read *The Times*."

He thrust Mr. Lucton into a narrow passage divided by a pitch-pine screen into two compartments: a rod- (or gun-) room and a lavatory. The outer was so dark and so thickly infested with "sporting" implements, shot-guns and deer-stalking rifles; fishing-rods of many lengths and descriptions; gaffs, telescopic and fixed; walking-sticks and shooting-seats, waders, brogues, creels, decoy-pigeons, landing-nets, gum-boots, jacks, cricket-bats and pads—to say nothing of festoons of lines dressed and undressed, hung out like lianas in a tropical forest between the shelves on either side of the impeded fairway to dry—that he knocked several of them over before he reached the inner chamber.

Even here an overflow of similar junk restricted his movements. He picked his way through it cautiously, trailing behind him a spinning-trace armed with triangle-hooks, which his coat-sleeve had picked up on the way, and found himself face to face with an apparition—his own image reflected in a cracked mirror above the old-fashioned wash-hand-stand. This was the first time Mr. Lucton had seen himself since the day when he had glanced at his reflection in the showcase at Malvern. The effect was no less encouraging than surprising. He was pleased to find himself by no means a bad-looking fellow: the loss of his grizzled moustache had reduced his apparent age by at least eight years; his eyes looked clearer than before, and the week's exposure had given his features, which had been lax and puffy, the bronzed, sinewy air of an active countryman's.

Though the borrowed trousers still resisted every attempt to make the button at the top, his waist was certainly slimmer, and the Harris coat, for all its age, looked well-cut and was strictly in keeping with his present surroundings. What pleased him even more was the effect of the Authentics tie. That he had no right to wear it, and that it was the cause of the equivocal position in which he now found himself, did not detract from the fact that it not merely suited him, but completed what was already a most effective disguise, in which he doubted if any of his friends could possibly recognize him. He found it hard, indeed, to recognize himself.

Fortified by this cheering discovery, he made his way to the study and waited with confidence for his host. The room so closely reflected its owner's personality that it might almost be said to have absorbed a part of it. It was, like the Rector, a mid-Victorian museum-piece, from the frayed red carpet to the macramé-fringed mantelshelf; from the deep maroon curtains, edged with chenille, to the hanging oil-lamp with its shade of opaline glass; from the flowered wallpaper to the embroidered carpet-slippers propped-up by the heavy brass fender. The wall-space above and on either side of the fire-breast was thickly hung with faded photographs of college cricket-teams, two emblazoned shields—one representing the University of Cambridge and the other Trinity Hall—and a number of others supporting moth-eaten trophies of the chase—masks, brushes and rudders of otters and foxes, and the swollen, supercilious face of an unfortunate hare which had lost its whiskers after being bowled over (as Mr. Lucton discovered) the year before he was born.

What attracted him more than these was the range of built-in mahogany bookshelves on the opposite walls. These were crammed not only with sporting and theological works and a considerable well-worn library of the classics, but also with a haphazard but representative selection of poetry, essays and fiction covering a period which began in the eighteen-seventies and ended, abruptly, at the date of the Boer War. They were the choice, one felt, of an eager and lively mind which, for some unknown reason, had become crystallized in middle age and, thereafter, discarded all intellectual curiosity. Yet, in spite of these tokens of deterioration (if the hard word were justified), this comfortable room was that of a man whose life, in its prime, had been cultured and civilized in a manner to which Mr. Lucton still wistfully aspired. It had acquired the patina of prolonged and peaceful habitation.

Among those books (so many of which he wished he had read); in those snug carpet-slippers; at that orderly desk, with its pipe-rack of seasoned briars and ample tobacco-jar, where the summer breeze, warm with sunshine and charged with wafts of roses and honeysuckle, stirred the torn lace curtains and fluttered the folded *Times*, the sheets of blank sermon-paper and the pages of an open diary blissfully innocent of engagements; in that ancient aura of homely-scented tobacco-smoke with which the whole room was impregnated; a man who had taken his fill of the world and learnt wisdom might well do worse than spend his declining days in virtuous indolence. Happy was the nation, men said, that had no history. Happy was the man, Mr. Lucton thought, whose serious history had been written, whose struggles were over, who had earned the right not to put away childish things, but to return to them without any guilty consciousness of levity. A counsel of resignation? At heart Mr. Lucton did not feel resigned. The bronzed, well-set-up, clean-shaven man whose reflection had lately startled and encouraged him had no business to feel resigned. He was, perhaps, still a trifle disorientated, a little tired. This mood would pass.

His host, returning, broke in on it. He had exchanged his shabby tweeds and clerical collar for a pair of extremely shrunken flannel trousers, yellow with age, which had once been white, a shirt of the same hue open at the neck to disclose a scraggy throat, and a faded Crusader blazer.

"Ha, here we are!" he roared heartily. "Had a look at *The Times?* Any news? How's Worcestershire doin'? A promisin' team, but unequal. Wants a couple of openin' batsmen to stiffen it. Not that county cricket's worth worryin' about nowadays. All this scramblin' for points . . ."

Mr. Lucton, excusing his lack of interest in things that mattered, pointed to the bookshelves. The old man laughed and nodded.

"Interested in books, are you? Ha . . . Never buy any now. Can't afford it, what with income-tax and the rest. When I was a young man I wasted a lot of time and money on them; but now, though you'd hardly believe it, I've no time for readin'." He laughed. The grizzled face, with its ruddy cheeks, had a charming innocence. "If I open a book at night, it sends me to sleep, and by the time I've finished a page I've forgotten what it's about, so what's the use of it, ha? By the way, do you want me to fit you up with a pair of bags?"

Mr. Lucton revealed the significant gap at the top of his trousers.

"Ah, I see you'ld never get into mine. Well, what does it matter? The game's the thing. But, mind you, a man of your age ought to take more care of his figure. Ten minutes of exercise every morning before your cold tub. That's what you want, my boy. By the way, I've been thinking things over. If we win the toss, I shall put you in first. All you'll need to do is to stick in and take the edge off the fast bowling. They've a young fellow named Perkins who's really quick for three overs. And you'ld better field silly mid-on when I bowl. They've one or two hardish hitters, and it frightens these village lads when the fielders stand in to them."

Mr. Lucton's heart sank. He had been hoping to be put in last and to be allowed to hide his lamentable fielding somewhere in the deep.

"It's a long time since I played cricket," he timidly suggested. "So if you don't mind . . ."

The old man nodded approvingly.

"That's it, that's it. I knew you wouldn't. Frightens the life out of 'em. You didn't hear a gong, did you? It's time we had luncheon. Just ring the bell, will you?"

Mr. Lucton tugged at a porcelain bell-pull. He heard the wires scrape, but no following tinkle. Yet, somehow or other, the signal must have been conveyed; for a moment later, a flustered old woman in a white apron and a cap with streamers announced that luncheon was served.

The old gentleman certainly did himself well. The food, for

which Mr. Lucton felt himself more than ready, was delicious: a dish of Wye trout, fried golden-brown in oatmeal; a home-cured ham, golden too, which the parson carved wafer-thin with a knife worn fine by half-a-century of expert sharpening; cream cheese, with crisp, but not overgrown, lettuce, and home-baked bread, made of stone-ground flour from Kington's mill and barm from the brewery at Builth. In addition to this, the old man had brought up from the cellar a bottle of *Château Latour*, which, while he was changing, had been set out in a basket on the sunny dining-room window-sill to acquire the perfect degree of mellowness. He was reasonably proud of his cellar.

"Thought the occasion worthy of a bottle, my boy, ha?" he said. "It's not every day one has the privilege of losin' a fish in water as low and clear as that."

The wine was, in fact, rather above Mr. Lucton's palate; but he drank more than his share of it gratefully, in the hope of raising his courage to face the ordeal that lay ahead. The old man talked of nothing but 'varsity cricket: a subject in which Mr. Lucton's enthusiasm exceeded his knowledge. Out of respect for his guest's supposed origins, he spoke mostly of Oxford.

"Were H. K. Foster and Charles Fry up in your day? No, no, what am I thinking of? They must be a bit older than you. But Tip Foster might have been there. He was the best of the bunch. A terrible tragedy, that! I must look you up in Wisden . . ."

It was fortunate that, whatever questions he asked, he never waited for answers, cheerfully accepting the certainty that he couldn't hear them. It was for this reason and no other that—with tactful smiles and non-committal mutterings and emphatic nods of assent to everything that wasn't a question—Mr. Lucton contrived to steer clear of the humiliating dénouement which he felt was his due. By the end of the meal, indeed, the admirable claret had done its work so thoroughly that he no longer feared it. The old man was so gay and confiding, so pleased by the prospect of a close game, that it would have been unkind to disillusion him, and as long as this Dutch courage lasted he felt himself fit to face any fast bowler in the world.

Unluckily, it didn't last nearly so long as he had hoped, and by the time they reached the pavilion its effect had completely evaporated. In this new light the whole scene—the church with its elms, the friendly rectory, the green width of the field in the middle of which the wickets had already been pitched—assumed the threatening atmosphere of a bad dream. His host, who had left him for a moment to talk with his parson friend, the opposing captain, returned to startle him out of this unhappy state.

"I've won the toss," he said. "Hurry up and get your pads on, and see that you get a good pair of gloves: that fellow Perkins *is* playing. I'm glad you're here to take the first ball, my boy. My friend Hallows, the vicar of Felindre, who's our regular Number One, ain't turned up. Been off fishin' this week-end. Car broken down, I expect."

If the Vicar of Felindre's car were anything like his colleague's, Mr. Lucton reflected, that wasn't improbable.

"What about boots? I'd forgotten that," the old man was saying.

Mr. Lucton showed him that his were soled with crêpe.

"That's all right—but be careful not to slip when you're running," he said.

Mr. Lucton felt doubtful if there would be any running. In a blacker extension of the same nightmare he put on his pads and accepted a bat which was handed to him. The umpires were out, and the opposing team were throwing each other catches and taking them with an expertness he knew he could never emulate. They were so gay and careless about it that he couldn't help feeling they knew his secret and were chuckling over his approaching discomfiture. He found himself walking out to the wicket side by side with the red-faced young farmer with whom they had almost collided at the turn in the lane. To Mr. Lucton, this journey seemed endless, the intervening space horrible in its emptiness. His hands were clammy with sweat inside his batting-gloves, and the bat itself seemed leaden and badly-balanced. He heard his companion speaking.

"This here Jim Perkins," he said: "by all accounts he's a

proper beggar—if you'll pardon the word, sir. They say he can't last more than three or four overs; but he's liable to bump 'em more than a bit, so you'ld better look out for some body-line stuff at the first go-off."

Mr. Lucton would have liked to ask this expert how he should deal with the problem; but by this time they were nearing the wicket, and there was no time for consultation. With a fluttering pulse and a feeling of giddiness, he walked to the crease and took guard, while the opposing captain, who looked almost as old as his friend the rector, but was clean-shaven, tossed the ball to a spidery youth with a shock of red hair and excessively long arms, like an anthropoid ape's.

Mr. Lucton took heart at this. Such a frail creature as this could hardly be the redoubtable Perkins, whom his anxious eyes had already identified in the shape of a black low-browed giant who spat on his hands and glared at him from first slip. The bowler paced out a long run and paused for a second. In the next, he had leapt into the air and flung himself forward through it like a high-speed projectile. Mr. Lucton had a momentary vision of tossing red hair and a flushed face twisted into a grimace of ferocious hostility. He could not see the ball nor even guess at its flight until the bat was almost wrenched from his hands and the invisible missile went streaking away through the slips to the boundary. From the pavilion he heard an encouraging bellow: "Well hit, sir! Well hit!" Four runs. . . . Without being aware of it, he had broken his duck.

The second ball was well pitched-up to the off. As it passed, Mr. Lucton made a half-hearted jab at it, only to discover that it had already reached the wicket-keeper's hands. The third, a short one, rose and whizzed by his left ear; the fourth shaved the seat of his trousers and went for four byes: the "sporting" wicket was showing what it could do. While the fielder ran to search for the ball in the hedge behind the boundary, Harry Kington advanced to the middle of the pitch and began to pat it solicitously with the flat of his bat. Mr. Lucton felt it was incumbent on himself, as an expert, to do likewise. As they stooped together, his partner whispered hoarsely.

"You didn't ought to go nibbling at them short ones," he said. "If you'll pardon my saying so, sir, you'd ought to leave them alone. That's what makes these quick beggars savage."

Mr. Lucton was not at all sure that he wanted to make the red-headed fury more savage than he was already. However, Kington, no doubt, knew what he was talking about. As for "nibbling at them short ones"—there was no time to explain that all lengths were alike to him and that he had no intention of hitting the ball if he could possibly avoid it, being engaged in the unpromising task of trying to keep it from hitting him. He returned to the crease determined, so far as he could, to leave well—and ill—alone.

The trouble was that the accursed Perkins wouldn't leave *him* alone. The next ball, an in-swinger of which he caught a brief glimpse, appeared to be flying straight at the pit of his stomach, but failed to rise, and despite (or rather because of) his attempts to avoid it—came to rest with a brutal thud on the fleshy part of his unprotected calf. Through a blur of pain, he heard Jim Perkins's triumphant yell:

"How's *that?*"

"Thank God!" Mr. Lucton thought. "I'm out."

He picked up himself and the bat he had dropped, and started to limp away from the wicket. Harry Kington's voice recalled him.

"It's all right. Come back! You're not out, sir."

Mr. Lucton gazed at the umpire appealingly.

"Look here, I *was* out, you know. I'm perfectly sure I was."

"If you was out, I'ld 'ave guv you out," the umpire answered indignantly. "And if you think as I don't know my job . . ." He turned on Jim Perkins: "You ought to know better than go appealing like that, Jim. L.b.w., my face! The poor beggar 'ad got 'alf way to square leg before you 'it 'im. Backed into it: that's what 'e done."

Mr. Lucton was not merely hurt but angry now. The next ball was the last one of the over, and he had no intention of waiting to let it hit him. As the bowler hurled himself up to the crease he rushed out to meet him. He slashed at the ball in mid-air and, to his own surprise, hit it.

"Come on . . . *run!*" Harry Kington shouted. "He's bound to drop it."

Mr. Lucton ran like a hare. In a backward glance he saw the ball rising up and up, shooting vertically into the blue above the church-tower, so high that they had actually run one before it began to fall. He was so entranced with the magnitude of his hit that he ran full tilt into the wicket-keeper, who stood waiting calmly for the catch, and bowled him over.

"How's that, then?" Jim Perkins shouted again. "Obstructing the field."

The umpire put up his finger.

"Well, thank heaven that's over, anyway," Mr. Lucton thought.

But he knew it wasn't over, alas!—it was only beginning. He had still to face his host; to account as it were, for that excellent lunch and the bottle of *Château Latour*. Explanations? His performance explained itself only too clearly. There was nothing he could say—even if it could have been heard—which would mitigate that. This solitary return to the pavilion seemed longer and more full of foreboding than his outward journey. It relieved him somewhat when, anxiously scanning the group of men on the boundary, he distinguished the rector's blue, black and white striped blazer hurriedly retreating toward one of the canvas screens behind the wicket. For the moment he would not have to be faced after all; but his thin old back, as he walked away, was eloquent with the scorn and disgust Mr. Lucton could see undisguised in the eyes of the players in front of him. Not that he cared a damn what they thought of him, or needed their sympathy. All he wanted to do was to get off his pads and see what sort of a mess that red-headed devil had made of his calf.

With a glowering face he limped up to the pavilion rails, where the incoming batsman sat hurriedly tightening the straps of his pads. No doubt he was the Vicar of Felindre, whose car had broken down. He rose, and Mr. Lucton stood aside to make way for him. Their eyes met; and immediately Mr. Lucton forgot his angry humiliation and the pain in his battered calf. He was face to face with danger once more. This was the hook-nosed old tyrant who had presided at the dinner-table at Llandewi. As he stared at Mr. Lucton his cruel eyes narrowed, his nose appeared even more predatory, his thin lips twisted in a malicious smile.

"Hello, hello," he said with a menacing softness. "This *is a* surprise. I fancy we've met before, sir. We must look into this. Yes, decidedly, we must look into this."

"Met before? I don't know what you mean," Mr. Lucton spluttered.

"Oh yes, yes, you do, my friend," the old man chuckled. "Ever listen in to the wireless?"

One of the umpires was bawling: "Next man in, please! Hurry up there!"

The parson picked up his bat.

"I look forward to seeing you later, Mr. . . . what was it? . . . Mr. Owen Lucton," he said with a sinister smile.

Mr. Lucton stumped up the steps as fast as his numb leg would let him and entered the dressing-room. A lantern-jawed youth, who was waiting impatiently, demanded his pads.

"That beggar Perkins copped you all right by the look of it," he said gloomily, gazing at the livid egg-shaped swelling on Mr. Lucton's calf. "He's a killer, he is. They didn't ought to play him, not on a hard wicket like this. I reckon you're lucky you're out."

Mr. Lucton agreed with him fervently. He would have been luckier still, he felt, if he had never gone in. His bruise, though the pain continued to grow more acute, was a negligible matter compared with the urgent necessity of making good his escape before Perkins had dealt with the Vicar of Felindre according to his deserts. His mind was divided between his anxiety for that wicked old man to suffer the pain and humiliation he had suffered himself, and an even greater desire that he should keep up his wicket just long enough to allow him to disappear.

Mr. Lucton was taking no chances. A hurried glance through the pavilion door showed him that the rector, having walked off his rage, was returning from the sight-screen with rapid strides. There was another door, fortunately, at the back of the dressing-room. Mr. Lucton turned and slipped through it. Under cover of the pavilion, he ran, as fast as his legs would take him, for a hedge that separated the cricket-field from some sort of road. As he pushed his way through it, he heard, from behind him, a whoop of triumph which made him look back. The Vicar of Felindre was out. Jim Perkins had bowled him. He was returning to the pavilion, Mr. Lucton thought, with an unnatural haste.

(XI)

THE DAMOSEL OF THREE SCORE

THERE was a ramshackle four-seater touring-car left standing at the side of the road. Its back seat supported a cricket-bag, and the remainder of the space behind was crammed with a jumble of all sorts of fishing-gear and a shabby rod-box painted black, with white lettering. The owner's name was hidden by a fold of tarpaulin, but his address was easily legible: *The Vicarage, Felindre.*

At this sight Mr. Lucton was tempted of the Devil. What vengeance, he asked himself, could be more just, more poetic—what means of escape more swift, more effective than to jump into that car and drive away in it? The temptation was grave. He had very nearly succumbed to it when it came to him that the mere fact of his having entertained such a lawless idea was a sign of panic. So far, in his travels, he had never transgressed the law. To have done so now would have been to make his first false step, a fatal slip which would have laid him open to arrest.

That would never do. Already this wild project had wasted valuable time. Glancing over the hedge, he saw that the Vicar of Felindre had not returned to the pavilion to take off his pads, but had made a bee-line for his friend. Now he was talking vehemently and waving his bat, while the other old man listened with his hand to his ear. In another moment they were both of them hurrying towards the pavilion. Mr. Lucton's mind worked swiftly. He knew his legs were no match for a motor-car—not even for such an old car as this. He must make pursuit impossible. On the near side, he found that the bonnet was tied down with string; on the other, fortunately, it was free. He lifted it hurriedly and turned off the petrol-tap—none too soon, for already the old men had searched the pavilion and were emerging, hot on his scent, from the dressing-room door at the back. As he raised his head, they caught sight of him over the hedge.

"There he is!" the Rector roared. "He's getting into your car."

Mr. Lucton refastened the bonnet and ran. Looking back from a distance of fifty yards, he saw his late host bent double in the dusty roadway, wrestling with the crank, while the Vicar of Felindre shouted encouragements and instructions from the driving-seat. Remembering his lunch and the *Château Latour*, Mr. Lucton's conscience was troubled. He hoped to goodness the poor old boy wouldn't strain himself. He would have liked to explain all this excited labour was useless; that, until some expert discovered the turned-off petrol-tap, they would not start that car if they toiled till doomsday.

But this was no time for scruples or sentiment. With a parting glance of triumph mingled with commiseration, he ran, limping, on his way: past the church, past the hospitable rectory, past the village police station—where the back-view of a red-necked constable, digging potatoes in his shirt-sleeves, made him slacken his pace—out on to a tortuous road which, so far as it had any direction, appeared to be heading for the blue line of the Radnorshire moors.

It was only when he had pressed along this for a couple of miles and gradually recovered his equanimity, that Mr. Lucton began to feel something was wrong, or, at any rate, missing. What he missed was the companionable weight of the bulging rucksack, which he had left hanging from the hat-stand in the hall at the Rectory. This lapse, as he quickly realized, was not compromising. There was nothing inside the rucksack connected with himself, and nothing of interest—unless that word could be justly applied to the *New Poems* of Alistair Shiel. He could imagine the shocked bewilderment of the two old men when they read them. This was the first laughable feature he had been able to extract from a distressing episode.

Not that he felt much like laughing even now. His left leg was beginning to stiffen. Turning up the trouser, he found it black from the fold of the knee to the ankle, and so swollen that he could hardly bend it. Much as he disliked the idea of another mountain adventure, he had determined, at the first opportunity, to make for the moors. Now he knew that climbing, or even rough walking, would be impossible: it was as much as he could do to keep going on a level road. His best plan, he decided, would be to try to scrounge a lift from a passing lorry or motor-car, to start "hitch-hiking", as they called it. So far, he had felt like congratulating himself that, on this obscure road, there was little chance of encountering a living soul, much less a motor-car. Now he would have thanked his stars for the sight of one.

During this exciting afternoon the hours had slipped by insensibly; the sun was already declining. By this time his bruised leg had become so stiff and painful that, in spite of the meagre distance he had covered, he felt he would have to give in. He sat down on the roadside and looked at his watch. It had stopped. Perhaps he had forgotten to wind it—he couldn't remember—but by the height of the sun he judged it must be at least five o'clock. In another hour or so, he reflected, the cricket match would be over, and some knowing yokel would have managed to make the car start. Even more probably, the parson would have called out the shirt-sleeved constable.

He pulled himself painfully to his feet and limped on for a mile or so. Now the road was beginning to climb, and each lift of his leg made him wince.

"When I get to the top of this hill," he consoled himself, "I shall look for a drink of water and settle down for the night in the bracken somewhere. By to-morrow the swelling may have gone down a bit."

He forced himself on till, at last, he breasted the rise. At this point the road was barred by a gate beyond which it ran vaguely northward, unfenced, over billows of sheep-walk or moorland. At any other moment of his life Mr. Lucton would have been overwhelmed by the magnificence of this open prospect. Full in front rose the dominant dome of Radnor Forest, deep-purple, bloomed like a grape; westward, lifted above the green lands that sloped to the valley of the Wye, the massif of Forest Fawr grew dark as the sun's rays dipped beyond its clear-cut horizons. There were other and mightier bastions of mountain, rolling away, peak on peak and wave on wave, to lose themselves in the cloudy confusion of the south; but Mr. Lucton saw none of these: his eyes were set on the long road before him, which followed the folds of the moorland with the graceful, easy curves of a bird that dips and lifts as it flies. The mere extent of those long undulations burdened his spirit with weariness; its emptiness was appalling. But was it empty? Midway, in the trough of one of those waves of moorland, a small black object stood in the middle of the road. Straining his eyes, Mr. Lucton identified it as a stationary motor-car with its bonnet pointing away from him.

Perhaps it had broken down and had been abandoned; perhaps it had merely been left there by some farmer visiting his shepherd or inspecting his flocks. Whatever might be the cause of its presence, Mr. Lucton's heart leapt and rejoiced to see it. It pointed a possible way of escape from this lovely, inhospitable wilderness of gorse and bracken and heather. His only anxiety was to catch up with it before it moved.

Gathering unexpected strength for the effort, he limped forward. For long stretches in which the road dipped, the car was invisible. The approach to every crest was a torment of anxious uncertainty; for each time it seemed more likely that, in his interval of blindness, the car would have moved on. But it did not move on. He was being drawn more and more toward the discouraging theory that it had been wrecked or abandoned, when he saw, on the bank of heather beside it, the figure of a woman sitting in an attitude of depressed resignation. At the sound of his footsteps she turned her head, and appeared to be contemplating his approach with increasing interest. Mr. Lucton slowly drew nearer—so near that he could now distinguish the brown tweed suit she was wearing and a ribbon of tarnished gold tissue bound about a head of wavy grey hair. As he came within speaking distance she rose calmly, stepped on the stub of a cigarette with a strong brogued shoe, and advanced to meet him. Mr. Lucton saw that she was a damosel of three score winters of age or more. He halted.

"Excuse me, madam," he said, "are you in any trouble?"

Just so, he thought, might Sir Uwaine have spoken.

She laughed.

"You look rather as if you'd been in trouble yourself."

"And you're not far wrong," Mr. Lucton thought ruefully.

"But, as a matter of fact," she went on, "I *am* rather bothered. This wretched car's gone dead on me. I've been stuck here for more than two hours, and it's such a lonely road I'd almost begun to give up the hope of seeing anybody. I suppose . . ." she hesitated. "I suppose you don't happen to know anything about motor-cars?"

"Well, I do happen to know a bit," Mr. Lucton said modestly.

"Then perhaps . . . if it wouldn't be keeping you back, and you would be so good . . ."

"It won't be keeping *me* back," Mr. Lucton laughed. "At this moment, it'ld be a lot harder to make me go on."

"It looked as if it were hurting you to walk. Have you had an accident?"

She lit another cigarette and offered the case to Mr. Lucton, who thanked her and shook his head.

"A crack on my leg, that's all," he said, "it's nothing to worry about. Let's have a look at this car."

It was not good to look at. From the day's experience it appeared to him that Radnorshire must be a sort of home for incurables to which all the low-powered cars of the early nineteen-twenties were sent to die. This was a venerable Austin. He knew the model well, and had actually owned one in the relatively humble years that followed the war. Considering its age, time had not dealt hardly with it. Compared with the two clerical rattle-traps he had had to do with that day, its exterior was fairly presentable. Though the varnish of its body and wings was cracked—it had been built before the era of cellulose—it was well-kept and highly polished, as were the plated fittings from which, through persistent cleaning, the surface of nickel had been rubbed away. As he gazed at it, not unmoved by the memory of its near relation which had once belonged to him and done him such good service, it struck Mr. Lucton, as it had sometimes struck him before, that motor-cars, long possessed, had a faithful way of absorbing and then reflecting their owners' characteristics. This particular vehicle was a good example of that fanciful theory. Though it was getting on in years, it was well-preserved. No attempt had been made to give it a spurious up-to-dateness or pretend that it was what it wasn't. This, together with its scrupulous cleanliness, lent it an air of dignity, one might almost say of good breeding, even of graciousness. It was a car that knew its station, and its station was one which commanded respect, being that of an owner of modest means who lived well within them and was unlikely to challenge ridicule by vain social pretensions. By the look of it, it had never been in a collision or suffered any violence: it had led a sheltered life. The sight of it made him a little ashamed of having owned a Pearce-Tregaron—the only personal extravagance on his part which could be considered "swank". He looked from the car to the lady—she was decidedly that—and smiled. He liked them both.

"Of course I'll do what I can," he said. "First of all, just tell me what happened."

"Well . . . I hardly know. You see, going down this hill, the engine started spitting; and then at the bottom, it stopped."

"You've not run out of petrol by any chance?"

"Oh, I hope not," she said.

She removed the cover of the petrol-tank and peered inside it. Mr. Lucton gasped at her carelessness. The ash of her cigarette fell within an inch of the opening.

"Please don't smoke when you're doing that," he said sharply. "Petrol vapour's inflammable."

She jumped at his vehemence.

"I'm sorry," she said. "You're quite right—and I smoke too much anyway." She extinguished the cigarette firmly. "This is my fourth to-day."

"That's all right. Just put the ignition control back a bit while I give her a swing."

"That's the lever on the right, isn't it? We never move it. We just leave it half-way up."

Who were "we"? Mr. Lucton wondered. He swung the engine violently without any result but considerable loss of breath and an agonizing twinge of pain below his left knee.

"She's dead enough," he panted. "Are the plugs firing all right?"

"I'm afraid I don't know. You see, I look after the outside and do the driving. My sister does all the oiling and that sort of thing—all the things it says in the book—and the garage in Lesswardine looks over the car two or three times a year. Nothing like this has ever happened before. She's very dependable."

"Yes, that's what the advertisements say. Where's the tool-bag? Ah, yes, I remember. Now hold the screwdriver, just like this, to each plug, while I turn her over, and tell me if there's a spark."

He swung the engine again. Though the compression was low, his heart went back to the pitiful sight of the poor old rector.

"Well, how is it?" he gasped.

"I don't see any spark. I really need my glasses. But there's a sort of crackling."

"That's good enough. It shows the juice is coming through."

He lifted the needle-valve of the float-chamber to flood it; petrol bubbled through.

"It's all clear up to that point," he said. "It must be the carburettor. Choked jet, I expect."

He extracted the main jet and blew through it.

"Yes . . . Choked, I'm afraid. Got a hairpin—one of the kind they call invisible?"

"Will this do?"

"Perfectly." He extracted a tiny black speck. "There you are. That's the cause of the trouble. Funny, isn't it, how an atom like that can bring fifteen hundredweight of machinery to a dead stop? And we're just the same. Some wretched little artery in the brain gets blocked by a clot, and there you are—speechless and paralysed. And you can't poke it out with a hairpin either, worse luck."

"What a horrid idea!"

"Yes, it is. But it's true." He screwed back the jet and assembled the carburettor. "Now I'll flood her and give her another turn. What'll you bet me she won't start this time?"

She laughed. "I'ld rather not bet with you. You know too much."

Mr. Lucton hoped to goodness the car would start: it was difficult to get down to the handle with a stiff leg. He pulled the engine over three times; at the fourth turn it fired and began to tick over regularly. He listened intently.

"She runs like an angel," he said. "Not a sound of a knock. Just a bit of piston-slap. This engine's been well looked-after. Do you know how old she is?"

"I'm afraid I don't. You see, the car was left to us by our uncle. I think he looked after it himself; he was fond of machinery."

"Well, I'm with him there. You'd better try her now: there may be some more bits of grit or water in the petrol, and you might be held up again. If this were my car, I should want to go right through the petrol supply and have a good look at the filters before I took her out again. Just drive on for a hundred yards or so, and see how she runs."

The grey lady hesitated.

"I don't know how I can thank you," she said. "I'm enormously in your debt."

Mr. Lucton saw her fidgeting with her handbag, from which she nervously extracted a leather purse.

"No, no, please . . . I don't want any money," he said. "I only want to make sure that she's running all right."

"I'ld much rather . . . You've been so helpful. If you hadn't turned up, I really don't know what I should have done."

"Don't mention it," Mr. Lucton said bashfully. "Let's see how she goes."

"Would you mind coming with me—just in case anything happens?"

Mr. Lucton laughed.

"You bet I wouldn't! I'd meant to beg for a lift in any case. I couldn't manage another mile with this wretched leg."

"Come along, then. That makes me feel rather less in your debt. Where do you want to go to?"

"To tell you the honest truth I haven't the faintest idea. I was just going on . . . exploring, as you might say. Where are *you* going?"

"Home to our cottage at Chapel Green."

"Chapel Green sounds as if it would suit me. Is it far?"

"About fifteen miles."

"Is there a pub there, where I can get some food and a bed?"

"Well, yes. There's the 'Buffalo'. I can't say if it's comfortable . . ."

"That won't worry me. It couldn't be worse than sleeping out on the moors without anything to eat."

"Very well, then."

She let in the clutch and the car moved forward. Mr. Lucton stretched out his lame leg in search of an easy posture. It was aching even more ferociously now, and his mind, which he tried to relax, was no more at ease. He was so used to driving himself that he hated being driven by anyone else. Not that this drive had the hair-raising quality of the morning's adventure when he had steeled himself to face death in a crash at every cross-roads: on the contrary, his companion crawled along with a care and timidity that were even more irritating than the old rector's furiousness. She drove at a pace that wasn't fair to the engine, hanging on to top-gear until the poor thing had lost speed, and finally "changing-down" with a grinding of pinions that made his heart ache for the tortured metal. At last he could stand it no longer.

"You know," he said mildly, "when you change down into second, you really ought to accelerate and double declutch."

She sighed. "Yes, I know; but somehow I never remember. It's so difficult to think of a number of things at once, and I haven't a mechanical mind."

"Do you mind if I show you?"

"I'm afraid that won't do any good. But I do wish you'ld drive."

"All right. But you'll have to direct me."

Mr. Lucton took the wheel, and instantly his anxieties vanished. During the last week he had often told himself that he would be perfectly contented never to handle a car again;

yet the sensation he now experienced was as great a relief as the first pipe of a man who has tried to give up smoking and failed. The driving of motor-cars—even such an inadequate motor-car as this—was a habit so deeply ingrained as to be part of his nature. With the steering-wheel in his hands he realized what he had missed, and became himself again. He opened the throttle and felt the immediate response of the willing engine. "That's more like it; that's what I'm meant for," it seemed to be saying; "for heaven's sake loosen me up!" Mr. Lucton glanced at the speedometer. The needle was motionless. He tapped the dial.

"This thing doesn't seem to be working," he said.

"No . . . It's never worked since we've had the car."

"I don't suppose there's much wrong with it. Pinion out of gear, I expect. I could soon put that right. It's probably not knowing your speed that makes you drive so slowly."

"Aren't *you* driving terribly fast?"

"Not more than thirty. She ought to do forty-five. The acceleration's quite good for a car of her age."

"Wouldn't that use up a lot of petrol?"

Mr. Lucton explained what he meant by an economical speed. The elderly lady was an excellent listener; and this flattered him, for the female members of his family were not, where he was concerned. Considering the shortness of their acquaintance, he felt astonishingly at home with her; she didn't strive to make an effect or continually remind him that she was a woman, yet she sacrificed nothing of her essential femininity; her company was soothing because it made no demands on him; she was, in short, an ideal companion for a man of his age.

Still, whatever his age might be, Mr. Lucton was still a man, and these reflections didn't prevent his realizing that she must have been an extremely attractive woman. Though she was, perhaps, a little too tall for his liking, she had none of the lanky woman's angularity. Her body was slender and straight and still supple; the cut of her tweed suit showed that it was well-proportioned; the ankles above her rough brogues were slim and elegant but well-moulded; she had a thoroughbred air that made him a little conscious of his own uncouthness. He liked her speech, too. It was purer than his own, without any trace of an accent—purer even, he thought, than the speech of the girl on the mountain, with its hint of a Mayfair (or was it an Oxford?) drawl. And it certainly wasn't "county": she didn't drop her final "g"s or say "ain't", like the poor old rector. Once again he fell back on the lame word "natural" to describe it.

He also liked her voice. It was so low and quiet, compared with the strident voices of most of the women he knew in North Bromwich. A voice like hers would never get on one's nerves. And he liked her hands. They were neither too small nor too big, and young for her age as he guessed it: the brown skin smooth, the nails well-kept and not talon-shaped nor smeared with carmine like blood dried on the claws of a bird of prey. Yet, though these hands were shapely, there was nothing pampered about them. They were alive because they had been used. He noticed, with interest, that she wore no ring.

He was getting "the hang" of the old car now; beginning not only to find out what the engine could do, but also to estimate by ear the frequency of its revolutions and their ratio to the road-speed so accurately that he could slip from one gear to another without a scratch. He felt rather like a concert pianist displaying his virtuosity on a tinny "upright" of the sort that survives in the "drawing-room" of a country inn. They reached an open stretch of main road, and he whipped the car up to a burst of forty or more. In the midst of this his conscience smote him.

"I say, I hope I'm not frightening you?"

"Not a bit. I'm enjoying it."

He watched her face as she spoke. Though her hair was platinum grey, he doubted, on second thoughts, if she were much older than himself or than Muriel. Except in certain lights it was not an old face. Their openness, their innocence—he couldn't find the right word—gave her features, and particularly her mouth, a singular sweetness. Her cheeks, flushed by the moorland air, and now further brightened by the exhilaration of what must have seemed to her a precipitate speed, owed nothing of their lively colour to art. There was, he noticed, a network of crow's-feet wrinkles at the corners of her eyes and her lips; but these were the marks, he decided, of a woman who often smiled—not with a social grimace switched on automatically whenever she spoke, but because she was frequently amused, and generally happy. There was an intimate relation between happiness and true beauty, Mr. Lucton thought.

In spite of these minute observations, he still found it hard to "place" her, to guess who and what she was, and she didn't help him. That was reasonable enough: he could hardly expect her to talk about herself to a strange man, lame and dishevelled, who had accosted her by the roadside and of whom she knew nothing except that he understood motor-cars. She would have a right to resent inquisitive questions, and his own delicacy forbade him to ask any. All he could gather, indeed, from what he had noticed and the little she gave away in their desultory converse, was that she lived with her sister at Chapel Green in a house that had probably been left to them, together with the motor-car, by a bachelor uncle; that their means imposed a careful economy, and that, at the time when he met her, she had been on her way home from interviewing a prospective maid—they kept only one—at a moorland farm.

There was so little on which to base further speculation that he surrendered himself to the pleasure of taking a rest from the road and to the enjoyment of the countryside through which he was passing. It was not long before they had left the moorlands behind and dropped down into a tangle of watery valleys and wooded hills. In its physical features this country was not very different from the lonely land which had oppressed his spirit on the way from the Forest of Arroy to Mynydd Savaddan. It was equally wild and lonely, but by no means sinister. It was, he thought, the greenest he had ever seen, preserving even now, in the midsummer drought, thanks to the rains condensed by the surrounding hills and gradually released from their spongy reservoirs of moss and peat-hag, the delicate hues of spring. And now, in the evening light, these tender greens were enriched and transfigured. It seemed almost as if the sinking sun, reluctant to see the last of such beauty, stood still in the sky; as if the flow of life in those valleys were momentarily subdued or suspended; as if all living things held their breath. Mr. Lucton himself felt an urgent desire to share in this rapt suspension. Even the rhythmical throb of the engine seemed an offence to its quietude; for the car was the only thing in it that moved, and her movement seemed an irreverence. He quietly slipped the gear-lever into neutral, and let her coast until she came to rest on the crown of a bridge under which a dark brook flowed in silence.

"What's the matter? What are you doing?" the grey lady asked anxiously, breaking-in on his trance.

"I'm sorry," he said. "Do you mind if we stop for a moment? I can't quite explain. This light . . . this extraordinary stillness. I feel as if I shall never see anything like it again, and I want to take it in while it lasts."

She smiled and regarded him curiously. "As well she might," Mr. Lucton thought. "The poor soul probably thinks she's picked up a criminal lunatic, and that I've chosen this spot to murder her." He laughed shyly.

"Look here, it's all right, you know," he said. "I'm not cracked, and I'm perfectly harmless. It's just that this country of yours—or this bit of it—has gone to my head. Reminds me of something I read long ago."

He murmured softly the lines he had quoted to Miss Jenkins in his office in Sackville Row a week before.

"In valleys of springs of rivers,
By Ony and Teme and Clun:
The country of easy livers,
The quietest under the sun . . ."

She stared at him with surprise.

"That's Housman," she said.

"Yes . . . *A Shropshire Lad.* Good, isn't it?"

"But how . . . (he felt she was going to say: '. . . does a man like you . . .' but she quickly corrected herself.) "How do you happen to know that poem?"

"Oh, I read a bit in my spare time," he laughed, "and things like that come back to me. That's the beauty of poetry. Fifteen miles, did you say? We must be near your home now."

"Yes, there are only two more valleys to cross."

Mr. Lucton drove on in silence. He wished they had farther to go: he wished he could go on driving like this as long as the magic light lasted. The last rays, of a deeper gold, flushed with rose, were fading when they reached the third valley. It was wider and shallower than those they had crossed, less jealously guarded by woods and hills, although mountain and moorland encircled it. Through the midst ran a lively stream—not one of those secret alder-shadowed brooks, but a stripling river of smooth slides and stickles that flashed in the sun. They crossed a stone bridge of three piers: over the pool below it myriads of spinning ephemerids danced in golden clouds; on the surface trout were dimpling.

"Turn left," his companion said. "Just half a mile more."

The road kept loose company with the river, which, from time to time, swerved away from it and returned, like a dog scampering round a man on a walk. Though the valley was flat, the air had an upland savour. Curlews whimpered and whinnied in the clear sky, mobbing a heron that flapped upstream with laboured wing-beats. In the distance, humble against the dark background of folded hills from which the river emerged, Mr. Lucton saw a nest of grey cottages, marked by a group of tall poplars, which he supposed must be the hamlet of Chapel Green.

"Our house is the first on the left," the grey lady said. "It's called Poplar Cottage."

It was a charming house, Mr. Lucton decided, neither too large nor too small, with a well-kept garden in front of it and, behind, a green-painted wooden shed which he took to be a garage. From a wicket-gate, on which there was a notice that said "Beware of the Dog", a flagged footpath led to a trellised porch. The path ended in a flight of stone steps descending to a green slope, half lawn, half orchard, that declined to the river-bank. At the porch a woman stood waiting. The grey lady waved to her.

"That's my sister," she said. "She must have been getting anxious."

She was slightly the elder of the two, Mr. Lucton decided, and so unlike his companion that it was difficult to believe they were sisters. She had none of the other's distinction of form or feature. She was short—one had almost said "squat"—and her figure, concealed by a sackcloth apron, appeared as shapeless as her hands, made clumsy by tough gardening-gloves. She, too, was grey-haired; but the grey was of iron, not of platinum, and her hair, disordered and coarser in texture than her sister's, looked as though she had clipped it with garden-shears by candle light. Her rather amorphous face would have seemed entirely unattractive but for her eyes, which were of a vivid blue, like a Siamese cat's, and an expression of disarming benevolence, which not even her present suspicions of Mr. Lucton could harden.

"I thought you were never coming, Catherine," she said reproachfully.

Mr. Lucton's companion laughed.

"I was afraid you would, Susan. Still, here I am."

"Any luck?"

"That depends what you mean by luck, Susan. That wretched girl won't leave home unless she can go to a town; but I don't think you'ld have liked her. In another way I've been terribly lucky. The car broke down and I should have slept on the moor if this gentleman hadn't kindly found out what was wrong."

"Not at all, not at all," Mr. Lucton murmured. "Only too delighted. Shall I run the car round to the garage? I see the door's open."

"Please don't trouble about that."

"It's no trouble at all."

Mr. Lucton moved on to the gate. He was anxious to do anything he could for them: a couple of old maids—such pleasant, superior women, too—living alone in the heart of the country and finding it hard to get servants, most probably because they couldn't afford to pay decent wages. He ran the car into the shed and levered himself out of it with difficulty: during the drive his knee-joint had stiffened to immobility. The old ladies were still standing at the gate, and appeared to be engaged in an anxious consultation. As he approached, he heard the words "half a crown". He felt certain they were discussing how much they should pay him. That subject must be avoided at all costs.

"All correct," he said cheerfully. "Now, if you'll show me how to get to that inn, I'll say 'Good evening'."

"I've been talking things over with my sister," his grey lady said, "and she quite agrees with me that it was wrong of you to refuse any . . . remuneration for your kind help." Mr. Lucton shook his head, but she took no heed of him. "You see," she went on, "if you hadn't put the car right, we should have had to pay the garage for a man to come out, and that would have been very expensive. So we both think it's only fair . . ."

"Please don't say any more about that," Mr. Lucton broke in. "I'm much more in your debt than you are in mine, you know. With this stiff leg I couldn't possibly have got to the inn. And I don't want money, anyway—really and truly! Why not call it quits?"

His lady—he privately called her "Catherine" now, and felt the name suited her—shook her head in despair.

"There you are, Susan. . . . What did I tell you?"

"Well, well: if he won't, he won't," the other said briskly. "What have you done to your leg?"

It was hard not to tell the truth in face of those honest blue eyes.

"Just sprained the knee-joint, I think. It'll soon be all right."

"It looks pretty stiff. Better sit down and rest while I get you some supper. Then my sister will drive you round to the 'Buffalo'. You oughtn't to use it unnecessarily."

She bustled away, Mr. Lucton limping behind her. There were two chairs on the stone-flagged terrace.

"Sit down here, and don't try to bend it?" she said. "I'll bring you a tray in a moment. Come along, Catherine."

They both disappeared into the house. It struck Mr. Lucton

as odd that they didn't invite him to follow them, until he realized that this slight was the obvious result of his uncouth appearance. After all, lonely maiden ladies could hardly be expected to invite a ruffianly, unshaven stranger who looked like a tramp to sit down to supper with them. He began to regret the loss of Alistair's rucksack. Though he was well quit of the tie which had landed him in such difficulties, he would have been glad of a shave to restore his self-respect.

In the meantime he was happy to surrender himself to the tranquillity of this sublime evening and the soothing homeliness of his surroundings: the trim garden, so piously kempt and weeded; the modest house—every polished window of which reflected an orderly habitation; the well-known orchard lawn, the sweet-smelling flower-borders. No traffic went by on the road. The only audible sounds—which contributed to his sensation of peacefulness rather than disturbed it—were a whimpering of late bird-song, subdued and tender; the bleating of invisible lambs; the persistent murmur of the river rippling at the foot of the orchard. He envied those two old ladies.

"This is the kind of place for a man of my age," he thought. "It's only in places like this one has time to live. No irksome distractions; no hurry; no telephone; no foolish ambitions; no futile expense. One could buy a house like this for a thousand pounds, and live in it on less than I pay my head-gardener. If I had any sense I'd have bought one long ago, instead of letting myself be dragged by the nose into a blasted suburb. Well . . . it's not too late. What I ought to do now is to dig myself in for a week or two at the inn, provided it's habitable, and have a quiet mooch round to see if I can find a cottage that suits me. A few books, a good wireless set, a cosy arm-chair; a small car to jog about in when one feels so inclined; a bit of gardening to keep one's figure in trim, and a dog for company—I'm damned if I know what more a sane man could want!"

The answer was, obviously, "nothing". Yet, behind it, he could not help remembering how, no less than three times in one tempestuous week, which already seemed like a lifetime, he had been betrayed into harbouring similar idyllic desires, only to see their fulfilment snatched away from him; and, with this threatening reminder, he became conscious of less pleasant things: the dull ache in his knee and the irritation of midges which, even in this paradise, had penetrated his socks and set to work on his ankles.

The elder sister came bustling out and set a tray laden with hunks of bread and cheese on the vacant chair beside him. Mr. Lucton quailed at the quantity.

"I hope there's enough," she said doubtfully. "The bread is home-made. I expect you'ld prefer to drink beer, but we haven't got any. Only lemonade or water, so you'll have to put up with it. Besides, beer would be bad for your leg, in any case. When you've finished, I'm going to have a look at it. You needn't be frightened: I happen to be a trained masseuse. And it's no use scratching those midge-bites," she added brusquely; "you'll only make them worse."

Her tone was kindly but dictatorial—the tone of a "managing" woman who was used to having her way. While he ate the meal she had thrown at him, rather resentfully, on the darkening terrace, lamplight bloomed in the little dining-room to emphasize his enforced segregation. He resented that too.

The conversation-piece framed by the square of lighted casement was one of an intimate domesticity that made him vaguely homesick—not for Alvaston Grange (God forbid!), but for the minute, idyllic existence for which his heart yearned. He longed to be part of that intimate scene, in its gracious setting of polished mahogany, of old glass and silver and fine napery. Though he was eager to satisfy his stomach's material greed, he was even more hungry for the quiet companionship, the unexciting routine of an established home life which these two enjoyed and which he was arbitrarily denied. He was by nature, he supposed, a sociable animal. Never before had he felt quite so lonely, so much of an outcast. Though he had freed himself from the shackles of all his existing human relationships, he realized that such freedom was not enough—that however free, he could not be happy alone.

No doubt this sombre mood was a natural reaction to the

accumulated excitements of the past week. He was fortunately not allowed to indulge it at length; for he had hardly devoured his last crumb and swallowed his last drop of lemonade before Miss Susan emerged like a benevolent hurricane.

"Now pull up your trouser," she said, "and let's have a look."

Mr. Lucton obeyed, and she rolled up the sleeves of her blouse, disclosing formidable forearms. Her hands looked strong enough to tear the leg in two, but as soon as they reached his skin he knew that she was an expert. Their cool touch was as delicate as that of an artist's pencil; they moulded themselves to the shape of the burning joint as closely as if they were boneless.

"Does that hurt?" she asked.

"Not exactly hurt. Your hands feel cold. Rather nice, as a matter of fact."

She laughed: "It's your leg that's hot. You oughtn't to have walked on it. I don't think there's any fluid in the joint; the swelling's below it; but there's a terrific bruise: it looks as if you'd torn a small blood-vessel. And it's not fit for massage yet. The best thing you can do is to go to bed and lie still with a cold water compress till the swelling goes down. Now stay where you are: don't start jigging about. My sister will drive you round to the 'Buffalo'. Go and get the car, Catherine."

A good sort, Mr. Lucton decided, in spite of her brusqueness, and womanly for all her disregard of appearances. While her sister went round for the car, she continued her advice.

"Get Mrs. Malpas to give you an extra pillow, and slip it under the knee. And don't try to straighten it. Do your best to relax, and don't try experiments. She'll have to bring all your meals upstairs."

"Won't she find that rather a nuisance?"

"Mrs. Malpas? Not she! She'll be glad of the chance of making a little money. The poor thing is an elderly widow with none to spare. Her husband was a waster, and left her with nothing but the house. And by the way, talking of money, are you sure you've enough to pay her?"

"Plenty, plenty," Mr. Lucton smiled. "Don't worry about that. I'm not broke."

"Are you quite certain? Your not having any luggage looks rather odd, doesn't it? I'ld much rather you'ld be candid, because, if you *are* hard up, my sister and I would feel it our duty to . . . do something about it."

"No, no. That's all right. Honestly," Mr. Lucton protested.

"Well . . . I will say you *look* fairly honest. But that wasn't a sprain. It was a blow, and a pretty heavy one." Mr. Lucton was silent. "And I don't think you're quite honest in other ways," she went on. "I can't make you out, you know, and neither can Catherine. You speak like an educated man; but you certainly don't look like one. Of course, it's no business of ours. Ah, here comes the car. You'd better lean on my shoulder and keep your leg off the ground. And don't forget what I told you. Drive slowly, Catherine."

The last injunction was hardly necessary, Mr. Lucton thought. After the usual lost battle with the long-suffering gears, the car crawled away. The grey lady was silent and, as it seemed to him, far more distant and cautious than she had been on their former journey. No doubt Susan had been giving her a lecture on her rash behaviour in picking up unknown ruffians on a lonely road. Once again—as before on the mountain—he experienced an urgent desire to justify himself, to confess, to convince her that the ruffian in question was not what he seemed —not only for the sake of his own self-conceit, but also because frankness seemed to him the only fair return for the spontaneous kindness these two women had shown him. It was fortunate for his subsequent peace of mind that the shortness of the road to the "Buffalo" made confession impossible. Within a couple of minutes they had reached the inn door.

"Here we are," she said in a business-like voice. "Don't try to get out till I've spoken to Mrs. Malpas. Then Morgan, her son, will give you a hand."

She slipped into the inn. Mr. Lucton heard her talking in the passage to a pale-faced, elderly woman who listened and nodded her head. He caught the whispered words: "If there should be any difficulty . . ." and flushed with annoyance. They were talking about money. Even his own grey lady didn't believe in his honesty: and this hurt him acutely, for he had already began to regard her as his particular friend and ally.

The two women came to the door, and the landlady bowed to him.

"Good evening, sir," she said.

Her tone was polite, but a trifle forbidding, and he fancied the "sir" came out reluctantly. Mr. Lucton summoned all the elegance of diction of which he was capable.

"It's extremely kind of you to give me a bed at such short notice," he said.

"Not at all, sir. Any friend of Miss Armitage . . ."

Friend of Miss Armitage be damned! He was in no need of recommendation from anybody. The situation demanded a gesture of independence.

"I've had an unfortunate accident," he went on, "and in the confusion I lost my haversack with all my things in it. It would hardly be fair to expect you to take me in without any luggage; so, if you don't mind, I'ld much prefer to pay for a week's board and lodging in advance."

"Oh, really, there's no need for *that*, sir."

"Perhaps not; but I like to see things done on a business basis," Mr. Lucton persisted, "and I prefer to pay my way. Here's three pounds to be going on with."

"That's enough for two weeks, sir."

"All the better," Mr. Lucton laughed.

"Well . . . It's not really necessary."

In spite of her protestations, he could see that she was relieved as she folded the notes and slipped them into her apron pocket. Then he turned to Miss Catherine, to see the effect of his studied magnificence. He was disappointed to find that she looked amused, not ashamed.

"I can't tell you how grateful I am," he said, rather grandly, "for all your kindness—to say nothing of the lift and the supper. Please thank your sister, too, for her . . . moral support. Tell her I hope to come over and thank her in person to-morrow."

"To-morrow?"

He laughed. "Oh, you haven't finished with me yet. You've forgotten my promise to put that speedometer right. *Au revoir*, and thank you again."

Rejecting the landlady's offer of help, he crawled out of the car and entered the inn.

"That'll teach them!" he thought to himself.

In the bar, while he waited for Mrs. Malpas to make up his bed, he ordered a pint of beer to solace his ravaged feelings and drown the after-taste of Miss Susan's maidenly lemonade.

PART THREE

QUIETEST UNDER THE SUN

(I)

THE "BUFFALO"

Mr. Lucton slept the clock round between sheets that smelt faintly of lavender, and awoke refreshed, with a feeling that he had cleared-off all his arrears of nocturnal discomfort and sleeplessness. His bruised knee, too, had made a miraculous recovery: though he respected Miss Susan's command to refrain from experiments, he discovered that he could bend the joint easily, and could even put his foot to the floor without pain. Moving cautiously to the bedroom window, he pulled aside the lace curtains and looked out.

In the dusk of the previous evening he had acquired no more than the vaguest conception of the geography of Chapel Green, and what he saw now delighted him. It was a hamlet of five or six buildings—including the inn and the Wesleyan Chapel from which, he supposed, it took its name—grouped about a few level acres of common-land scattered with flaming gorse-bushes and two flocks of geese which, against the green background, appeared as white as the washing that flapped in the breeze from a line, slung between two posts, in the immediate foreground beyond the road. It was natural, he thought, that both the geese and the washing should look preternaturally white: the whole common was so drenched with bleaching sunlight, so swept by the cleanest and coolest of air drifting down from horizons of heathery moorland, that it would have been hard for any impurity to survive its influence. Mr. Lucton inhaled this vital elixir luxuriously, and felt that the tissues of his lungs—his whole body, indeed—were being equally cleansed. This air was not unduly thin and exciting, like the air of the mountains, nor yet somnolent, as that of the plains, but of a quality that combined the virtues of both, and produced in the breather a sense of mild exhilaration innocent of reaction, whose after-effects resembled those of a well-seasoned wine of choice vintage. It was, to mix beverages and metaphors, his "cup of tea": of its kind a perfect example of that Golden Mean which, in airs as in everything else, was his ideal.

"The sort of air," he reflected, "which makes one feel young —but not too young for one's age. Born again, as somebody said, in an expurgated edition."

In this matter, as in several others, the experiences of the last week had taught him a lesson; yet he was not so resigned as to be able to resist the temptation of looking at himself in the mirror, embellished with paper hair-tidies, on Mrs. Malpas's dressing-table. The result shocked him. No wonder that the Misses Armitage had shrunk from admitting him to their dining-room! The light of mountain, moorland and river-side had scorched his face lobster-red; his nose and his cheeks were peeling, and through the blistered cuticle, for lack of two days' shaving, there sprouted a villainous stubble which was actually grey but looked almost white against its flaming background. It was, in spite of its air of rude health, an extremely gross face, from which women less delicate than they might have recoiled in terror. He must certainly put this right before he revisited Poplar Cottage.

He dressed hurriedly, and limped down the stairs with surprising agility into an atmosphere of stale beer enlivened by the smell and sound of sizzling bacon. At the foot of the stairs the landlady met him with reproachful eyes.

"I was just going to bring your breakfast upstairs, sir," she said. "Eggs and bacon. The moment I heard you moving about I started preparing them."

Mr. Lucton laughed gaily and rubbed his hands.

"Eggs and bacon? That's splendid. I can tell you I'm ready for them the moment they're ready for me."

"But Miss Catherine told me . . ." she hesitated, ". . . that Miss Susan gave orders you weren't to get up on any account."

"Have I got to take orders from Miss Susan?" he asked, with mock indignation.

"Well, most people do, sir," she answered solemnly, though there was a hint of a smile on her lips.

"H'm . . . I'm not altogether surprised to hear that. But my leg's nearly all right. I feel good for a game of football."

She laughed. "There's a cricket-match on the green this evening, if that would serve, sir."

"No, not cricket. Anything but cricket," Mr. Lucton said firmly.

"Well, since you've come downstairs, sir, I won't be a moment."

The parlour was exactly the kind of room he liked: neither too big nor too small. On the sill of the open window, which looked over the green, were ranged pots of geraniums whose warm scent diffused itself in the sweet morning air. On one side of the hearth stood a well-padded arm-chair which might have been made to measure for him; at its right hand, just within reach, a well-filled book-case. He picked up a book by Nat Gould, an author unknown to him, but much more comprehensible than Alistair Shiel, and glanced at it idly while Mrs. Malpas laid the table. Her linen was speckless, the silver bright, the china obviously her best. On the centre of the table she placed an imposing, elaborate, silver-plated vinaigrette which, however unnecessary, gave to the whole a formal air of Victorian solidity. He noticed the quiet precision of all her movements. A neat-handed woman, who must surely once have been pretty and was still, in a tired way, attractive. Perhaps she had been in "good" service. In any case, she gave the impression of having "seen better days". Remembering the tragic story Miss Susan had hinted at, he felt kindly to Mrs. Malpas. He liked her, as he liked her house: the lavendered sheets, the arm-chair, the cosy parlour. There was really no need, he told himself, to look round for a cottage and shoulder unnecessary responsibilities when such charming quarters as these were available, with excellent beer on tap on the other side of the passage and his kind friends of Poplar Cottage just over the way. Chapel Green itself, isolated in its wide ring of moorland, seemed to offer an admirable refuge: neither too much in the world nor too solitary. He must think this over.

"Do you get many visitors here, Mrs. Malpas?" he asked.

"Well, no, sir. Very few, apart from an occasional fishing gentleman." Mr. Lucton winced; "but we don't even see them nowadays. We used to rent a nice little stretch of our own; but since my husband died the river's preserved. Mr. Delahay —that's the squire, you know—lets out rods."

"Rather out of the world, I suppose?"

She smiled. "No, I don't feel that, sir. You see, I've lived in these parts all my life."

"And, of course, there's always the wireless," Mr. Lucton suggested.

"No, I don't think there's any wireless at Chapel Green— unless the Misses Armitage have one. My boy Morgan used to have a crystal set years ago; but it was generally out of order —and then, all this changing of batteries: Morgan had to take them to Lesswardine to get them charged, and we really don't miss it."

Mr. Lucton sighed with triumphant relief. Most decidedly Chapel Green was the place for him. When he had eaten his fill of home-cured bacon and eggs, he was even more convinced of its desirability. Only one thing troubled him: the lack of a tooth-brush and shaving-gear and a change of clothes. This was a subject that had to be dealt with tactfully.

"I'm in rather an awkward position, Mrs. Malpas," he said. "You see, I lost my haversack at the time of my—er—accident and forgot all about it; and if I stay here some time, as I hope to do, I must really fit myself out with one or two necessaries —pyjamas and shirts and a razor and things of that kind. And I can't walk very far, as you see. Where are your nearest shops?"

"Well, Lesswardine, sir, is where I do most of my shopping; but it's not much more than a village."

"Could I get there by bus?"

"Oh no, sir, only on Saturdays. The carrier from Mainstone goes into Ludlow twice a week, and this is his day, but I'm afraid he's started by now. If I'd only known . . ."

"A razor's the most important thing—and perhaps a necktie. I don't fancy looking like this."

"Oh well, if that's all you want, sir, I can let you have our, Morgan's razor, and welcome. It's the old-fashioned kind though."

"I'm an old-fashioned man, Mrs. Malpas. When you've known me a little longer you'll realize that."

"And I could lend you one of his cricket-shirts and a necktie, too, sir. Provided it isn't too skimpy," she added, with a modest glance at Mr. Lucton's figure.

The razor might have been sharper, but he managed, without drawing blood, to scrape away a great part of the two-days' growth from his cheeks, together with most of what was left of their epidermis—the resulting surface resembling one of those fiery Herefordshire cornfields which had been raped rather than reaped by a broken-down machine. Morgan Malpas's cricket-shirt was a great success, being roomily cut. Though it refused to meet at the neck, Mr. Lucton managed to fill the gap with a vivid green tie which made the scarlet of his scarified face more staring. If it looked like that of a brewer's drayman on the verge of apoplexy, at least he felt reasonably clean and able to face Poplar Cottage with confidence. He told Mrs. Malpas that he was going there and would be back for lunch.

"I'm afraid you won't find the ladies in, sir," she said. "I saw the car going out towards Lesswardine half an hour ago. I expect they're still looking for a maid. They're hard to find, these days."

Mr. Lucton resigned himself to the anticlimax. After walking round the green, inspecting the Wesleyan Chapel and the cottage gardens, he returned to the barren bookshelves of the inn parlour. There was no book in them that he hadn't either read or thought not worth reading, so he made his bored way to the back of the house where Mrs. Malpas sat shelling peas in the shade. He found it pleasantly hypnotic to sit and watch a mechanical task being performed unhurriedly by somebody else, and she seemed glad of his company and willing to talk. When he questioned her, guardedly, about the Misses Armitage, she answered without any reserve.

They had been living at Chapel Green, it appeared, for four or five years, having inherited Poplar Cottage from their uncle, a very old gentleman, who, she thought, had been a bank manager. Nobody knew where they came from, but everyone liked them. They were real ladies, and never put on "side". "You can always tell the difference, can't you?" she said.

"Of course," she went on, "Miss Susan's rather a handful. My boy Morgan says she ought to have been a man. A bit 'bossy', if you know what I mean—but then, it's the heart that matters, and if anyone's in trouble Miss Susan's the first to help, though she has to have everything her own way, mind. I expect that comes of her having been a schoolmistress."

"A schoolmistress, was she?"

"Why, didn't you know, sir? I thought they were friends of yours. They were both of them schoolmistresses. Miss Catherine taught English and foreign languages in a big school at—let me see—I think it was Oxford, and Miss Susan was a teacher of gymnastics and physical training somewhere near London. When they came into old Mr. Armitage's money—I don't think there was very much, by all accounts—they decided to retire and set up house together. It must have been a bit of a break for both of them, never having kept house before or lived in the country; but they must have enjoyed it. I've never seen anyone happier. Almost like a young married couple, they were: just as if they were starting life all over again. And then, only look what Miss Susan's done to the garden! In old Mr. Armitage's time it was a regular wilderness. Now folk walks that way on a Sunday afternoon to look at it."

"And where does Miss Catherine come in?" Mr. Lucton asked.

"Well, she's practical too—at sewing, and that sort of thing. Everyone likes her, and nobody's frightened of her, like they used to be of Miss Susan. She drives that old car of theirs beautifully, too" (Mr. Lucton knew all about that), "and of course she's the life and soul of the Women's Institute. Nothing seems any trouble to her. The only thing is . . ." She paused. "Well, it does seem a pity that neither of them have ever been married, doesn't it, sir? That makes such a difference."

Mr. Lucton gazed at her, remembering the "tragic story". One would hardly have thought that a woman who had suffered so much from a drunken husband would regard married life as a blessing. But there it was: one of the many incomprehensible things about good women was the way in which they pathetically persisted in loving the worst of men. Mrs. Malpas was certainly a good woman.

She was also, as he had reason to regret, an excellent cook. He ate far too much at luncheon, and again, in the afternoon, fell a willing victim to an enormous tea which, for the want of the violent exercise to which he had become accustomed, made him feel liverish. He determined to walk it off in the cool of the evening by making a bee-line for the nearest horizon of moorland; but, lacking the customary stimulus of being pursued, abandoned the idea. He was not attracted by walking for walking's sake. . . . He found himself wandering, still surfeited in body but hungry in spirit, along the road on the other side of the green that ran past Poplar Cottage. The little house still pleased him: it was so neat and clean and friendly, with bees buzzing in the trim garden and the murmur of the river rising from beyond the green orchard slope. The front door and all the windows of the house were flung open—as open, he thought, as the owners' gentle, innocent lives. But it was empty, and empty, too, was the garage shed. The spirit had gone out of it. Its vacancy repelled him, it made him feel himself an intruder.

"What a fool I should look," he thought, "if they came back and found me hanging about. Probably think I was trying to cadge another meal."

So he returned, disconsolate and overfed, to the "Buffalo" and its barren bookshelves, and then restlessly moved on again to the "back", where he found Mrs. Malpas preparing his dinner.

"I expect you've got a big appetite after your walk, sir," she said cheerfully. "All the gentlemen who stay here are like that. They say it's the air being so strong."

"I'm afraid it's your cooking. You spoil them, Mrs. Malpas," he said.

At the moment the very smell of more food revolted him.

"Well, supper will soon be ready, sir."

He went back to the parlour and sank into the comfortable arm-chair.

"Unless I can do something or find something to read," he thought, "I shall go mad in this place."

Though he was loath to admit it, the fact of the matter was Mr. Lucton was bored.

(II)

POPLAR COTTAGE

THINGS began to look a bit brighter later on in the evening when "my boy Morgan", the owner of the shirt and the razor, came home. Mrs. Malpas introduced him with a glow of pride that transformed her placid face. It seemed strange that this dark little woman should be the mother of a man of forty with broad Saxon head and wide-set blue eyes. He had been out at a moorland sheep-shearing, and was, perhaps, just a trifle lit-up, to judge by the warmth of his greeting and the strength of his enormous handclasp. Though his mother held the license, Morgan relieved her of much of the heavier work at the inn, and, in his spare time, cultivated a smallholding and ran a few sheep on his own account. In intervals between serving drinks in the bar, he brought in Mr. Lucton's dinner, and stood gossiping, with a towel hung over his arm, in a deep, musical voice.

"It's a treat for Mother to have someone staying in the house. Since my sister Gladys got married, she's too much alone, and this time of the year I've a pretty busy time of it what with the shearings and then the harvest, so as I don't often get home before evening. Just one moment, sir . . ."

A farmer had ridden up to the door. Morgan took him out a pint of beer and joked with him in Welsh.

"That's Evan Meredith, the Cefn," he said, returning. "They'll be sheep-shearing there the day after to-morrow, and he called to say he was sending down for the beer. If you've never seen a sheep-shearing, you ought to come along with me."

"Are you sure I'ld be welcome?"

"Why, bless your heart, sir, everyone's welcome at a sheep-shearing. Plenty of beef and pease-pudden and beer."

"I heard you talking Welsh. You don't look like a Welshman."

"A Welshman? *Me?* I should think not. You'll have to be careful about talking that way in these parts. If you call a Clun Forest farmer a Welshman, he's liable to knock your block off before you've finished speaking. Chapel Green's in Wales, worse luck—no Sunday opening; but I was born at a place called Wolfpits, just over the border in England—in Shropshire, to be exact. Anything more you want, sir?"

At the moment Mr. Lucton wanted nothing more in the world. When he had taken a stroll to and fro in front of the "Buffalo" and smoked a pipe, he sidled into the bar. The company were talking English and Welsh indiscriminately, and the staple of all their conversation was sheep. Even their clothes, Mr. Lucton noticed, smelt of sheep. Though they seemed to be friendly disposed towards him, Mr. Lucton felt rather out of his depth in this highly technical subject and was drowning in boredom, when Morgan, to brighten things up, proposed a game of darts and invited him to take part in it.

Mr. Lucton had never played darts before, but was ready to try. The game, which seemed simple enough, was apparently as full of cunning technical refinements as sheep-farming. Once more, he found himself an amateur among experts and lost six games running: an achievement which immediately set a seal on his popularity, since each loss, it appeared, implied a round of drinks, which included everybody but Morgan, who only drank water. By the time Mrs. Malpas poked in her head to say it was closing-time, Mr. Lucton had accepted invitations to two more sheep-shearings and made half a dozen new friends who offered him rabbit-shooting whenever he had a mind to it and the chance of a pot at Squire Delahay's pheasants, come October. He had even, in an access of rashness, promised to play cricket for Chapel Green on the following evening, before, convinced that he had never in his life met a more agreeable lot of fellows, he lit his candle and went upstairs at peace with himself and the world.

It spoke well for the quality of the Chapel Green air that next morning he woke none the worse for the results of his dart-playing. Once more he slept soundly. The only thing he regretted on waking was his promise to Morgan to play cricket for Chapel Green. Supposing, for instance, he were to find that the match was against Norton Lacey? Such a situation would not bear thinking of. He must manage somehow or other to wriggle out of it. His game leg would serve as an excuse, though, indeed, by now, there was no pain and hardly any stiffness left in it. He was altogether in better shape than on the day before. Even the ordeal of shaving with Morgan's blunt cut-throat razor proved easier and its result less humiliating, the hue of the lobster having been toned down to that of a crab.

He made a careful toilet, and after breakfast crossed the green to Poplar Cottage. The little house had regained its lost soul. As he lifted the latch of the wicket, a clock in the hall struck ten with a silvery chime. Miss Susan, in her gardening gloves and apron, stood with her back to him, picking a basket of roses for the house. At the clink of the latch, she turned.

"Oh, it's you," she said. "How's your leg?"

Mr. Lucton demonstrated its flexibility.

"That's all very well. Let me look at it." She took off her gloves, and Mr. Lucton obediently rolled up his trouser. "Yes, it looks very well," she admitted. "That comes of doing what you were told. Well, what are you going to do now?"

"I'm proposing to mend your speedometer."

"I don't see why you should. We've got on without one perfectly well for five years. However, if you think you can manage it . . ." She went to the door and called: "Catherine!"

Her sister came out with a pen in her hand. She wore reading-glasses which magnified her fine grey eyes. They surveyed Mr. Lucton kindly but with surprise, and echoed Miss Susan's words.

"Oh, it's you," she said—but not forbiddingly.

Her sister wasted no time.

"Look here, Catherine," she said, "Mr. . . . what is your name, by the way?"

Mr. Lucton said "Owen".

"Mr. . . . Owen"—the tone, Mr. Lucton felt, implied that she didn't believe him—"Mr. Owen wants to mend the speedometer, so you'd better go with him while I get on with my flowers."

"Of course. I'd forgotten," the grey lady said. "I'll fetch the key of the garage."

Mr. Lucton felt they were being packed off to play like a couple of children who were likely to get into mischief. Miss Susan continued to gaze at him with doubtful eyes. Once again, as on the day when he had failed to gaff the salmon, he was aware of a scrutiny directed not at his face, but just below it.

"Where on earth did you get that awful tie?" she demanded.

"It belongs to Morgan Malpas."

"Well, you really shouldn't wear green with a red face like that. Complementary colour, you know. When you've finished the car I'll try to find you a more modest one of my own. Otherwise, you look fairly respectable now. I'm afraid I was rather rude to you the other evening," she added, with a smile.

"Well, you know, I really *am* fairly respectable," Mr. Lucton said.

Miss Catherine led him to the garage, and he started work on the defective speedometer. It was an easy job. As he had guessed, the pinion-drive from the shaft was not engaging, and he soon put that right. She watched him with frank admiration.

"I hadn't the faintest idea how it worked," she said, "but you make it seem quite simple. I do wish Susan were here for you to explain it to her."

Mr. Lucton wasn't at all sure that he shared this desire, though the compliment pleased him. While admitting that Miss Susan was intelligent, capable, and even kindly, he was aware of a sub-acid flavour in her attitude towards him—something vaguely defensive and sceptical, of which there was no trace in Miss Catherine's admiring eyes.

"Well, that's that," he said. "Now you'll know how fast—or rather how slow—you're driving; but while I'm about it, don't you think it would be just as well if I gave this old bus a general look-over? I fancied, the other evening, that one of the cylinders wasn't firing too regularly. I'll just yank out the sparking-plugs, if you don't mind."

He unscrewed them, and found that in one the porcelain insulation was cracked.

"There you are! What did I tell you?" he said. "Have you got a spare?"

Miss Catherine shook her head hopelessly.

"I really don't know; but, of course, my sister will. I'd better go and fetch her."

Miss Susan looked none too pleased at being fetched.

"I'm sorry we let you loose on the car," she said. "I believe you're the kind of man who pulls everything to pieces."

"If I do, I'll promise to put it together again," Mr. Lucton assured her. "First of all, I want a spare sparking-plug. This one's gone west."

"It didn't prevent her running all right," Miss Susan complained.

"That depends what you mean by 'all right'. The second cylinder's firing intermittently, and this cracked plug's the reason."

"Well, I haven't got another," she said almost sulkily.

"Then we'll get the carrier to bring one from Ludlow."

"What do they cost?"

"Oh, you needn't worry about that," Mr. Lucton said airily.

"We *have* to worry about it. Couldn't this be repaired? The man at the garage never said there was anything wrong."

"Wait a moment, and I'll start her up and show you exactly what *is* wrong," Mr. Lucton said. "Now just watch the points while she's running. At one moment the plug is sparking; the next it goes dead. And what's more, it's a wonder it ever fired at all. The whole thing's caked with carbon. How long is it since this poor engine's been decarbonized?"

"I think it was done just before my uncle died. About four or five years ago."

"Then no wonder the plug's in a mess," Mr. Lucton said sternly. "That's sheer cruelty. If you don't have this engine decarbonized at once, you'll be asking for trouble—pre-ignition and so on—and the valves ought to be ground in as well.

There's no compression at all, and I'll swear they're badly pitted Just think of the power you're losing."

"There's quite power enough for us, thank you very much."

". . . and the waste of good petrol."

That argument appeared to move her rather more. She gazed at him questioningly; her eyes, Mr. Lucton thought, were like those of a doubtful child.

"Are you sure you know what you're talking about, Mr. . . . Owen?"

"Perfectly sure. I owned a car just like this one in nineteen-twenty. I had her decarbonized regularly every ten thousand miles."

"But that's a big job. It means taking the engine down. We couldn't possibly afford it, could we, Catherine? It might cost five or six pounds."

"You needn't afford it."

"What do you mean?"

"Why, I'll do it for you myself. I've time on my hands, and I should be only too glad of any excuse for using them, so long as you don't mind my taking my time over it."

Miss Susan looked at her sister inquiringly. Her eyes were still dubious; but Miss Catherine smiled, and Mr. Lucton saw that the battle was won.

"I think what you offer to do," Miss Susan said, "is a great deal more than we have any right to accept from a stranger; but since my sister seems to approve . . ."

"You'll have to put up with it. Was that what you were going to say?" Mr. Lucton laughed.

"I was going to say, we shall both of us be very grateful."

"No more grateful than I shall be, Miss Armitage. I can't see a job like this, you know, without wanting to get my hands into it."

"Of course, I'll do all I can to help."

"I'm quite sure you will. First of all you can help by showing me what tools you've got. After that, it will be a one-man job more or less, though, of course, I shall be glad of your company. If you *do* own a car, you ought really to know just a little bit about what's under the bonnet."

"Yes, I'm sure you're quite right," Miss Susan said. "But there are so many other important things to do that we never seem to have time for anything."

"No time!" Mr. Lucton thought enviously. "Lucky, lucky women!"

"I'll come down as soon as I've finished my lunch and start work right away," he said, "and what's more, if you'll give me plenty of rags, I'll promise to make no more mess than is necessary."

Mr. Lucton rejoiced for the next five days in the atmosphere of motor-oil and black grease smelling of metal which was the principal element in the climate of his spiritual home. The re-conditioning of a crock was the sort of job for which he had often yearned, and which had never been granted him, during his later years of prosperity. The task was a good deal tougher than he had foreseen. When he came to examine details, it seemed a miracle that the old car had continued to run for so many years without falling to pieces: that it had survived the jolting of Radnorshire roads and the persistent misuse of Miss Catherine's driving was almost more remarkable, for many of its component parts appeared to be held together by nothing but the Grace of God and the indurated collars of rust and mud and grease with which their junctions were coated. When he saw this he looked back with horror on the burst with which, in his ignorance, he had "worked her up" to the reckless speed of forty miles an hour.

Mr. Lucton was happy at last. In the oleaginous heaven of that little garage, over whose earthen floor he swarmed and snorted in the dungaree overalls Morgan Malpas had lent him in the absorption of methodical manual labour, he forgot his old discontents—forgot even that he was still a fugitive on whose ears the baying of the hunt had barely died. He was at the same time fulfilling a thwarted vocation and renewing the delights of a penurious youth; pleased and, even more, proud to discover his mechanical resourcefulness and powers of improvisation in tackling a difficult task with wholly inadequate means. There was no question of stress or hurry. Time, his ancient enemy, whose harsh voice had boomed at him every quarter of an hour from the campanile of the North Bromwich Art Gallery, held no sway at Chapel Green. His working hours were determined by nothing but inclination, and conscience had no say in them; yet he was actually working harder than ever before in his life.

It mattered nothing to him how long the job lasted—the longer, indeed, the better. By the end of the five days he had calculated as its probable duration, he had done little more than scrape the accumulated carbon from the pistons and cylinder-head and grind-in the pitted valves. If the car had been his own, he would have wired to Austin's at Longbridge for new washers and gaskets; but in this case it was a point of honour to cut down expense, the only thing that cost nothing being his own time; so he tapped out every one of them laboriously from sheets of copper and asbestos which he obtained in secret, with Morgan Malpas's collusion, from the garage at Lesswardine, and made, in the end, a professional job of them. The taking-up of big-ends was more complicated; but by the time he came to this he had made friends with the Chapel Green blacksmith, one of his dart-playing boon-companions at the "Buffalo," who allowed him the run of his tools and his forge and his lathe.

So the five days stretched to a fortnight, and still the job was not within sight of its end. The transmission, as might have been expected, was in a lamentable condition. The task he had undertaken was practically the equivalent of dismantling and re-assembling a wrecked car on a desert island. It was no use spoiling the job for want of a ha'p'orth of toil, so he continued to go through with it systematically, in the virtuous consciousness that, by the time he had finished it, his "old ladies" would be left with a car that, however ancient, was mechanically sound from radiator to tail-light.

Even in the working-day there were, of course, diversions. In the middle of the morning, as a rule, Miss Catherine would carry out a cup of tea and a plate of delicate home-made scones to the garage. Mr. Lucton, sitting on an upturned packing-case in his oil-soaked overalls, devoured the welcome snack greedily, and generally managed to engage her in half an hour's talk.

At first she was inclined to be shy. It took them a long time to recover the frank relationship which had been established so quickly and naturally at their first encounter on the moorland road and then dispelled by the cold douche of her sister's scepticism. He had to coax her back to that delightful mood, and, even when he had done so, the monitory shadow of Miss Susan dominated its background. But, little by little, she thawed—she had never been naturally cold—and they began to talk not only about the minute preoccupations of her own domestic life, but also about the books—and particularly poetry—which played so large a part in it.

Up till then Mr. Lucton had never had any intimate contact with a cultured woman. The culture, such as it was, of his own womenfolk and their North Bromwich friends, was of a stop-press variety and, even so, evanescent. Though they subscribed to libraries, and considered it their duty to be aware of such books or plays as had impressed themselves, by sheer weight of sales, advertisement, or box-office receipts, on the tough hide of the city's limited artistic consciousness, though they patronized "Celebrity Concerts" precisely because the performers were "celebrities", they showed little interest in the arts except in so far as a superficial acquaintance with them might possibly serve as a social asset. They read the new books to kill time, did not regard even these as worthy of that deplorable function unless they knew "everybody" was reading them, and, as soon as their value as conversational small-change was no longer current, forgot all about them. To them, Mr. Lucton's devotion to his limited library of English classics, many of which he read over and over again, appeared an odd foible, and, since it typified his unelastic dislike of everything "up to date" save machinery, a trifle discreditable.

But Miss Catherine, he soon discovered, was not only conversant with those old favourites which, at home, he was almost ashamed to admire: she was also an adventurer into dizzy realms of modernity which would have scared his up-to-date family stiff. If she knew her Milton and Matthew Arnold backwards, she was equally well-read, though less interested, in twentieth-century verse, a province in which Mr. Lucton could not pretend to keep pace with her. In a vain attempt to hold his own, he mentioned Alistair Shiel.

"Alistair Shiel? But how on earth . . . ."

"Go on. That's just what you said when I quoted Housman."

"Ah, but I didn't know you then, and I'm sure I apologized. But Alistair Shiel. . . . Such a very obscure young man!"

"What do you think of him, anyway?"

"I think he's sensitive to the beauty of life, but grudges it and refuses to look at it because he thinks he'll make more impression by dwelling on its ugliness. That's all very well when you're old and disillusioned, like us, but in youth it seems to me such a waste of life. I know nothing about him personally: he's probably an extremely well-fed young man and enjoys life no end; but if he often feels as he writes, I shouldn't like to be in his shoes."

"Any more than I like being in his damned trousers," Mr. Lucton thought.

"But why are you so interested in Alistair Shiel?"

"He just happens to be the only one of that lot whose work I've come across," Mr. Lucton answered guardedly.

"Well, he isn't the best of them by a long way," Miss Catherine said. "If you'd like to have them, I'll lend you some of the others."

Mr. Lucton embarked on a course of Communist verse. He didn't make very much of it. Indeed, when he had finished his day's work at the garage and dined well and played a couple of games of darts, in which his growing prowess decreased his popularity with the "Buffalo" cronies, he was not in a mood for reading of any kind. The strong air of Chapel Green made him begin to yawn long before closing-time, and the "Buffalo's" brew, though light, was soporific.

Still, if he didn't always read the books she lent him, Mr. Lucton profited a great deal from Miss Catherine's tuition. She must, in her early days, have been an excellent teacher, and still possessed the power of communicating her enthusiasm for the things she loved. It was a tender glow, which accorded well with his middle-aged distaste for anything violent, and had the effect of transfusing and transforming her, making this sweet-faced, low-voiced, elderly woman resemble a young girl, after the manner in which some radiant days of autumn recall an April tenderness and seem full of green hopes. They did not only talk about books—the old ones which they both loved and the new ones that puzzled him. She had a passion for modern painting, and taught him to understand many pictures which, because they did not conform to his desire for representational detail, he had previously dismissed as insolent or merely incompetent. Mere perversion of anatomical shape no longer made him scornful. He discovered what "these beggars were driving at", and was finally assured that they were not "pulling his leg".

In music, her other principal passion, Mr. Lucton could not follow her. He had always supposed that what was called "classical" music was "above him", and had therefore avoided listening to it, while the kind to which he was more accustomed, that of the dance-bands, which his children adored, and which, churned out by radio and gramophone, had supplied a perpetual wailing background to the moments when he most longed for silence at home, merely irritated his ears and made him want to howl like a dog. Miss Catherine's music at least had the virtue of softness; and, though he couldn't pretend to understand or enjoy it, the notes of the little upright piano in the drawing-room were as much an element in the atmosphere of Poplar Cottage as the murmur of the river. Sometimes, when he stopped work in the middle of the afternoon, and sat on the stone-flagged path sipping the tea with which Miss Susan refreshed him, he could see Miss Catherine as she sat playing Mozart or Scarlatti; and though the music itself meant little to him, he relished the delicate pattern of sound as yet another expression of her sensibility, the fineness of perception which he had come to admire and venerate in everything she said or did—those qualities which had not only impressed him, from the first, with a sense of her spiritual distinction, but had also awakened in him the desire to protect her as a creature of finer clay than himself, appealingly fragile in her exquisiteness. If she had been a young woman he could not have felt like this.

Miss Susan certainly stood in no need of protection: she was more capable of "looking after herself" than anybody, male or female, at Chapel Green. But, oddly enough, his discovery of Miss Susan was the most remarkable outcome of Mr. Lucton's work at Poplar Cottage. At first she had appeared to receive him on sufferance, as though she were still unconvinced that he wasn't a plausible fraud; but as the work went on, though she maintained her sceptical air and her brusqueness of manner, he began to notice a reluctant softening in both. She was, in fact, intensely interested in what he was doing. Her mind, no less acute than her sister's, had a mechanical bent; her sharp eyes and wits were engrossed, though she wouldn't admit it, in the problems with which he was dealing; she longed, though her shyness deterred her from asking, to know the reason for everything he did.

Mr. Lucton, smiling to himself, encouraged her curiosity. The process was rather like that of tempting a shaggy mountain pony—which, in some ways, she resembled—to eat out of one's hand. It involved extreme tact and patience; but by the end of a week he noticed that Miss Susan's visits to the garage became more frequent and longer; that she was less inclined to bustle away with a toss of her iron-grey mane and a contemptuous smile. He answered her questions with the seriousness that their intelligent nature demanded, and with some pride—for the anatomy of motor-cars was (with accountancy) a subject in which he could claim to be an expert. Then he put subtle temptations in her way, asking her to pass him a particular tool that was out of his reach or to hold a locking spanner.

"I'm afraid you'll make a dreadful mess of your hands," he told her.

She accepted the mischievous challenge as he had anticipated.

"My hands are accustomed to dirt, and I'm capable of washing them," she answered indignantly. "Do you think they're not fit for this work because they're a woman's?"

They were, as he had noticed before, far better adapted for

tasks of this kind than Miss Catherine's. Her fingers had great physical strength, a nervous precision that made Mr. Lucton's look clumsy, and a slenderness that enabled them to penetrate the most unapproachable recesses of the mechanical labyrinth.

"Do you think you could engage the thread of that nut?" he would ask. "It's just a bit awkward for me."

"Of course I can. Give it me. I can reach the bolt quite easily. There! What did I tell you?"

"My word, I wish my hands were as steady as yours!"

She laughed.

"You needn't waste compliments on *me*, Mr. Owen."

But she relished them, all the same. It was a greater danger, he saw, to appear to be patronizing her; she wanted to be treated as an equal. What she wanted even more, but was still too suspicious to ask of him (or of any man), was a comradeship in which her sex was forgotten or tacitly discounted; and this, so far as he was concerned, was not difficult to achieve, for her age and her nature alike discouraged a sentimental relationship. Her company, Mr. Lucton thought, resembled that of an eager, shy, intelligent boy, and as such, to her relief, he accepted it, with the result that, by the time the long job was drawing to an end, they had become friends as well as fellow-labourers.

In addition to her capability she possessed a sharp sense of humour; and when once they had begun to share jokes, a friendship which Mr. Lucton found increasingly charming was sealed. He began to address her as "Miss Susan", and would almost have been justified in borrowing Bert Hopkins's word and calling her "partner". Now Miss Susan's face and her wide blue eyes lit up with a friendly smile whenever she saw him: and this warmed Mr. Lucton's heart; for he knew it would be impossible for a creature so candid as she to feign a friendliness that she did not feel. When he came to Poplar Cottage he knew he was welcome and liked—"for himself alone", as the story-books put it. Was there any other house in the world of which this could be said of him?

It could almost, he was proud to feel, be said of the "Buffalo". Though Mrs. Malpas still treated him with professional deference and Morgan persisted in calling him "sir", he was accepted as one of the family. He was as much at home in the kitchen, where the Malpases ate, as in the room which was supposed to be his own, and, indeed, was happier there, in that charming company, than when he was left in the solitary dignity of "the gentleman in the parlour". More usually, he was the "gentleman in the bar", where he always spent his evenings, while in the village he was known at first as "Mrs. Malpas's gentleman", and later on as "Mr. Owen, the 'Buffalo'."

The "Buffalo's" bar, in fact, was the very heart of Chapel Green; the focal point on which all its social life converged and from which it was directed; the centre of business; the meteorological bureau; the exchange of news and opinion; the stronghold of immutable custom; the court of final arbitrament on all matters of human behaviour. It was also a club—a more likeable club, Mr. Lucton thought, than his own in North Bromwich and actually better behaved—for whereas at the Constitutional he had often seen prominent citizens, who should have known better, in a state of mild alcoholic elation, he never saw any of the cronies of Chapel Green the worse for liquor. Mrs. Malpas and Morgan saw to that. And whereas, in North Bromwich, the hierarchy of age and position insisted on its prerogatives in the bar of the "Buffalo" (as in the church or the grave) all men were equal.

Mr. Lucton made many friends there. If he had been assertive or flamboyant or "chucked his weight about", he would have received politeness, no doubt (for these border village folk had excellent manners), but not the friendship by which he felt he was honoured. He had never before had any intimate acquaintance with the English peasant and, as townsman born, had been inclined to regard him as the agreeable but comic yokel who provided snobbish jokes for *Punch* or was travestied on the music-hall stage by comedians practising synthetic dialects. But the men, young and old, with whom he talked and played darts in the "Buffalo" bar, had a natural dignity rarely seen in the cities or suburbs. Their humour, of which they had plenty, owed nothing to the music-hall, but much to the sources from which

Shakespeare drew his great comic characters. Their dialect particularly on the lips of the older men whose values had not been falsified by the refinements of school-teachers or the vulgarities of the cinema, was a living language, full of vigour and colour.

Nor yet were they fools: he found them not only shrewd judges of character and rich in experience of human behaviour, but also sharp-witted and lively in observation, on which, in their conflict with nature, their existence depended, and skilled in a dozen highly specialized crafts, evolved through the practice of centuries, and demanding far more intelligence and concentration than those for which their clock-punching, machine-minding industrial equivalents were paid double the agricultural wage. They were a cheerful people too, and rarely malicious. Perhaps the community of Chapel Green was too small—as the thronged cities were too big—to permit of life being possible in a quarrelsome atmosphere. There was a quality of "live and let live" in their judgment of human follies and frailties, and, with this, an acceptance of facts—even of facts that were sordid—in which wisdom and charity and fatalism each had a part.

As he got used to them, and they to him, Mr. Lucton ceased to be a lone hand and became, for the first time since his army days, a member of a team, a community. He played darts and swapped stories and drank beer with them; he shot rabbits (not very efficiently), rode ponies, went ferreting, and joined, with a decorum befitting his age, in the fertility festivals called sheep shearings. If he had been a fisherman, he could have had the choice of a dozen trouty streams. He was "a good sport" and "game for anything", as they said: game for anything, that was, except cricket.

On this point, for all Morgan's persuasions, he remained obdurate.

"No, no, I'm too old and stiff in the legs and short-sighted," he said, "to keep up with young chaps like you."

"Old? What are you talking about?" Morgan said scornfully. 'Why, this coming Saturday we've got an 'away' match over in the Wye Valley, and their captain, the vicar that is, must be pretty near seventy, if not over: a grand old sport, too: used to stay at the 'Buffalo' and fish when Dad had the water. The Reverend Harrowby: that's his name."

"What's the name of his village?"

"Norton Lacey. A pretty place, too. You ought to see it. If you won't play, sir, you might come along and umpire. They've got a bowler named—what was his name, Joe?—ay, Perkins, that's right, Jim Perkins, who ought to be no-balled for throwing, by all accounts, but none of the local umpires has had the courage to do it. Norton Lacey's a goodish way from here, so the bus'll leave early, just about dinner-time."

Mr. Lucton would have liked nothing better than to "no-ball" Jim Perkins; but Norton Lacey was much too near Felindre, and to balance this pleasure he saw a terrifying vision of a spare, hook-nosed figure stalking out on the ground and fixing him with a vindictive eagle's eye.

"Well, I'll think it over," he said; "but you mustn't count on me: I may not be able to make it. I want to finish that job on the car down at Poplar Cottage."

"We'll look for you, anyway," Morgan Malpas said hopefully.

They looked for him in vain. On that day he did not return to lunch at the "Buffalo" until he had seen the brown bus go rattling past on its way to the lion's den—or the eagle's eyrie.

(III)

STILL LIFE

So July passed away in a welter of warm, drenching thunder-storms, fulvous sunsets turning the slopes of dark green bracken to bronze, the rain lodging acres of corn and saturating the hill-side foxgloves, which were now in their pride, until their sturdy stalks sagged beneath the weight of sodden bells. The river roared turbid and bank-high past Poplar Cottage, and Mr. Lucton armed with tackle borrowed from Morgan Malpas, achieved his latent ambition of catching a basket of trout. His clerical friends would have been deeply shocked by his heretical use of the local lure, a red worm dug from Morgan's manure-heap; but the thrill of fighting a fish in heavy water was as acute as if he had hooked it on a home-dressed fly, and the result, a dish of plump, red-speckled beauties, was welcome to the old ladies' larder and filled his heart with inordinate pride. The experience made him a fisherman for life. One of these days, he decided, he would go into Ludlow and buy a fly-rod.

It was all very well to think about buying anything. Moderate as her charges were, Mrs. Malpas's weekly bills had been a steady drain on his limited capital. He was not used to deliberate economy, and slow to realize that, in his present circumstances, a penny was the equivalent to a pound in his former condition. In his first week at Chapel Green, he had been compelled, by sheer decency, to renew his wardrobe; to buy trousers that fitted him, new shirts and pyjamas and socks and shaving-tackle. He had spent even more, surreptitiously, on materials necessary for the reconditioning of the Misses Armitage's car. In addition to this, his social obligations as "Mr. Owen, the 'Buffalo'," had involved him in what Stevenson called "a lapse of coin", which was not merely "spontaneous", but persistent, though hardly noticeable until, at the end of the month, he came to examine his resources.

Out of the twenty-five pounds with which he had started his adventure—not counting the unnegotiable two thousand on the integrity of which his continued freedom depended—he had less than seven left; and three more weeks, at his present rate of expenditure, would see this balance exhausted. He might possibly have confessed to Mrs. Malpas that his funds were running low and asked her to house him on a more modest scale, giving up his snug sitting-room and taking his meals with the family; but such a step, he feared, would compromise his position and might arouse speculation, while, even if she consented, it would only mean putting off the day of reckoning.

Moreover, now that his job on the car was completed, he had no valid excuse for continuing to frequent Poplar Cottage. And he could not bring himself to forgo what had now become as much a matter of routine as his former morning drive from Alvaston to his office in Sackville Row. He had become attached to the place, and even more attached to its owners. Each, in her complementary way, supplied a necessary ingredient in the life which he found so pleasant. He would have felt lost and disorientated at Chapel Green, in spite of his "Buffalo" friends, if he had been deprived of Miss Susan's frank, human companionship and the elusive æsthetic background which Miss Catherine contributed.

For a few days, at least, he found the excuse of "trying out" the revived and reincarnated car, and was able to gain time by tinkering with a number of adjustments. Miss Catherine was still scouring the countryside unsuccessfully in search of a maid, and in these fruitless expeditions to remote villages and small farms on the moors, which the heather and the smooth-leaved Welsh gorse now made splendid with Assyrian trappings of purple and gold, she insisted on Mr. Lucton's driving.

"If you don't really mind," she said, "I feel much more confident with you at the wheel. I never really liked driving, you know, and the car seems to go so much faster now, that I'm almost afraid of it."

"What a pity you haven't a uniform cap for me," he said. "I should fancy myself as your chauffeur."

"People like Susan and me don't have chauffeurs," she told him; "we know our station. I sometimes wonder if we've any excuse for employing a maid: we've so little money to spare, and really we've managed to rub along quite well without one. After all, a maid spends most of her time washing-up for herself, and is more expensive to feed than the two of us put together."

Mr. Lucton leapt at this opportunity.

"I believe you're right. What you really want is a man to do the rough work. Men are equally useful and far less temperamental."

She laughed. "What a fantastic idea! A manservant, looking after two old maiden ladies!"

"You may laugh; but I'm perfectly serious," Mr. Lucton said. "It's a comfort, they say, for women to 'have a man about the house'."

"What do you mean? A cook-general-butler-chauffeur-gardener?"

"No. I mean an odd-job man, who can turn his hand to anything. I don't like the idea of your living alone and unprotected. You haven't even a dog, in spite of the warning on the gate."

"That was Susan's idea. A deterrent to tramps and gipsies."

"That's just what I mean. Supposing the tramp or the gipsy weren't deterred?"

"Well, they always have been, so far. And what you suggest is ridiculous: we couldn't afford it. Besides, Susan doesn't like men."

"She doesn't like me, for instance?"

"Present company is always excepted. As a matter of fact, she's quite reconciled to you, and I didn't need to be. But why be so personal?"

"Because I thought of offering my services."

"My dear Mr. Owen, don't be foolish."

"I'm not being the least foolish. I mean what I say. I've nothing to do. I've taken a fancy to Chapel Green and would like to stay here; and—mind you, this is a secret between you and me!—I've got to do something for my living."

"A capable man like yourself could easily find work."

"I don't want to find work. I'm not young; I've worked hard for the greater part of my life and I think I've a right to enjoy the rest of it, and this is exactly the kind of job that appeals to me—keeping a car in good running order and driving it now and then; pottering about and doing odd jobs, like putting a new washer into a leaky tap or knocking up a fowl-pen—you ought to keep a few fowls, by the way—and mowing the lawn, and . . . oh well, there are dozens of things that want doing. The doors need painting, for instance, and the windows, too, want painting and puttying in places, or you'll find the wood will go rotten. I can see enough work to keep me busy for a year at Poplar Cottage."

"I know, I know. Susan's talked about painting those windows herself."

"She hasn't the time, and it isn't a woman's job, either."

"Don't tell Susan that—unless you're looking for trouble! Like everything else with us, it's a matter of money. You probably don't know how poor we are, Mr. Owen. When we've put all our savings and uncle's legacy together, we can only just manage to live at Poplar Cottage, and we've certainly nothing over to pay a man's wages as well."

"What did you pay your last maid—if you don't mind my asking?"

"Very little. We catch them young, you know, and I train them. Their first place after leaving school. Eighteen pounds a year: that is thirty shillings a month."

"Seven and sixpence a week. Well, that'ld suit me all right."

"What nonsense! It wouldn't even pay for your lodging. And, naturally, you couldn't sleep in the house."

"No—that's quite understood; but I needn't, any more than I need stay at the 'Buffalo'. This isn't exactly a new idea of mine. I've been thinking it over a lot during the last few days. A man at the 'Buffalo' told me that when your uncle was alive he employed a sort of handyman, who looked after the car and did what I'ld like to do, and lived in the loft above the old stables."

"But you couldn't do that. The roof leaks, and it's full of dust and spiders."

"I had a look round and mended the roof the other day: there was nothing much wrong, just a tile or two out of place. That's a jolly nice little room, with a fireplace of sorts. If your uncle's man made himself comfortable there, why on earth shouldn't *I!* All I'ld want is a bedstead—the maid's would do, and a table. I can knock up any other bits of furniture I want out of packing-cases. There's a lot of available junk there, too, including a Primus stove, which I can soon get to work."

"And what about food?"

"Oh, that needn't worry you. I could cook for myself. As a matter of fact, Mrs. Malpas feeds me too well: I'm putting on far too much flesh. Well, what do you think of it?"

"I think it's the maddest idea I ever heard of. If we could pay you a reasonable wage . . ."

"It isn't wages I want, Miss Catherine: what I want is a home."

"But you can't call a loft a home."

"Let me give it a trial. That painting ought to be done before autumn sets in. If you leave it much longer the job will be twice as expensive. I could tackle that right away."

Miss Catherine shook her head.

"I still think it's all wrong, from your point of view as well as from ours. You're too shockingly unambitious. A man of your kind, in the prime of life, a man with your education, has no business to be asking for a part-time job that's fit for a feeble old-age pensioner, for that's what this amounts to. I quite agree that a handyman would be useful; but if we ever were able to employ one, we should want to do the thing on a business footing and pay him a proper wage. I'm sure my sister will agree with me. As things are at present, we couldn't possibly do that. Later on, perhaps, when our ship comes in . . . *if* our ship comes in . . ."

Mr. Lucton clutched at the possibility of reprieve.

"Your ship?"

"Our investments."

"Ah, yes. I see. Your investments."

Investments. . . . At the sound of the word Mr. Lucton had felt a stab of anxiety. The protective instinct which Miss Catherine always aroused in him was on guard—for he could not help remembering a number of cases—one read of them every day in the newspapers—in which innocent, solitary women such as these had been tricked out of their slender savings by fraudulent conversion or criminally bad advice. They were the natural prey of the bogus company-promoter, the outside broker and the shyster. He could not let the subject pass.

"I hope you won't think me impertinent, Miss Catherine," he said, "I've no intention of prying into your affairs; but . . . well, in my time I happen to have had a good deal of business experience, and I've learnt how important it is for the inexperienced to have good advice in money matters. I suppose your uncle's will appointed trustees?"

"Trustees? Oh no. My sister and I were sole heirs and joint-executors. Of course, Susan has much the better head for business, so I leave all those things to her."

"Yes, that's natural, quite natural," Mr. Lucton said approvingly. "I quite understand. All the same, these matters are sometimes complicated. Conditions in the stock-market change from day to day. It's no business of mine, of course; but I do hope your sister has a sound man, a reputable lawyer or stock-broker, to advise her and manage your affairs."

Miss Catherine laughed.

"Did you say 'manage'? Can you see my sister letting any man manage anything for her?"

Mr. Lucton couldn't.

"To tell you the truth," he went on, "I don't like the idea, if you'll forgive my saying so, of a ship coming in. It sounds rather as if some of your investments may be speculative."

"Oh no, I don't think they're that. Susan's very hard-headed."

"I agree . . . but, oddly enough, it's often people who know they're hard-headed who make mistakes. Self-confidence is sometimes a danger." He hesitated. "All right, Miss Catherine," he said. "We'll leave it at that, and we won't talk any more about money: it's a dull subject, anyway. What's much more interesting is my idea of painting those doors and windows. I quite realize that you're not in a position to pay me; so let's cut that out. But, as I've said, there are jobs that are crying to be done which would keep me busy for a couple of months, and I'ld like to set about them. Don't you think, if it implies no other obligation on your part, your sister might let me rig up a bed in the loft and carry on till they're finished? I'm not a big eater. Why, I could even buy my own food, if it comes to that . . ."

Miss Catherine shook her head.

"You're kind and you're generous, Mr. Owen; but it's ridiculous to talk, as you do, about our not being under any obligation. We're under a big one already."

"I can't see that. You'ld be giving me valuable lodgings in return for my doing odd jobs here and there. It won't cost you anything, and it will tide me over a difficulty and give me a great deal of pleasure. That seems to me fair enough."

"I don't think for a moment my sister will agree. She's so independent."

"Will you ask her, anyway?"

"Yes, I'll ask her," Miss Catherine said.

Mr. Lucton passed an anxious night. In the morning, as usual, he crossed the green to Poplar Cottage, with the excuse of washing the car and polishing the fittings, which were, in fact, none the worse for the drive on the previous day. It was not a pleasant morning. The rainy July had given way to a stifling August of charged clouds that brooded heavily on the hills but would not break. The river, running away rapidly, had exhausted its mountain springs and declined to a trickle: under the weight of the sunless noon he could not even hear its companionable voice. He was rather hurt that Miss Catherine had not come out to tell him the result of her mission. This silence on her part seemed as ominous as the burdened sky. And neither of them had brought him his usual cup of tea. That was another bad sign.

He finished washing the car, and stood back to observe his work with reasonable pride. The sight of the old crock inspired affection too: after all, he had rescued it from the verge of the scrap-heap and given it a new lease of life; it was sad to think that he must say good-bye to a piece of machinery he had recreated. He was still wrapt in these sentimental reflections when he heard Miss Susan's voice.

"Here's your tea, Mr. Owen."

He thanked her. Her tone was not promising. She stood and watched him in silence. There was, he thought, an indignant, contemptuous look in her eyes. That was one good thing about them: you always knew what she was thinking.

"I should put it down for a moment if I were you," she said, "unless you want to scald yourself; and why don't you sit down?"

Mr. Lucton subsided on his packing-case.

"You're a very odd man, Mr. Owen," she went on. "I've a bone to pick with you. My sister's given me your message."

"Oh yes, Miss Susan? That's good. Well, what about it?"

"I think your proposal is monstrous. No wonder you hadn't the nerve to speak to me for yourself."

"But really," Mr. Lucton began, "I only intended . . ."

"Don't talk to me about your intentions. You ought to be ashamed of yourself. You've been working here for a month doing a job that I'm sure would have cost us fifteen pounds, without receiving a farthing in return or anything else but an occasional cup of tea, and now I hear you propose to paint the house for us on the same conditions! Very kind of you, no doubt, but hardly flattering to us. We may not be rich, but there are limits to what we are prepared to receive in the way of charity—particularly from a man who's apparently even worse off than we are."

"I assure you, Miss Susan, I meant no offence," Mr. Lucton said mildly.

"But I *am* offended. I've a right to be offended. Here you are, out of money, and up to your ears in debt with poor Mrs. Malpas, for all I know, offering to go on in the same silly way. As I've said already, it's monstrous."

Her tone was still indignant; but Mr. Lucton thought he noticed the tremor of a smile in the corners of her eyes. He smiled too.

"Well, you know as well as I do, Miss Susan, those windows want painting," he said.

"How like a man to get away from the point! I hear you've made all sorts of plans: going to sleep in the loft and the rest of it."

"Well, I believe I could make it quite comfortable."

"And cooking your own meals, too! You may be a good mechanic; but I'm ready to bet you'ld ruin your stomach for life or poison yourself in a week. We don't want a Coroner's Inquest," she added scornfully.

Mr. Lucton sighed.

"All right, all right, Miss Susan. If you feel as strongly as that we'll say no more about it."

"Not at all. I've a lot more to say. I entirely agree with you that the doors and the windows want painting. How much paint would it take and what would it cost?"

Mr. Lucton laughed. "I haven't the faintest idea."

"Well, you'd better drive into Ludlow and try to find out this afternoon. Better still, I'll go with you and inquire for myself."

"Then you'll let me do it?"

"That depends on whether you're sensible, Mr. Owen. We're prepared to pay you three pounds a month and your food. You can take your meals in the kitchen, and sleep in the loft if you really think it's inhabitable.

"If you'll give me a hand, Miss Susan, we'll soon make it that. With a mattress to sleep on, and a couple of blankets and enough food to live on I shall be perfectly happy. If you'ld cut out the question of money altogether, I should be even happier."

"There you go again! I think you're the most obstinate man I've ever known. Our terms are fifteen shillings a week with board and lodging, and a week's notice on either side. You can take it or leave it."

"All right, all right, I'll take it, Miss Susan," he said.

Thus "Mr. Owen, the 'Buffalo' ", became, in a night, "Miss Armitage's Mr. Owen."

Chapel Green adapted itself to the altered description far more easily than Mr. Lucton himself, or, indeed, his employers. This was the first time since the day on which he had been demobilized that he had not been the master of his own time. Hitherto his position at Poplar Cottage had been that of an amateur, conferring favours that were gratefully (if not always willingly) accepted. Now, in spite of his protests, he had become a professional, a paid servant.

Miss Susan made no bones about it. She was out for her money's worth. Though she was always polite to him and still called him "Mr. Owen", like Bert Hopkins, she "knew her rights", and her orders, though reasonable, were orders. Mr. Lucton, fortified by the humour of the situation, obeyed them implicitly, and was forced to confess that she organized his working hours much more capably than he could have done himself.

His relationship with Miss Catherine was rather more complicated. She naturally found it difficult to treat a person with whom she had been in the habit of discussing art and literature and sharing an intimate companionship as though he were a hired servant. The sudden change in their relative positions made her shy—charmingly shy, Mr. Lucton thought. The few orders Miss Susan forced her to give him were in the nature of timid requests for which she felt a need to excuse herself. When they were alone in the car, which Mr. Lucton habitually drove, she became, with relief, her old self; but in her sister's presence she was awkwardly and distressingly remote. Mr. Lucton felt sorry for her.

He was not, in the least, sorry for himself. His new quarters, thanks to Miss Susan's domestic thoroughness, were comfortable. His loft was his castle, even more particularly his own and more homely than Mrs. Malpas's front bedroom. Miss Susan had furnished it with a carpet, old glazed chintz curtains through whose brilliant pattern the sun shone as through ancient glass, and a well-cushioned Oxford chair in which he could sit with his legs propped up and smoke his pipe and read the books he borrowed without question from Miss Catherine's library. It was pleasant to fall asleep between smooth linen sheets with the murmur of the river in his ears.

If he missed the genial company of the "Buffalo" bar, which he rarely visited now, there were compensations. He had known for years that, even in moderation, beer was not good for a middle-aged liver, and felt brighter and better for an abstinence which was almost complete. Again, the delights of Mrs. Malpas's lavish table had encouraged a natural weakness for overeating, which Miss Susan's estimate of a working man's appetite kept in check. On the whole, he was a cleaner, a healthier, and therefore a happier man.

There was no more lying in bed in the morning. By seven o'clock he was up and busy with the foundations of the day's routine: pumping water from the well into the cistern at the top of the house, sweeping the yard, opening the garage, looking over the car, and cleaning the shoes which were put out by the kitchen door. This task, though it was entirely novel to him, he rather enjoyed. Miss Susan's blunt-toed brogues were always in a mess; she had an invincible tendency to plunge them into soil or mud; but Miss Catherine's reflected the delicacy of her slim-ankled person, and it was a labour of love to enhance their elegance. By this time Mr. Lucton was ready for his breakfast, which, in spite of its meagreness, had a daintiness and an incalculable variety which made it more appetizing (if appetite were lacking) than Mrs. Malpas's heaped orgy of bacon and eggs.

At ten o'clock, to the tick, Miss Susan came out in her overalls to give him his orders, and the main work of the day, the painting of the windows, began. As soon as he had accustomed himself to the smell of paint, which clung to his nostrils even when he was in bed, Mr. Lucton enjoyed this too. By the end of a week he had acquired a professional dexterity in handling a brush and making the paint go farther than he had imagined was possible. When he had mastered the process, it became purely mechanical, with the result that, perched on the ladder he had borrowed from the "Buffalo", he was able to surrender his mind to a pleasant nescience through which vague thoughts wandered as aimlessly as the cumulus whose shadows dappled the distant moors sailed across the sky. Sometimes he remembered fragments of verse which he had been reading when he turned to blow out his candle on the night before, sometimes a phrase of music that had strayed into his mind and been lost there as he listened to the faint notes of Miss Catherine's piano; sometimes, for an hour at a time, he would think of nothing at all, his mind being no more than a mirror, unconsciously reflecting the quiet beauty that surrounded him—the hushed voice of the stream, the faint shiver of the three poplars—which transformed themselves into a general sense of warmth and bodily well-being and spiritual content.

So the placid days passed, with no more than one embarrassing moment, when, on the first Saturday at dinner-time, Miss Susan, quite unembarrassed, put into his hand an envelope containing a ten-shilling note and two half-crowns.

"Here are your wages," she said. "If you'd rather be paid by the month, you've only to say so."

Mr. Lucton blushed. His first instinct was to refuse; but Miss Susan's face warned him that she was prepared for this, and he pocketed the money good-humouredly.

"Are you satisfied that I've earned it, Miss Susan?" he said.

Her blue eyes twinkled.

"Yes . . . considering the wage, we think you've been quite satisfactory. Though you're thorough, you've used a terrible lot of paint, and you don't seem to be in much of a hurry to finish the job."

He wasn't. He foresaw with anxiety the day when it would be finished and he would find it difficult to put in an honest day's work. Yet, so far, he could satisfy his conscience that he had worked honestly and saved them a good deal more than the money he earned.

Another fortnight went by with a startling rapidity. Whereas the first week of his flight, with its swift succession of emergencies, had seemed an eternity, the rhythm of life in this backwater, where nothing happened and the steps of time should surely have dragged, had quickened to a degree in which days flashed by like minutes. A similar phenomenon appeared to be manifesting itself in the outer world. So far, Chapel Green had hardly been sensible of the political events which were distracting and terrifying Europe. It had submitted to a number of serious but, as it seemed, quite unnecessary Air Raid Precautions (in which Miss Susan, naturally, had taken a leading part) such as attending Ambulance Classes and fitting on gas-masks whose grotesque shapes afforded a good deal of harmless merriment. But now, even at Chapel Green, the folk who had been told, after Munich, to go home and sleep in their beds, assured of Peace in their Time, were beginning to feel that war was no longer an uncomfortable possibility, but an imminent danger swiftly and surely approaching, its shadow encroaching on their lives as relentlessly as that of the earth itself spreads over the moon in a lunar eclipse.

Mr. Lucton had not read a newspaper for nearly two months; but, in spite of this deliberate abstinence, which had been begun out of fear and continued because he felt none the worse for it, the backwash of news had reached him in his weekly visit to the bar of the "Buffalo". Not that his cronies there allowed international politics to interfere with their game of darts; they continued to play, as Drake played bowls at Plymouth. Czecho-Slovakia had seemed a far cry from Chapel Green, and Poland was even farther; but the general opinion expressed itself in the mild irritation they felt when a wasp determined to drown itself in their tankards of beer.

"If that beggar gets up to any more of them tricks," they said, "I reckon he'll have to be stopped."

And, annoying though the prospect might be, there was not much doubt in their minds who would have to stop him. This war, if it came, was unlikely to affect Chapel Green any more than the last, in which it had only contributed a couple of names to the roll of honour carved on the Lesswardine memorial. Farming folk, on the whole, had "done remarkable well out of it", and their sons, for the most part, were now in "reserved" occupations.

Mr. Lucton's composure was rather more disturbed than theirs. Apart from his friend the blacksmith and Morgan Malpas, both of whom had served in the Shropshire Light Infantry, he was the only one in the company who had had any experience of fighting, and he could not face the prospect of war so easily. Though he was well over military age himself, his sons were not. Rupert, the younger, with his passion for aeroplanes, would certainly volunteer, and Leith, for all his cautiousness, be dragged in later; and if Leith went, he asked himself, what would happen to the business—and, if the business suffered, what would become of Dorothy and Muriel?

It was the first time for nearly two months that he had allowed himself to think of his family; and even now he determined not to allow his peace of mind to be broken by anxieties that led nowhere. In the newspapers he had read in the past, and among his business friends, it had generally been agreed that Hitler, annoying though his hysterics might be, was Europe's main bulwark against the arch enemy of all business—Communism. Only on the day before he left home he had overheard in the club that the next meeting of the Steel Cartel was to be held in September at Düsseldorf. That didn't sound much like war—in the West, at any rate. German industry didn't want war any more than we did. It consoled him to think that the Prime Minister was, like himself, a North Bromwich business man.

But the shadow, unconscious though he might be of its growth, was there. It continued to impinge on that August's sunny serenity. Try as he would, he could not insulate his mind from the high potential of anxiety that strained so many millions of human hearts and whose waves were propelled, hour by hour, through the insentient ether.

Even his old ladies at Poplar Cottage appeared to share in the universal uneasiness. He didn't see much of either of them nowadays. When he had finished his day's work, he usually retired to his loft to read the books he had borrowed from Miss Catherine. They were as much "out of the world" as he was, and he felt it would have been cruel to inflict his own—possibly needless—alarms and anxieties on their tranquil lives. None the less, he could see that something was worrying them. Miss Susan was no longer inclined to stand at the foot of his ladder, her hands on her overalled hips, and gossip with him as he painted. More sinister still: Miss Catherine's piano was silent. In its place he heard the restless tapping of her sister's typewriter.

The climax of this disquietude was reached one afternoon in mid-August. Mr. Lucton, lazily painting the frame of Miss Catherine's bedroom window, to which he devoted a sentimental care, heard the sound of voices raised in an urgent discussion from the drawing-room window beneath him. In the middle of it, somebody—Miss Susan, he guessed—closed the casement violently. ("As if it mattered a damn what I heard!" Mr. Lucton thought.) But the debate still went on. He could not distinguish a word, and indeed didn't want to; but it sounded to him, at one point, as if somebody were crying. Half an hour later Miss Catherine emerged and called his name. Her face, at the foot of the ladder, looked drawn and pale and old.

"Will you bring the car round, please, Mr. Owen?" she said in a hard, controlled voice. "We have to go to Ludlow at once."

"Do you want me to drive?"

"Oh yes . . . *please.*"

Mr. Lucton climbed down with his paint-pots. He washed his hands and tidied himself methodically and started the car. The engine was now in perfect condition: it fired on the first pull-up. Then he drove round to the wicket-gate. Miss Susan was waiting impatiently, and Miss Catherine came hurrying along the path out of breath with a bundle of documents.

"I thought you were never coming, Mr. Owen," Miss Susan snapped.

"I'm sorry. I hope nothing's wrong?" he answered mildly.

"Oh, Susan, you've forgotten your hat!" Miss Catherine cried, with a nervous laugh.

"Shall I wait?" Mr. Lucton asked.

"No, drive on. I don't want a hat." Miss Susan tossed her

grey mane defiantly. "And please don't dawdle. We want to get to Ludlow as quickly as possible."

Mr. Lucton accelerated. The old car ran like a dream; the needle of the repaired speedometer touched and passed forty-five, and he began to consider Miss Catherine's nervousness. He looked over his shoulder to see if the draught were too strong for her.

"I hope I'm not going too fast?" he asked anxiously.

"Fast? You're not going fast enough," Miss Susan answered for her.

They had been rattling along for forty minutes before they saw Ludlow tower. It was market-day, and the streets were thronged with droves of Clun Forest and Kerry Hill sheep, dipped canary-yellow. Mr. Lucton swarmed his way through them, conscious all the time of Miss Susan's growing impatience.

"Drive straight to the square," she said, "and stop outside Mr. Burwarton's. You'll see the brass plate."

"A doctor's!" Mr. Lucton thought. "I hope to God it's not anything serious." Then he saw the brass plate: *Craven and Burwarton, Solicitors*, and his momentary panic was eased.

For more than an hour he loitered in the square, enchanted by the carillon, yet vaguely apprehensive. He would have liked to explore the castle ruins, remembering how Miss Catherine had told him that it was here that the magical words of Milton's *Comus* had first been spoken. *Sabrina fair, listen where thou art sitting, under the glassy, cool, translucent wave.* "That's poetry, that was," he thought, borrowing from Bert's facetiousness: "Rings the bell every time." It was odd how, in periods of emotion such as this, great poetry seemed to gain in intensity and even in beauty. He walked to and fro, trying to dredge from his imperfect memories of *Comus* the lines he loved best, and, failing these, with better success, the poems in *A Shropshire Lad* that had Ludlow for a scene—pretty melancholy they were on the whole, and most of them connected with the idea of war. Fifty years had passed, he reflected, since Housman wrote them, and here we were, thinking of war again! *Danzig: New Nazi Moves . . . Poles Mobilize*, the blood-red newsbills shrieked at him from the stationer's over the way. As if human life were not complicated enough without wars!

But here they were. Miss Susan came out first. Mr. Lucton smiled to greet her, but she did not see him. Her stalwart, plump little figure appeared to have shrunk; her plain, courageous face had lost its boyish youthfulness; even her eyes had grown old. Miss Catherine, hurrying up behind her, was a grey wraith. When he opened the door of the car for her to step in, she did not thank him.

"Drive straight home, please," Miss Susan said. "You needn't hurry this time."

They drove away slowly in a forbidding silence. Nobody uttered a sound until they had left Ludlow behind and crossed the Ony at Bromfield. Then Mr. Lucton spoke.

"I ought to have taken the opportunity of picking up more green paint to finish the job. I don't think I shall have quite enough for the garage doors. Shall I stop in Lesswardine and see if I can find an odd tin?"

"What did you say?" Miss Susan asked sharply. She had not been listening.

Mr. Lucton repeated his request.

She gave a dry little laugh.

"Didn't I tell you to drive straight home?" It was only a flicker of the old Miss Susan. "I suppose we ought to use up what we've paid for," she went on, in an oddly lifeless voice, "but after that there won't be any more painting. The cottage will have to be sold; and you, I'm afraid, Mr. Owen, will be out of a job. We said a week's notice on either side, didn't we? Well, I suppose your notice will have to begin to-morrow."

Mr. Lucton was silent for a moment.

"Look here, Miss Susan," he said at last, "I'm a man of the world and a friend. Won't you tell me what's wrong? I might be able to help you."

"I'm afraid it's no good; we're past helping, Mr. Owen," she said.

(IV)

DEA EX MACHINA

WHEN they reached Poplar Cottage they left him without a word. Mr. Lucton ran the car into the garage and looked at his watch. It was well past his normal tea-time and he was feeling hungry; but nobody appeared to be moving about the kitchen; the life of the little house had stopped dead, like that of a clock that has run down. He debated whether he ought not to go into the kitchen and make them a pot of tea without consulting them. No doubt it would "do them good"; but the delicacy of the situation deterred him. People in trouble often preferred to be left alone.

He climbed the ladder to his loft and sought among the books for Miss Catherine's Milton, with the idea of recovering the lines in *Comus* which had eluded his memory. But he could not be bothered to search for them. His snug little room had lost its familiar tranquillity: it was full of restless thoughts that circled and fluttered like bats round the light of his mind. He sat in his Morris chair gazing out of the window across the slope of the orchard lawn where ripening cider-apples now gleamed red and golden in the sun. He had looked forward to seeing it in the spring when daffodil-spikes thrust their way through the turf he had mown and the river-bank lay dusted with primroses. It hurt him to think that this miracle might now be denied him; that, for him, those pale galaxies would be strewn in vain. He felt cheated, and even angry with Miss Susan for having rejected his offer of help and advice. If, as he supposed they must be, their troubles were financial, there were few men more highly qualified to deal with them than himself: his knowledge of affairs was certainly likely to be better than that of the small-town lawyer to whom they had appealed. He reproached himself for having been put off so easily. He should have stopped the car and insisted on being told what was wrong.

"The cottage will have to be sold," Miss Susan had declared. Which meant, he supposed, that they had had a big loss of some kind. Probably it hadn't occurred to them that, if they were in need of cash, they could easily raise three-quarters of what the house was worth on a mortgage which wouldn't carry interest at more than four or four and a half per cent. He remembered Miss Catherine's rosy expectations of the ship that was going to come in. He hadn't liked the idea of it at the time; it had sounded far too speculative; but a bad investment didn't necessarily imply immediate ruin. There were ways and means of turning an awkward corner, which it had often been his job to discover for clients in difficulty. Besides which, in such a minute estate as theirs, this loss couldn't amount to much on his usual scale of reckoning. Poplar Cottage, as it stood, could hardly be worth much more than a thousand pounds. How the poor dears would gasp if they knew that he was carrying double its value in the bank-notes which still lay folded in his breast pocket!

"The price of my freedom," Mr. Lucton reflected. At a pinch it might be the price of their freedom too.

At the moment, thank heaven, there was no necessity to face the bitter dilemma which this reflection implied. Until he had persuaded them to confide to him the nature and full extent of their difficulties, he need disclose no more of his secret than the fact that he was something of a financial expert, and that his advice was worth having. He determined to risk so much without further delay, and went down to the cottage in search of Miss Susan, who, however difficult she might be (and he feared the worst) was more likely to be able to supply precise information than her sister.

He walked through the empty kitchen to the front of the house and tapped at the closed door of each of the living-rooms. Nobody answered; but whether they were vacant or occupied he could not guess, and was too shy to ascertain. A sound of faint rustling upstairs suggested that somebody was moving in one of the bedrooms.

"I mustn't rush them or scare them," he thought. "The only

thing I can do is to hang about until one of them happens to come down."

He stepped out cautiously on the flagged path. The afternoon sun was still fairly high in the summer sky. Its rays beat on Miss Susan's bedroom window, revealing the part of the frame that was still unpainted.

"I must finish that anyway to-morrow morning," he thought.

The idea that he might be discovered and watched on the terrace disquieted him; so, still walking on tiptoe for fear of his steps being heard, he passed along the front of the house to the orchard. The grass still grew strongly, and needed another scything.

"I must see to that, too," he told himself. It was odd how he had almost begun to regard this little place as his own.

He walked down the slope to the river with greater confidence. There was a big trout lying in a swirl at the root of an alder on the opposite side, which usually began to feed at this hour. He wondered if it was rising. There were several other sizeable fish on which he had had a greedy eye lying under the bank. With the sun still on the water and the river running clear, he knew he would have to stalk them if he wanted to catch a glimpse of the speckled bodies before they arrowed away. Seeking cover, he remembered a willow-trunk on the verge of the stream, from behind which he had often watched them; so he dropped to his knees and crept forward on all fours. As he reached his hide he heard a quick movement and an exclamation of surprised alarm, and saw that Miss Catherine was sitting there, her head bowed in her hands.

"Mr. Owen! Oh dear, how you startled me!" she said, with the wannest of smiles.

"I'm sorry . . . terribly sorry. I had no idea you were here."

She shook her head without speaking. Her lips twitched. He could see she had been crying. He sat down on the bank beside her and took her hand—the hand whose elegance he had so often admired. It was an old woman's hand, limp, unresponsive, cold, yet the sensation of holding it filled him with an overwhelming compassion, a desire to shield and to save.

"You'd better tell me what it's all about, my dear," he said. "Your sister's too proud to allow me to help you, as I believe I can; but you and I have always been good friends, haven't we? And I think you might trust me."

"Of course I trust you," she said. "But that won't do any good. It's just that we've lost the little money we had, and shall have to leave here and go back to work. I don't mind so much for myself. I love teaching, and have all sorts of interests. But I'm heartbroken for Susan. She won't easily find another physical-training post at her age; we're both of us over sixty; and her life is so wrapped up in this little place, her garden and all that. After all, she's practically made it. It's like losing a part of herself."

"Are you certain that things are so irretrievably bad?"

"Mr. Burwarton says there's practically no hope of recovering anything."

"I'm not sure a lawyer's advice on financial matters is what you want."

"It is, I'm afraid, in this case."

"I take it that some investment has turned out badly. Could you tell me exactly what it was?"

"Yes," she said. "It was Mushrooms."

"Mushrooms?" Mr. Lucton gasped.

"Yes, Mushrooms," she repeated. Even in this extremity, his surprise and her sense of the ridiculousness of the word compelled her to smile. "I know it sounds ludicrous. We both of us laughed at the idea when the circular came; but Susan went into all the statistics thoroughly. I'm a perfect fool at figures myself, and always have been; but everything was set out so clearly and simply that even I was able to understand. The figures proved that he was certain of making big profits, and that it wasn't a speculation."

"He? I haven't quite got the hang of this yet," Mr. Lucton said.

"The head of the company who sent out the circular. I know what he looks like, because his photograph was on the outside; but I've forgotten his name—I always forget things like that. It was a hyphened name, anyway."

"I see, I see," Mr. Lucton said sympathetically.

"The idea seemed most reasonable. All he had to do—of course he was an expert—was to rent disused tunnels and wine vaults and cellars, which he knew he could get for next to nothing. The big salesmen in Covent Garden wouldn't support him, because it's in their interests to keep mushroom prices up, and, though he'd put all his own money into it, that wasn't enough to finance the affair on a big scale. Apparently, he had found himself up against all sorts of—what do you call them? —Vested Interests. Even the Stock Exchange was against him. So he decided to give the small private investor a chance. I can't think how he came to hear of us. We don't often get circulars."

"There are always such things as County Directories, you know."

"Yes. I suppose that was it. But we were quite unimportant compared with the prominent people—even generals and members of the nobility whose names we knew—who had taken shares according to the list at the end. We didn't pay much attention to that—my sister's a Fabian, you know—but names of that sort *did* give one a certain sense of confidence."

"I quite understand."

"We didn't do anything rash. We thought it all over for several weeks. Susan worked out the figures again and again and found there was nothing wrong with them, and that there was practically no risk of the company not being able to pay the dividends they promised."

"And what did they promise?"

"Let me see . . . Let me think; my head's in a muddle. I believe—yes, I'm sure it was fifty per cent."

"Fifty per cent? You must be mistaken!"

"No. I'm quite sure I'm right. We put in our money a year ago, and they've sent us two interim dividends already, making twenty per cent, and an offer of a bonus if we could introduce more capital—though, of course, we couldn't do that, we knew so few people. The final dividend was due at the end of last month. We were counting on that when Susan decided to take you on and to have the house repainted. But the money didn't come on the day they promised it would, and we began to feel a bit worried."

"Naturally."

"Then, last week, we wrote to Mr. Burwarton, our uncle's lawyer, and asked him to find out all he could about it. And this morning a letter came back from him asking us to go and see him. And this afternoon he broke it to us that our money was gone. The whole thing was a fraud. There'd never been any mushrooms at all; and the man who said he'd been doing so well and paid us those dividends had vanished. Mr. Burwarton says the police are after him, but I'm afraid that's not much consolation," she ended, with a feeble laugh.

"How much money did you put into this . . . er . . . company, if you don't mind me asking?"

"Practically half of what we possessed. Uncle left us nothing but the house, you know; he was living on an annuity; but Susan had saved nearly two thousand pounds—she was always much less extravagant than I, in dress and books and things of that kind. I had nearly twelve hundred."

Mr. Lucton made a rapid calculation. Three thousand two hundred. Half of that was sixteen hundred. After all, it wasn't so bad.

"And you still have the house, of course," he said.

She shook her head.

"That's the awful part. We haven't. When they wrote last year and offered a bonus, we both thought the opportunity was too good to be missed, so Mr. Warburton raised a mortgage on it for six hundred pounds."

"You didn't tell Mr. Burwarton what it was for?"

"Of course not. It was hardly his business. And they sent us the bonus all right. It was having received the two dividends before that made us feel confident. Poor Susan was planning to do all sorts of wonderful things. She's always wanted a green-house to grow tomatoes, and next year we hoped to put up a revolving summer-house. We'd looked forward to that so much.

I'm only thankful to heaven we didn't buy them. Things like that go for nothing in a sale."

Mr. Lucton sighed heavily.

"I hope your other investments are sounder than this one."

"Oh yes, I hope so. What's left is in four-per-cent War Loan. That's fairly safe, isn't it?" she added anxiously.

"Yes, you needn't worry about that," Mr. Lucton assured her. "In fact you'd much better not worry about anything. Things often turn out a lot better than you expect."

"Do you really think so?" she asked, entreatingly.

"Yes, yes, I'm practically sure they will," Mr. Lucton said. "You never know. I must go and think this over."

"Mr. Burwarton was so solemn and hopeless."

"Lawyers generally are. Don't take any notice of that. Now go and look after your sister, and try to buck her up a bit."

He smiled and nodded and pressed Miss Catherine's hand with a reassuring tenderness.

"You're a good friend, Mr. Owen," she said.

"Don't say that. I'm very fond of both of you."

With these words, which moved him as much as an avowal of love and brought foolish tears into his eyes, Mr. Lucton left her.

He followed the river bank down-stream. Since he came to Poplar Cottage this had been his favourite evening walk, for he had never before been intimate with running water, and he had fallen in love with it. The scene was always full of movement and variety—not merely in the caprices of the river itself, but in the multitude of creatures which depended on it for their lives: the trout that leapt in still pools or wallowed in inch-deep shallows hunting minnows; the dragon-flies, mailed in red or kingfisher blue, that broke from the caddis-shell to sun their trembling wings on the blades of corn-flags or lie motionless along reeds; the myriad ephemerids, olives and spinners (a hatch of "pale-wateries" and "August duns" was on the water now) that hovered in sunlit clouds or dipped to the surface daintily; the birds that built in the banks—kingfishers and martins and delicate yellow wagtails—and dippers that bobbed their white breasts from an island pebble; the old heron, standing so still as to be invisible, and so wary that he always rose in flight before Mr. Lucton could come within fifty yards of him; the lapwings that mewed and screamed and tumbled in the air; the whinnying curlews. All this life was now dear to him and familiar, yet, that evening, he was hardly aware of it. His mind was obsessed by a single question that must be answered unequivocally before it could know any peace.

It was in his power at that moment to save Poplar Cottage and to restore the lost happiness of two innocent human beings, both of whom he regarded with compassion and tenderness, and one with peculiar affection. The two thousand odd pounds in his pocket, representing no more than the cost of a new Pearce-Tregaron motor-car, was sufficient to make good their losses and give them the security they deserved for the rest of their gentle lives. But the money he possessed, and could spare, was only negotiable on one condition: the surrender of the personal freedom he had fought for and won and enjoyed during the last two months.

The sacrifice he contemplated implied even more than that. It meant that he could never again set foot in Chapel Green; that he must say good-bye to the place he had grown to love and the people who had taken him so generously to their hearts. It meant—and this seemed even more bitter to him—that he must even forgo the pleasure of enjoying the friendship in which he delighted and the fruits of a sacrifice which must remain anonymous; since he knew that if his gift were thrust on them in any other manner, their pride ('or at any rate Miss Susan's) would compel them to reject it. It meant, furthermore, an abrupt return to North Bromwich, to a life which he loathed even more in retrospect than when he had left it, to cares and reponsibilities from which he felt he had earned his release. It meant —and the prospect of this was more intimidating—it meant Explanations which he could not possibly evade: Explanations to Muriel, whom, even if she had been indifferent to his presence, his absence had humiliated; Explanations to Leith, who had been bearing the embarrassments his departure had inflicted on the business; Explanations to his club-mates and business acquaintances, to whom (including the Chief Constable) his disappearance must have provided a nine days' wonder and an opportunity for all kinds of amused speculations; Explanations to Mr. Fowler, the butler. (No, whatever might happen, he was damned if he was going to explain anything to Fowler!) It meant that he would be condemned to walk through the streets of North Bromwich, a city in which he had been respected for thirty years, as a marked man no longer entitled to respect a man who had divagated, who had shown himself as an unreliable oddity, the object of obscene sniggers and pointing fingers. It would take him years—in all probability the rest of his life—to live down the reputation earned in those two short months. Could he face this embarrassing future, this loss of pride? Was he justified in accepting them under a compulsion no more urgent than his desire to satisfy a romantic whim?

"Well, I am romantic," he told himself. "I just happen to be made that way. If I had been the hard-headed business-man I'm supposed to be, and that people want me to be, I shouldn't be where I am now. I've done things by halves all my life. I've been too damned timid and conventional; butter wouldn't melt in my mouth. If I choose to chuck away a couple of thousand pounds for the sake of a gesture, it's my own business and nobody else's. I've had a good run for my money, and that's more than most of them can say."

Another aspect of the question presented itself. This freedom, which, in spite of his spontaneous romanticism, he was still so reluctant to surrender—how far could he rely on maintaining it in any case? Apart from the unnegotiable hoard, he had little money left. If Poplar Cottage were sold, and the old ladies departed, he would be forced to find employment of some kind, and could hardly expect to fall on his feet so easily a second time. Living on the most modest scale, he could not count on paying his way for more than a couple of months; and, in a couple of months, he told himself, if another Munich were rejected (as he felt it should be) the whole world might be plunged into war. If that dreadful moment arrived, it would become his duty, no less than a necessity, to return to North Bromwich, to stand by his family and by his business, from which Leith would almost certainly be snatched away.

By the time he had reached this hypothetical conclusion, and was wavering, in spite of its complications, towards his original plan, Mr. Lucton had walked two miles down-stream and reached a point where the Lesswardine road, running close to the river, suggested an easier way of returning to Chapel Green.

"I won't finally make up my mind till I get there," he soothed himself. "A brisk walk may help me to think a little more clearly."

At this moment it seemed as if the forces of nature were mischievously conspiring to make the decision more difficult. The sun had now almost reached the dark rim of the western hills; the wide upland basin lay drenched in a flood of golden light which threw every irregularity of the landscape into sharp relief, and cast lengthening shadows, velvety black, upon the green meadows on either hand and on the road before him. It was a moment of warm stillness, of suspension, resembling that in which, after their first meeting, he had allowed Miss Catherine's car to coast and come to rest on the bridge, and quoted the lines of Housman that had marked the beginning of their companionship. Never in all his time at Chapel Green had the valley appeared more lovely, its rapt quietude more consoling. Its beauty tugged at his heart. This place was his spirit's home. He rebelled against being compelled to leave it.

He paused for a moment drinking in that beauty, savouring that quietude. He stood there, enraptured, until the sun dipped behind the hills and the landscape, losing its magic light, became flat and unenchanted. Then, bracing himself to face the last mile to Poplar Cottage, he stepped out briskly.

The long road lay empty before him--he was glad of this, for in his present mood he was loth to meet any acquaintance—until suddenly, in the far distance, he perceived the figure of a woman on a low-geared bicycle who appeared to be treadling towards him at an inordinate pace. It was probably, he imagined, the district nurse hurrying to a maternity-case at one of the neighbouring farms. She was a particular friend and ally of Miss Susan's, so he prepared to greet her.

As she drew nearer, still pedalling furiously, he saw he had been mistaken. She wasn't the district nurse after all, and yet, though he couldn't place her, there was something about her that seemed to him vaguely familiar. When she came within twenty yards, she lifted her eyes from the front wheel on which they had been concentrated. He couldn't discern her features, for the light was fading and, such as it was, against him; but the sight of himself appeared to affect her strangely. She was losing control. The bicycle began to wobble. It swerved from one side of the road to the other and, in spite of his attempt to evade it, finished up with the front wheel wedged between Mr. Lucton's legs, while the rider collapsed ignominiously in the dust, as though she had fainted.

Mr. Lucton disentangled the bicycle from his legs and bent over her. She picked herself up to her knees and stared at him, speechless, her eyes wide, with horrified amazement. Then she put her hands to them and burst into tears.

"Miss Jenkins, Miss Jenkins," he said, "you mustn't do that. It's all right. It's only me."

"I know it's you, sir, I *know*," she wailed. "But I couldn't believe it. I thought you were a ghost. Oh dear, dear, dear, I shall never get over it."

She shook her head helplessly and broke down again. Mr. Lucton did his best to console her. He took her arm and hoisted her on to her feet.

"There, there," he said. "You mustn't cry like that. I'm a long way from being a ghost, I give you my word. What a mess you've made of your skirt." He dusted it clumsily. "Ah, that's better. No damage done to the bicycle either. I caught it just as it fell. Now you're feeling better, aren't you?"

Miss Jenkins assented tearfully.

"It was too much," she wailed. "I just couldn't believe it. Seeing you there, like that, all of a sudden, when I looked up. I'm afraid I . . . I lost my head." She laughed feebly. "So unlike me, too. Oh dear, dear, dear . . ."

"What are you doing here, Miss Jenkins?"

"I've come on my holiday, sir. I think I told you, my mother lives at Mainstone."

"Ah yes. I remember now. That was a long time ago."

"Just exactly two months, sir. It was the very day when you . . . you . . . Oh dear, oh dear . . . I shall never get over it."

"Oh yes, you will," Mr. Lucton told her encouragingly. "You'll be perfectly right in a minute or two. How are things going on at the office?"

"They were all right when I left, three days ago, sir. At first, of course, it was dreadfully difficult; but Mr. Leith has been perfectly splendid; you've no idea how splendid he's been."

"Oh, yes, he's capable enough," Mr. Lucton admitted, with less enthusiasm.

"And now everything's running just as smoothly as if . . . well, you know what I mean, sir."

Mr. Lucton helped her out.

"Yes, yes. That's most satisfactory."

"We've even been getting new clients—as the result of the sympathy, you know, that everyone felt."

Mr. Lucton fell back on a cliché.

"It's an ill wind that blows nobody any good, Miss Jenkins," he said. "How's my wife, by the way?" he added casually.

"Oh dear, Mr. Lucton, my mind's gone quite blank. Let me see. Oh yes. I remember what Mr. Leith told me. Mrs. Lucton and Miss Dorothy have gone to the Rivvy-era, to Antibes, I think, the place where the poor Duke of Windsor goes. They say it's so good for the nerves—sun-bathing, I mean, and Mr. Leith thought they'd better take the opportunity of getting some during the alterations . . ."

Mr. Lucton broke in: "Alterations? What alterations?"

"Oh, I really don't know," Miss Jenkins said. "Just some work the builders are doing up at the house."

"I've heard nothing of this," Mr. Lucton began . . .

"Well, of course, sir, you wouldn't, would you?"

Mr. Lucton uttered something between a snort and a sigh. "I forgot to ask about Rupert," he said.

"He's somewhere in camp, I think, sir, with the Auxiliary Air Force. It's dreadful all this talk about war, sir, isn't it? If it gets any worse I'm sure Mr. Leith will join the Territorials. That's what's been worrying us at the office, with you away."

"Well, you needn't worry any more. When does your holiday end, Miss Jenkins?"

"I've four more days left, sir."

"You'd better make it a week. You'll need that to get over this upset."

"Oh, I couldn't, really, sir. You see, Mr. Leith will be expecting me. Besides, I'm quite all right again now. It's wonderful, isn't it?"

"What's wonderful?"

"That . . . well, that it should have been *me*."

"I don't understand even now."

"That it should have been me, running into you, that brought back your memory."

Mr. Lucton laughed.

"Yes, yes. Delightful for both of us. Much obliged, Miss Jenkins. You arrived, rather violently, I admit, at a critical moment. Now you'd better ride home before it's quite dark and enjoy the rest of your holiday."

"Oh, I enjoy every single minute of it," Miss Jenkins glowed. "It's so lovely here, sir, isn't it? So peaceful! Whenever I arrive here I always say 'Thank heaven nothing can happen'. And there you are: something did! Like a miracle, wasn't it?" She paused awkwardly. "Now, I think, as you say, sir, I'd better be getting along. Mother will be excited to hear about everything. She's over eighty, you know, sir. A great age, isn't it? And all her faculties."

Mr. Lucton nodded his satisfaction at old Mrs. Jenkins's state of health. Her daughter mounted her bicycle, and with a tremulous smile was off again, pedalling like mad. She didn't look any too safe even now, Mr. Lucton thought. No wonder so many cyclists were killed on the roads.

It was nearly dark when he reached Poplar Cottage. In the

kitchen the lamp had been lit and turned down, but his supper was laid on the table. Miss Susan (or was it Miss Catherine?) had made amends for his scamped tea by putting on a piece of cold bacon, which was one of his favourite foods, to carve for himself. He cut himself a couple of slices and then retired hurriedly to his loft. Now that Miss Jenkins's discovery of his whereabouts had forced his hand, he felt he would rather leave Chapel Green unobtrusively, without running the emotional risk of protracted farewells. This was the night of the week on which he generally went to the "Buffalo", so that his early disappearance would not seem unusual.

Alone in the loft, he lit his candle and ate his supper. It was important, he thought, to go to bed early and get as much sleep as he could; for he planned to set out soon after dawn before anybody in Chapel Green was stirring and likely to see him. By the time he had finished his supper it was half-past nine and pitch-dark outside. First of all, for Miss Susan's sake, he was anxious to leave the room tidy; so he made a perfunctory spring-cleaning which, so far as he could see by candlelight, appeared to be fairly thorough. Next he spread out his surplus clothes on the bed—they included Alistair Shiel's shirt and grey flannel trousers—and tied them up in a bundle which he addressed, without comment, to Morgan Malpas. The books he had borrowed from Miss Catherine's library came last. He was sorry to be parted from these, and handled them tenderly. There was one, a volume of poetry she had lent him only a few days before, which he had not even had time to glance at. He opened the book and turned the pages haphazard. A single line, the beginning of a poem, caught his eye: "*Look thy last on all things lovely.*" He read no more. There was no place in his present plans for sentimental regrets. He closed the book with a snap, and set it with the others in an orderly pile on the table. Then he found an odd sheet of paper and a pencil and sat down to write.

Dear Miss Catherine (he wrote),

This means "Dear Miss Susan" too. I put you, Miss Catherine, first because, but for you, I should never have come to Poplar Cottage.

When I say "dear", I mean what I'm writing literally; for I think I am old enough, and you know me well enough now, for me to say without impropriety that you're both of you dear to me. In this rather dirty envelope—I have no other—you will find the wherewithal to put your affairs in order and repay the money you borrowed on mortgage. It's no use being angry with me, Miss Susan. As you've told me, I'm an odd man—in both senses of the words—and I can be just as obstinate, when I want to, as you. Please don't think there's anything fishy about this. The money isn't false, and I haven't stolen it. Take it to the bank and pay into your account, and when you re-invest it put it into Insurance Stocks or four per cent War Loan, or, better still, buy yourselves a Joint Annuity, on which you will probably get half as much again. Your bank manager will see to this for you. I'm going away from Chapel Green without saying good-bye, and you'll probably—almost certainly—never see me again. By the way, I think there's just about enough paint to finish that bedroom window if you use it carefully. I don't think I have any more to say, except that I remain,

Yours gratefully and affectionately,
"Owen."

Mr. Lucton folded the letter along with the notes, all but ten pounds' worth, which he put in his pocket for the expenses of the journey. He closed the bank envelope and addressed it: *The Misses Armitage*, and propped it up against the books on the table with the key of the garage. Then he lay down on the bed in his clothes—he had packed the two pairs of pyjamas in Morgan's parcel—and fell asleep, for the last time, with the music of the river in his ears.

He awoke with the first light of dawn to a misty morning; lit his candle to shave by and to make sure that he had left nothing undone, and stepped out of the yard on to the road to Lesswardine. At this early hour the mist gave the air an autumnal savour, like that of a day in early September. In the white light, the dew on the verges resembled frost, and he found the coolness exhilarating. It was a mysterious journey. He knew nothing of what awaited him in North Bromwich, save the fact that it was bound to be difficult and embarrassing. The thought of those Explanations continued to worry him, until he remembered that, in his successful encounter with Miss Jenkins, he had explained nothing at all. That, no doubt, was the right line to take. He wondered how far it would carry him.

But it was no use wondering. He was as little the master of his immediate fate as a bullock carried along to the slaughter on the moving platform of a stockyard, or a criminal marching to the dock. It was some consolation to know that he was physically more vigorous and fitter to deal with the unknown emergency than he had been for years. Not many men of his age could have covered the eight miles from Chapel Green to Lesswardine in less than two hours.

He reached the village, in fact, a good deal earlier than he need have done, for nobody in it was awake. He hung on the bridge that spans the Teme, waiting for the garage to open, and watching the early rise of trout in the shadow under the piers.

"Next year," he thought, "I shall have to rent some water and tackle this dry-fly business properly. It'll give me an excuse for getting away at week-ends. I wonder how much it would cost to take a rod on a river like this?"

It came to him suddenly that this was a problem that need not worry him. He was no longer poor, and could take his choice of all the best water in England. There was something to be said for material wealth after all.

He heard the scrape of the garage door, which a sleepy youth was dragging open, and hurried away from the bridge.

"Here, son," he said. "What time does your boss turn up?"

"He'll be here any minute," the boy said sulkily.

"Where does he live?"

"First house round the corner."

Mr. Lucton knocked at the door. As he did so, a clock inside the house struck seven, and the proprietor of the garage, whom he knew, emerged in his shirt-sleeves.

"Hello, Mr. Owen," he said. "What are you doing here at this time?"

"I want you to take me to North Bromwich as quickly as possible."

"North Bromwich? Good Lord! What d'you want to go there for? Nothing wrong, I hope?"

"No, no. Just a matter of business. Can you manage to take me?"

"I dare say I might. It'll cost a good bit, though. I can't do it at less than sixpence a mile, and it's sixty-four. That's three pound four counting the return."

"That's all right. Can you start at once? I want to get there as soon after nine as possible."

The garage-man laughed.

"Come into a fortune, by the look of it."

"Well, not exactly that; but I'm not going to bilk you. I'll pay you in advance if you like."

"Get away with you! Don't talk like that. We're old friends, you and me, though you did me out of the job of decarbonizing Miss Armitage's Austin. I told that old lady again and again it ought to be done, but she wouldn't heed me. Want to get there by nine, do you? I doubt if that can be done. The clock's just struck seven. That means averaging thirty-two, and the road's not a fast one."

"Well, do your best anyway."

"I'll take the V eight Ford. She's done fifty thousand miles, but she's still good for seventy. Wait a moment while I get an overcoat; it's a bit fresh this morning, but I reckon the mist's for heat."

They left Lesswardine at ten minutes past seven. Mr. Lucton remembered very little of that journey, save that in the first ten miles he was frozen and in the last ten sweltering with heat. It was five minutes past nine by his watch when they reached the outskirts of Alvaston. With every moment of the last half-hour, Mr. Lucton's nervous apprehensiveness had been increasing. Now, suddenly, as he saw the familiar names of the Alvaston roads, a new anxiety seized him. Within a week the story of his wild extravagance would have reached the "Buffalo". If he allowed the man from the Lesswardine garage to drive up to Alvaston Grange, Chapel Green would also be informed of his exact destination.

"This will suit me quite well," he said hurriedly. "You can put me down here."

"What's the good of that, after driving all these miles? Tell me where you want to go, and I'll put you down at the door."

"You needn't trouble to do that," Mr. Lucton said. "I shall have to look about for the house I want, and I can do that much better on foot. Sixty-four shillings, wasn't it? I'm afraid I've nothing but notes. Here's four pounds."

"I'm blest if I've any change either."

"That doesn't matter. You owe me fourteen bob. The next time I see you will do."

The man laughed.

"Well, you may not have come into a fortune, like I said, Mr. Owen; but you're pretty flush by the looks of it. Fourteen bob. I won't forget. I'll tell the lad to give it to you any time you're passing."

He turned the car at a corner. Mr. Lucton waved him good-bye. He was less than five minutes' walk, as he reckoned it, from Alvaston Grange, and it was now a quarter past nine. By this time Leith, with his Spartan regularity of habit, would have left for the office, so it was fairly safe to approach the house without any fear of meeting him. Fear . . . Why should he fear meeting Leith? Yet fear it was.

It was strange, after so many weeks of country roads, to be treading the smooth asphalt pavements. He had always boasted that Alvaston was a model suburb: "It's almost like being in the country," he had often said. It was very different from being in the country, he felt now. The very dust of the country roads smelt sweeter than these barren streets; the tarnished leaves of laburnums and lilacs and horse-chestnuts had no life in them; even the houses which he had most admired looked dim and grimy compared with Poplar Cottage.

And here, at the corner of the road, was Alvaston Grange, with its Victorian Gothic mullions of sooty freestone. One side of the house was beset by scaffolding which surrounded a new structure of staring red brick which had already reached the level of the first-floor windows.

"What the devil do they imagine they're doing here?" Mr. Lucton thought angrily. "It was high time I came home!"

He approached the front door, found it unlocked, and entered. Nothing had changed, except that, for some odd reason, the hall looked less spacious and shabbier than he had imagined it. Perhaps that was because there was no air in it, though that could hardly be the right explanation, since the door that gave on to the garden was open wide. The second gardener was mowing the lawn as usual, with a motor-mower that seemed to be dragging him unwillingly in its wake. All the beds were set with bedding-plants, geranium and lobelia and calceolaria, disposed with a geometrical precision. He felt he would have given the lot for one corner of Miss Susan's ungeometrical wilderness. He saw a man in shirt-sleeves sitting in a deck-chair smoking a cigar—a very good cigar by the smell of it—and luxuriously contemplating the second gardener at work. Mr. Lucton drew back for a moment. Was it possible that Leith was entertaining a visitor? Then the man in the deck-chair spat, with remarkable precision, into the flower-bed in front of him. He poked his head round the corner of the deck-chair and gazed full into Mr. Lucton's eyes, and his lard-like face grew even more ghastly than the face of Miss Jenkins.

"Good morning, Fowler," Mr. Lucton said pleasantly. "Enjoying a morning off?"

Mr. Fowler hurriedly ground his cigar on the crazy pavement and thrust the smouldering remains into his trouser pocket. Even in this emergency his grand manner did not forsake him.

"Good morning, sir," he said. "Well, if I may say so, this *is* a surprise, and no mistake. Would you be requiring anything in the way of breakfast?"

Mr. Lucton laughed.

"No, thank you. Mr. Leith's gone to town, I suppose."

"Yes, sir. Mr. Leith left the house as usual at nine precisely."

"Shall I find my clothes in my room?"

"I'm afraid they're not put out, sir. Not having had any notice . . ."

"Never mind. I'll find what I want."

Mr. Lucton ran upstairs three steps at a time. He went straight to his room and flung open the door. A strange sight and a whiff of strong perfume greeted him. It wasn't his room any longer. It was a bathroom, fitted with an array of chromium-plated pipes and showers and douches and oddly-shaped receptacles that might have been inspired by a modern plumber's Freudian nightmares. In the midst stood an enormous black marble bath, and the walls were covered with rose-coloured mirrors. He returned to the head of the stairs and bawled at Fowler, whose sluggish movements had brought him to the bottom step:

"Fowler, where the hell is my bedroom?"

"I was on my way to inform you, sir. Your bedroom is now Mrs. Lucton's bathroom; but your things have been transferred to Miss Dorothy's."

In Dorothy's room Mr. Lucton found his old chest of drawers and wardrobe. He would not have been surprised if he had found that Fowler had sold his clothes; but, apparently, he had not even brushed them. The black city coat and the striped cashmere trousers hung exactly where he had left them two months before, at the back of the wardrobe. His shirts, collars and ties were in their accustomed drawers, his shoes on the rack.

It took him less than ten minutes to change. On the whole, he was pleased with the result. The clothes were well cut and suited him. He was, he felt, a much better-looking man than when he had last worn them. At the foot of the stairs he found Fowler, also transformed, in a starched collar, with a black tie, and a coat with tails.

"Excuse me, sir," he said, "would you be requiring luncheon and dinner?"

"I shall be out for lunch and probably back for dinner. Is there a car in the garage?"

"I'm afraid there isn't, sir. Mr. Rupert has got the Bentley in camp; Mr. Leith has drove his to the office as usual, and the mistress has taken the Daimler on to the Continent. I could telephone for a taxi, sir."

"Don't bother. I'll take a bus," Mr. Lucton said.

Fowler hurried, so far as he was capable of hurrying, to open the door for him. As he passed Mr. Lucton caught a whiff of stale cigar-smoke. He could have sworn, from what he had smelt on the terrace, that Fowler had been enjoying one of his Corona Coronas.

He caught an omnibus in the Halesby Road. Oddly enough, he felt less nervous now that he was properly clothed. He rode on the top of the bus and noted with satisfaction that Alvaston, after all, was neither so begrimed nor so shabby as he had thought half an hour ago. Perhaps it was his change of clothes that accounted for this too. All the familiar buildings he passed appeared to welcome him, as though they were old friends, and prepared to overlook his divagation. He found a certain zest in feeling himself so much at home. In these grimy surroundings he had lived the greater part of his life. They belonged to him, and he to them. For better, for worse, he was a North Bromwich man, and proud of it.

He left the bus at the Post Office, opposite the Corinthian Town Hall. As he crossed to Sackville Row, the clock of the Art Gallery campanile chimed a quarter to ten. He looked up at the solemn face affectionately. Its voice, too, was familiar: the sound which had measured his days for nearly forty years. In Sackville Row itself he began to feel more self-conscious. Every yard of it carried the danger of an astonished stare. But nobody stared at him, though many must surely have known him. North Bromwich was going about its daily business unstirred by his presence. It was less concerned with him, apparently, than he had imagined.

So he came to the crossing just short of the club and forty yards from his office. There was a check in the traffic here. A policeman, superb as ever, stood there controlling it with a white-sleeved arm. Mr. Lucton found himself in the midst of a thick knot of pedestrians waiting to cross. The policeman held up the Sackville Row traffic and waved to them, permitting them to cross. As he hurried over with the rest, Mr. Lucton caught his eyes. The man smiled and quickly brought up his hand to the salute. Mr. Lucton, acknowledging it, could not have sworn that he didn't also wink. But the salute of the law had restored his confidence. He had become once more a prominent citizen of no mean city. He mounted the stairs that led to his office with a springy step.

THE END